THE ANTIGALLICAN

Causeway Books,
Bushmills.
07776075176

THE ANTIGALLICAN

Tom Bowling

OLDCASTLE

This edition published in 2009 by Oldcastle Books,
P.O.Box 394, Harpenden, Herts, AL5 1XJ
www.oldcastlebooks.com

A CIP catalogue record for this book is available from the British Library.

ISBN 978-1-84243-321-8

2 4 6 8 10 9 7 5 3 1

Typeset by Ellipsis Books Limited, Glasgow
Printed and bound in Great Britain by J F Print Ltd., Sparkford, Somerset

To the memory of William Milne. A sailor, like his father and brothers, he was a charitable man in every sense, and a pleasure to know.

An`ti-Gal´li`can

a. 1. Opposed to what is Gallic or French

1

The light was dazzling. The sea was calm. There were no waves. The Gulf Stream's swell met the cold northern water and caused the great ocean to rise and fall as a body, as if it were breathing. But that was the only movement. The black hull of the fishing boat *L'Imprevu*, a small, brigantine-rigged Terre-Neuveian wallowed in the swell, her stays creaking, a dirty grey tarpaulin suspended limply over part of her deck to serve as shade. A man and a boy hung in the rigging above the tarpaulin, sweating. The air around them felt thick and warm. The boy sang a ditty in Jerrais, Jersey French.

'J'nos'nallons pour Terr'neuve, C'hest nouot pays d'Esden,' he almost whispered. 'We're going to Newfoundland, it's our garden of Eden.' The man did not respond. The Newfoundland banks were not an 'Eden', even in summer.

The boy repeated the line, then wiped his forehead with his sleeve. He was called Thibault, and was just twelve years old. His hair was streaked blond from the sunlight and his face was ruddy. He wore just a shirt and breeches, like the rest of *L'Imprevu*'s crew. Thibault was the ship's boy, and was acknowledged as the best pair of eyes aboard.

The man was Jean Cotterell. He was the captain of *L'Imprevu*. Cotterell was thirty. He had light-brown hair, blue-grey eyes and an angular, pointed face with broad cheekbones. His hair, like the boy's, was bleached by exposure to the sun. Cotterell's family claimed to be descended from the original Viking Jersey stock. He looked the part.

Cotterell scanned the horizon. To the south and west the sky met the sea in a great, seamless white and metal-blue expanse, full of startlingly bright light. Only dark, distant anvil clouds broke the scene's calm consistency. *L'Imprevu* could have been in the English Channel in midsummer, not thousands of miles into the Atlantic. Below the clouds, fifteen or twenty miles away, an even darker smudge marked rain.

L'Imprevu was neither big enough nor rigged so as to have a masthead proper. Above them stood just the bare masts and rigging. Cotterell and the boy hung in the ratlines on the mizzen of the fishing boat. The big red fore and aft sail flopped beside them. Thibault's usefulness as a lookout was beyond doubt. But he talked too much.

'It's hot,' he said.

'It's May,' said Cotterell.

'My grandfather used to talk about the cold.'

'You don't remember that.'

Thibault's brown eyes looked hurt. 'He died before I was born. He told my mother,' he whispered. 'She gave me woollen hose.'

'You'll need them in the winter.' Cotterell was softer. 'Look after them.'

'They are in my sea-chest.' The boy was outraged at the idea he should scorn anything provided by his mother.

'She knit them herself?'

'Of course.' Cotterell imagined Thibault's mother by the fire at la Grange, knitting for her son, surrounded by the other women, gossiping, clacking the needles. It seemed very remote from the deck of his boat in this great flat windless ocean, thousands of miles to the west. He looked again at the dark cloud on the horizon. That would change things.

'We will still be here in the winter?' asked Thibault.

'That's the plan, God willing.'

'Fishing? Or looking for Frenchmen?'

Cotterell didn't answer.

'Are we going to fish *ever*, Jean Cotterell?' Thibault asked.

Cotterell didn't reply, but pointed to the south west, where the tall dark cloud promised a storm later. For now the southern sky and sea were welded together in shimmering, steely sunlight and only the very softest of airs blew. The oily surface of the swelling sea moved and shivered. L'Imprevu's spars clattered as the sails received the zephyr, then spilled it. The vessel swung slightly and the rig creaked and clattered again as the breath of wind fell from the sails.

'Imagine for a moment that you're the captain of this vessel, Thibault.'

Thibault imagined. Cotterell suppressed a smile.

'Would you put out boats and lines with that coming?' Thibault looked at the dark cloud.

'No.'

'Why not?'

'Strong winds. We'd have to fetch them in again soon.'

'Good boy. So there's your answer.'

He touched the boy's head with affectionate familiarity. It was Thibault's first season on the Banks and Cotterell had undertaken to educate the boy as a seaman. Cotterell looked down to the deck, to his other charges. L'Imprevu's crew lay prone, looking for all the world as if they'd been struck by some giant hand. A tarpaulin was rigged over part of the deck, but still Cotterell could see parts of their bodies, feet and hands beyond it, unshaded. The sailors, he knew, were in shirts and breeches. Of course none wore shoes. Their clothes were old, sun-bleached and poor. Bright light shone down on the crewmen, as it did upon the fishing lines which were neatly rolled on the larboard side of L'Imprevu's deck. An empty bait tub lay open, forward. The lines were not baited, and weren't about to be. The vessel's fish holds were empty and her boats were firmly chocked and lashed above them.

Cotterell and the boy hung in the rigging, sweltering under the burning sun. Cotterell looked to the horizon again. He almost wanted the gale to come. The air would clear. The decks

would dampen and swell. The men would be busy. In the gusts
and gales of an Atlantic blow, however brief, they would find
the lack of fishing easier to bear. Action ends reflection in men.
He began to sing in English:

'Ye zephyrs fair that fan the air,
And wanton thro' the grove,
O whisper to my charming fair,
"I die for her I love."
This lass so neat, with smile so sweet,
Has won my right good will,
I'd crowns resign to call her mine;
Sweet lass of Richmond Hill.'

'What's that?' asked the boy.
'It's a song.'
'What does it say?'
'You must have heard it.'
'No. Where does it come from?'
'I learned it on a big ship. The *Asia*. When I was your age.'
    Cotterell began to translate for the boy. As he did so he looked
at the base of the cloud on the horizon again. Something there
drew him. Some anomaly. He couldn't be sure what it was. He
stopped translating and looked through his telescope, but could
pick out nothing of significance. If the wind blew hard any
French ships in that quarter would have to run before it. They
would have to run towards him. Cotterell wasn't on the
Newfoundland Bank to fish, but to look out for French ships.
Other fishing boats waited farther south and east, invisible beyond
the horizon, but Cotterell and his sailors knew they were there.
As soon as the French fleet was in view *L'Imprevu*, or one of
the others, would pick up her skirts and run to the nearest British
frigate. Cotterell's men knew that was why they were sitting on
the Banks without fishing. Cotterell's men also knew that on
other fishing boats over the horizon the lines stayed flaked, the
hooks bare, the pulling boats chocked. The bait tub sat empty.
The line of fishing boats – it couldn't be called a fleet when the

vessels were so far apart – were on the edge of the Grand Bank, between cold and warm water. It was where the best fish were found. But they would wait without working until the French had passed, as they had been ordered. The small fleet of fishing boats had to keep their holds empty if they were to outrun . . . well what? French warships, perhaps. For certain a fleet of French grain ships.

The crew of *l'Imprevu*, and those of the boats over the horizon, suffered loss of earnings in the same way. But release from competition didn't help the men's mood. Each day that passed cost the fishermen a day's money. Would King George's English admirals pay their losses? No promise had been made. Cotterell knew there was a fine balance between the men's loyalty and their need to earn money. There was no point in their spending a year in Newfoundland and then returning to Jersey without a bag of money.

L'Imprevu's spars clattered again. The ship's wheel made small staccato movements as its chain links moved across the tiller below the deck, rocking back and forth; click, click, click-click.

Antoine LaRoche, a middle-aged man with black hair and a grey beard, stood, looked up and pointed towards the storm clouds. He called towards the masthead.

'Shall I reduce sail, Cap'?' Antoine spoke Jersey French. He had stepped back from the awning as he looked up, but he couldn't see Cotterell. The sky was too bright. To Antoine his captain looked like a black paper cut-out against an almost unbearably white-hot sky.

Cotterell called, 'It may go round.'

'Shall I fetch water?'

'We have water. Get in the shade again. Rest.'

Antoine took a last long look at the threatening cloud on the horizon, then obeyed. He lay on the deck. But his body didn't look at ease. Cotterell could see the older man perfectly well looking down, his raised face round like a plate, his hand casting a blue shadow as it shaded his eyes. Cotterell smiled.

He knew Antoine wouldn't be satisfied until they were sailing or working or fishing or scrubbing decks. But Cotterell wanted them to rest. They were a small crew, six men, including the boy and himself, and *L'Imprevu* might have to hold station like this for weeks.

'How long will we stay here?' asked Thibault, reading his thoughts. The older men mightn't have dared question Cotterell, but Thibault was full of self-confidence. The boy felt certain of his place next to Cotterell. Fishing the Banks was a trade handed down from Jersey father to Jersey son. Cotterell had learned it from his father, Jean-Jacques Cotterell. Thibault Dumaresq was the grandson of Jean-Jacques' long dead mate.

'As long as we need to,' Cotterell replied quietly.

'Damn the French,' said the boy.

'Watch your tongue. Your mother . . .'

'My mother says damn them all and may God kill them all. She wrote it in the letter I received from her in St John.' Thibault was deadly serious. 'My mother says kill all lying, stealing, cheating colonials too, who are thieves and disloyal to their king.'

'Does she?'

'You could see the letter if you wished.'

Cotterell leaned back from the rigging, taking his weight on his hands, thinking and looking at Thibault. 'Kill them all, she wrote?' he asked.

'Yes. But foremost the French.

'She is very antigallican, your mother.' Cotterell laughed. 'Be patient and you may get your chance to kill Frenchmen.'

'Here? What will I use? A fish gaff?'

'Join the King's Navy. They'll be glad of the company. I hear there are openings for young men.'

'I couldn't.'

'Oh?'

'She wouldn't allow it.'

'Damn the English too?' Cotterell was laughing at Thibault. 'Your mother says damn everyone.'

'Her life is hard. She doesn't want me to suffer on the lower deck of a warship.'

'Perhaps one of His Majesty's ships will force the issue.'

'How?'

'They could press you and place a gun in your hands.'

'Press?' said the boy, outraged, 'I'm a Jerseyman.'

'And they would have your mother to answer to. The prospect will keep their Lordships awake at night.'

The boy held out his hand. Cotterell passed the telescope. Thibault lined it up with the horizon.

'Bang. Bang. Bang,' he said as he swung the instrument across the horizon. 'Death to the French.'

'Death to King George's enemies,' replied Cotterell.

'She says I could do it if I could be sure to be an officer.' Thibault was still looking through the telescope. 'Join the King's Navy, that is.'

'How can you be sure of that?' asked Cotterell, aware that though the boy's eye might be to the telescope he, Cotterell, was being observed.

'I could get a place as a Midshipman.'

'You need interest. Do you have any?'

'What is it, exactly?'

'Someone to look over you.'

'Like an angel?'

'Something like an angel.'

A silence, then Thibault asked, 'Don't you have interest, Jean Cotterell?'

'No. Why would I? I'm a poor fisherman.'

'My mother says you do.'

'I thought you didn't know what it meant?'

The boy was silent for a moment.

'Your mother is a good woman and a friend of my family . . . but,' continued Cotterell, 'she says a lot for a woman on the other side of the ocean.'

'She talks about you in her letter.'

'Then I am obliged and flattered.'

'She asked me to remember her to you. Did I tell you?'

'Many times.'

'She says she hopes you are looking after me.'

'Did you write back?' asked Cotterell.

'We left St John's harbour in a dash.'

'So we did.'

'I'll show you the letter if you would like.'

'It's in the sea-chest with the Jersey hose?'

Thibault looked suspicious. 'Yes, it is.'

'I think she meant this momentous document just for you, Thibault. Keep your eye on the horizon.'

'She says you were seen with Captain d'Auvergne in St Helier.'

'I am not familiar with that person.'

Thibault took the telescope from his eye and looked at Cotterell, eyes screwed up against the light. Cotterell looked back, expressionless.

'She says if you have interest . . .'

'Is he in Jersey, this Mister Overn?'

'Captain d'Auvergne. Yes. I'm sure you know him if Mother says you do. She wrote it . . .

'. . . in the letter you received in St John. Do you see anything?' Cotterell pointed to the south west.

'Clouds,' said Thibault.

'Does he live in Jersey, this man?' Cotterell repeated.

'Yes.'

'Where does he live?'

'In Gorey, her letter says.'

'So Captain Overn is as far away as Veuve Dumaresq, your mother?'

'Yes.'

'And therefore just about as useful as a lookout on this fishing boat. Do not reduce yourself to the same condition.'

'Which is?'

'A person of little use. Be careful that I do not land you the

next time we reach St John, leaving your mother to arrange with
this Captain Overn to transport you and your weighty letters
back to Gorey as best she can. Clear?'

'Yes Jean,' said the boy.

'Captain,' prompted Cotterell.

'Yes, Cap'. Sorry Cap'.' The boy returned to his telescope.
Cotterell began to descend. The ratlines were hot to his touch.

Thibault looked at the base of the anvil cloud. 'I can see a
sail,' he said quietly. Cotterell was beside him again in an instant.

'Where?'

'At the foot of the clouds.'

Cotterell looked.

'I see nothing.'

'It's dark there. But I see a sail running towards us.'

Cotterell looked down for a moment. The crew had heard,
though the boy had spoken in little more than a whisper. They
were on their feet. The fishing boat creaked in expectation.
Cotterell took the telescope. He looked through it at the foot
of the cloud formation.

'What sort of sail? A fisherman? A warship?'

'Just a sail,' the boy said. 'A white patch.'

'I see nothing.'

Thibault smiled. 'Perhaps I'm wrong.'

They both knew he wasn't.

As the ship on the horizon drew closer the boy eventually iden-
tified that she bore an American flag. While Cotterell went on
deck, Thibault watched her approach through the telescope. He
reported she flew an enormous stars and stripes. Closer yet and,
Thibault called down to them, he could see every sail looked in
perfect order, the whole was spick and span.

'She's beautiful!' he called from his perch in the rigging, and
meant it. The men were on deck wedging the hatches to the fish
hold in anticipation of rough weather. They paused for half a
second and looked at each other; some beauty.

'Is she a warship?' a voice called to the boy.

'What else?' Antoine answered from the deck. Cotterell and the crew of *l'Imprevu* sat in almost still air. The American vessel was under the heavy clouds, running under reefed sails. She aimed at *L'Imprevu* like an arrow. The clouds seemed to aim at *L'Imprevu* too. They promised a full Atlantic blow.

The weather arrived first, beating the American frigate by hours. First rain fell. Large droplets of water landed on deck, splashing back as if the deck were a hot plate. Each drop left a dark mark on the bleached oak surface. There were spaces between the dark marks. Next the clouds gathered overhead. The sky grew gloomy. The dark rain marks on the sun-whitened wooden deck closed and became one. When the first airs came *L'Imprevu* ran too, both from the storm and from the American frigate, which was now less than ten miles away. *L'Imprevu* pointed north and east for Avalon and St John, her crew hoping the British frigates were there and not out on the Flemish Cap.

'Rain before wind,' said Antoine to Cotterell. 'Things will become interesting if we keep all this sail up . . .'

'We'll keep our sails up while the American chases. With any luck he will lose interest in us and pick on someone else. Or night will come and save us.'

'Why is he chasing?'

'Shall we stop and ask?' said Cotterell, regretting his sharpness as soon as he had spoken. Antoine deserved a proper answer. 'At the very least he will scatter us fishermen back to Newfoundland,' Cotterell continued, 'so his French friends shall have a clear and unreported passage in our absence. But his appearance alone tells us the French fleet have set sail. We have to find King George's frigates and tell them. The American, meanwhile, will want to detain those he can. He may even make Yankee crewmen of us.'

Now the wind blew and the sails filled on *L'Imprevu*. The American was three miles away, but now both vessels had power in their sails. *L'Imprevu* ran for her life. As she ran, the sea around her grew first into waves; then the waves heaped up and spray flew. After an hour the waves were large, big enough to bury the bow of the little fishing boat each time she descended a trough, big enough for the crew to feel the wind ease across her deck on the downhill slope of the wave. The wind never eased in her sails and her captain never let up his search for speed. Cotterell kept up every scrap of sail – mizzen over the starboard quarter, brigantine square-sail sweeping the deck. The spars screamed complaint. The cords, halyards and sheets were tight as a musical instrument. The wind beat against the sails, creating a thrumming running through the vessel, as if some tune was about to groan out of her. The sails stretched. The sheets hummed. Rain beaded on the sailcloth filler. Cotterell fetched Thibault down from his vantage point. The boy was almost lost in finding the safety of the deck, tripping and floating on the spume of a wave that broke over *L'Imprevu*, banging his head and his leg against the scupper. Two men fought the wheel, slipping and sliding in their struggle to hold their course. A false move during a gust meant they lost control of the wheel momentarily. The mizzen flipped to larboard then back to starboard, gear crashing on the mast as it did.

'Hold your course,' bellowed Cotterell. 'We'll lose the lot if you broach.'

'We will lose control if we don't reef now,' Antoine shouted, clutching Cotterell's shoulder and shouting in his ear. The American ship was behind them, clear for both men to see, now perhaps two miles off.

'No.' Said Cotterell.

Then there was a report like a gun. At first Cotterell thought the Americans must have aimed some sort of bow chaser at them, but the frigate was too far away to fire a gun and the seas were too rough to allow one to be aimed. He looked up. The mainmast angle on *L'Imprevu* seemed to be wrong. The rake was too much. The mast moved of its own accord, separately from the ship, he thought. Realisation of the awful truth came slowly

to him. The mast was breaking. As Cotterell understood he turned
to the men on the wheel to warn them. As he turned, a wave
washed over the fishing boat, soaking the men on the wheel
anew, sending Tomas, one of the crewmen, sliding forward like
a man on a waterfall. Cotterell clutched a deadeye and held on
for his life. The deck tilted as the bow buried. As the vessel
stalled the mast snapped. The bow came up while the mast
descended in a tangle of rigging. Another wave swept them and
this time the helmsmen lost control of the boat entirely. *L'Imprevu*'s
mizzen drove her stern on while her bow remained buried at
the bottom of the trough. The broken mainmast and mainsail
fell over to larboard, catching water there like a purse or a bucket
dropped in a stream. The weight of water in the sails could only
bring one result. She broached. Another wave broke, the vessel
turned, the wind and sea seemed to roar in victory. Cotterell,
standing on the starboard and holding his deadeye, found himself
propelled through the air, off the deck and into the sea. The
fishing boat, having broached to larboard, stayed on that side
for a second, then rolled with the next wave and disappeared
under the seas. Apart from that second of obscenely exposed
hull, like a maiden aunt bowled over, skirts awry, arse exposed,
L'Imprevu sank without a pause, without hesitation. She left no
sign she'd ever been there, except Cotterell alone in the sea.

Jean Cotterell never saw the American pass, if she ever did. He
never even confirmed for himself that she was American. But
he saw his own vessel sink. There was a moment when he was
in the water and he saw her hull nearby. Upturned, *L'Imprevu*
was covered in barnacles and weed. He believed he could smell
the black hull. Another wave washed across Cotterell, making
him tumble. When he rose again, also tumbling, she was gone.
He looked around himself but there was nothing. He was alone.
There was no sign of *L'Imprevu* and no sign of the American
vessel. There was no Thibault, no Antoine, neither of the two
Tomases, no Michel, no Yves. He allowed himself to take the

information in again. The vessel, the men, their hopes and prayers were gone. Surely not. Cotterell looked about himself. He was alone in the sea. For a moment he felt sorry for himself. Cotterell wondered how he would tell little Thibault's mother, Widow Dumaresq, that he had lost her son. It would be too much to bear. She had already lost her father and her husband to the sea. Then he laughed at his own vanity. He would never tell her. Cotterell knew he was going to die. He prayed for the souls of the other sailors, then prayed for his own. Salt-water spray whipped around his head. It frothed over him, snatched at his mouth, stole his breath and stung his eyes. It tossed him head over heels, over and over. It clutched him and released him, first in one element, then the other. Out of the water his ears were beaten by the rushing of the wind, by the crashing of tons of water in the giant empty North Atlantic. Under the water was warmer, almost noiseless. Under the water was as safe as a womb. But Cotterell knew the water would kill him.

The wind eased as quickly as it had begun. Slowly the waves ceased to thunder and break so violently. Eventually, as the afternoon went on, the storm ended completely. Only the swell continued. Cotterell looked about himself. He was amazed to find a wooden spar from his foundered fishing boat. He forced his arm and head under some cord lashed to the wooden spar. Now he couldn't be washed away again. The spar was his home, however temporary. He recognised it. From now until the end of my life, this is my home, he thought, then banished the idea. Down that path lies despair. But he was in a despairing situation.

Time passed. He called in English until his voice was hoarse, hoping the Americans would hear him, but there was no response and no sign of the American ship. Cotterell eventually began to believe he was completely alone. Knowing is one thing, truly believing is another, he thought. Now I believe.

'Is this all that's left?' he said aloud, as if to fend off the thought. Only an hour, perhaps two before he spoke Cotterell had been standing on the deck of his fishing boat, where men had cried and fought the storm. Now they were gone.

The green swell carried him north and east. Cliffs of water peaked and collapsed. Cotterell rode the swell. Over and over he fell into a green abyss. Over and over he rose again as if by a miracle, still clutching his wooden spar. Each time he rose he looked for his fishing boat, *l'Imprevu*, as if by the same miracle she could rise again and sail. *L'Imprevu* wasn't there and neither were his crew. Logic was swept aside. His mind was for a long time unable to accept the truth his senses told him. Had his time and his world, his ship and his men, had all of his experiences really been snatched away from him? Was this a nightmare? Cotterell was trapped between drowning and not drowning, between life and death. If it was a dream, he couldn't wake. Cotterell wept bitter salt tears into the ocean. He didn't want to think about the other sailors. He imagined their faces begging him to save them as the ship turned and foundered. He had never seen it but they must have done it. Save us. He was their captain. He'd let them down.

The fishermen's faces were real to him; their voices too. How far now was the Newfoundland coast? He wondered aloud, but no answer came from the fishermen. He knew the answer, anyway. Two hundred miles. Where was the rest of the fleet? He knew the answer to that too. A day's sail, if they hadn't been scattered in their turn by the sight of the American warship's sail. Self pity coursed through Cotterell for a moment, like a false heart beat. There was no hope of rescue. He set the thought aside. He determined to remain rational and hopeful. He closed his eyes and concentrated on remaining alive as long as he could.

By the end of the afternoon the chill of the green water had driven rational thought from his mind. Only the very core of Cotterell lived now. He had no energy for imaginings or nightmares, for drowning sailors and sinking ships. He had lost most of his clothes. The cold seemed to have soaked his skin, penetrating to his bones. His whole being, limbs, heart, mind, and

even soul seemed to have frozen past numbness, to have slowed
beyond dullness. Cotterell was barely able to hold his face out
of the sea. He relaxed, little by little. Cotterell dozed towards
death, spluttering awake each time he fell asleep into the water.
The sea, now the long Atlantic rhythm he knew so well from
his years of fishing, prepared to accept him. The sky overhead
was as sharp and blue as a polished gem. He saw a gull, sitting
in the water, turning its head, one beady eye after the other
choosing the best place to strike. He knew when he died he
would be consumed between the fish below and the birds above.
Was the gull really there, so far out to sea waiting to feed on
him? Cotterell couldn't tell. He didn't know if he was dead or
alive. His body was completely numb. The spar and the cord
had ceased to hurt. His eyes were red and sore, almost impossible to open. Only pain differentiated between opening his eyes
and dreaming it. His mouth wouldn't work. His lips wouldn't
part. His tongue was stuck to the roof of his mouth. He was
desperately thirsty. Finally his raw eyes refused to open at all.
He was beaten, like a prize-fighter who'd done twenty or thirty
rounds with Mendoza or Humphries. This is how the end comes,
he thought. Cotterell's arms hung over the spar, tied by the cord,
trapping him, refusing to let him drown. Now nothing but the
cord kept him from slipping under the water. Sometimes pain
came like flashes of light, but its source was inside him, not
outside. Spasms of cramp sometimes woke Cotterell from his
dream of death, but he knew he would die soon. He wondered
if he already had. If he lifted his head brilliant pink light flooded
his mind. He felt that if he could just swim through the light
he would meet his makers, his Lord and his long-dead father.
He repeated the words of the Nicene creed to no one at all,
unspoken words addressed by his otherwise silent, dying mind
to the inside of his own skull, 'I believe in one God, the Father
almighty, Creator of all things visible and invisible . . .'

He heard voices.

Cotterell couldn't understand what the voices said. There was another sound. He realised he could hear the creak of rigging. Ropes ran, sheaves squeaked. Next he heard the greased slide and splash of a ship's boat entering the sea. This is a fantasy, come to taunt me, he thought. So this is how a man dies, in a dream. An age passed, then the splash of oars was near him. A voice called in French, 'Lift oars.' Rough hands grasped Cotterell and lifted him from the sea.

'Careful now. Careful. Is he alive?' A gruff voice near Cotterell's head spoke French with a strong English accent. Other men's hands wrapped him in what felt like a large rough woollen blanket. He was like a baby, held in their arms.

'Is he alive?' the voice repeated.

'No.'

Cotterell couldn't reply, not even as much as a movement of the head or a blink of his eye. He couldn't even open his eyes.

'He's breathing.'

'He's dead.'

'Pinch him.'

If they pinched him Cotterell didn't feel it.

'He's dead,' repeated a gloomy French voice. 'Put him back.'

'He's not.'

Someone punched him in the stomach. Cotterell vomited a warm stream of salt water. He could feel it run between his teeth and out the corner of his mouth.

'Do it again.'

The punch came again, this time in the solar plexus. Cotterell vomited again, this time warm salt water ran up the back of his throat, exiting through his nose. He gasped.

'See. Breathing. I told you. You give up too easily.'

The owner of the voice punched Cotterell one more time for good luck. Cotterell gave a dry retch.

'Don't kill him.'

'Would I be down here fishing for him if I wanted to kill him?'

Cotterell still couldn't breathe steadily or speak or open his eyes. They bathed his face with fresh water from a keg held near his head. They ran the water over his eyes and lips. Cotterell could smell the fresh water as soon as they uncorked the keg and was greedy for it. But he couldn't move his head, and neither could he ask for it. He couldn't speak. He couldn't drink. His lips wouldn't move. He felt a soaked rag held against his mouth for a few seconds, like a baby's pap-feeder. Fresh water from the rag dribbled between his lips. Still Cotterell didn't have the strength the take the kind man's hand and hold the rag to his mouth and suck on it, which is what he wanted. Cotterell couldn't see his rescuers, just felt himself stretched across their knees in a small boat while bright red light filtered through his eyelids. He coughed sea water and sweet water mixed.

'Don't give him any more now, you'll kill him.'

Then shadow was cast over the boat. Whatever wind there had been calmed. The boat rose and fell and Cotterell couldn't see, but he could feel the presence of a ship close by. They were in its lee. A canvas sling was tied about Cotterell and he was lifted from the boat to the ship, swinging free in the air as he rose, one arm dangling. His free hand felt rough manila netting. His fingers slipped around the netting, grasped for a second, then fell open. On deck they removed the sling. Under his body he could feel the comforting solidity of the oak deck of a big ship. He was certain he was either dead or dreaming. 'What comes next?' he wondered, and then allowed the swaddling warmth of sleep to smother his conscious mind.

2

After death comes life. Cotterell slept and dreamed, but his dream was obscene and surprising. He was in a cot in a dark place, naked except for a rough blanket over him. His arms and legs were like lead on the cot. His skin burned as if it was on fire but he couldn't move. A lamp approached, shone into his face. Two women leaned over him. They were both under thirty, but not much. One was a coarse-looking countrywoman with red brown hair and a shawl over her shoulders. She had rosy cheeks and a friendly face. The other was thinner-faced and more serious looking, with grey eyes, a dirty red cap over her hair and a blue tunic. She was dressed like a man in a picture shown to his mother by a French priest. They had been in his mother's parlour. Cotterell had been there and held the grubby picture while the old man and his mother talked. The priest had referred to the soldier as a *sans culottes*. It meant the revolutionary rabble. But it meant more. Just before Cotterell had left Jersey the *sans culottes* had left Paris under arms to defend their Republic. The priest had merely picked up his skirts and run to Jersey. Cotterell remembered the French priest's eyes gleaming by the firelight.

'Devils. Very devils.' The old man had whispered. He'd felt at home with Cotterell's mother, one of the few local Catholics on the island. 'They believe in nothing. Imagine. Such people as there never were before.'

Later the priest offered Cotterell's mother a benediction. He had a little nub of incense in his cloak which he lit and placed in a bowl. Cotterell had gone outside the cottage while they did it. Cotterell had said he would keep watch. The scent seemed to fill the air outside the cottage. Cotterell could smell it still, when he tried to remember. Refugee priests were banned from giving services and from prozelytising on the island and he'd been fearful someone would pass. What would he say? Jerseymen were Protestants, and Cotterell was a good Jerseyman. His Breton mother's Catholic faith was tolerated on the island, but no more, and the parts of it she'd taught him had been in secret.

Cotterell lay in the cot with his eyes closed. His limbs were leaden. Had he slept? Was it a dream? Was he dead? He didn't know. He raised his eyelids a little. The women were still there.

The two women by the cot talked quietly. They were discussing Cotterell, he knew. He couldn't make out the words. Their lips moved but the words came out as if spoken through a muffler. The sans culottes lifted the blanket that covered Cotterell's body. Both women laughed like girls. The countrywoman's smile gaped. She had no teeth. They talked again, the sans culottes holding up the blanket all the while. The countrywoman gave a gummy grin as she felt for Cotterell's penis. He felt it grow in her hand. He felt as though he was pinned to the cot but the penis rose with a life of its own, the only part of Cotterell's body able to move.

Both women laughed again while the countrywoman worked him and the woman in the red cap looked on.

'I told you,' said the woman with no teeth. 'I told you.'

'Will he stay up?' asked the revolutionary.

'I think so.'

'Go on then.'

The sans culottes slipped out of her pantaloons and climbed onto the cot. 'Voila!' She took his penis inside herself. 'Voila!' The sans culottes bounced up and down on him.

'Bravo!' hissed the woman with the red cheeks. 'I told you.'

'Fetch them . . .'

A noise behind them turned both away. A man's voice spoke.

'Told her what? Fetch who? What are you doing here with a light? Do you want to blow us all to pieces?' The darkness came on again. The women's voices laughed in the darkness, just once, and Cotterell's vision ended. His mind drifted untrammelled in the complete darkness. He wondered if this was what madmen's minds were like. Am I unhinged? Has the sea kept me alive to make me mad? His eyes were too heavy now. Cotterell slept.

He awoke, perfectly sane and sentient in a wooden cot on the orlop of a warship. Though his body caused him pain, Cotterell welcomed it as the affirmation that he was neither mad nor dead. He looked about himself. There was just one light on the deck, a large candle in a big glass case. Cotterell looked at the flickering flame. It was an expensive glass case, carefully carved in mahogany. A candle was mounted inside on a specially constructed holder. Cotterell knew that meant they were next to the filling room, the gunpowder store. By the slowly flickering light he could make out the whitewashed wooden walls which surrounded him. To one side was a companionway leading to the next deck. The feeling of his skin being on fire was still there, but now he could just about move his limbs, though they ached infernally. Cotterell's hearing worked too. He could hear water trickling past the hull of the ship. The vessel was like a musical instrument. The creak of the rigging was conducted down to him by the mast. Even so far below deck Cotterell could hear and feel the ship was moving easily across the ocean, sailing large.

'Awake?' asked a voice in English. Cotterell focussed. A black man's face was leaning over him. The man had large firm lips, high cheekbones, flashing whites to his eyes. He was very handsome and perhaps a little vain. Close cropped black curly hair jutting out beneath an incongruous, immaculate powdered white wig. The black man was in his mid-thirties. His eyes held Cotterell's for a moment, then looked away. Cotterell allowed his own eyes to close. He tried with an almost physical effort to clear his mind. Was this another dream? Was he dead? Behind the black man a voice spoke.

'What do you think?' Another voice asked.

'I don't know.' The black man replied.

'He'll live?' asked the voice.

'I said, I don't know.'

'He's lucky.' A pause, then, 'Have you been on deck today Citizen Charles?'

'Not since daylight,' replied the black man.

'There are still sheep in the sea, even now.' Both voices were speaking French. French seamen say '*moutons*' where Englishmen would say 'white horses.' Apart from the single word 'awake' Cotterell had heard nothing but French since he'd been on the vessel. The black man, Rasselas Charles, spoke good French with a definite but lilting English accent. The other voice was a country French accent – Cotterell recognised that it came from the Norman Cotentin. He'd heard that accent many times before, from fishermen around Jersey, from Frenchmen on the Gaspé or even Nova Scotia. But there was something else. It was extraordinary. Cotterell didn't only recognise the accent; he recognised the voice that spoke it. Cotterell didn't trust his senses. Was he still in a dream of death? He wondered. His dulled, slow-awakening brain worked through the logic. The world was becoming concrete again. The gunpowder filling-room with such a grand lamp meant he was on a warship. That he was by the gunpowder filling-room meant he was in the bowels of the ship, on the orlop deck or cockpit. The voices meant it was a French warship. The smell confirmed it. Down here upon the orlop, above the ballast, the ship stank. English warships do not stink in any quarter, or else someone would pay for it. Cotterell was a fisherman but he knew that much about the King George's Navy. Now Cotterell heard another French voice, this time refined, sounding as if it belonged to a man of education, without the marks of a region in it. 'It's a miracle we saw him. If night had come . . .'

The Cotentin voice harrumphed. Apparently it did not much care for the opinions of the refined voice.

'Or fog.' Continued the refined voice, lecturing. 'Fog is partic-
ularly common in the seas around the Banks.'

'Really? Common?' said the Cotentin voice in a tone which
said 'be quiet.'

The black man Charles leaned closer to Cotterell's exhausted
face. 'How are you?' he whispered in soft West Indian English.
Cotterell couldn't reply. 'You were like a drowned rat when we
took you out of the sea. You surprised us. We thought you were
dead.'

Cotterell held the black man in his gaze for a second.

'Don't whisper. What are you saying to him, Citizen Charles?'
said the refined French voice. The word 'citizen' had an unpleasant
taste for the man behind the voice, as if it was spoken with a
mouthful of stones.

'That everyone thought he was fish bait.' Charles replied.

'He may well have been bait. But for which fish?' responded
the refined voice. 'He owes his life to France and the sharp eyes
of our sailors.'

'He is indeed a lucky man.' Charles agreed. He took a piece
of pale clean cloth and dipped it in a bowl of liquid, then wiped
Cotterell's eyes. Cotterell blinked. His eyes felt as if they had
been scrubbed with sand. The liquid relieved the pain.

A man clumped forward in leather seaboots which creaked.
He leaned over the black man's shoulder. He was dressed as an
officer of the French Navy, with long flowing black hair and a
large, grey moustache stained brown by tobacco. The black hair
was patently and cheaply dyed, making the officer look for all
the world like an actor playing a ship's officer. The uniform tunic
didn't fit very well. It looked as if the man would only need to
give one good swing of his elbows to split it. Though he had
been a child when he last saw the face, Cotterell immediately
recognised it. The man leaned over Cotterell and spoke. He stank
of cheap tobacco and brandy.

'Chance fell for you, young fellow. The end of Floreal, Prairial
approaches. You must have fallen into the warm current. Any

earlier in the year or the current's course changed by even a point, you would have died from cold within an hour.'

This was the Cotentin voice. He wore the clothes of a French naval captain but didn't sound like one. Cotterell understood the words but not the sense. What the hell was Prairial? The Captain pawed at the skin on Cotterell's face like a farmer examining a plough-horse's mouth.

'We lack seamen, that's for sure. Don't we Citizen Auchard?'

The refined voice, its owner still out of sight, agreed. 'We certainly do, Commandant.'

Charles reached into the cot and pulled Cotterell's hand from under the blanket. He showed the soft hand to the Captain in the flickering, dim light.

'He's no rough-handed seaman,' said Charles.

The Captain ignored the hand. 'Then we'll make him one.'

Auchard came forward, a thin face, a prematurely balding head with a fine brow and almost non-existent eyebrows above one grey eye, the other covered by an eye patch. He was a perfect picture of a French maritime officer. Clean, precise, meticulous. Auchard took Cotterell's hand into his own, felt the soft skin across Cotterell's palm, then let him go again. He addressed Cotterell in French, 'Which ship?'

No reply came. Cotterell could barely think, let alone speak.

'Stop playing games with me. Which ship? How many men? And who are you? Passenger? Officer?'

Again no reply.

'He speaks English in his dreams,' supplied Charles. Auchard repeated the same words in strongly-accented English. Cotterell tried again to answer but no words would come and the effort exhausted him. Cotterell closed his eyes. He heard the French Captain's's voice behind Auchard. 'I know the English. They like red meat to eat and the wind in their sails. Take him on deck. He'll improve.'

'Later would be better. Don't you think?' Charles answered. He spoke quietly.

The Captain didn't argue. 'You're the doctor.'

'Not I,' replied Charles.

'What is a doctor but a man who consults his books and mends a fellow? There is no man on this vessel better read than you, sir. You be the doctor,' said the Captain. 'What do the books say about nearly drowned men?'

'Nothing.'

'But he'll live?'

'I expect so. I don't know.'

'Well . . . do your best.'

'Keep him down here?'

'As you see fit.'

Charles held a small cup to Cotterell's lips. He allowed liquid to dribble from the cup into Cotterell's mouth. It tasted bitter. Cotterell opened his eyes. The black, Charles, and the Frenchman, Auchard, looked at him for a moment in silence, then a voice called down the companionway, 'Citizen Commandant! Citizen Commandant!'

'On the faux-pont,' called the Captain.

A boy of about twelve tumbled down the companionway. He was barefoot, wore trousers and shirt made of un-dyed canvas and a little blue muffler. He straightened himself on landing, like a cat. For a moment, looking out of the corner of his eye, Cotterell thought it was Thibault.

'On deck, Citizen. Sail sighted.'

'You saw it, Erique?' asked the Captain.

'No Citizen. Yannik is up there. I . . . Citizen Lefèvre called me down.'

'Which point?'

'South-west quarter, Citizen.'

'Was it the *Vendôme*?'

'Too far to see, Citizen.'

'Just one sail?'

'I believe so.'

'Was it a fleet? Vanstabel's fleet?'

'He couldn't see, Citizen.'

'No signal? No flag?'

'He said it was too far away.'

'You'd have seen it, Erique. You'd have told me exactly what is out there.' The Captain put his arm about the boy's shoulders and addressed Charles. 'This boy is a little gem. He has the best eyes in the maritime service. And probably the best ears too. Eyes and ears make a captain. One day he'll be an admiral.'

Erique smiled, pleased. 'Thank you Citizen.'

'Which way was this vessel headed?'

'Yannick just said he saw a sail, Citizen, with the hull down below the horizon.'

The Captain considered this. He sat on a chest.

'Could it be your grain convoy?' asked Charles.

'It could,' answered the Captain, 'or it could be a British frigate waiting for the convoy.'

'Mon Commandant.' The boy was hopping from foot to foot. He had something else to say. The Captain waved him to speak. 'Are we in a hurry?'

The Captain frowned. 'What?'

'Citizen Lefèvre said we were in a hurry and you are to come up immediately . . . sir.'

'Says? *He* says?'

'Yes, Citizen Commandant.'

'He commands the *Hortense* or I do?'

'You do. I suppose, sir. Captain sir. I mean . . .' Then he corrected himself, 'Citizen Commandant.' The boy could feel a trap opening under his feet.

The Captain thought for a moment. 'You go up the mast for me, Erique, and join Yannik. Keep your keen young eyes on that ship. As soon as it shows the slightest sign of belonging to that foul tyrant King George, or of getting any closer to us, you let me know straight away.'

'Yes, Citizen.'

'*Me*, mind you,' said the Captain. 'You tell me.'

The boy scrambled up the companionway again. When he'd gone the black man broke the silence, 'Will we run?'

Auchard and the black stood around Cotterell, who was, for all outer purposes, unconscious in the cot. The Captain watched them from across the cabin. Auchard answered for his chief, all stiff formality. 'It is not for you to question a Captain of the French maritime service.'

The black man didn't reply. The Captain's sense of humour returned. He laughed. '. . . no matter how he came by his command.'

'I'm sure I don't understand, sir,' said Auchard, though he did.

The Captain confided, 'Citizen Auchard will defend the honour of this uniform to the death, no matter who wears it. Isn't that the case, Auchard?' The refined voice didn't answer. 'And I happen to wear it.' The Captain continued. 'He doesn't like revolutionaries and he doesn't like negroes. The idea of his beloved maritime service being taken over by privateering scum, then used for transporting Jacobin niggers across the ocean in places reserved for officers revolts him.'

'Citizen Commandant, I beg you,' said Auchard.

The Captain continued to speak 'confidentially' to Charles. 'Allow me to apologise on behalf of my officer, Citizen Charles. Don't be uncomfortable with him. There are plenty of ex-slavers in our crew. Perhaps the very men who took you to America are among them.' He paused as if a thought had occurred, though it was clear to them all that what came next was deliberate. 'Perhaps you travelled in one of Auchard's *negriers*."

'I have no slave ships,' said Auchard, exasperated. 'I never did.'

'Your father's then,' replied the Captain.

Charles said very quietly, 'I was born in Jamaica.'

The Captain was reassuring. 'Auchard has an excess of military zeal, but that's his only fault. He's not to know that one word in the right ear from a man like you could lop off his head. Indulge us, I beg you Mr Charles. We're not savages. We're not Englishmen, drinking the blood of French babies and enslaving all before them. You saw how I pulled this one from the sea. How kind we are to the boys on board. No one is allowed to so much as lift a hand to them. This is a people's navy, run on proper revolutionary principles.' And then the Captain spoke softly to the other officer. 'On deck now, Auchard. On your way up give orders for dinner to be prepared early, then fires dowsed. And make sure the off-watch rests. They will need it.'

Second officer Auchard left them. Charles disliked the mock humility. He disliked the way the Captain toyed with his second in command. It meant trouble. The Captain stayed sitting on his wooden chest, apparently lost in contemplation. Charles busied himself with jars of ointments. He had no idea what they were or where they went in the surgeon's kit. After a while the Captain spoke. His voice had lost its mischievous tone. He was clearly talking to a possible ally, wanting Charles to understand his reasoning. 'I won't run, but I won't engage him unless I have to. We'll move north to see if he follows. If he's French he'll stay on his course. If British he'll follow, in case we're part of the grain convoy.'

'I am pressed for time,' said Charles. 'I travel to France at the express invitation of members of the Committee of Public Safety, Captain.'

'I know.'

'Do you know which members in particular?'

'Citizen Robespierre wrote my instructions to fetch you from Maine. But I have other orders from the Committee, too. Jeanbon St André's name is on them.'

'Whose writ runs?'

'We are at sea. Citizen St André has a representative on board whose sole task is to ensure we follow those instructions word for word.' He paused for effect. 'Nothing is more important than the American grain. Each and every French vessel will make protection of the grain convoy its most urgent priority, above

all other considerations. Without the grain France will starve.
Without the grain our Revolution will have been in vain. If we
fail, the British, the Bourbons and their aristocratic friends will
lord it over us once more. Neither of us wants that, Citizen
Charles, surely.'

'You will need to find the Chesapeake convoy.'

'Perhaps I have.' The Captain rose and mounted the companionway.

Charles leaned over his patient. The eyes were closed. The
man seemed to be asleep. One man murmuring English in his
dreams shouldn't represent a danger. But Rasselas Charles knew
there were powerful British ships roaming the North Atlantic
looking for them. Was this man from one?

When Cotterell opened his eyes once more he was alone. The
candle behind the glass in the big mahogany case was much
lower. Many hours had passed, perhaps even a day. Cotterell had
no way of knowing if it was the same candle. He clambered
out of the cot. His head was full of the Captain's voice, as if
he had the man by his side all that time. Had Cotterell really
seen him or had it been a dream? Did the voice mean he was
actually aboard the wretched *Galipétan*? Cotterell was naked. He
sat on the edge of the cot and examined his body, hardly daring
to believe he was all still in a piece. Everything ached. His limbs
ached. His head ached. From the feel of his guts, his liver and
lights ached too. His eyes were still sore but there was no acute
pain from keeping them open. As he moved Cotterell noticed
he had a long wound across his back, then inside his oxters and
under his arms. He felt and examined it. The wound was a burn
where the rope had held him to the spar. It would mend. The
muscles in Cotterell's aching limbs shot pain through him when
he moved. But they would mend too. Cotterell gave thanks for
the pain. It was life affirming. He was alive when he hadn't
expected to be. He stumbled on aching feet to the mahogany
lantern case and peered past it into the filling-room, sheltering

his eyes from the flame inside the glass with his hand. There were powder kegs inside but no person. He was completely alone. He turned and looked about himself. He had no clothes. Cotterell fumbled about the dim orlop until he found a long, dark, seemingly starched-linen smock on a surgeon's chest. He pulled it on. Even the linen felt as if it tore at his skin. He wrapped the woollen blanket from the cot about his shoulders and made his way to the companionway. Cotterell ordered first one foot then the other up the steps. They obeyed reluctantly. At each step he had to repeat the order. But he moved. Slowly, painfully, he climbed.

Cotterell emerged on the ship's lower deck. Another companionway rose above him. The deck was in darkness, save for one sailor sitting cross-legged, carving a bone by a scrap of candle. The carver put down his piece of bone and carving knife. He stared at Cotterell but said nothing. Above the bone-carver's head, dozens of men slept in hammocks slung between the beams. The hammocks swung in time to the movement of the ship. If any of the sleeping crew so much as opened an eye, Cotterell did not see it. Dozens more hammock spaces were empty, which was a puzzle to Cotterell. Perhaps the French Navy arranges watches differently, he thought. His eyes adjusted to the comparative darkness of the deck. Two more men sat under a knee, speaking softly to each other. They stopped when one saw Cotterell. Both stared. All three waking men watched Cotterell climb slowly, painfully and carefully up the ladder. None spoke to him.

Fresh air reached him now. The head of the companionway emerged on the gun-deck, which was open to the stars on a frigate, having only a quarter-deck and foredeck above it. Cotterell stood on the very concrete gun-deck, sails, ship's boats, dark sky and endless, unreachable veil of stars above his head, solid wooden deck beneath his feet. He looked up and watched the stars for a moment. He could make out the constellations, looked for, then spotted, Polaris. They were heading a little north of east.

He could feel the breeze and sense the waves. His escape from the sea and a lonely death still seemed like magic. Cotterell turned about himself, taking in the universe and the vessel he was on. He felt as if he was on a magic ship sailing in a sea of stars. But the magic ship had guns. He counted twelve on each side. He knew there would be more, probably short-range guns, on the quarter-deck. The gun deck had been cleared as if for action, partitions folded, furniture cleared and stacked away. Buckets, sponges and shot sat ready, all lit by a tiny, soft red glow radiating from a covered brazier in the middle of the deck. Cabins, hammocks, furniture and possessions up here were stowed lashed against the ship's wooden walls and rails. The guns were lightly manned. A few crew sat or lay on the deck by them. The gun-ports remained closed. The vessel was prepared for an action which wasn't about to happen. Cotterell was no expert on warships but this, with the crew below, did not seem normal.

The men sitting on deck or by the guns looked at him with curiosity. None reacted otherwise. Near the brazier stood the sans culottes and her toothless companion, large as life. They hadn't been a vision. He turned again; there was something else. Apart from the brazier, which was hidden by rails and wooden walls from outside view, not a light glowed. The ship presented almost complete darkness to the sea outside and any ship which happened to be on it. The only lights Cotterell had seen were the filling-room lamp, deep on the orlop, and the scrap of candle on the lower deck, which was closed from the outside world anyway.

Above Cotterell on the public side of the quarter-deck stood a small group. The Captain in his clumping sea boots and uniform paced alone, a few steps away from the others. Cotterell could hear the steps. The figure of a young woman could just be made out the near the Captain. She was leaning on the rail. Even in the near-dark, covered by a cape, her curves were still obvious to Cotterell. The Captain paused by the young woman and pointed to the north sky, his voice growling softly in English.

'Great Bear, Little Bear, Cepheus, Polaris. To the south . . .'

He turned to point to the south and in so doing spotted Cotterell lit by the dim red glow of the gun-deck brazier.

'Ah. The survivor of the storm.' He waved at a young slim man in a sword and hat. 'Mathelier . . .'

The slim man turned at his Captain's command, saw Cotterell and leaned over the rail to call, 'You there. Up here on the gaillard.'

They watched as Cotterell painfully climbed the steps to the quarter-deck. The ship's lanterns were unlit. There were no lights on the quarter-deck, just a tiny glow from the ship's binnacle, and again a brazier ready for use by gun crews up here. The brazier's soft red glow was reduced by a cover and hidden completely from seaward view, behind a rail. Cotterell could neither see nor sense gun crews around the quarter-deck, attending the guns which should be there. He could hear hens clucking away in a coop behind the helmsman's figure.

Very little light came from the binnacle. Cotterell knew the helmsman might be steering by a star, he'd done it enough himself. But still he was surprised at the almost absolute darkness both on deck and, apart from the stars, in the sky. Where was the moon? There was no cloud to cover it. That meant some considerable time had passed since Cotterell had last kept watch on the deck of his own fishing boat; days, perhaps a week. As he pulled himself up to the quarter-deck Cotterell could just make out the domed brow of Auchard, then the outline of black Charles' powdered wig. By Auchard's side stood a short stout woman. Cotterell couldn't see her features. Her matronly figure made her about forty. With her was a small man. This man turned to whisper something to the Captain. Cotterell fancied he saw a big beard and moustaches.

The young woman to whom the Captain had been showing stars was a dark figure on the rail. Mathelier, the young man wearing a sword and hat, stood at the top of the steps. He made no attempt to help Cotterell or even get out of his way.

'Bloody naval officers,' Cotterell thought, 'always conscious of their position.'

Cotterell looked along the gaillard. He was accustomed to the dim light now. He reckoned dark shapes around the rail made eight more guns. On an English ship they would be carronades.

'What is your name?' Mathelier asked abruptly.

Cotterell hesitated for a moment. His brain turned slowly. He still hadn't completely recovered from the near-drowning. The slim young man asked the question again in English. Cotterell replied, 'I speak French.'

'Then answer.'

'John, sir.' Cotterell decided to go for ignorance and obeisance.

'Ship?'

'The *Maude*, sir,' he lied. 'Which is this ship?'

'I ask the questions. Provenance?'

'I boarded her at Halifax, New Scotland,' he lied again.

Auchard's voice came from the darkness. 'Where is 'alifax?'

'Le Havre en Acadie, to the French. Jipugtug to the Micmacs,' answered Cotterell.

'Micmac?'

'Indian, sir,' replied Cotterell. He knew very well French seamen were familiar with the name 'Halifax,' an English fort built specifically to protect Nova Scotians from the French. Auchard was testing him.

'Bound for?' asked the slim young man in the darkness.

'I was going to Plymouth.'

'What happened?'

'There was a storm.'

He waited. No one spoke. Cotterell went on. 'She sank in a storm. Turned on her side, then didn't return. She rolled over. I was standing on deck. Holding on, like this,' he held the rail, 'and the next thing I knew she rolled completely and I was in the water. Please what is this ship?' he repeated.

'The *Hortense*,' said the young officer. 'A frigate of the French

Navy.' Cotterell was confused. He had feared he was on a privateer. He had thought he had recognised the privateer's captain.
Had the near-drowning so addled his senses?

'What sort of ship was this *Maude*?' asked the young officer.

'A merchantman, sir.'

'Captain?'

'Adam.'

'Home port?'

'I don't know. She was British and going to England, that's
all I cared.'

'What was her cargo?'

'I don't know.'

'You must have some idea.'

'I was a passenger sir.'

'Were there other passengers?'

'Some.'

'Soldiers?'

'No.'

'Did the ship flood before she capsized?'

'The crew were pumping and we had no sails out. I really
don't know. I just hung on to the rail.'

A silence. Cotterell could hear someone moving about on the
mast above them.

'You must have been in the storm?' Cotterell said.

'There was a storm,' agreed Mathelier.

'We were overwhelmed,' said Cotterell.

'You are the only survivor of this sudden disaster?' asked
Auchard.

'I don't know.'

The French officers whispered to each other. Then Auchard
spoke again.

'Where were you born?'

'Ashford. In Kent.' Cotterell lied again. He knew if he said
he was a Jerseyman they would interpret it as 'fisherman',
'sailor' or even 'pirate.' He'd never been to Ashford and chose

the town because it seemed unlikely any French officers would have either.

'A seaport?'

'No sir. It's inland.'

'You have family?'

'My father farmed pigs and apples.' Doesn't everyone in Kent, he thought, and expected to be safe.

'Bravo!' came the Captain's voice. 'Bravo! *Vrai fermier! Vrai paysan!*' He made it sound like a qualification. '*Chapeau*, Citizen. *Chapeau!*'

Now Cotterell was sure. The voice was that of the privateer captain he had last seen hanging like a monkey from the rigging of the *Galipétan*, almost twenty years ago. The Captain obviously had not recognised Cotterell, but that was no surprise. Cotterell had been a boy when he had last clapped eyes on the man.

Auchard's voice in the darkness continued as if his commander had said nothing. 'You decided not to follow him.'

'My father died and my mother sent me to the New World to better myself.'

'As a clerk?' Auchard asked in English. He obviously found the idea of a man who thought being a clerk was 'bettering' himself extraordinary.

'Yes sir. We all have to make the best of the skills God gave us to find our place in the world. I could write, my mother couldn't support me, so she sent me to the new Halifax to use my skill, as her cousin was in business with a man who was opening a store there.'

'Again from Kent?' asked the Captain.

'Yes sir.'

'And we have plucked you from the sea,' said the Captain, 'so your mother may see you again.'

'Thank God.'

'There is no God,' interrupted Mathelier. 'There is no logic in believing power comes from outside of men. It has been established.'

There was a silence. No one on the quarter-deck rushed to support Mathelier's youthful voice.

'You'll forgive me if I don't share your confidence, young sir.' said Cotterell. 'As your Captain says, you have picked me from the sea. And you may be assured I did not go into it and lose all my clothes and all my possessions from choice. So if there is no God, who saved me? And whose hand drowned all those men on the ship with me?'

'Nature,' came a voice from the darkness, another voice. The man with the beard. 'Nature is what we modern men call God.'

Cotterell had never been on the quarter-deck of a French warship before and hadn't expected to be tested on philosophy when he did.

'Where did you learn French?' asked Auchard.

'In Nova Scotia. In the hardware store in Halifax.'

The small man with the big beard huffed and puffed at each answer Cotterell gave.

Auchard said, 'You learned well.'

'Thank you.'

The men in the darkness whispered to each other.

'How long did you live in 'alifax?' Auchard asked.

'Since I was made apprentice to the storekeeper. Eleven years sir.'

'Wife?'

'No sir. That's why I was going back to Kent, sir. To find one.'

'Are there no women in Nova Scotia?'

Before Cotterell could answer the Captain's voice cut in, booming across the dark quarter-deck. 'There are thousands of women in 'alifax. The place is full of women. Every other man is a woman. Dutch cows with long faces. Whores, harlots and fishwives . . .'

'Emily,' said Auchard in English, commanding the young woman in the cape. 'Go below.'

She didn't move.

'. . . Bar-girls, waitresses and no doubt a schoolteacher or two,' continued the Captain. 'And then there are the miserable Protestant fanatics. Bitter daughters of British loyalists. American émigrés. They would look down on a little clerk in a little store selling nails and lamp-oil. Am I right?'

'There are American loyalists in Halifax, yes sir.'

'But are there any women a man would *want?*'

Cotterell didn't reply to the booming voice.

The Captain went on, 'Loyalty to the British crown isn't much of a qualification in a wife, is it? It doesn't compare with a warm breast, or a generous physical nature. Who wants a wife who loves King George but keeps her knees clamped together? There is no one in Halifax a young man full of vim and vigour would want for a wife.'

'You sound like you know it, sir,' said Cotterell.

'Oh I know it,' replied the Captain, but offered no more.

Cotterell continued his answer to Auchard. 'I was not introduced to wealthy loyalist circles, sir. Owing to my station.'

'You should have gone south, sir.' The Captain couldn't resist another interruption, speaking English in his thick Cotentin accent. He sounded like he was enjoying whatever gloom came upon young men in Halifax. 'South to the former British colonies. Charleston. Georgetown. The women down there are impeccable. Proper English women, but raised in America. Georgetown women. Isn't that true, Auchard? Women with pink cheeks and dewy rose lips. Like one of your Kent apples gone on an adventure. *Les femmes de Georgetown.*'

He bowed deeply towards the woman Auchard called Emily. Someone giggled. Emily curtsied in the darkness. Cotterell could see her head bob.

Auchard said in English, 'Go below, Madam.' He was addressing the dark shape of the curtseying woman.

The dark figure did not reply, but left the rail and moved almost silently across the quarter-deck. As she descended the companionway her perfume drifted across to Cotterell again.

Everyone except Auchard and Cotterell seemed to have found the Captain's comments amusing. Even the hens clucked in their coop. Cotterell didn't understand the joke. Auchard's voice became if anything more formal.

'You were eleven years in 'alifax. So you know all about the sea?' Auchard asked.

'I know nothing about the sea. I was a clerk in a store.'

At this the bearded man could contain himself no longer. 'Why should we believe you?' He was a Breton.

'Sorry?'

'Logic says you're obviously some spy the English planted in the sea. Why else were you there?'

'Planted?' said Cotterell, disbelieving his ears.

'Posed. Put. Left for the *Hortense* to find.'

Cotterell tried to see the man's features in the dark, but couldn't. 'My ship sank.' He said.

'Ridiculous.'

'Sir?'

'We saw no sign of a ship.'

'It sank, sir.'

'We only have your word for that. You even speak French. Why?'

'So I could sell ironmongery to French farmers and fishermen, sir.'

'There are no Frenchmen in Halifax,' said the small bearded man.

'The country is full of Frenchmen. The inshore fishermen are French. The farmers are French,' countered Cotterell.

At this the Captain laughed aloud.

'Liar!' roared the small bearded man. 'It is a fact universally acknowledged that the British forced the French from Arcadie more than thirty years ago. Those who were not transported were murdered in their beds by British redcoats. Isn't it?'

'Undoubtedly, Lefèvre,' said the stout middle-aged woman by his side. 'A fact universally acknowledged.'

'With respect sir,' said Cotterell to the small bearded man, Lefèvre, but addressing all of them, 'From the very bottom of my heart I thank you all for saving my life. That I stand before you and live and breathe is no doubt thanks to you. I am grateful. But you have clearly never been to Nova Scotia. If you had you'd know it's full of your countrymen, whether they have been expelled or not.'

'He'll be telling us it's full of blacks next. Don't thank me. You owe that to the Captain. I would not have saved your life,' said Lefèvre. 'I would have left you to drown as soon as I heard the first English word from your mouth.'

The Captain spoke again. 'Enough. I decided what I decided.'

Cotterell stood in silence. No-one spoke for a while, then the Captain said, 'And your ship sank?'

'Yes sir.'

'How very sad. Very, very sad. How much did you pay as fare for your passage, Mister John?' He used the English word Mister. It sounded sarcastic in his mouth.

'My employer paid. But I know he paid twenty-seven guineas for the fare and another two pounds fifteen shillings for food. Of which I received only the barest ration of the poorest stuff.'

'That was very cheap.' Said Auchard.

'On account of how it wasn't a very good ship, I expect,' said Cotterell. 'But I found that out later.'

A silence. The Captain spoke again. 'Mr Lefèvre and my Second are all for hanging you from the *vergue*, sir.'

'I'm afraid I don't know what the *vergue* is,' replied Cotterell.

'What would it matter, if you were hanged from it? The information would be surplus to requirements, since your ears would be that much further from your shoulders. The yardarm.' He said the word 'yardarm' in English and pointed up to it. He continued in English, spoken through his strong Cotentin accent. 'So what do you say, Citizen John from Kent? The yardarm, the sea or a little bit of work for the French Navee?' He made the rhyme sing. He laughed again. He was close to Cotterell now, so that Cotterell could smell the brandy on his breath once more. He couldn't see the face clearly in the darkness but he could imagine it. He'd carried the image of that face in his head for years, since childhood.

'On deck!' came a call from the mast above. Cotterell recognised the voice of the boy, Erique. 'A light on tribord.'

'Lieutenant, get up there.'

'And another, Capitaine!' Erique called again from above.

'Sir.' The slim young man made for the rail and ratlines. His sword clattered as he moved. The Captain's voice stopped him.

'What are you going to do up there, make steak haché?'

'Sir?'

'Put the sacred sword down.'

'Sir.'

The Captain had made up his mind about Cotterell. 'You're lucky, Englishman. I need some lucky men on my ship, my God I do. Can you write French?'

'No sir. Just English.'

'More is the pity.' The Captain called over the rail. '*Chef d'equipment!*'

A voice called a reply from the gun-deck, '*Mon Commandant!*'

'Quiet man. To stations. Whisper it. No noise, no drums, no bells. No lights to show.'

'*Capitaine!*' The boatswain acknowledged again in a hoarse whisper.

'And issue this man with some clothes. Put him with English Tom.'

'Yes Citizen Commandant,' called the boatswain in another hoarse whisper, then, 'English Tom up on the galliard, now!'

A man stirred on the gun-deck.

'Are you fit?' The Captain asked Cotterell. His voice was even. He gave no sign at all of recognition.

'I believe so now. Yes. Thank you.'

'Thank France, young man. Not me. Clerk!'

'Citizen.' A quiet voice spoke in the darkness behind him.

'Put him in the book. One *terrien*,' and then softly to Cotterell, 'That's 'landsman' to you. A sailor entirely without skill.' The Captain raised his voice again a little for the benefit of the clerk, 'One landsman, found at sea, name of John . . .'

He waited for Cotterell to finish it. Cotterell had decided long ago that to reveal his identity would probably end his life there and then. But he was beyond fear.

'Cotterell. John Cotterell,' he waited. The Captain turned away.

3

In the late morning the French warship drew by their side.
Cotterell could see her through the shaft of light the gun-
port admitted under the foredeck, where he sat with his back
to a limed wood partition and his feet against a black painted
gun carriage. The warship was a three decker, much bigger than
a frigate and even at this distance towered over *Hortense*.

'You had better turn your mind to this,' said English Tom.

English Tom was teaching him to whip and serve rope and
Cotterell was doing his best to look like he was learning. Behind
Cotterell's head, beyond the partition, he could hear cattle moaning
and lowing. Beyond the three-decked warship he could see the
masts of other ships. By twisting he could see they were warships
and merchantmen both. These were the lights the boy Erique
had seen from the mast-top. By day the vessels all had plenty
of sail set but the breeze was feeble. The ships made way but
when the wind fell away they rocked in the long Atlantic swell.

The *Hortense* had stood down from her alert not long after
dawn, when it had become clear the vessel with which she had
kept company overnight was a friend, part of the Captain's
expected grain convoy and not a British reception party laid on
to meet it. The watch, now including Cotterell, went about its
business in the normal way of a military ship, constantly checking
and repairing the fabric of the vessel, trimming sails when ordered,
busying themselves with the thousand small jobs needed to keep
a warship at sea. But she was lightly crewed, that was clear to
any eye, and Cotterell wondered how such a small crew could

possible handle the ship and fight at the same time. The first
English warship to meet *Hortense* would serve her out in some
style, he thought.

Cotterell was now, at least in dress, every bit the French matelot,
though the boatswain had made it clear he was not required to
fight should they meet a British vessel. Tom remained in his Royal
Navy clothes, right down to the tarred straw hat, though Cotterell
discovered later that Tom had relieved a dying English merchant
sailor of it – waste not want not. To the outside eye, Cotterell
was a Frenchman. It was that or serve naked. They'd taken the
smock he'd found – it had been the surgeon's and in daylight
could be seen to be so covered with blood it was stiff to the
touch – and instead he wore second-hand canvas slops, called
frusques in French, and of worse quality than their English equiv-
alents, a neckerchief and a seaman's cap. The cap and neckerchief were stained and stank of the previous owners, but the
slops were sanitary, having been bleach-washed in a urine and
sea water mixture the French called *lessive*, then thoroughly dried
on deck before storing. His feet were bare, which was just as well
because the boatswain had had enough trouble fitting him out
with slops, on account of his height. Cotterell was six feet tall
and broad. A belt had been found for him and was cinched tight
about his waist. Hanging from it was a leather pouch containing
the small steel knife and spike every sailor on every ship needed.
The original owner of these implements, like the original and
various owners of the clothes he wore, had long since gone aloft
to join his maker. Below, on the lower deck, Cotterell, like every
other seaman, also now owned a bag made from old sail and a
rolled hammock formed of the same material. The bag hung on
a wooden peg hook. It contained a grubby and faded tunic jacket
and nothing else. Since Cotterell had found himself aboard the
Hortense as Abraham-naked and lacking in belongings as the day
he was born, possession of second-hand clothes, a knife, spike
and belt, a blue tunic jacket and a worn sailcloth bag was an enormous improvement on his position.

The sunlight through the gun-port caught Cotterell's face. He could feel it on his skin. He was amazed when the Captain hadn't recognised his name and doubly amazed when, encountering the officer by daylight, there had been no recognition of his face. He looked very like his father and grandfather, he knew. That face may have carried down the generations since the original Viking stock. Jerseymen were proud of their Viking seafaring heritage, none more so than Cotterell's father. He had told his son imaginary stories of Viking sailors during the long weeks they spent together on the ocean, fishing, building racks and drying their cod in remote bays on the Gaspé, in Acadie or on the Terre Neuve, as his father had always called them, whether he was talking to a Frenchman, Briton or Breton.

English Tom was short, broad and immensely strong. He lost no time in telling Cotterell he had been in the King George's Navy for more than twenty years, since he was nine. He had yet to explain how he'd ended up on a French vessel. The two sat by the foredeck gun-port so that Tom was able to demonstrate a whipping, opening the lay of a rope and pushing tarred twine through on a big needle.

'You can just unravel the lay on a small cord to get it through, but if you do that with one of these big buggers it stays unravelled, so you have to do it with a needle and turn the twine with a serving mallet.'

He showed Cotterell the worn mallet with the groove on top and the curved face. 'The French call this here what we are doing '*matelotage*', but I suppose you know that.'

'Why should I?'

'I have heard you speak their lingo. You sound like one of them.'

'I was a clerk . . .'

'I heard that and I heard you. Look close now or you'll never learn.'

Cotterell watched Tom turn the tarred twine neatly around the rope. Tom spoke confidentially, 'This is called an Admiralty whipping, but we don't mention that for fear of upsetting certain persons aboard, who cannot abide mention of anything British.'

'So what do you call it?'

'Just a whipping, or *surliure* in their lingo, and if any man asks for more intelligence I feigns ignorance.' Tom smiled.

'Why are you making your admiralty whippings on a French man-o'-war?'

Tom stopped turning the twine and looked closely at Cotterell. 'Because they made a prisoner of me.'

Cotterell waited. Behind him the cattle scuffled at their straw.

'I was on the *Veteran* commanded by Captain Nugent, in Sir John Jervis's expedition. Have you heard of Captain Nugent?'

'Should I?'

'He is a fine man. It was an honour to serve under him. I was captured in Guadeloupe,' continued Tom. 'Sir John raised a siege on Basse-Terre. We were ordered under the Midshipman Mr Wills from the *Veteran* to cut out a gunboat, round the corner in Pointe-à-Pitre harbour. Except this fellow. He pointed at the deck to indicate the *Hortense*, 'was in the harbour when he shouldn't have been, so took us by surprise, caught us, fought us, captured me and the officer. Killed the others.'

'Where's the Midshipman now?'

'He died of his injuries. Cutlass wounds in both arms and a pike wound in his leg here.' He indicated the lower inner of his right thigh. 'He fought like a lion but you get the stink quick in the Indies, and poor old Mr Wills' wounds fair stank, they did.'

'Was he young?'

'No. Thirty-three. The cutting out would have made him a lieutenant at last.'

'There was no surgeon on here?'

'Oh yes. The *Hortense* had a surgeon. And he took his saw to the poor fellow. He lopped bits off Mr Wills like he was pruning an old apple tree. I'm surprised he didn't flower and bear fruit. But the poor beggar died in a week, on that cot where they kept you.' An irrational chill went through Cotterell. 'And so I was left all alone, prisoner on this here French vessel. Then, when the landing came on Guadeloupe and Basse-Terre cried quarter, *Hortense* cut and run for Cuba and all points north, for fear of being trapped there. I ended trapped in my turn aboard her, prisoner on a runaway Frenchie ship, never knowing whether to be pleased or afrightened when we see a British one, since I know what a mess this one is in.'

'You've been here ever since?'

'I spent the first month in the *nask*, that is in irons, on the lower deck, with the Frenchmen messing and sleeping all about me.'

'You were mistreated?'

'Like a dog. Vile, but you can't kill me that easily. You are a lucky man they have neither the time nor spare men to keep you chained up too.'

'Then?'

'They captured an English merchantman down Jamaica way, a vessel what had been in the Honduras. And we soon found out why she was so easy to catch. Her crew brought the flux aboard, killing men more freely than if they had swept the decks ten times with canister shot. So that Captain ran short of men to work the ship and set me free.

'I take 'that Captain' to mean 'not this fellow?''

'You are correct. *That* Captain was an aristo, according to the crew, and jumped ship like a pressed butcher's boy as soon as we reached America.'

Cotterell had heard in Jersey of French Captains deserting their ships, but that was from French aristos who'd also run from the Revolution. This was the first time he'd heard directly of a commander deserting.

'Where did this one join?' Cotterell asked.

It was an odd question and Tom raised an eyebrow. But Cotterell needed to know about this French Captain.

'Georgetown. Some French agent sent him down from Charleston, where there is no shortage of French cut-thoats.'

'And privateers.'

'Exactly. You are well informed, Mr Halifax-living Cotterell.'

'What is this Captain's name?' Cotterell asked, though he knew the answer.

'Dubarre, and despite all the Frenchie bonhomie he's a real bastard, as you will no doubt see for yourself. He gets his officer boys to do his bully work for him, but everyone knows whose ship this is. Before the Revolution he was one of them Charleston privateers, and would cut a man's ears orf and stuff them down his throat as soon as look at him, according to his reputation, which he can't do now because beating and executing sailors has been more or less forbidden.'

'By?'

'What they call the Convention. Which is some parly-ment arrangement they have in France. They are in love with it. Convention this, Convention that.'

'But they use the guillotine in France.'

'There is always the guillotine, but we haven't got one handy. For shipboard matelots that comes later.' Tom said this with the air of a man laying a trump. 'On the pavey, in Brest, little Lefèvre says.'

Lefèvre again. To Cotterell it appeared Dubarre didn't have complete control of his own vessel.

'What's the First Officer called?'

"'Seconde' is the First Officer, in this arse-about-face way of running a ship they have. His name is Auchard.'

'Was he aboard throughout this cruise?'

'Throughout.'

'So he must be asking himself, why am I passed over? Why is a privateer captain of a French navy ship?' asked Cotterell.

'You understand seamen.'

Cotterell turned his eyes to the whipping in Tom's hands, then said, 'I just know men's nature.'

'It's the Revolution, of course.' Tom spoke softly. 'It's the world turned upside down. If you're the Mr St André of Paris little bearded Lefèvre keeps talking about, you would as soon trust a rabid dog as the 'Seigneur de this' or the 'Comte de that.' But you can trust Joseph Dubarre, who is a Norman innkeeper's son turned Charleston privateer and scourge of the British merchant fleet.'

'Who is Mr St André of Paris?'

'You must be the only man on this ship who hasn't heard of him. Mr St André is some form of naval grandee under the Convention. I think he must be the MP for the Navy or whatever is the equivalent for the Frenchies. If Lefèvre is the finger, St André is the arm, if you catch my drift. Lefèvre never stops talking about him.'

'You have listened carefully.'

'There often is no choice. You will see. I have discovered a great deal on this ship by listening. There is no outlying cause or dispute in French politicking I haven't had from messmates who speak a bit of English and I'm sure they will cut my throat before allowing me back to England to report it all to the Admiralty. Or yours.'

'My?'

'Throat. Once on board this vessel, according to our hosts you are here come hell or high water. You are a French sailor.'

'And you?'

'I pray every day for the blessed barky to be blown out of the water.'

'You joined Citizen Dubarre and his *Hortense* with these British merchant prisoners?'

'I did not 'join' the vessel at all, I'm sure. But things will go easier for me when we meet our British fellows,' he said. 'I am what I appear to be. You are the one wearing French sailor rig-out.'

Tom tore the tarred twine off the cord, unravelling his work, pulling it free of the rope. He offered the unravelled rope-end to Cotterell.

'You do it.'

Cotterell took the rope-end in his lap, turned the twine into a loop and began to feed it through the large needle. Tom watched carefully. Cotterell pushed the large needle through the rope.

'I did not mean to imply anything untoward,' said Cotterell.

'Is that so, Mr Cotterell?'

'You sailors have a special meaning for 'join.' Like a wedding. I just meant you were here on this ship. I apologise.'

Tom nodded assent, then, after a few seconds watching Cotterell begin the whipping again, he spoke. 'The captured merchantmen all died of the disease they brought with them, as well as half the crew of the *Hortense* herself, which the Frenchmen have not been able to replace because we were denied the coast of Louisiana and anywhere else west of the Floridas by British ships. They chased us as far as the straights between Cuba and Florida and only gave up when American warships came out to meet us off the Carolinas. By that time, though, we were aground at a place called the Frying Pan, where we were stuck and I thought we would all drown, as soon as the Almighty took his eye off the weather, which he kept calm, until our own boats and others from the American warships pulled us off. Then we went to Georgetown for repairs. You know it?'

'No.'

'It is entirely American, and it is most peculiar they still call their town after King George, since they can't find a good word to say for him. It is also a place where unattached maritime Frenchies to man the ship could not be obtained for neither love nor gold coin.'

'Apart from a captain?'

'That took over a month and the French have special agents down there arranging such things.'

'And the agents can't organise crew? No Carolinian volunteers?'

'Merchantmen pay better. There were plenty of merchantmen hiring, the Americans have no navy to speak off, except ships hired from the French. And I don't see one of His Majesty's

press gangs operating in Georgetown. No, the merchant way is
the best option to a skilled seaman in America.' The cows lowed
again, as if to interrupt him. Tom said, 'They can smell the girl
that feeds them.' Cotterell could see no girl. 'They always start
moaning if she's forward.'

'She feeds them now?'

'Cows do not carry pocket watches, Mr Cotterell. Just as
sailors don't. Aren't you hungry?'

'Starved.'

'I'm not surprised. You must have been on your back in that
orlop for over a week.'

'A week?'

'The blackie told me you didn't eat but they gave you water
dosed with some plant supplied to him by Indians. You were
delirious.'

'He confides in you?

'Not confides. He is far too grand a nigger to confide in a
little Jack Tar. We exchange English talk from time to time, since
he found out we share a native tongue. And I was on the boat
that lifted you out of the briney, so I was interested later to
discover whether the Good Lord had seen fit to save you. As
is natural.'

'Indeed. Does anyone else on this vessel speak English?'

'Only one, properly. An American lady. Though plenty of the
Frenchies speak it for purposes of trade when you have something they want. You'll see the lady . . .'

'I already have.'

'But I would not speak to her if I were you.'

'Why?'

'She is the Second, Auchard's, American wife, that he found
in a big house on the Waccamaw River.'

'You were there long enough for him to woo her?'

'I think it was arrangements rather than wooing that got him
the girl.'

'He walked her out?'

'He did. We spent our winter having planks repaired and hoping to find Frenchmen for a crew. Which there were none, apart from the Portuguese carpenter who was willing to serve and la belle Hélène ...'

'Who is ... ?'

'A whore come aboard for the crossing. You must have seen her. No teeth? She was beached there and was short of the blunt, I believe. She was smuggled aboard by a sailor, though I believe the Capitaine may have connived at it. You can rely on sailors to find the Cyprians, eh?'

'Tell me about Auchard's American wife.'

'Her family deals in Africans, as does his. The crew believe they found each other by correspondence between the families, the one shipping the Africans for the other. Like a marriage arranged between families of grocers or farmers.'

'What does Auchard say?'

'No one would dare ask him, but that's not her story. She told Charles, who talks to me, that they are completely in love and that Auchard is taking her to his estate in France and giving up the sea for good.'

'You believe that from the surgeon, Mr Charles?'

'He implied he did not believe it and the lady spoke for form's sake. I have no opinion. And he's no surgeon. The ship's surgeon died of flux with the others, though you would have been unlucky if you had found him for a healer, what with his endless bleedings and prunings of parts in case they become infected. A lot of good it did poor Mr Wills.'

'So the African was his assistant?'

'Not at all. He came aboard later, on the Penoboscot River in Maine, and the crew was glad to have him.'

'Why?'

'Why?' English Tom repeated. 'Why?' It seemed an incredible question to him. 'Did you forfeit your brains in the sea? Isn't it obvious? Blacks are natural doctors. You don't meet Africans what don't know about medicine, what with their muds and poultices and teas of barks and spices. Have you never been in the Indies?'

'Never.' Cotterell lied.

'Well if you had you'd know. If you want my opinion, the nigger saved your life.'

Cotterell tightened a turn of the twine on the rope, then passed the free end through the standing loop of the whipping.

How?' he asked at last.

'You had a fever like I'd never seen a man survive. You were on fire. You were coughing up your guts and gizzards. You don't recall?'

'No.'

'Perhaps it's a mercy. We thought you were rounding the cape, in a manner of speaking.'

Cotterell had finished his whipping. He held it out to Tom and asked, 'This American wife converses with Charles, even though she's from a slaver family?'

'She does.'

'What does her husband say?'

'I don't know. The gentleman concerned is the ship's First Officer, or Second in their own lingo. He don't discuss his family dealings with mean little matelots like me. But if you want to know what I think . . .'

Cotterell raised an eyebrow. Tom looked disappointed. Cotterell smiled disarmingly. 'Tom, you have had your native English tongue locked up for too long.'

'If it doesn't please you . . .'

'Continue. Please. '

Tom did. 'If the ship's harlot gave birth in there,' he indicated the manger behind Cotterell's back, 'would the child she bore be a calf or a baby? Just because Miss Emily's father is a dealer in Africans don't mean she's one too.'

Tom took Cotterell's whipping and examined it.

'You have whipped that uncommon well for a man who has never done one before. More like the work of a man who's been at sea for twenty years or more, that there is.'

Tom waited. Cotterell didn't answer. Tom went on. 'I look at those soft hands. I look at the way you tie that whipping and I think, I am talking to an officer in the King's Navee. That's what this gentleman is. Hiding his identity, for fear of becoming a barter piece. Or worse. Perhaps I should stand and salute you, sir.'

'I'm not an officer and I'm not in the Royal Navy.'

There was a silence before Tom relented. 'Anyway, if you want Capitaine Joseph Dubarre and his crew to think of you as a landsman or *terrien* or whatever way their Frenchie lingo calls it, you'd better start behaving like one.'

He threw the whipped rope back into Cotterell's lap. But he had lost Cotterell's attention. The Jerseyman was looking through the port at the ship beyond, sailing in company with *Hortense*. There was no wind to speak of and the 'sailing' was minimal. 'Why are they launching a boat?' Cotterell asked.

The frigate's crew had swung out a boat and were crewing it with oarsmen. The swell was light and there were no waves but still it was odd to send men to board *Hortense* by boat rather than signal messages by code flag.

'That'll be a signal officer, no doubt. The surgeon wasn't all the *Hortense* lost to the flux. She was struck dumb when she lost both our cadets.' said Tom. 'We'd be there all blessed day waiting for the Second to pore over his signal books and Lieutenant Mathelier to tie the bunting to the halyard, leave alone reading what the other fellow says.'

'<u>Our</u> cadets?'

Tom was silent for a moment. 'Just a way of speaking,' he said. 'Anyway, they were both good kind boys who made sure I was fed when I was in the nask, which is more than you can say for they other beggars. And now they have gone aloft to Frenchie heaven, leaving their earthly selves below.'

On the nearby frigate two men descended to join the oarsmen in the boat, one a seaman with a bag, tunic and cap, the other a very young officer with the features and figure of a boy. An iron-banded wooden officer's sea-chest was lowered to them.

'The officer will read the book and the man will raise the flags,' said Tom. 'Meanwhile this vessel is a hundred fighting men light. I have seen a better organised game of pell mell than the way these beggars arrange themselves.'

Cotterell didn't reply, but again he noticed Tom saw things as if he were a Frenchman. A whistle sounded on the deck behind them.

'Nosebag.' Tom stood. Cotterell smiled at the image, which pleased Tom.

'That's what I am lacking about my messmates on the old *Veteran*,' said Tom. 'French is not a very funny language, leastways not as I speak and hear it. And these French beggars have no sense of humour at all that I have noticed.'

4

On the lower deck of the *Hortense* the men ate off square boards on the deck below their sleeping place. There were of course no hammocks slung while they ate. Tom didn't like it.

'They eat like beasts,' he said.

The men were served from a group pot, each sitting cross-legged on the deck. There were other differences from Cotterell's previous experiences at sea. On a merchantman or a fishing boat the food provided to the crew would have been fresh as long as it lasted. The *Hortense* had not long since been in Penoboscot Bay, Maine, and had the chance to take on supplies which could have lasted for weeks, picked-over every day by the cook's assistants. But she had not done so. Captain Dubarre had neither permission nor money to go far outside the contract provisions arranged by correspondents in Brest. The ship had fresh cabbage, onions and potatoes in plenty, as they were permitted to purchase on the American market, but otherwise she relied on stores provided by French commissaries, of which there were few in America, and stores she looted from combatant ships which fell in her way, of which there had been just one, the British merchantman which had brought the flux disease, along with prisoners and food. *Hortense* carried salt pork, beef and a great deal of salt fish in barrels, not only Atlantic fish but barrels of North Sea herring too, taken from the British merchantman which the *Hortense*'s men had looted and plundered with a thoroughness peculiar even by the standards of French Republican sailors. There appeared to be no beer on board *Hortense* and there was little spirit available to the sailors. Though brandy was carried it wasn't rationed out under regulations, as rum would be on an English ship of war. Wine was available, kept in giant casks in the hold, where it was tapped, brought on deck and served to the crew along with water, both wine and water being carefully measured. The ship carried eau de vie too, but Dubarre didn't have it issued.

Cotterell was supplied with a horn cup for drinking and a wooden platter from which he might eat; dead men's belongings again. He sat opposite English Tom, pressed between other sailors in a circle around a pot and lifting slabs of warm fish cake to his mouth using his knife and a piece of bread, since he lacked a spoon. The fish cake was a mixture of salt cod, oil, potato and garlic, and this first taste of fish since his near drowning, despite his hunger, reminded Cotterell of the fate of the men on his own fishing vessel. His mood fell.

'Are you well, brother?' asked Tom as he saw Cotterell's face become thoughtful. Their messmates had laughed at Cotterell when he sat to eat. As he and Tom had descended the companionway to the mess the sans culottes had stood, a few feet away, to take a bow from the others. The watch had applauded and shouted 'Bravo.'

Tom told Cotterell she was called Liberté, and that with her toothless but voluptuous constant companion, Hélène, she had taken bets all round that she could 'raise the dead', meaning Cotterell. No one had expected him to live when he left the water. The bets had been paid out.

Cotterell found the presence of women crew extraordinary. Neither he nor his father had carried women on their fishing vessels; to his knowledge neither had any other Jersey fishermen. Merchant ships big enough for numbers of officers and skilled crew might carry one or two wives, and of course women were carried on ships as passengers, but in Cotterell's experience a semi-official ship's harlot was unique to the military service,

French or English, and usually confined to port or coasting. Sailors' 'wives' did not usually cross the Atlantic but, for whatever reason, Hélène was crossing, while Liberté seemed a normal crew member. The other sailors advised him – unconcerned as to whether Cotterell was or was not interested in the information – that Hélène conducted her business either behind a raised piece of canvas or in public, but in either case usually upon the deck on which they ate. The canvas was raised or not according to the shyness or otherwise of the crewmember using her services. Hélène did not have a preference.

Liberté was a different creature altogether, small, slim and intense. Her chestnut hair was short under the red cap, her eyes grey, her features fine and her smile was full of her own white teeth. Her real name was Cecilie but she had changed it and abandoned skirts for the pantaloons of a revolutionary soldier in '91. Tom, who knew everything, despite his indifferent French, had found out she was a regular member of the ship's crew, carried on the books but with her sex unspecified. She was rumoured by the cook's assistant, a black-haired, olive-skinned Provençal who insisted the mealy-tasting fishcake was '*brandade*', to have followed Kellerman's artillery to Valmy and, when her husband was killed before her very eyes, had taken his place and fired his cannon at the Prussians. The cook, also black-haired, also olive-skinned, also Provençal, but surly, told Cotterell and Tom – they were at the stove fetching their group's numbered portions – that Liberté was merely heroic. But the assistant cook overheard and insisted, poetically, that implacable revolutionary hearts like Liberté's were the real source of the '*furia francese*' of noble reputation in both Italy and Provence. She was insatiable in every sense, and he hinted, a little frightening. To emphasise this he sang a new French song:

'*Aux armes, Citoyens, formez vos bataillons,*' and the others immediately joined in. The deck echoed to the *Marseillaise*. The crew sang about battalions in a citizens' army and farrows filled with the blood of their enemies. Cotterell had never heard anything so extraordinary. Liberté sang loudest, looking like she'd dipped her hands in the blood of their enemies.

Tom told Cotterell both women manned guns on the *Hortense* in the same way as male members of the crew. Liberté went aloft in the afternoon in just the same way as the men. No one would dare refuse her. But the belle Hélène, as she was popularly known, was excused yardarm duties both on account of her precious skills and of her luxurious and voluptuous shape, which was designed by God, or his modern and more logical revolutionary replacement, better to lie on a Charleston or New Orleans *chaise-longue* than hang over a yardarm furling or unfurling sail. 'Up there she'd have been a danger in several ways at once!' said Tom.

The furthest aloft the belle Hélène went was the gun-deck. It was she who fed the cattle there and no doubt continued with her other 'duties' in the comfort of the ship's manger. Sometimes Liberté joined Hélène in the manger. When she did the other sailors stayed away, for fear of provoking one of the tempers that ran through Liberté's arteries like channelled forces of nature.

'If she chose you the way they say, every man on this ship is jealous. You were where they all want to be.' Tom had observed of the sans culottes.

'What's to stop them asking?'

'She'd cut their throats for their trouble. She's a real spitfire, that one.'

'Does she hate men?' Cotterell said

'She was married.'

'I expect the husband took the Prussian shot with some relief.'

5

Above Cotterell sailors spread canvas canopy to shade the deck. Half a dozen sailors rolled it out. Two pushed a narrow boom into the device while the others held the canvas corners, then the whole was raised eight feet or so off-deck by halyards until the guys they'd attached to chain plates and lower-rigging tensioned.

'The Captain takes care of his crew.' Cotterell motioned to the awning.

'That is neither for your benefit nor mine,' said Tom. 'The world has changed, but not that much, especially where Capitaine Dubarre has command.'

Later they were lined up on the gun-deck with the rest of the crew to take part in an extraordinary theatrical event convened by Lefèvre. It took the form of a sort of pantomime with the quarter-deck as a stage and Lefèvre in the role of a garrulous Harlequin.

'He does this every day and the Captain puts up with it, laughing all the while behind his back,' said Tom. 'Who says the French have no sense of humour?'

'You did,' answered Cotterell. 'In the forenoon.'

'Watch, landsman,' replied Tom. 'Listen and learn.'

Lefèvre stood on the quarter-deck pulling his red beard and looking excited; commissioned officers and Dubarre behind him, matronly Citoyenne Lefèvre by his side. The new signalling officer and crewman were on the quarter-deck too, but busy attaching flags to a halyard. Apart from them, the helmsman and the look-out, the whole crew was devoted to the event. The boy Erique stood before Lefèvre holding a thin book up to him, so the red-bearded firebrand could read it in comfort and have his hands free to refresh himself from a flask of wine or just to wave about for emphasis.

Captain Dubarre's dyed hair and theatrical uniform, allied with the languid postures of his officers, formed a tableau above the sailors. Lefèvre's demeanour made them look even more like a company of quarter-deck actors, with Erique the human lectern as prompt. The officers looked out over the crew on the deck below them or stared out to sea.

Tom whispered, 'He reads the work of Master Tully to improve us.'

'Who is?'

'A famous Roman. Know him?'

'No. Have you read him, Tom?'

'Myself, no. I can't read very well. Charles, the black, has read him, of course. What hasn't he read? He told me his master's wife had him educated in Latin as a boy in Jamaica. Imagine! I don't believe he ever did an honest day's nigger work in his life. He is all reading, writing and languages. You must have heard him speak French.'

'I have. Can't you?'

'He has tried to teach me but no matter what I do I end up sounding like a baby.' Tom looked troubled at the thought of his own attempts at French. He continued. 'When first he came aboard he used to stand next to me and translate what Lefèvre said.'

'Why?'

'For my improvement. Charles is a great believer in improvement.'

On the quarter-deck above them Lefèvre was flicking though the pages of the book that Erique held out.

'When I was on the *Veteran* Captain Nugent read to us from the Old Testament because we had no priest to hold services.

Now *that* has stories to satisfy anyone. But this Roman,' said Tom, 'this is their religion.'

'You dislike it?'

'It's poor stuff. It lacks either wrath of God or temptation or any of the other stuff the good book has in it.' Tom dropped his voice further, and beckoned Cotterell towards him. 'I think it may contain the logic that killed their King and Queen. In which case the antique Roman who wrote the book is a useless advisor, for that is the worse day's work they've ever done.'

'A Royalist . . .' said Cotterell, and would have continued, but Tom clapped his hand over Cotterell's mouth. 'Don't tempt fate, Mr Cotterell. You would be better whistling down the wind than mentioning that word among this lot.'

The crewmen around them stared. Tom released Cotterell.

Lefèvre had found his text. He was willing to wait till he had the crew's attention, so that he had to compete only with the creak of the rigging and the slop of the sea against the hull. It took some time and none of the officers offered to help quieten the crew, who talked among themselves.

'You are not one of these unmentionables?' asked Cotterell quietly.

'Ever so, as is every true Englishman loyal to his own King. But it's clear for all to see they Frenchies have not had a moment's peace since Mr Bourbon lost his head. Now there's a lesson they could learn instead of all this philosy-fizing with Romans.'

The crew on deck had fallen silent at last and Tom's voice was heard by all. Cotterell thought there must be half a dozen men on the gun-deck who understood what he had said, but no one acknowledged it.

Lefèvre seized his moment and began to read, raising his voice to a hectoring, wavering trill as he spoke, and allowing his hands to wave around like a man trying to catch a fly.

'I dreamed of Scipio Africanus,' Lefèvre read, 'and he said that the earth is surrounded with certain zones, and those two that are most remote from each other, and lie under the opposite

poles of heaven, are congealed with frost; but that one in the
middle, which is far the largest, is scorched with the intense heat
of the sun. The other two are habitable, one towards the south
– the inhabitants of which are your Antipodes, with whom you
have no connection – the other, towards the north, is that which
you inhabit, whereof a very small part, as you may see, falls to
your share. For the whole extent of what you see, is as it were
but a little island, narrow at both ends and wide in the middle,
which is surrounded by the sea which on earth you call the great
Atlantic Ocean, and which, notwithstanding this magnificent name,
you see is very insignificant.'

Citoyenne Lefèvre restrained herself from applauding with
difficulty. Her husband had raised them all to the level of Roman
philosophers merely by reading a book. Lefèvre rambled on, at
least to the men's ears.

There was a sound behind Cotterell. A chair scraped on the
foredeck. He turned and saw a beautiful young woman up there,
about to sit on a wooden backed, upholstered chair held solic-
itously by the boatswain, Derray. They were under the canvas
awning. Intense light reflected from the sea to the canvas and
glowed down again across Derray and the woman. The woman
had dark hair, dark eyes and a smooth almond face. She wore
a spotless, long, cream-silk dress, an extraordinary form of attire
on a warship full of tar and oil and grease. The dress came up
to her neck with a little ruff, an old-fashioned look. The sleeves
reached right to her wrists. Its fullness would have been oppres-
sive on such a hot day, but she was impassive as she sat with
reflected light across her face and breast. Charles climbed the
companionway towards her.

'Madame Auchard,' whispered Tom, who had also turned.
This was the woman Cotterell had seen as a shadowy figure
on the quarter-deck at night. Cotterell watched Charles' back
until he was beside the woman, then turned and bent to whisper
in her ear. Her gaze met Cotterell's. She didn't look away and
Charles went on whispering. Cotterell turned again to the

quarter-deck, feeling the woman's gaze on the back of his neck.

Lefèvre warbled like a small fat bird. He was now in full flow. In his imagination he really was Cicero, the man Charles had called Tully, addressing the Romans. When he wasn't waving his hands to explain some part of Cicero's dream, he threw his arm across his chest, hand flat and pointing straight out in line with the arm, like a man giving directions to a horseman in a hurry. As he spoke, Lefèvre glared with eyes a-popping at his audience. Lefèvre had seen French lawyers do this when prosecuting anti-revolutionaries in Brest, and their audience had found it very convincing. In fact, before his very eyes his mentor, the former priest Jeanbon St André, had congratulated lawyers who held forth in such a way as champions of the people, tireless protectors of the Republican cause, thirsters for victory, implacable opponents of the nation's enemies. Not everyone present at the occasion, before a guillotine set up on the strand in Brest, had been so sure of the value of St André's recommendation, especially those less logical and less well-educated inhabitants of the Breton hinterland, who had watched their relatives arrested and executed with only a condemning speech in French, a language they could neither speak nor read, to serve as judicial process. But St André, like Lefèvre, like all mountebanks, was only dimly conscious of other men's opinions.

And so on the quarter-deck of *Hortense*, Lefèvre stood next to his admiring but apparently dim wife and played at Cicero while his bemused fellow travellers, the ship's captain, officers and crew, looked on without even a glimmer of understanding. They understood the pantomime; it was the speeches which confounded them.

'Why,' Lefèvre blundered on, reading from the book held by Erique, 'if you have no hopes of returning to this place, where great and good men enjoy all that their souls can wish for, pray tell me, of what value is all that human glory, which can hardly endure for a small portion of one year?'

The sailors' faces looked up to Lefèvre, uncomprehending. Behind him on the quarter-deck Captain Dubarre stood, stretched, and walked over to the quarter-deck drum. He thrummed his fingers softly on the skin. He stretched again, then yawned. Dubarre knew what he was doing. Within seconds half the crew stifled a yawn in response. Lefèvre noticed the crew yawning, and paused in his reading to look down at them. The signal halyard sheave rattled as the newcomers raised their bunting, the officer ticking off flags against a message on a slate. Cotterell looked at the men around him. There were country Frenchmen, Parisian Frenchmen, Marseillais, two Provençal cooks, Picards, Savoyards, Gascons, Basques, Spaniards, Algerians, blacks, whites, Danes, Swedes, Slavs, one Russian, men from the Dutch provinces. Tom had pointed them out on the mess-deck. There were men from so deep inside France they spoke French with accents almost entirely impenetrable to Cotterell. The *Hortense* had a renegade Hanoverian gunner, a Parisian boatswain and a Portuguese ship's carpenter, the last having been beached from a Rio merchant vessel in the Carolinas for argumentativeness and lack of sobriety. He was, Tom had implied, their sole acquisition in Georgetown apart from the Second's wife and belle Hélène. There were no marines aboard *Hortense*, since they had been commandeered for the futile defence of Guadeloupe. Lefevre continued to read. To one side, on the gun-deck, the belle Hélène and Liberté were arm in arm, hearing the little man's 'speechifying' but not necessarily listening.

From their look in the burning late afternoon sun the crew appeared hardy enough, healthy and well fed after their months in America. They were the fat-stock version of Frenchmen. Cotterell had seen them handle the ship well and answer the boatswain's orders sharply. But they were too few in number. They would never manoevre the ship and fight at the same time.

Sweat ran into men's eyes and beards, dripped off their noses. Liberté freed her chestnut hair from her red cap for once and dabbed at her face with the cap. Beyond them Cotterell could see Vanstabel's great convoy spread across the horizon, ships of the line leading what looked like hundreds of merchantmen. The two warships were to *Hortense*'s starboard, the merchant ships beyond stretching right across the great Atlantic Ocean, as far as the eye could see.

On the quarter-deck Lefèvre continued from his book. 'When he had ceased to speak in this manner, I said Oh, Africanus, if indeed the door of heaven is open to those who have deserved well of their country, I will from henceforth strive to follow you more closely. Follow them, then, said he, and consider your body only, not yourself, as mortal. For it is not your outward form which constitutes your being, but your mind; not that substance which is palpable to the senses, but your spiritual nature. Know, then, that you are a god – for a god it must be which flourishes, and feels, and recollects, and foresees, and governs, regulates and moves the body over which it is set, as the Supreme Ruler does the world which is subject to him. For as that Eternal Being moves whatever is mortal in this world, so the immortal mind of man moves the frail body with which it is connected.'

Lefèvre stopped reading and took the book from Erique, folding it closed and tucking it under his arm. Lefèvre composed himself for a moment before speaking in what were apparently his own words. '"Know then that you are gods," wrote Cicero. The Revolution demands each of you should be a supreme being. Each man here carries the fate of France in his hands. When I look out across you, that's what I see, a crew of immortal men.' He looked around them. 'You don't believe me perhaps? Sailors of France, imagine the mouths those ships will feed with the corn in their holds.' He threw his pointing arm towards the distant convoy. Every head turned towards them. 'Imagine the need on the streets of Paris. Imagine a starving child in Nantes or Calais. You have the power in this vessel to fetch their food. France is surrounded, blockaded, starved. Only you can bring relief, you and these other sailors. Imagine! What an enormous thing! France depends on you. You can feed your fellow free Frenchmen.'

They imagined, as required. He pointed to the empty ocean on the other side of *Hortense*.

'But . . . out there somewhere is a British fleet, placed in our path by King George and those who conspire with him, conspire against the people of France. Conspire against your infant Republic. See them!' he commanded, and they all turned to look where he pointed, though there was nothing to see. 'The British fleet intends to stop us. They want to dash the food from the mouths of our children. To steal the bread from their hungry lips. To what end, you may wonder? How have the children of France offended King George? By throwing off their chains? By executing the traitor Bourbon and his salope?'

The sailors cheered, giving Tom and Cotterell sideways looks. Auchard cheered too, Cotterell noticed, though he appeared to be doing it for form's sake. Auchard was no revolutionary. On the *gaillard avant* Madame Auchard sat motionless and expressionless.

'The fires of freedom and of revolution burn in the hearts and bellies of the children of France. They will be stoked by the grain on those ships. The children will be fed, and will man our armies and carry the banner of freedom all around Europe. No tyrant will sleep safe in his bed. A British fleet may attack us, but we cannot be defeated. Cannot?' He bared his breast theatrically, twisting from side to side so that they should all see it clearly. It was like parchment. Its paleness shone. 'I may be shot. I may die. But if I die, it will be with the words of the great philosopher ringing in my ears, "consider only your body, as mortal". Sailors of the *Hortense*, consider only your bodies as mortal. You are immortal. Your eternal being is France. You are invincible. *Vive la France!*'

The crew huzzah-ed.

'Sailors of France, you are France!'

They huzzah-ed again.

'Vive la France!' cried Liberté. The drummer on the quarter-deck played a roll. Belle Hélène put her wooden teeth in her mouth and beamed as the others replied.

'Vive la France!' Basques, Spaniards, Berbers, Danes, Dutch and others among the ranks joined in the rallying cry with enthusiasm. *'Vive la France. Vive.'*

Cotterell stood impassive. Tom waved without enthusiasm.

'Vive la France!' cried Lefèvre.

'Vive la France!' answered the sailors again.

'Vive la Révolution!' cried Madame Lefèvre, unable to contain herself any longer, her voice wavering with passion, hands trembling, breast heaving under her dark, full gown.

'Vive la Révolution!' answered the sailors again. A cruel-looking matelot with a pock-marked face and black hair tied into a red kerchief swung in front of English Tom.

'Vive la Révolution!' he cried, spittle on his lips. The others joined in. *'Vive la Révolution!'*

'Vive.' said Tom.

'Vive la Révolution!' cried the man again, this time confronting Cotterell. Cotterell ignored him.

'Vive la Révolution!' cried the man again.

'*Vive!'* echoed the others. Cotterell was silent. The cruel-looking matelot pulled a knife from his belt. He held it up to Cotterell's throat. Their faces were inches apart.

'Vive la Révolution!' the man spat. Cotterell put his hand on his own knife. Every eye on the ship watched Cotterell. Tom closed his giant fist over Cotterell's.

'Just say it,' he said quietly. 'Just say what he wants.'

'Vive la Révolution!' cried the man again. He moved the knife, just lightly lifting the skin on Cotterell's throat and drawing a smear of blood with its keen edge.

'Vive la Révolution.' Cotterell replied. The pock-marked man spun away. Tom's grip on Cotterell's hand tightened for a moment until the man was well out of reach. A small, ferret-faced sailor with a fiddle emerged on deck from the companionway. He

began to play tunelessly. But it was a simple and repeated song. Tom relaxed his hand. Cotterell wiped his throat and looked at the thin, light bright smear of his own blood on his hand.

'I reckon he was measuring you up,' said Tom.

'For?'

'The blade. They love the blade. They are not like Englishmen, with open hearts and clean hands. Pay him no heed. No harm done by a little bit of claret.' He meant the smudge of blood on Cotterell's hand. 'You have the upper hand. He bet you was as good as dead when you came out of the sea and you had breathed your last.' Tom laughed and shouted over the fiddle music. 'He lost his money to Liberté on you being raised from the dead. As if that wasn't bad enough I do believe he wanted to hang up his hat with her.'

'He's jealous?'

'Well, you've had her and he hasn't.'

'I had no part in the matter.'

'That's not strictly true, John Cotterell. Anyway, she used you as a bulwark against him.'

'A bulwark?'

'A message then. You are a walking message to the other sailors. She chooses, not them. Women don't change they nature when they become revolutionaries, it seems.'

Cotterell looked at the pock-marked sailor again, who spat and turned away.

'I reckon he wants to send you back to hell's gates,' said Tom.

'Why hell?'

'We're sailors, ain't we?'

Liberté led the singing. The quarter-deck drummer beat the time.

'Ah! ça ira, ça ira, ça ira,
Les aristocrates à la lanterne!
Ah! Ça ira, ça ira, ça ira,
Les aristocrates on les pendra!'

This was a well-rehearsed performance for the crew, and they played their part to the full, singing verse after verse of *'Ça ira'* and cheering. Cotterell turned and looked at the foredeck again. Charles and Madame Auchard had gone. All that remained was the empty chair.

6

Days passed in this routine; chores, ablutions, matelotage, ship's food and Roman republican pantomime, followed by communal singing of the songs of the barricades; '*la Marseillaise*,' '*allons Francais au champ de Mars*,' '*la prise de la Bastille*.' Especially popular were the bloodthirsty '*la Carmagnole*,' in which the crew danced in the foot-stamping style of Bavarians and sang of the treasonable Madame Veto's promises to cut the throats of the people of Paris, and '*Ça ira*,' where the brave sans culottes return the compliment by promising to hang aristos from lamp-posts. Madame Veto had long since gone to the guillotine but they sang about her anyway. English Tom and Cotterell were not excused attendance at these performances, though they were not expected to link arms and dance the *Carmagnole* with the crew. Tom treated the matter like a long nightly round of unusually bloody nursery rhymes, and would join in the singing to amuse his shipmates much as he would have recited Mother Goose or Puss in Boots, had they asked.

'That I say something does not necessarily mean it exists,' he told Cotterell in a flash of philosophical insight. At dinner the cook, Pascal, delayed Cotterell at the range. He explained Madame Veto was the dead French queen Marie-Antionette and that many of the crew believed all foreigners – that is, all who held themselves separate from the crew and the Revolution – deserved the same fate. He demonstrated with a long cook's knife on a dead chicken he was preparing for Dubarre's supper. The cook pointed out that Cotterell had already been sized for the blade by the pock-marked man, Eustache. The cook had decided he liked Cotterell and wanted to ensure 'the second Englishman,' as the crew referred to him, knew what he had to do. By singing, Cotterell would prove he was one of them. Why shouldn't he? Cotterell owed them a life. He was no longer a subject of the British King. He had been born on the *Hortense*. Cotterell smiled, but said nothing. Next morning he found the dead chicken's head protruding from his bag on the peg hook and turned to see pock-marked Eustache grinning at him in a shaft of light. That afternoon, after dinner, Cotterell sang unasked, reflecting that debts are best settled in cold blood.

Days passed while the *Hortense* sailed in company with the fleet of grain ships and her crew, whose presence was meant to warn of the English, comforted themselves with savage songs and dances. They reminded Cotterell of a man whistling in the dark. The American woman didn't appear on deck again at revolutionary singing time. She didn't appear with her husband either. Dubarre, in an act of unfathomable nobility, had given Madame Auchard his sleeping quarters. The Captain slept, when he slept, during the day in a cot made by the Portuguese carpenter in the great cabin. Second Auchard spent his days on the quarter-deck running his single eye over the ship. Emily Auchard spent the days alone, gliding rather than walking about the ship. She didn't encourage conversation. The Auchards seldom spoke in public. If Cotterell hadn't heard English Tom's intelligence about the marriage on the Waccamaw River, he would never have associated her with the Second. Madame or Citoyenne Auchard's demeanour made her unapproachable. The crew avoided her, not knowing what to make of such a class of American lady. They did not have enough English, nor she enough French, to find any common ground. Emily Auchard certainly didn't pass the day with Citoyenne Lefèvre. She looked, and to an extent behaved, as if she were the class of person the Lefèvres' revolution had intended to sweep away. She was silent, distant and, had she been French, might easily have been thought haughty and Royalist. But Emily Auchard came from the American Republic. She was impeccably republican and egalitarian. And over the days Cotterell saw, in glimpses, that she had friends on the ship: Dubarre, the Captain, who had an eye for a woman and liked to educate her about the maritime world; Derray, the boatswain, who thought her comfort his personal responsibility; la belle Hélène, who fetched tea from the ship's range for Emily to sip while she read in the shade, and Charles, who clearly enjoyed conversing with her.

Cotterell supposed Charles offered the attraction of education, having some experience of America, and of being, like Madame Auchard, a supernumerary on the *Hortense*. The black man and the white woman spent many apparently happy hours on deck, talking in hushed tones in whatever quiet corner they could find. Her frosty husband, Second Auchard, seemed to ignore them. Auchard was more interested in the behaviour of his crew, the lack of gunpowder on *Hortense* and the condition of his unused and unpractised guns than in his beautiful young wife.

The Captain and Auchard kept regular day and night watches. Dubarre preferred the night, when he paced his quarter-deck, or stood by the helmsman's shoulder from dusk till dawn. Sometimes he even took the helm. The sailors loved him as one of themselves, though an infringement of one of his personal rules would leave them tied to the rigging for two or three days at a time and a serious contravention of ship's rules would leave them in irons on the mess-deck for weeks. Days found him cat-napping. The daytime running of the vessel was Auchard's. The Second was an able navigator, seaman and organiser, though he lacked the charm and presence of a leader. His one good eye missed nothing on deck. Auchard navigated, assisted by the Lieutenant, Mathelier. There were no cadets to teach and the two men reduced the sights and found their position alone, not inviting the newly-acquired cadet officer and signaller, Merlet, to assist. Since cloud had closed in on Merlet's fourth day on the *Hortense* the teaching would have been impossible anyway. There were no sights to reduce. Dubarre knew his stars all right and wasn't slow to point them out to the helmsman when the sky was clear at night. No one steered *Hortense* without being able to spot Polaris. Cotterell never saw Dubarre so much as check his Second's navigation though, and he found that surprising.

Meanwhile, on the foc'sl, Cotterell's 'education' continued.

'A waister like you would never get this interest on a British ship,' said Tom. 'I 'spect you do know what a waister is?'

'Enlighten me.'

'A man unfit for seamen's work. Someone like you, sir. But a ship needs strong lads for the lines here and this vessel is woefully short of them. Strong lads. Also I'm here, so the boatswain knows you have an experienced eye on you, to correct you and make sure you don't fall into bad habits.'

Tom said this last deadpan. On deck, for practice, Tom and his messmates the foc'slmen had taught Cotterell with a bit of canvas to hand the leech of sails, 'like lifting a girl's buntlings,' then to reef them to the boatswain's or his mate's orders. Since the winds were light and steady, trips up to the spars would have been only for the sake of practice, which they could not afford for fear of losing their station in the convoy. Sail handling was confined to dumb practice on deck and 'bracing', setting the spars and canvas with brace lines or ropes to best receive the wind and drive the ship. Cotterell and English Tom helped the sail-maker too. 'They call this a fuck,' said Tom as they stretched a sail on the foredeck. 'What a language.'

'Foc,' said Cotterell. 'French for foresail.'

'Fuck this, fuck that. French for beard-splitting, I say. You sell a lot of them, fores'l fucks, in your oil-shop in Halifax?' Tom laughed. Cotterell ignored it. They were spreading the second best fores'l for the benefit of the sailmaker, who wanted to ensure it wasn't half eaten or full of mildew or rats' nests. Above them signal flags flew.

'That is how they compare wittels,' said Tom.

'Victuals?' asked Cotterell.

'There is no other intelligence to pass over. The master of that vessel there now knows we had French burgoo for breakfast and we'll have French burgoo for dinner, now the landbread has run out. What do you say?'

After a flurry of flags and decoding by his new signalman, Dubarre had the look-out double-manned, one on the foretop, one on the artimon. He also drew *Hortense* even further north of the fleet of merchant ships. Cotterell overheard Charles ask Dubarre why they had changed course, but this time the Capitaine was unforthcoming.

'Orders,' he said gruffly. 'Orders.'

When Cotterell was next on deck the merchant fleet was on the horizon.

'Is it usual to be so far away?' Cotterell asked.

'It makes us the eyes and ears for the French Admiral, at least in this direction.'

Derray was behind them. 'The Captain wants to see you two.'

Dubarre waited, bootless and minus his military frock coat at the foot of the mainmast stays. Lefèvre was also there, also unshod.

Tom tugged his forelock.

'Mon Commandant.'

Dubarre pointed at the ratlines. 'Aloft,' he said. He offered no further explanation or command.

English Tom and Cotterell began to climb. Lefèvre followed, slowly, inexpertly. His wife watched from the foredeck.

'*Allez, Lefèvre*,' she said.

Hirnan Lefèvre rose, climbing the ratline, hands clutched white to the lines, nose pressed so close to the stay his beard looked like it would tangle.

'Take care, Hirnan.' The voice came from below again. They rose and rose, Tom in the lead, Cotterell following, Lefèvre clamped to the stay below Cotterell's feet, Dubarre below that.

'It's just under a hundred feet,' said Dubarre, encouragingly.
'One hundred French feet, not English,' he called in English for
the benefit of Tom and Cotterell. And so they rose again, up
and up, creamy pale sails billowing by their side.

'Don't look down.' Dubarre was speaking to Lefèvre, who had
almost frozen. 'Only another fifty feet to the cat-hole. We'll stop
there.'

Tom and Cotterell reached the mainmast-top. Cotterell followed
Tom's instructions and climbed round rather than through the
cat-hole as sailors do. They made their way out onto the spar to
make room for Lefèvre and the Captain. The mast-top was
unmanned. The twin lookouts were on the mizzen and foremast.
Above Cotterell and Tom the main-top stretched into the sky.
Below them the ship, reduced by perspective, rolled in the long
swell which took it on the side. Cotterell noticed the swell and
knew there would have been a storm far to their south, perhaps
many miles beyond the horizon. There was no sign of a change
in weather here. A soft white veil of cloud covered the sky.

Below them the ship was visible all of a piece. Cotterell could
see the tops of men's heads as they went about their work, and
the faces of Madame Lefèvre, Lieutenant Mathelier and, for some
reason, Liberté looking up at them, eyes shaded from the sun
with their hands. On the rigging Dubarre was struggling with
Lefèvre who wanted neither to go up nor down. Dubarre looked
like he would throw the smaller man overboard for the price of
a rotting dog's body.

'Why has he brought us here?' asked Cotterell.

'Us? I don't know. Him? Because the old man wants to take
that one down a peg or two, and this is the place he has chosen
for it.'

Dubarre had clamped his hands over Lefèvre's and was moving
them one at a time on the rigging.

'Look yonder, since you are so full of questions.' Tom said.
He indicated the horizon to the north. 'That is why we have
moved away from the generality of the fleet.'

'I don't understand,' said Cotterell, though he did.

'From this advantage we can see the fleet and the fleet can see us. Also we can see the horizon. A vessel on the horizon though will only see us, not the fleet.'

To *Hortense*'s larboard or north side the sea was empty. To the starboard or south the sea was full of ships. Cotterell had never seen so many big ships at once, not even when he'd seen a fishing fleet on the Grand Banks. He thought there were over a hundred and fifty ships in view. They were sailing large, white sails full, drawing them over the glistening sea. Though he was sure they were all armed he could only see one other vessel which was obviously a warship. He was certain about the ships close by, but who knew what the dark wooden walls and hatches of the ships further away hid. He turned and looked north again.

'What's over the horizon?' Cotterell asked, though he knew.

'Iceland. If you keep going. There are British ships in Iceland,' said Tom. 'Warships and whalers.'

'Have you been there?'

'In their sea. Protecting whalers.'

Cotterell looked down. Below them they could see the ship's guns, then closer, on the ratlines, Dubarre seemed to have Lefèvre's hands free and was guiding him.

Cotterell indicated the northern horizon again. 'What happens if a vessel is spotted there?'

'What do you mean – what happens?'

'What do we do?'

'Am I the Captain?' asked Tom. Cotterell agreed he was not, but still Tom ventured an opinion. 'We will engage it, to delay it from the fleet.'

'And if there are two, or three, or four?' asked Cotterell.

'Well let's hope there are a dozen and they're His Majesty's ships and they defeat us, because that will get us both back to our rightful places. Me in his Navy and you back to your clerk's bench. God willing and preserve us in the battle.'

'They will defeat us,' said Cotterell.

'I know,' replied Tom, 'the way this vessel is armed and exercised, a bum-boat full of starving Lascars with blunt pikes could take it.'

'Do they ever practise the guns?' Cotterell asked.

'Never.'

'Is that usual?'

'I don't know. This is my first cruise on a French ship.' Tom answered. 'The Captain believes that firing them against the occasional merchantman is sufficient. He is an old privateer. It could be that the habits die hard and he is only willing to engage those he can bully. It may be he doesn't have much powder. I expect the Americans charge dear for it. Tell me . . .' Below them there was a cry as Dubarre punched Lefèvre. Tom continued as if nothing was going on. 'Is ships' guns such an important subject on the store clerk's bench?'

'I'm interested in ships' guns because I'm on a ship.'

Tom looked at the Captain, twenty feet below, and then spoke quietly. 'I don't believe Dubarre intends to fight for a minute. I think we are a sacrifice to be offered up to His Majesty's ships if they approach us from Iceland, to draw them away well before they get to the convoy. It is a common ruse in convoy. We on the *Veteran* did it for an East Indiaman convoy once, in company with a couple of frigates.'

'Did it work?'

'Yes. But the *Veteran* is sixty-four guns, which is twice what this barkey sports. And those guns were run out by prime seamen and gunners. Approach her at your peril.'

'And will the British approach from Iceland?'

'You tell me.'

Lefèvre came though the hole like the proverbial scalded cat. Dubarre climbed over the top. Cotterell thought Dubarre looked more at home here, a hundred feet above the deck, than he did on the quarter-deck, where he looked as if it was his dearest wish to wrest the wheel from the helmsman and steer in a manner he considered proper, or seaman-like.

'Well?' Dubarre asked Cotterell and English Tom.

'Yes, Captain,' replied Tom through habit. He had no idea to what he was agreeing.

'Isn't it magnificent?' Dubarre swung his arm over the enormous French fleet.

'Yes, mon Commandant,' answered Cotterell. He stretched for the shroud to steady himself. As he did Dubarre looked closely at Cotterell's hand.

Lefèvre gripped the mast and rigging firmly. His mouth was still working, though his face was pressed against the mast.

'The glory of the Republic,' Lefèvre gasped, 'is spread below you. This is the reason France may never be defeated.'

'Since such a fleet has never before assembled and may never do so again, Citizen Lefèvre wanted to see it for himself.' The Captain informed them, 'and thought it was – what was the word?'

'Propitious,' supplied Lefèvre.

'There you have it,' said Dubarre, 'propitious. Propitious that we should take you to the mast-top and have you see the power of France spread before you.'

'Thus we will confound our enemies,' Lefèvre uttered.

'Indeed.' Dubarre agreed. Was the Captain laughing at Lefèvre? It seemed so to Cotterell. Lefèvre looked aware of it too. 'Fix it in your mind's eye, Englishmen, and make sure everyone in England knows about it when you return.'

'Will we return?' asked Cotterell.

'There are always packets between Calais and Dover, war or no war. Does your family have money?'

'No.' Said Cotterell.

'I have no family,' added Tom.

'Well,' said Dubarre, 'we'll see what we can do. We might exchange you, like a pair of officers and gentlemen.' That smile again. Dubarre enjoyed toying with their discomfort. No one would exchange a couple of little sailors and he knew it.

'You have no right to promise that, Citizen Commandant,' said Lefèvre, confidentially.

Dubarre answered in full booming voice. 'I will say what I think fit on my ship, Citizen.'

Lefèvre continued quietly. 'And I will report it to Citizen St André if I see fit, Citizen.'

'Do you think the Committee of Public Safety will listen to every little bit of tittle tattle you drag up?'

'Yes.' Lefèvre smiled his answer through clenched teeth.

Now Dubarre answered quietly and with confidence. 'On the deck of a warship there is no democracy, Citizen. One man rules on it alone like a king. The Captain. Isn't that true, English Tom?'

Tom didn't understand him for once. Cotterell translated, looking at Dubarre's thin smile as he did so. He knew the sign was dangerous. If Lefèvre knew, he didn't betray it. Cotterell had seen that smile on Dubarre's face before, many years ago. He had been a boy. His father had stood by his side. They were on a beach in Newfoundland, setting out fish to dry. His father's old fishing boat had been drawn up on the beach. Dubarre's privateer vessel had bobbed at anchor in the bay.

Dubarre interrupted the translation.

'Where did they come from?' he asked Cotterell. He was close, and he stank of alcohol. Cotterell considered how easily the Captain could slip. He was tempted to push. Dubarre was looking at Cotterell's hands again. Then their eyes met. 'Citizen?' Cotterell asked.

'Where did you get those scars on your hands?'

'I fell through a skylight as a boy, Monsieur.'

'Mon Commandant,' Lefèvre corrected Cotterell.

'A skylight.' Dubarre considered.

'Yes sir.'

Dubarre continued to look into Cotterell's eyes. Eventually he asked, 'What does that look mean?'

'Look?'

'Don't glare at me man.'

'I don't glare sir,' said Cotterell. 'At least I don't mean to. I will look where you wish, sir.'

'You will. Look at the sea.'

Cotterell did. Dubarre continued, 'I fished you out of the sea. I can put you back where I found you.'

'Yes sir,' said Cotterell. 'At your service, Monsieur.'

'That's enough. He's to be addressed as 'Citizen' or 'mon Commandant.'' said Lefèvre.

'I rule the ship and will be Monsieur if it pleases me,' said Dubarre, clearly wanting to demonstrate he would accept orders from no one.

'The Republic has no place for Mon-sieur this and Ma-dame that. There are no ranks in the Republic.'

'I outrank you, Lefèvre, just for now.'

'I represent the Committee . . .' Lefèvre began.

'This isn't a republic, sir, though we serve one. This is a ship. You will do as I say, not the other way round.'

Lefèvre's nerve may have left him on the ascent, but he was fearless in politics.

'Even the King in France lost his head, Captain,' he replied. 'I hope you will remember.'

'I remember it's a long way down,' responded Dubarre. They were quiet for a moment, then the Captain indicated the deck below. 'After you, Citizen.'

The cat-hole yawned at Lefèvre's feet. Lefèvre went backwards through the hole, moving slowly, holding tightly to the wooden edges of the platform. Dubarre smiled again, this time in genuine pleasure at the little red-bearded man's discomfort. Lefèvre began to descend the ratlines, trembling. Cotterell looked down at the raised faces on the deck below. They reminded him of the crew of *l'Imprevu*. It seemed like a year since he had looked down on those faces.

The Captain ignored both Lefèvre's descent and those watching, instead scanning the horizon. Tom and Cotterell shared a look. About twenty feet below them Lefèvre froze.

'He is stuck fast, mon Commandant,' said Tom.

Dubarre looked down the shroud at the ratlines. 'Move,' he cried.

'I cannot,' answered Lefèvre.

'You must.'

'I cannot.'

'Then you will spend the night there. We will descend by the other side.' Dubarre turned to Cotterell and English Tom. 'En bas.' He pointed. They climbed onto the tribord stays and began to descend. Cotterell was soon at the same level as Lefèvre.

'Go down, sir,' called Tom. 'He means it.'

'Hold the stay,' advised Cotterell. 'One hand at a time. Use the ratlines as a ladder and the stays for your handhold. You'll be safe.'

But Lefèvre was inconsolable. He closed his eyes and seemed less likely than ever to move.

'Move, Citizen.' Dubarre leaned over the platform, taking most of his weight on his hands so that he could shout and bully better. One slip would plunge him to the deck, but Dubarre was oblivious of his precarious perch. 'One foot, then the other. Come on. Move.'

Lefèvre was like a sleeper awaking to the shout. He began to move again, first one foot then the other, then one hand then the other. He let his hands hang on to the safety of their purchase too long, so that he was constantly over-stretching his arms, then fumbling for the next grip on the stay. The Captain watched from the masthead, Cotterell and Tom from the matching tribord stays, his wife, Lieutenant Mathelier and Liberté from the deck. But there was nothing they could do. There was nothing anyone could do. Lefèvre was on his own. He managed another ten feet or so in this way, arms stretched too long for their grip, feet and toes fumbling for the ratlines. In seeking utter security he seemed to stretch too far, pressing his body against the stays and lines, trying to flatten and make himself as one with them. Then, inevitably, Lefèvre slipped. His leg went through the gap in the ratline, his stretched fingers lost their grip and he tumbled backwards, twisting his knee with his whole body weight. Lefèvre screamed, hanging there upside down for a second, the leg supporting him at an unnatural angle, then he fell a further twenty feet, turning a full somersault as he did so, but never really losing contact with the shrouds. His hands grabbed and he stopped, ending hanging in the rigging half-way up the stay, right leg still twisted in an unnatural position, left leg and hands holding his weight. He continued to scream in pain. Liberté and Mathelier sprang to the rigging, Liberté with a loop of light cord. They raced up the ratlines.

'Bosco! Bosco!' cried the Captain to the boatswain. 'Fetch a halyard!'

At a movement from the boatswain's hand a sailor belayed a halyard from the pins at the foot of the mast. The boatswain took the free end of the cord, swung himself outside the stay and began to carry it up the ratlines.

'Help him!' cried Citoyenne Lefèvre. Her husband screamed again, as if in answer. Now Dubarre was above Lefèvre and the agile Liberté was by his side. Lieutenant Mathelier swung inside the rigging so he could meet Lefèvre face to face. Between them the Lieutenant, Dubarre and Liberté rigged a pair of large bowlines around Lefèvre. The boatswain passed the heavier halyard to Liberté and she made it off to the loops, then climbed inside one, intending to descend with Lefèvre.

'Belay!' cried Boatswain Derray to the deck. Men were on the halyard now and they could lift or lower Lefèvre and Liberté at will.

Cotterell and Tom were at deck level now, standing on the ship's rail and looking up. Belle Hélène had her arm around Citoyenne Lefèvre, who sobbed with her face in her hands, unable to look aloft again. Auchard had the ship, standing next to the helmsman. Even he was looking up to the rigging.

Two more sailors held the halyard and with the other took the strain on a belay pin, one sweating the halyard on the pin, the other two hauling.

'Steady, Bosco!' cried the sailor sweating the halyard.

'Steady!' replied the boatswain. And then to the Captain and officer. 'We have him.'

'You are safe. You have to let go now.' Lieutenant Mathelier told Lefèvre, whose answer was another scream.

'I said, let go. We have you.' The younger man was still, hanging on the interior of the shroud ratlines, face to face with Lefèvre, most of his weight carried on his arms. Mathelier was out of balance, his feet some way outboard of his head. But he was young, strong and agile. He spoke calmly. 'We have to swing you inboard to let you down, Citizen.'

Lefèvre sobbed and held the shroud in a vice-like grip.

'Let go, Citizen,' repeated the Lieutenant.

But he wouldn't. The boatswain and men on the halyard waited.

'Let go,' commanded Lieutenant Mathelier patiently. But Lefèvre did not let go. Mathelier looked up at his Captain for instructions.

'Make him,' said Dubarre.

Mathelier tried to prise Lefèvre's fingers off the shroud. He couldn't. Liberté tried too. She pulled, pushed, twisted and finally bit, but still Lefèvre hung on, blinded and deafened by pain. His knuckles bled where Liberté had bitten into the flesh. Eventually the Lieutenant began to punch Lefèvre. Once, twice, three times he swung. On the third punch Lefèvre opened his eyes and punched back, a straight blow through the ratlines which caught Mathelier square on the jaw. The younger man was stunned for a moment. His grip loosened and he fell forty feet to the deck, spinning as he fell. He broke his head like an egg on the carronade below as he landed and spattered the hysterical Citoyenne Lefèvre with his brains.

'You bastard,' said Dubarre. He put his foot firmly on Lefèvre's head and pushed. Liberté and Lefèvre swung, Lefèvre still screaming. Now they were free and the sailors began to lower them to the deck.

Cotterell looked about himself. Black Charles was with Mathelier, who was past aid. Citoyenne Lefèvre had fainted clear away into the arms of the belle Hélène. Auchard stood by his helmsman. Emily Auchard stood on the gun-deck companionway, watching, not moving. The crew remained almost frozen, every head turned towards Mathelier's broken body on the deck. Dubarre rattled expertly down the shroud, landing on the rail at the same time as Liberté and Lefèvre arrived on deck.

Liberté rushed towards Cotterell.

'You could have stopped that,' she said.

'How?' he replied. But she threw herself upon him, punching and scratching.

'Be quiet!' ordered Dubarre. Liberté stopped. Then Dubarre turned to Charles, who was bending over Lieutenant Mathelier. 'Leave him. He's dead.'

Lefèvre was rolling and screaming on deck as they took the bowline loop off him. His lower leg lay almost at right angles to the upper.

'Set his leg.' Dubarre commanded.

'I don't know how to do that,' said Charles.

'Set it.'

Charles bent over Lefèvre, who was still rolling.

'How?' Charles asked.

Dubarre took a bronze belay pin from the rail and smacked Lefèvre behind the ear with it. He lay still and silent.

'Set it,' repeated Dubarre.

'We could fetch a doctor from another ship.' Charles tried again.

'There is no question of it,' responded Dubarre. 'I have my orders and we must keep our station. A patriot like Citizen Lefèvre will understand. I can't put one man above France.'

Lefèvre was in no state to permit or understand any course of action. Charles waved at Cotterell and Tom. 'Help me.'

7

On his third day moving about the *Hortense* Cotterell had been declared fit enough by the boatswain to haul the cook's stove-wood from the hold and to scrub out la belle Hélène's manger, activities fitted to a landsman, and an English one at that. By the fifth day he was hauling a line for the forecastlemen too, as a consequence of his size. On any ship a man as big as Cotterell would likely be claimed by the forecastle. On a ship as lightly crewed as *Hortense* it was a certainty.

It was decided by Auchard that if the ship beat to stations the two 'Englishmen' should assist Jamaican Charles to 'doctor' on the orlop. This had been organised so that they should not have to stand on deck and fight their own countrymen. The arrangement was not out of sympathy for their feelings but because they could not be trusted. The other nationalities aboard might be equally reluctant to battle their countrymen, but the only ships *Hortense* was likely to find herself fighting were British.

So Tom and Cotterell had been given the role of mates to the surgeon, who was not one. They were present when Mathelier fell to the deck and Charles went to his aid. Nothing could be done for Mathelier. But Charles was expected to help Lefèvre, which meant his English assistants would follow his orders. The first part was simple. The three men borrowed battens from the carpenter and splinted Lefèvre's leg on deck. Then, aided by other strong sailors, they carried him deep into the heart of the ship. When at last the three were alone with the unconscious man Charles poured each a large cup of ship's brandy from the surgeon's stores, then set about examining the knee. Tom had to cut off Lefèvre's pantaloons which were bursting, so gross had the knee become. The full weight of the body, twisting, tumbling, falling, then caught, had been taken by the joint. The cap was floating. The leg was entirely disjointed at the knee and could move unhindered from side to side, though naturally the unconscious man whimpered if they did it.

'We don't have very long until he wakes, I fear,' said Charles. 'What do you say?'

'I don't know,' answered Tom promptly, though the question was aimed at Cotterell. 'I thought I'd seen every injury a man could suffer. I saw a fellow crushed by an anchor once, when they dropped the blessed thing right in his whaler.'

'Was it a similar injury?' asked Charles.

'It killed the man next to him outright. And it bent his knees the wrong way, like it had stove in a thwart. The surgeon took 'em off.'

'It sounds similar,' said Charles. 'With a saw?'

'Yes sir.' He mimed the action over the leg, then stopped as Lefèvre moaned.

'Did he live?'

'For a day or two, certainly. After that I don't know. They put him ashore as unfit for the service, which he certainly was, apart from potato peeling and the like. No one is going to carry a man up and down to the lower deck just to peel potatoes and turnips.'

'Do you believe he will lose the leg?'

'Undoubtedly, sir, from the look of it,' said Tom.

Cotterell agreed, 'How could it be repaired?'

'You don't believe it will mend of its own account?'

Charles didn't believe it either. He was grasping at straws.

'No. He'll either lose it now or later,' said Tom. 'On the sea or on the shore. We have to choose. Cut it orf or no.'

'We are a long way from putting anyone ashore. And a long way from expertise with the saw.'

'There's a former pork butcher among the maintop-men,' suggested Tom. 'And there's always da Silva the carpenter, though he is not so clean living as he might be, and I wouldn't want his mucky Portuguese arse sitting on me while he sawed off my leg. I reckon the pork butcher is the best bet.'

'What happens where the knee and shin join? Is it in your books?' asked Cotterell.

'They are not *my* books, Mister Cotterell,' replied Charles frostily. 'They are just here because they're here. Like you – or I.'

He passed an illustrated book to Cotterell and opened one himself.

The two began to thumb through the pages for clues while Tom looked closely at the knee. Charles poured himself another brandy and pointed to an anatomical plate in his book. 'That front part is meant to be holding the whole together, and in the patient it has abandoned that proper role.'

'Very professional if I may say so, sir. Quite the doctor,' said Tom, standing from his scrutiny of the knee.

'How come?'

'Patient, you called him, sir. Now if ever I had enough money to be treated by a proper doctor that's how I would like him to call me. 'The Patient.' Not 'Jack Tar here,' or 'Tom Lad' but 'The Patient.' It feels right. You'd make a good doctor.'

'Except I lack the skill,' reminded Charles.

Cotterell had taken Tom's place in inspecting the ballooning knee. The leg was mottled with blue marks from the impact. It was red and white in the distension, which was swelling by the minute.

'So what is your diagnosis, Jack Tar?' asked Cotterell.

'If he carries on like that, he will have a second arse grown on the front of his knee within the hour.' Tom pronounced. 'In other words, no one has any idea what to do. We can ask him when he comes round what he wants.'

'I'd prefer he stayed asleep,' said Charles. 'He will be uncontrollable if he wakes.'

'You must have laudanum,' said Tom, fumbling through the surgeon's bottles as if he could read. 'The sawbones on the *Veteran* gave out laudanum.'

'For?'

'Almost anything. But he gave it to sick men to help them sleep, I know.'

'Did it work?'

'In its fashion. Double or triple issue grog helped too.'

'What are you looking for?' Cotterell asked Tom, who was staring at the labels on the bottles as if everything might suddenly become clear.

'It's a blue bottle.'

'You can't give him the contents of any blue bottle you chance upon.'

'I wasn't going to.' Tom was outraged. 'I'd have the doctor here examine the contents.'

'I am not a doctor!' exclaimed Charles. Lefèvre moaned again. Tom put his finger to his lips. 'You will wake him, sir.'

'What would you do, Mr Cotterell?' asked Charles.

Cotterell had more than once set a broken arm on one of his fishing crew, but this had been a simple business with a wooden splint and bandage. Cotterell had actually assisted his father remove a crushed leg from a sailor who'd been caught under a falling boat. But he couldn't reveal that, and anyway the man whose leg they'd taken off, Cornelius Shea, an Irish fisherman, had died where they were, becalmed hundreds of miles from anywhere, in the Atlantic. Cotterell was saved from answering by the soft swish of light feet descending the companionway. A pair of silk slippers, then the skirt of the cream dress and finally all of Emily Auchard appeared.

'How is the injured man?' she asked.

Tom tugged his forelock. Cotterell stood still. It was the first time Cotterell had heard her speak. Her voice was warm but soft, deeper than he had expected. Her accent was pure Carolina.

Charles answered, with a little bow of greeting. 'Captain

Dubarre's pacifier seems to have done the trick for now, Ma'am. Have you ever seen such an injury as the knee?'

'Not directly, Mr Charles,' she replied, which Cotterell thought a strange answer. She made it sound as if she had some special knowledge in the matter. 'I have merely come to enquire for Mrs Lefèvre, who is almost deranged from anxiety that her husband will lose his leg.'

'Just what we were discussing.'

'Will he?'

'He may. We don't know.'

'Do you have medical expertise?' She asked Cotterell.

'None at all, Madame. I'm a clerk by trade.'

'Nor I,' added Tom, though no one had given any sign that they thought he might.

Lefèvre struggled towards consciousness. He began to moan.

'Soon he will be raving,' said Tom. 'Then you'll have to tie him down and do it.'

'Is there a barber?' asked Emily.

'No. There are several men who can handle a saw.'

'Will they have the skill required?'

'No, Madame,' answered Charles, 'they will not. But there are rudimentary instructions in this manual of surgery. And from the looks of this knee our man will soon be so desperate we will have to take action.'

He was right. The knee was now more than twice the size of its fellow and the leg and toes below were white from lack of blood.

'I've seen that before,' said Tom. 'When a tackle slipped and an eight pounder dropped on a man's leg. The passageway for the blood is trapped.'

'How did they cure it?' asked Emily.

'There's only ever one cure at sea, Madame, where there are no teams of medical men to consult. If the hand offends thee, cut it off, and cast it out,' quoted Tom.

'Matthew's Gospel. You are well educated.' Emily smiled at him. Tom looked embarrassed.

'Not at all, Ma'am. I have sat in church and listened often enough, when I was a boy. But I don't recall whose gospel it was, apart from the priest's.'

More footsteps sounded, boots this time, and Auchard appeared. He ignored the other men at first and gave Emily his one-eyed glare.

'What are you doing here, Madame?' he asked.

'Seeking news.' She replied.

'Do you have it?'

'Yes.'

'Then adieu.'

Auchard waited in silence for Emily to leave. She hesitated, looked around the men on the orlop, then curtsied to Auchard. He gave a little bow and she climbed the steps. Their eyes never seemed to meet.

'This is not the right place for a lady, with rough men and you.' Auchard spoke to Charles, without making any particular effort to wait until she had gone. The 'you' was significant. 'You'll refuse her entry for the future.'

'What your wife does and where she goes is her affair. I cannot give her orders,' answered Charles.

'On the contrary, what my wife does is my affair,' retorted Auchard, 'and I give the order. I say she is not to come down here. You will ensure my order is complied with.'

Charles didn't attempt to argue further.

Lefèvre moaned. Auchard indicated him. 'What is this man's condition?'

'We think our hand will be forced within hours,' replied Charles.

'We?' said Auchard. 'You say we? Does that mean you take advice from these two?'

'I'd take advice from the devil if he knew better than I. None of us knows what to do. I was on my way to ask the Captain . . .'

'He is no surgeon.'

'Nor am I . . . I was about to ask would he permit us to remove the leg if needed?'

'That's not the situation now?'

'It will be soon.'

'Have you become an expert in amputation since you came aboard the *Hortense*?'

'I already said, sir. I am no surgeon. But his leg is dislocated and it is not apparent how it should be put back in the right place. And his blood does not appear to be flowing in the limb. If his blood remains stuck in the leg he will die. It doesn't need a surgeon to tell that.'

Auchard didn't reply, but just glared first at the leg, then at Charles. What Charles said was obviously true. No one could survive with a leg in that condition. Professional surgery was enough risk. Cutting by unskilled amateurs would almost certainly kill Lefèvre. The tension between the two men; one a former slave, the other the son of a slaver, seemed to hang in the air, a physical presence.

'The Captain . . .' Charles began again patiently.

'The Captain is concerned with the military and maritime affairs on this ship.'

'The Captain doesn't wish to be consulted?'

'Do-as-you-see-fit.' Auchard spoke slowly, as if he were addressing a cretin. 'Understand?'

There was a silence. The two men looked at each other. Lefèvre moaned louder below them.

'You'll indemnify me?'

'I'll do nothing of the sort. You must take responsibility for your own actions. If you kill the Citizen I've no doubt his wife will see you hung from the yardarm. If you leave him and do nothing then his death will be your responsibility and no doubt his wife will want to see the same result. In my opinion, not a moment too soon.'

'I come with the authority of the Committee of Safety,' said Charles.

'So does this man.' Auchard indicated Lefèvre. 'But he is a French citizen and you are a jumped-up slave.'

Charles bowed slightly, but did not reply. Cotterell admired his coolness.

'Is it your intention to remove the leg now?' asked Auchard.

'I don't have the skill.'

'Does either of these?'

'No.'

Auchard turned and addressed Tom and Cotterell. 'Then you are not needed. To your duties.'

8

When they had been high above *Hortense*'s deck, at the maintop, Cotterell had genuinely considered killing Dubarre. He carried a knife in his belt, like all sailors. The Captain had stood on the top with his defences open. Dubarre's hands had been full of yardarm or cordage. He hadn't been expecting a blow. Cotterell had stood by the French Captain on the yardarm, waiting for an opening. He'd put his hand on the knife handle and watched Dubarre's movements as he swayed on the little platform. There had been plenty of opportunity, but still Cotterell hadn't acted. He didn't know what had stopped him. He had reason enough to kill the ex-privateer. His duty as a loyal subject of King George directed him to do it. The opportunity had presented itself. But still he'd waited. Dubarre had turned his back, presenting a fine target for the sliver of steel. But even then something held Cotterell back. He'd told himself that it wasn't the British way to stab a man in the back. That was the reason. Later, as he swung in his hammock in the dark below-decks, Cotterell had closed his eyes and remembered why, when the moment came, he would plunge the knife into Dubarre's chest, face to face, and tell him exactly who he was, and exactly who he was avenging. Nothing less would do.

In the seventies, as a youth, Cotterell had accompanied his father on the first *l'Imprevu* to the fishing grounds on the far side of the ocean, just as he had accompanied his grandfather as a boy to the shoal fishing grounds around their Jersey home. The trips with his grandfather had been informal, arranged to please themselves. Sometimes his sister Marie even came too. They would take mackerel off the headlands or *loup de mer,* sea bass, from the shallower waters. They would even fetch *ormers* from L'Ecrehou, where all sorts of crustaceans were plentiful. Guernseymen said ormers couldn't be found outside their waters, but it wasn't true. Cotterell's grandfather believed this lack of accuracy on the part of Guernseymen was nothing rare.

'Guernsey this, Guernsey that. Nothing exists for them apart from their blessed island. They are the most one-eyed patriots to be found anywhere in this world.' The old man had said. 'Excepting Frenchmen. Frenchmen are one-eyed and blind in that one eye.'

Jean Cotterell's grandfather, also Jean, but invariably called Pepe, or Grandad, was a slim little man with grey eyes permanently shaded by a blue peaked sailor's cap. He had white moustaches and eyebrows which were dyed brown by the fumes of the pipes he smoked. His hands were lined with scars, evidence left of a lifetime spent on the deck of a fishing boat. Old Jean Cotterell had not a word of English, speaking only Jerrais. He could understand French, but never adapted his accent so that Frenchmen could understand him. He lived alone in a cottage in St Aubin. His wife had died during one of his long voyages to the fishing grounds. Old Jean, Pepe, had cousins near Avranches and some more distant relatives who had swallowed the anchor and left the sea several generations before and gone into the wood business somewhere near Fougères. That closeness and kinship, though, never stopped him referring to Frenchmen as if they were someone else. The Cotterells were Viking Jerseymen, according to the old man, and if other branches of the family had gone off to France for wives and woodyards, or to America for land, well that was their affair. It was true the girls in Normandy were pretty and that could turn a young fellow's head. It was also true, old Jean Cotterell would admit if cornered, that God had stopped making land in Jersey some time ago. Farmland on the island was almost unobtainable. The men who went out with

Carteret in Pepe's own grandfather's time had found land aplenty
in America. But at what cost? They had given up who they were.
They had made their children Americans. What advantage is that
to an islander? They were lost. They may as well have become
Englishmen or Frenchmen. Old Jean Cotterell's people were
Jersey through and through, back to the Conqueror and beyond.
He wished they would remain so, and had made this clear to
the youthful bearers of his family name. The grandchildren,
including young Jean Cotterell and his sister Marie, loved old
Pepe without reservation. If he'd said their people were men in
the moon who lived on cheese and should continue to do so
forever the grandchildren would never have argued, at least to
his face.

When the time came that Pepe Jean considered himself too
old to go to the fishing grounds on the Newfoundland Grand
Banks he had handed over the first *L'Imprevu* to his son, Jean-
Jacques. That had been when young Jean Cotterell was a baby.
As the child grew in his father's yearly absence his grandfather
took long-limbed and coltish young Jean and his dark-haired and
pretty younger sister Marie on fishing expeditions, sailing *Jolie
Fille*, a twenty-foot open lugsail vessel, around the coast of Jersey.
The old man and his grandchildren were the only crew. They
drifted around the bay of St Malo, following the circular tides
of the bay, finding all the counter-currents and back-eddies.
They wandered as far south as Cancale and as far north as the
Cap. They went up with the tide by the Cotentin and they came
back through the Race of Alderney, which spat them back to
the north of Jersey whether they wanted to be there or not. The
tides of the bay were not just mysterious, they were vicious. The
old man taught his grandchildren as he had been taught as a
boy. Sometimes they just drifted, fishing. No one bothered them.
Who was interested in two children and an old man in a little
boat? Sometimes they collected ormers or cleared lobster pots.
Sometimes they collected or delivered 'tax free' packages on the
Minquiers or Chausey, or even on the French coast, as Channel

Island fishermen had done in the bay since time immemorial. Grandfather Jean said it was a normal part of a fisherman's life to fish the rocks as well as the sea, and if a package was landed or collected there, well, a poor man has to make his money any way he can. Though they were better off than the landless or even the dirt-poor Jersey farmers, there was no spare cash for the Cotterells. It was all in the boats or in their cottages. Young Jean Cotterell's heritage was the ground he stood on, his patrimony the boat his father sailed. When old Jean Cotterell's rheumatism got so bad it wouldn't even let him sail the little lugger any more, he beached the boat at Belcroute Bay for the last time. He handed back his grandson and namesake to his son, a complete if youthful sailor, ready to be apprenticed as a fishing boat skipper. It would be a long process, but eventually young Jean would need to take over *l'Imprevu* from his father in his turn. There had never been any question of Marie using the skills she'd acquired at sea.

The next March, proud as could be, old Cotterell had walked down to the *grève* at St Helier with his Breton daughter-in-law to see off his son Jean-Jacques and grandson Jean in *l'Imprevu*. Jean-Jacques and little apprentice Jean sailed with a crew of four for the Banks in seventy-six. Two Jerseymen, Dumaresq and Gallichan, and two Cornishmen, both called Goff but unrelated (or so they claimed), made up the crew. *L'Imprevu* was part of a fleet, mostly consisting of much bigger vessels, even including a three-masted Grand Banks schooner built on the American style. The fleet was dressed in bunting and ribbons and the strand or grève was lined with weeping sweethearts, wives and mothers. A band played on the grève as the boats left and some women had climbed Noirmont to wave a last farewell. The women of Jersey cried a sea of tears as their husbands and sons left. Some of the men of the fleet had wiped away a silent tear too, once la Corbière point was far behind them, dipping on the horizon, and Guernsey was to their north, the last land they would see for many long weeks. No one could admit to tears.

It wasn't permissible for the men. Young Jean watched the men around him struggle. No man met another's eye until this surge of immediate homesickness was washed away by the seas. No one looked back until they knew Guernsey would be well out of sight. Then the open Atlantic was before them and the sailors in the little fleet around young Jean had to prepare themselves to become fishermen again.

On the Grand Banks, after a journey of weeks and thousands of miles, little *l'Imprevu* fished cod on long lines like the rest of the Jersey fleet, the crew laying out miles of line at a time, a hook and bait every few yards. It was hard work and could be cold, even in May. That first time out on the Banks young Jean Cotterell had worked as hard as the men, baiting hooks and pulling lines, while his father spent days at the wheel, keeping the fishing boat on a steady drifting course. The lines and the barbs cut the sailors' hands and the salt from the bait and sea water meant the wounds didn't heal. The fleet fished all day and all night, the men baiting and laying, or hauling and gutting in turns. Fish guts and oil soaked their clothes, their food, their water, their skin and their wounds, so that young Jean felt he had become part fish too, so much of him was soaked in it. At night they kept fishing, the oil deck lamps on the boats making the fleet look like a bobbing city, like St Helier, the biggest town he'd ever seen then, seen across the bay from his grandfather's house in St Aubin. The sailors kept talking too, stories, anecdotes, a whole cycle of frightening ghost stories from the younger Goff, Jacob was matched by similar tales of the ethereal in the Jersey parishes by Dumaresq, who came from a family which talked like magpies, as the Jersey saying goes. There was a great deal of translation to English by Jean-Jacques, since the unrelated Cornish Goffs spoke only that language. They amused themselves, and the other members of *l'Imprevu*'s crew, by teaching young Jean Cotterell to speak English properly. He was already almost fluent in the language but learned quickly to adjust his accent and to stress sentences in the English way. The Goffs were proud of their teaching and Jacob even declared that Cotterell had made a schoolteacher of him. Perhaps he should give up the sea.

'Perhaps you should,' said Jean's father, 'but until you do, bait the line. We are here to bait fish, not men.'

Jacob scowled and Jean Cotterell's father winked at Jean. But they went back to baiting. Days passed in this timeless, repetitive existence. Bait and lay, haul and gut, bait and lay, haul and gut until *L'Imprevu* had filled her salt-barrels with fish. She was the first, since she was smaller than the other vessels, and had to find the shore earlier than the rest of the fleet. Jean-Jacques Cotterell brought them to the nearest familiar land, Hope Bay, where they ran the boat ashore, cut wood, built split pine racks and began the process of air-drying the codfish from the Banks. Hope Bay is where Cotterell had first seen Dubarre, almost twenty years before. Dubarre had been captain then of the *Galipétan*, just as he was now of the *Hortense*. But in 1776 he had been a privateer.

Hope Bay, Terre-Neuve was an almost regular section of a circle, about three miles across the mouth and one mile deep from its chord to its arc. It faced east and was therefore mostly sheltered. It had a long sloping sandy beach. Hope Bay was deserted save for *L'Imprevu* and her crew. No one had ever called there apart from nomadic Indians who sometimes harvested mussels and inshore fish. Even they failed to appear on this visit.

The bay was guarded by rocky promontories and had a dense northern wood behind it. On the southern side there was running fresh water as a stream met the sea. All around the bay there was shelter under the trees. On this southern side of the beach lay *l'Imprevu* and nearby were the signs of old pine drying racks Jean-Jacques and Pepe Jean had used in years gone by. The old racks, formed of split pine branches tied to trestles, had been broken and bleached by the weather. Newfoundland winters are nothing if not weathering on any object left to fend for itself. Underneath the old broken-down pine racks was a thin crust of white salt, scatterings dropped from the cod which had been dried there.

To a cod fisherman the bay was perfect, and this far north should have been safe from prowling French privateers. There was security too. English fishing vessels were just over the horizon and British warships were in St John harbour. In nearby Petty Bay there was even a garrison, though Jean-Jacques knew they stirred little for fear of revealing their weakness.

Young Jean Cotterell allowed his face to turn in the sunlight. The day was warm with a soft breeze beginning to move from the sea to the land. It was balmy. The unrelated Goffs were taking fish from the salting barrels and hanging them on the newly-constructed racks. Jean and his father were helping. They were enjoying the work, laughing and playful in the English they were teaching young Jean. Below them, further down the beach, *L'Imprevu* was careened. Dumaresq and Gallichan were cleaning her undersides of the beard of weed grown on the Bank and the Atlantic crossing. Then Gallichan looked into the bay and called Jean-Jacques, 'Patron!'

They all stopped work. A ship slid into the mouth of the bay. She carried no ensign but her shape was clearly French. She wasn't a merchantman and she was missing the tidiness of a naval vessel.

'Privateer,' said the older Goff, simply. He was right. The privateer warship was handled expertly. Her anchor dropped and she swung to it. Jean Cotterell's young eyes could read the name painted on her, even at that distance – *Galipétan*. Ten of her twenty guns were pointing towards the fishing boat. A whaler dropped from her side.

Fifteen minutes later Dubarre – though at the time neither Jean Cotterell nor the others knew that was his name – strode up the beach, followed by half a dozen of his men. Other armed privateers waited in the whaler. Each, apart from Dubarre, was furnished with a pistol or blunderbuss and a cutlass. Dubarre was clearly the leader. He carried no weapon at all. His hair was dyed black, and he wore a strange and theatrical mixture of clothes, white pantaloons, a green frock coat with a high collar, a white cotton shirt whose tail flapped in the breeze whenever it could escape the coat tails and a long, curved French officer's cockade hat worn sideways. His feet were bare.

'*En provenance*?' he demanded of Jean-Jacques without preamble.

'Morbihan, Monsieur,' the older Cotterell replied. 'The city of Vannes. And I am addressing?'

Dubarre looked around his men before replying, 'You are addressing?'

'Your name, sir.'

Dubarre looked around his smirking men again. It was as if Jean-Jacques Cotterell was the victim in an entertainment they had witnessed before. Dubarre pointed at the ship behind him.

'Do you see the guns?' asked Dubarre.

'Yes sir,' replied Jean-Jacques.

'They mean I ask questions and you answer.'

'Of course, Monsieur. I presume you carry letters of marque?' Jean-Jacques responded.

Without a word of command one of Dubarre's sailors stepped forward and knocked Jean-Jacques down with the butt of a blunderbuss. Gallichan stepped aboard *l'Imprevu* and grabbed two gaffs, handing one down to Dumaresq from the beached fishing boat. The Goffs drew their knives. Jean stepped forward to defend his father, full of aggression. He held a knife too. Dubarre moved towards him and twisted it out of his hand in one easy movement. The blade fell on the sand. Dubarre laughed and put his arm around the boy's shoulders.

'Easy there, young one. Easy. Knives and boys are not much defence against cannons.' His voice was friendly and warm. 'There is no need for too much excitement. Help your patron up.'

'He's my father,' said young Cotterell, and punched Dubarre's hands away. Dubarre applauded. His crew followed, slapping one hand against their weapons.

'Bravo!' cried Dubarre. '*Chapeau*, young monsieur. This lad defends his father. We all admire a brave young man. Perhaps we should take him into our crew.'

'You will not,' said Cotterell.

'Spirit!' cried Dubarre, and laughed again. 'Spirit.' He grasped Jean's shoulder and led him away a pace or two. Then he slid his arm around the boy's head and held it in a side chancery with a grip like a vice, patting his cheek as he did so. 'Just give me an answer, boy.'

'What answer sir?'

'You're from Vannes?'

'I am.'

This was rehearsed among the crew of *l'Imprevu*. They knew they might meet French warships or privateers and they carried papers on *l'Imprevu* for a vessel of that name from Vannes.

'Is Vannes on the sea?'

Behind them Jean-Jacques was struggling to his feet. Cotterell turned and saw his father.

'You have to pass through the Morbihan to get there sir. It's an inland sea.'

Dubarre nodded and let the boy go.

'Where do you get the salt for the fish?'

'Redon, sir. It's sold on the quay there by the ton.'

'You take this vessel up there?'

'No, sir. The river Vilaine is impassable to a sea-going boat. It almost dries in parts and is rocky throughout.'

'It does indeed dry, young sailor. Do they speak Breton on the Vilaine?'

'No, sir. Gallo, throughout.'

'One more question. Who is Vannes and his wife?'

'A carving, sir. An ancient wooden carving.'

Jean-Jacques and his Jersey crew had sold fish in Vannes in the past and the boy had been there too. His Breton mother was from Auray. Both Jean-Jacques and young Jean spoke the Breton Gallo when they wanted. It wasn't so far removed from their native Jerrais. Dubarre let Jean go, walked back to the sailor with the blunderbuss and punched him in the face. The man fell. His mouth bled. Dubarre towered over him.

'How dare you assault that gentleman? I should let that fisherman stick his gaff up your arse.' He said, pointing at Dumaresq, still holding his long fish-gaff. The sailor Dubarre had punched, a big man with olive skin and long black tousled hair, didn't complain, but simply stayed on the ground and staunched the blood with the cuff of his old-fashioned jacket. Dubarre turned to Jean-Jacques. The fishing boat Captain was on his feet again.

'No doubt you have papers from the city of Vannes.'

'I do, Monsieur.' Jean-Jacques went toward *l'Imprevu*. Gallichan handed down a tied bundle of papers wrapped in a waxed-cloth. Jean-Jacques began to untie them but Dubarre stopped him and handed the package instead to one of his sailors. The man was small, thin and weak-looking. He wore a black coat tailored for a much bigger man and coughed almost incessantly into a dirty piece of rag. The sailor stuffed the rag in his pocket for a moment, pulled the package open, then used a pair of spectacles to read. The spectacles hadn't been ground for him, since he held them halfway between himself and the pages he read.

'Have you seen any English vessels?' asked Dubarre as his man read, moving his lips. He asked in a casual way, as if he'd just found Jean-Jacques by his side in a tavern. But he was watching the patron of *l'Imprevu* carefully.

'No warships,' lied Jean-Jacques. He knew there were English warships two or three days' sail away.

'What about fishing boats?' asked Dubarre, looking at him closely.

'None, sir.'

'You're not part of a fleet?'

'We've seen fishing vessels, but I don't know where they were from. We didn't approach them.'

'Very wise,' said Dubarre. 'In case they were English. The English are well known to be savages. They would take your cargo, make slaves of you and probably burn your boat.'

He looked at Dumaresq and Gallichan.

'Where does your crew come from?'

'These two are from the Morbihan. The other two are Cornish.'

'It's forbidden to carry English crew on a French ship.'

'They are Cornish, Monsieur.'

'Do they speak Cornish?'

'No sir. No one does, to my knowledge.'

'Do they speak English?'

'Between themselves.'

'Do they have a Cornish King?'

'No sir.'

'Do they have an English King?'

'Yes sir.'

'Then they are English,' said Dubarre. 'Where did you find them?'

'On the *quai* in Vannes, looking for work.'

After a while the coughing sailor pronounced, 'All correct, Capitaine.'

Dubarre indicated that the sailor should give the papers back to Jean-Jacques. He did so, coughing a fine spray of blood over them.

'Get rid of the Englishmen.' Dubarre ordered Jean-Jacques. His voice was calm and pleasant, but there was an edge to it. 'I could take your ship just for that one irregularity, French vessel or not.'

'Yes, Monsieur.'

Jean-Jacques waited for Dubarre's next command. It was an age before the privateer spoke. Then he moved his head close to Jean-Jacques. 'Command of a ship is a heavy responsibility. Command of any ship. Our *métier* is the loneliest, don't you find?' Dubarre confessed in a whisper. He had inclined his head to speak softly to Jean-Jacques and as he spoke his eyes met young Jean's, standing at his father's side. What was so threatening about those words, Jean wondered? It was as if the intimacy, the tiniest glimpse into the privateer's soul, was given just to intimidate the father and son who could hear the whisper. Dubarre turned on his heel without uttering another sound and strode back to the whaler. The whaler's cut-throat crew scampered after him.

*

Later, when the privateer *Galipétan* had weighed anchor and been towed from the bay by its crew in their whaler, Jean-Jacques took young Cotterell inland. They wore shoes against the rough stony ground and Jean-Jacques carried his precious boat's telescope, wrapped in a soft green leather bag. Jean Cotterell carried a little adze, a present from Pepe before they had left. The terrain rose as they walked.

'Did he believe us?'

'Who? The privateer? I expect so. He left. Put yourself in his shoes. We look and sound like French. The boat looks French and carries French papers. Why not?'

Young Jean considered it. Why not indeed?

'He wasn't wearing shoes.'

Jean-Jacques laughed and put his arm around his son.

'He is a creature of the seas, lad. He doesn't take many steps on land.'

'Is that what he meant, when he said ours is the loneliest trade?'

'I expect so.'

They climbed higher. The pines swayed in the breeze. They rustled like women's skirts. The fresh pine smell from their needles was so pungent that Jean felt he could almost see it, like snow.

'Will we put off the Goffs, Papa?' Jean continued. 'As the privateer ordered.'

'Certainly not. What would they do? Swim home?'

'And if the Captain of the *Galipétan* finds out?'

'How will he do that?' said Jean-Jacques. 'He can't. They're safe.'

His son wasn't convinced. Jean-Jacques went on.

'Be calm, son. The privateer will be caught by the King's Navy within days, and will be hung above his own quarter-deck for his impudence in sailing these waters.'

'How will he be caught?'

'Because the devil walks round him and leaves a track. And it is well-known God sees everything and dispenses justice. Now be quiet.'

They walked on. Young Jean wanted to speak more, so his father explained their mission.

'Twenty years ago,' said Jean-Jacques, 'when your grandfather first brought me here, the country was alive with Beothuk. Indians who painted themselves in red ochre from head to foot and went about as naked as a baby. They showed Pepe which pine bark you could use to make tea.'

'Tea?'

'Against the scurvy. We'll find some. That's why you have the adze.'

The climb was steep now and though both were fit, their weeks at sea had made them unused to the exercise.

'Were you a boy then, Father?' asked Jean.

'I was.'

'And you were with Pepe when he met the . . .'

'Beothuk,' supplied Jean-Jacques, 'Yes.'

'Was Pepe their friend?'

Jean-Jacques laughed at a memory. 'People like him. I some-times think that my father knows someone everywhere in the world. So they helped him. And in return for their help Pepe taught them how to salt fish for the winter.'

'They didn't know?'

'No.'

'Why is that funny?'

'They didn't want to know. They laughed. They said there had always been fish and there would always be fish. God had put the fish in the sea to feed the Beothuk. If we wanted to dry fish to take back with us across the sea that was our concern. There is plenty of fish for everyone. But the Beothuk would eat fresh fish.'

'Are the Indians we sometimes see Beothuk?'

'No. Mikmaks.'

'They are different?'

'They are untrustworthy. They use little ochre on their bodies. They would steal your eyes and come back for the lashes. Also they are in a confederacy with the French.'

They walked on. They were now at a height where they could see inland. The forests stretched as far as the eye could see with no sign of life or habitation. It was like looking at a pine ocean.

'Why have the Mikmaks not attacked us?'

'There are British soldiers at Petty Harbour.'

'They would protect us?'

'Unfortunately not, my son. They are too few. But the Mikmaks believe the British soldiers would avenge us, which makes it sufficiently dangerous to the Mikmaks that they do not attack us.'

'Where is Petty Harbour?'

'About ten miles that way.' He pointed inland. 'In another bay.'

They paused and looked back towards the bay and the sea. The privateer ship sailed slowly away. From this distance and height the sea was like a mirror, entirely lacking waves or even a swell. Jean-Jacques Cotterell unwrapped the telescope and looked through it at the privateer, then handed it to his son.

'Have a look with your young eyes. Tell me what you see.'

Cotterell looked through the telescope, sliding it slightly to focus. He could see the ship very clearly. He looked along the decks.

'I can't see the Captain.'

He lifted the telescope slightly to examine the rigging. On the maintop platform stood the large, unmistakable figure of the barefoot privateer captain, officer's hat still on his head despite the height. He too held a telescope. Or was it a musket? Even Cotterell's young eyes couldn't tell. It must be a telescope, he thought. After a while the privateer turned the long, pipe-like object onto the hillside where they stood. They would have been difficult to see against the woodland and shale but still a shiver passed up young Jean's spine.

'He's in the rigging,' he said. 'Scouting the horizon.'

'Looking for some other honest fisherman to prey upon, no doubt.' Jean-Jacques took the telescope from his son and wrapped it up again.

'Let's find this tree.'

They began to climb again. Soon they had crossed a ridge of broken grey shale and begun to descend again inland. The bay and the sea beyond were now out of sight.

Jean-Jacques and his son returned to Hope Bay many hours later. Both were laden with pine bark, the makings of the anti-scorbutic Pepe had discovered many years before. They had spent the afternoon cutting it with the adze. Even before they reached the shale ridge they could see something was wrong. A pall of smoke hung over the bay. Jean-Jacques dropped the bark and handed his precious telescope to his son.

'Wait here.' He took a step forward, then turned, 'whatever happens, don't follow me down there.'

Jean Cotterell watched his father descend from the ridge. The pall of smoke still rose from the bay below him. The French privateer was in the bay again. Its boats were on the shore. *L'Imprevu* was burning down to its ribs. Jean could see two bodies washing back and forth in the surf. The fish-drying structures were smashed and the salt fish scattered. The privateer captain was on the beach. Jean-Jacques approached him. They exchanged some words. They were much too far away for young Jean to hear what they were. Jean-Jacques raised his hand towards Dubarre. A sailor stepped from behind the privateer captain and struck out with a cutlass. Jean-Jacques fell. Now there were three bodies in the surf. Cotterell wanted to run down there too, but his father's instruction held him back. He watched his father floating in the surf. There was nothing he could do. He wept.

Years later, at night on board the *Hortense*, Jean Cotterell the grown man opened his eyes with his sobs still ringing in his ears. Even now he could barely breathe when he thought about it.

The memory of his father floating in the surf was as fresh as if it had happened a day ago. As a boy he'd buried his face in the shale of the ridge to erase the sight. Later he'd buried his father and the two unrelated Goffs on the beach with his own hands. Dumaresq and Gallichan were nowhere to be seen. Perhaps they were hiding in the bush nearby. Perhaps they'd run away. Perhaps the privateers had taken them. Cotterell lay in the dark and remembered building the cairn beside the charred remains of the fishing boat, then the long lonely walk to the British fort at Petty Bay. It took three days, and all the time Jean had felt he was being stalked by French-loving Indians he couldn't see, savages who would steal his scalp for nothing, leave alone the expensive telescope and adze he carried.

In Petty Bay, Newfoundland, Cotterell had arrived tired, starving and bleeding from the cross-country walk from Hope Bay. He had found his wooden stockade fort and his British soldiers, made his report of the privateer and met the Lieutenant off one of three British ships at anchor in Petty Bay. The Lieutenant was a fellow Jerseyman, Dauvergne, who had come ashore to deliver orders and take on water. Dauvergne was a dapper little man with bright, blue-grey eyes and hair already turning silver, though he wasn't over thirty. His ship – the *Asia* – seemed enormous to Jean Cotterell, easily big enough to chase, catch and smash *Galipétan*. Even from a distance he could see the Royal Navy vessels were scrubbed and trim, like the Lieutenant. Lieutenant Dauvergne knew the Cotterell, Gallichan and Dumaresq families by reputation in Jersey and listened carefully and politely to the boy's story, but he refused to impress on his captain the urgency of chasing down the privateer.

'We are bound for Boston. We have orders.'

'Then I'll wait till someone comes who doesn't have orders.'

Dauvergne shook his head. 'Everyone has orders, boy. No one comes to Newfoundland by chance. The soldiers here don't have rations for you and there is no one in the post who will take you on as a servant. You come with me to Boston. You

can work as a boy on the *Asia* and I'll make sure your mother
has news of you plus the hope of your eventual return, safe
and sound.' And he had made good on his promise.

Swinging in his hammock on the deck of the French frigate,
Cotterell reflected that no one knew what had happened to his
father's crewmen Gallichan and Dumaresq. Neither the Cotterells,
nor their own families, nor any other Jersey fishing people had
had any news of the missing sailors in all the long years since.
Awake in the near-complete darkness of the lower deck of the
Hortense, Cotterell knew why he had dreamed of the burning of
the first *l'Imprevu* in Newfoundland. It wasn't the vision of his
father's body in the surf, though that had occupied his mind for
years. It wasn't regret for not killing Dubarre on the mast-top
of the *Hortense* earlier, where he had been vulnerable and unpro-
tected. Killing in cold blood, even killing Dubarre, would be a
sin. Instead the dream had told Cotterell simply that Dubarre
couldn't read. He reflected on this fact. Cotterell had never seen
Dubarre read so much as a scrap of paper. He never took the
sun sights on *Hortense*, he'd passed the first *l'Imprevu*'s papers to
his blinking owl of a sailor to read on the Newfoundland beach.
It was incredible – an illiterate man a captain in the French Navy.
But of course an illiterate privateer captain was not incredible.
He just needed his own vessel, or be able to convince an arma-
teur, an investor and a ship-owner to supply him with one.
Dubarre's qualification for the role would originally have been
the ability to turn a profit on his letters of marque. Cotterell
considered it. If the French maritime service or Navy, which
according to Tom's Jack-Tar judgement and by Cotterell's observation was in a parlous state, was desperate for professional and
successful ships' captains, it would seek to make up the short-
fall from the merchant and privateer fleets. And who would ask
a man who was already a ship's captain to take a reading test?
Men who could merely read could be found anywhere, probably half the crew had the skill to some extent or other. There
would be three or four men who could navigate aboard any ship

and a Captain's clerk to write the log. On *Hortense* Auchard, Mathelier, probably the signal cadet Merlet too, could work up a position from sightings, the clocks and the books carried aboard. Before they'd gone down with the flux probably half a dozen more would have had the skill.

Mentally he crossed Mathelier off the list. He'd seemed a decent young man, if full of himself. Not many years ago, when Cotterell had first taken command of the family fishing boat, he'd probably been full of himself too. And he'd also taken risk lightly, just as Mathelier had when he'd scampered up the rigging to help Lefèvre. Cotterell looked about himself on the lower deck of the frigate *Hortense*, eyes penetrating the darkness. The only light was a single candle further along the deck. Like Cotterell the rest of the '*tribordais quart*,' or starboard watch, slept in hammocks slung athwart, swinging in time with the ship's nodding genuflexions to the sea. Cotterell's and Tom's hammocks were next to each other. Tom turned and whispered in the darkness.

'You're awake?'

'Yes.'

'Caulk or yarn?'

By which Tom meant, will you talk?

'Do I have a choice?'

'You cried in a dream.'

'Did I?' Cotterell had no intention of sharing his thoughts. 'Did anyone hear me?'

'No. I expect not. You were a quiet bawler. You'd never make a boatswain.' Not one sailor in the other swinging hammocks showed any sign of being awake.

'How many in the wardroom on this ship, Tom?' Cotterell asked.

'Wardroom is it now? First you was an oil store clerk, now you turn out to be a regular matelot.'

'How many?'

'Hardly none. The Second should be there, but he keeps his own company and has a wife to entertain him.'

'Which she doesn't.'

'We have seen. She doesn't even sleep in his cabin with him.'

'Has she ever since she came aboard?'

'Not as I have noticed, and it's a small ship. Back to ward-rooms. Mr Mathelier should be there but will not be requiring a seat at the table. There was another Lieutenant, but he died of injuries he received from my good Midshipman Mr Wills, when they were fighting to capture us. He never even made it as far as the Floridas. There was a regular sailing master but he died of the flux, so now the Bosco doubles as both boatswain and master. God knows you wouldn't want to introduce him to any important gentlemen around the supper table for he's a ferocious good seaman but lacking in genteel manners, and will scratch his arse and blow his nose wherever he wishes. Unless of course he is 'aristo mankey', as these fellows say, and altogether too eager to prove he is not an aristo for revolutionary purposes.'

'*Manqué*, and I doubt it. Derray is what he appears to be,' replied Cotterell.

Tom rubbed his chin, deep in thought. 'The two ensigns died of the same flux as the *Hortense*'s sailing master, which had come aboard with the merchant seamen. God rest their souls. The surgeon died from treating them, though from what I saw he might as well have died of too much brandy, eau de vie and laudanum. Cordell, the ship's clerk, is hale and hearty. He seems to be a regular warrant officer in the French Navee, though he wouldn't get a kiss my arse in the wardroom of a proper British man o' war. Imagine, a little scribbler eating with the officers.'

Cotterell imagined.

'There's Merlet, the new signal officer, of course. That's it. Just Merlet, Cordell and the Second are in the wardroom, I think.'

Cotterell considered it, then asked, 'So how many aboard in all?'

There was a silence, then Tom said, 'the *Hortense* is depleted everywhere. No surgeon, hardly officers to speak of, the ship's company should be more than two hundred and fifty . . .'

'So how many?'

'Why do you want to know?'

'You are the one who keeps talking about men dying of the flux,' said Cotterell. 'I wondered how many.'

'There are never more than a hundred and fifty men aboard the *Hortense* now. Still too many, shipmate, if you are thinking of taking her over.'

'I'm not.'

'So why are you interested?'

Tom waited for a reply or another question but none came.

Cotterell closed his eyes, as if to prove the conversation was ended.

After a while in silence they heard a muffled cry of pain from the orlop below them. Then there was sobbing, then silence again.

Tom could not resist speaking again. 'He has been making that noise all this time. Crying like a baby. Sometimes calling aloud for his mother – as if she could hear him.'

Cotterell could hear Lefèvre's voice calling and jabbering incomprehensibly. 'He scares the others when he cries out,' said Tom.

'Why?'

'His pain.'

'It's not theirs.' Cotterell's voice was matter of fact.

'We will all end in pain and sorrow, the good book says,' whispered Tom, gloomily.

'Where?'

'I don't know. But I'm sure it says it. What about ashes to ashes?'

'"In the sweat of thy brow shalt thou eat bread, till thou return unto the ground, for out of it thou were taken. For dust thou art and unto dust shalt thou return" That's from Genesis.'

'Remind me, was you a clerk or a cleric before we lifted you out of the ocean in the Miracle of the Grand Bank?'

'I was never much of a schoolboy, Tom, but even I contrived to stay attentive for the first book of the first testament. Anyway, it's not true.'

'What?'

'That bit of scripture.'

'Blasphemy now.'

'All around us is ocean. What chance we will "return unto the ground".'

'Not much, if one of His Majesty's ships finds us, unless there is a burial plot deep under this sea. You appear to have my nob in Chancery, John Cotterell. I feel as if someone is tightening a cooper's band around my head.'

Now Lefèvre was sobbing again, the sound reverberating up to them from the bowels of the ship. Men shifted uncomfortably in their hammocks. Cotterell closed his eyes. Whatever the merit of Tom's faulty theological memory it was true, the sound was awful. It was an uncontrolled, uninhibited sob as you might hear at the end of a life. Cotterell had heard men cry before, he'd seen them sob in pain and shame, but there was an extra quality to Lefèvre's sobbing. It was childish and full.

'The black is still down there with Lefèvre,' said Tom. 'I have been awake all this time and I have not seen or heard him come up. He is a good man. He has a conscience. Anyone else would leave Lefèvre to it. The Second would.'

'Auchard seemed more interested in his wife's doings,' replied Cotterell. Then after a while he couldn't stop himself asking Tom, 'It is supposed to be a love match between those two?'

'That's what she told Charles.'

'It is hard to believe?'

'Observation,' whispered Tom, 'would make a blind man think the Second and his wife are not a love match. They don't coo over each other like a couple who have not long been wed. They do not touch. They do not even seek each other's company. He gives her orders, as you have seen, and in the generality she ignores them, as you have also seen.'

'Then why is she here?'

Tom reached up and touched his nose, to indicate special knowledge. 'I was on old *Veteran* when we stopped a ship full of them Africans on their way to America. An English vessel, but she was still a slaver. They had thousands of the poor bastards chained naked below. Imagine this here lower deck with a thousand men on it instead of a couple of hundred, all chained down to the deck. They ate, drank, shit and died where they were chained. Those who wasn't dying of the shits was drowning in it. It was a terrible thing to see, Mr Cotterell. Terrible. And the stench.'

'What did you do?'

'What could we do? Set 'em free? The slaver was a mean bastard but he couldn't have a thousand free sick Africans tumbling about and screaming in their God-forsaken languages below deck or upon it in the middle of the ocean. No. And our Captain Nugent was shocked by the nudity of the Africans. Men, women and children, all mixed up and us naked as the day they walked out of the bush. What could he say to the slaver? Bring them on deck as they are? Let them take turns wearing sailors' skirts while exercising for their health? Our good Captain admonished the fellow, then let him go with a promise if he ever so much as showed himself in England again he would be persecuted.'

'Prosecuted.'

'You are an educated man, Mr Cotterell, and I a poor sailor who has spent twenty years on the lower deck without so much as a thankee and good-day from a schoolmaster. But I believe I have seen more of the evil in the world than you. I recognise the influence of the devil in men when I see it.' He paused, then, 'So reflect on this. If a man makes his living from the sale and purchase of a couple of thousand miserable naked niggers, would it trouble his conscience to sell his daughter to some passing rich Frenchie?'

'Put like that, no,' replied Cotterell. 'Though in so saying you sound like an abolitionist.' He smiled. Even on their short acquaintance he knew very well that Tom was salt of the earth English, averse to politics in theory and practice. If Tom had any political principles they reflected those of his secure English universe where his masters were his betters in every sense. Anything which suggested his thoughts had struck out alone made him anxious.

'What's right is right.' Tom harrumphed. 'And the Second bought his wife, which is wrong.'

Footsteps sounded behind them. Cotterell turned to see the dark shape of Charles approaching.

He called softly. 'Mr Cotterell!'

'Here,' replied Cotterell, and was out of his hammock in one movement. Charles squeezed between their hammocks so that he could pull their heads close before speaking in a whisper.

'Which is the pork butcher?'

9

Gaston, the former pork butcher, was from Mézières, a cradle as far removed from the sea as that of any man aboard the *Hortense*. He was a good Republican and, when asked, had refused to take part in the proposed amputation of Lefèvre's leg, claiming a shaking hand had excluded him from his earlier profession and the shake might well 'do for' Citizen Lefèvre if it were to be let loose on him. They all knew that in fact Gaston was wary of the consequences. Perhaps he was more confident than the others that the ship would reach Brest, where consequences might be applied to the head which had guided the hand which had wielded the knife on a revolutionary friend of Jeanbon St André. Perhaps simple fear was the reason for the tremor in Gaston's hand. He held it out and showed them. Gaston recommended they instead ask Pascal, the cook, who had once helped him butcher an injured cow and was 'a very confident and able man'. Pascal certainly had a high opinion of himself, and they had to admit he knew as much as any man aboard ship about sharp knives and animal physiology, which had at least some resemblance to that of men. Pascal might very well be the best-qualified man aboard for the job. Pascal knew the revolutionary Lefèvre well and may have been the closest thing the small bearded zealot had on the ship to a friend, leaving aside his wife.

Pascal was doubtful. Charles was persuasive. Pascal was promised brandy; he was promised the performance of the cut would be an act of fellowship and a Republican Duty performed. Other men had been swept up by the *levée en masse* to serve France, whereas Pascal could serve her conveniently just by removing a man's offending leg. It wasn't even his own limb he would have to sacrifice. Pascal went to the galley, put his assistant in charge of preparing the morning's breakfast to come (dried biscuit formed into porridge and 'coffee' made from other, black-burnt dried biscuit), wiped the worse of the grease off his hands with a tow of unravelled rope and was ready to operate. Tom wondered aloud if the sail-maker wouldn't come in handy too, for the successful conclusion of an amputation, but the little group left that individual to sleep undisturbed in his hammock. There was only so much room on the orlop.

Emily met the little group as they were about to go below. She held a dim lamp which she shaded from the open deck above her with her hand.

'It's late, Madame,' said Charles with a hint of disapproval. It convinced no one. 'And your husband . . .'

'. . . is on deck at his post, as always,' she said. 'I couldn't sleep and I could hear that man screaming. May I help?'

'Have you any bandages?' asked Charles.

'I can make some,' she said.

'Please do. I had intended to ask Citoyenne Lefèvre.'

'She is beside herself,' Emily replied.

'She is always beside herself,' said the cook, Pascal. 'But now unhappily she has some reason.' Pascal seemed to enjoy gloominess almost as much as Tom.

Charles ignored him, instead saying to Emily. 'Please send bandages down with a crew member. I don't want to cause any further inconvenience to the Second.'

Tom met Cotterell's eye. They all knew what Charles meant, even the cook Pascal who had not witnessed Auchard's coldtempered dismissal of his wife on the orlop. They descended, watched by Emily, before she turned and padded back to her quarters.

On the orlop Cotterell consulted the surgeon's sewn and bound manual with Charles, while Tom helped Pascal the cook to sort through the tools of the surgeon's trade in search of a good blade. Lefèvre was somewhere between death and dream, moaning softly, but never opening his eyes.

The knife blades had lain unused for a long time. Once Pascal had found a steel they thought would do for the task, Tom polished it with a leather until they'd satisfied themselves of its keenness. The two found some cat-gut and a needle, then set about pouring strong surgeon's brandy down the delirious Lefèvre's throat, after first tasting it and verifying the quality for themselves. Cotterell and Charles refused a ration, so Pascal took theirs too.

'We must leave a good surface for a wooden leg.' Charles put the book down and pronounced in French over Lefèvre's enormous naked leg. The knee was like another man's torso. It looked as if a pin would burst it. The lower half of the leg was white and deadly. No blood flowed there.

'We can make a good stump,' he continued, pointing at the book, 'and leave the gentleman almost as agile as before, with care. We have instructions on how to do so.'

'If not the skill. Let's not get in front of ourselves with talk of good stumps,' said Cotterell. 'Have you seen it done?' he asked Charles.

'No.'

'I have,' said Cotterell. He held out his hand. Charles passed him a knife. Cotterell felt the blade with his thumb. 'Is he ready?'

Tom gave Lefèvre's clenched teeth another good splash with the brandy bottle, then he and Pascal wrenched the moaning victim's jaws apart, by the means of Tom pushing on his brow, while Pascal held the lower jaw. Tom shoved a leather strap he'd found among the surgeon's tools between Lefèvre's teeth. Lefèvre's eyes opened and rolled when he was released again and his bite on the strap was weak, though whether that was due to inebriation or pain wasn't clear. He sweated a great deal and his hands clutched at the cot sides from their bindings. He moaned and babbled loudly, but was beyond following any instruction or responding to any command. He was secured all-round in the cot with belts and straps, though this wasn't very convenient for any cutting and sawing to come.

'A table would have been better,' said Cotterell.

'Let's just do it,' said Charles. He held out the book and read from it. 'The tourniquet should be put on the femoral artery, two-thirds of the way down the thigh, just before the vessel passes through the tendon of the triceps muscle.'

Cotterell asked, 'Does anyone know where the femoral meets the triceps?' Pascal pointed at the leg and held his finger where he'd pointed. Charles thumbed through the book till he found an illustration, compared it to the position of Pascal's finger, then moved the finger to a new point.

'There, I think,' he pronounced.

'Do we have something to mark it?' asked Pascal.

'No,' said Cotterell. 'Just remember it.'

Tom found the tourniquet, a webbing belt device with a leather pad and a brass screw attached to it by buckles. They put the webbing belt around Lefèvre's upper leg, over the femoral and triceps as the coloured engraving in the book indicated. Charles held out the book to Cotterell while he supervised the tourniquet, reading from it as he did. Charles tightened the screw. Pascal drank more brandy. Tom waited his turn for brandy.

'It says speed and skill are the most important attributes for a satisfactory conclusion. Do we have speed and skill?' asked Cotterell.

'I don't,' admitted Charles.

'He will,' said Tom, pointing to Pascal.

'We have to draw up the integuments,' read Cotterell aloud.

'What?' asked Pascal.

'I can't understand one word,' said Tom, wiping Pascal's spit from the bottle mouth, then taking a draw. 'Not one word. Integglements?'

'Skin,' said Charles. 'You pull the loose flesh and skin up for him and then . . .'

'The surgeon,' continued Cotterell, reading, 'should then divide the skin completely round the limb with one quick stroke of the knife.'

'There.' Charles showed Pascal an area just below the knee where he wanted the cut made. 'Will you do it?'

'If *he* has experience, *he* should.' Pascal meant Cotterell.

'I have seen it once,' said Cotterell. 'Whereas you are an expert with the knife.'

Cotterell handed the knife to Pascal, who made the sign of the cross with it, then drew on the brandy bottle again. So much for the Godless revolution, thought Cotterell. Pascal circled Lefèvre's leg below the knee with the surgeon's knife, releasing the skin and the loose flesh under it. Lefèvre screamed through the biting strap. Some clear fluid flowed from the cut flesh of the knee but not much blood.

Tom said quietly, 'My God.'

Cotterell read the manual again, then, 'you must cut it back clear of the joint, it says.'

Pascal made the cut with all the skill of a man used to boning meat. Lefèvre gave a suppressed squeal. Pascal took another draft of brandy. Lefèvre began to build up to a full-lunged scream. Charles grabbed the bottle from Pascal and poured into Lefèvre's face so that he gasped and spluttered and Tom had to shove the strap back in his mouth. He screamed through the strap, so that Cotterell had to shout to be heard.

'The surgeon should cut through the muscles of the calf, from the inside of the tibia to the fibula. This will form a flap from the calf which will be used to cover the stump. Are we clear?' asked Cotterell. He turned the book and showed them.

Pascal and Charles agreed they were clear and Pascal began to cut again. Lefèvre squealed anew, then began to flap like a landed fish, so Tom sat upon his chest while Pascal continued.

'Now you have to divide the muscles in the knee itself. Divide loose muscles first, then those which are intimately attached to the bone. Take care to cut completely through the deep muscular attachments. It says here to avoid dividing muscles more than once, to prevent repeating severe pain for the subject.' Pascal cut deeply and swiftly, avoiding a second divide. Lefèvre screamed through the strap and flapped even with Tom on top of him. Cotterell looked at the book again. 'And now you must separate something called the interosseous ligament, which I expect means the ligaments next to the bone.'

Charles nodded agreement. Pascal did as he was asked. Lefèvre fainted. More fluid and little blood came from the knee – the joint was entirely exposed now.

'I have seen lamb look like that.' Pascal said of the exposed knee knuckle. 'Though it's a finer joint, of course. Men are heavier built.'

Tom opened another bottle of brandy. 'There's plenty on board,' he said, 'and we need it.'

'Now there are two arteries which would supply blood to the tibia area and another called the peroneal behind the knee.' Pascal and Charles found them. Cotterell ordered, 'These have to be tied with ligatures.'

Charles and Pascal tied the arteries with cat gut.

'The limb may now be removed.'

Pascal cut through the last few sinews. Tom climbed down and removed the parted lower leg, wrapping it in a piece of sailcloth and placing it respectfully on the deck.

Cotterell read aloud again. 'After the removal of the limb, you must take the femoral artery and tie it, avoiding crushing the nerve behind. None of the surrounding flesh ought to be tied, though the ligature should be placed round the artery where it emerges. Is that possible?'

Pascal had another dig with the knife and freed enough of the femoral to tie.

'And now you have to do the same to the vein,' said Cotterell. They tied the vein.

'Clean the wound well, to reveal any blood vessel with its orifice blocked up, or which is concealed under haemorrhage, and when you are sure all are sealed slowly release the tourniquet.'

'The brandy,' said Charles. Tom took a good draw on it and passed it to Pascal, who did the same, then splashed the wound.

'What's that?'

'I'm cleaning.'

'Not with brandy,' said Cotterell. 'Use a rag.'

Tom took the bottle from Pascal's custody, tasted it, then closed it. Pascal took it back, like a jealous mother with a baby.

'Here,' said a voice on the companionway stair behind them. Emily stood with her arms full of torn petticoat. She held the strips out to them. Cotterell took some of the torn strips from her and wiped the wound, which was now running with spirit and blood. He continued to read from the book too. 'The skin and muscles are now to be placed across the face of the stump, sewn and supported in this position, by long strips of bandage, applied across the face of the stump.'

'You need an unguent,' said Emily. 'Whale oil, or at the very least butter, in order to keep them from sticking.'

'Have you seen this before, Madame?' asked Cotterell.

'Several times,' she replied.

'I have too,' offered Tom. 'I was the surgeon's servant boy on my first vessel. I should think I've seen half a dozen amputations.'

'You kept that quiet,' said Cotterell. 'What happened to them?'

'They died.'

'All?'

'Every man Jack of 'em.'

'And you need not to bind it too tightly,' said Emily. 'Or he will wind up with an ugly stump, which may never heal and which in any case will never support a wooden leg.'

'Thank you, Madame,' said Charles. 'Any more?'

'The slaves dressed stumps with earth from the river bank and wrapped them in a certain leaf.'

'We have neither river bank nor river water available, so we must just do our best with the unguent,' said Cotterell.

Pascal had been nursing the brandy bottle all this time. Suddenly he was drunk. 'What does she say?' he asked.

Cotterell translated.

'Why did the slaves have stumps?' Pascal asked.

'From gangrene leg, from being in chains,' said Emily, not needing, Cotterell noted, a translation.

Pascal was astonished. 'They chain the blacks so they get gangrene?'

'No. They chain them to stop them escaping. But the lady says it very often leads to the condition,' said Cotterell. 'It is an extreme and rare form of punishment carried out on incorrigibles.'

'It is an undesirable outcome, because it reduces the subject's capacity for work in the fields. Chaining a man so long he gets ulcers in his legs is only one step better than hanging, which of course prevents them from working in the fields entirely.' Charles replied, dead-pan, making them find the irony in his voice for themselves. 'However, inveterate absconders may be crippled so they could be kept in their rightful place.' Pascal slumped down on the deck, still holding the brandy bottle. He didn't spill any.

'This is stronger than I'm used to.' Pascal said. 'Or I'm getting weaker.'

Cotterell bent down to take the bottle and help him to his feet. Pascal grabbed Cotterell's collar as he bent, holding Cotterell close to him and said, 'Chain a man so he's poisoned, then cut off his foot to stop him running? Is it true? He's not joking?'

'I don't know,' said Cotterell.

Pascal shook his head. 'It's right what they say. The British are savages.'

Tom touched Cotterell's shoulder to remind him not to rise to it.

'The lady is American, so I believe these slave-holders were Americans,' said Cotterell.

'But what were they before they were Americans? British, hah?

British.' With this last bit of logic Pascal's eyes had lost their coordination, as if the effort had exhausted him. Cotterell let him slip back to the deck, next to Lefèvre's canvas-wrapped, dismembered leg. Pascal closed his eyes.

'He looks happy,' said Cotterell. He was referring to Lefèvre. It was true. He lay in a dead faint in the cot, taking shallow breaths and seeming peaceful at last.

'What about the remaining wound?' asked Tom.

'Can you sew?' Cotterell turned to Charles.

'I have done it before,' said Emily. 'Give me a needle.'

'And the leg?' Tom indicated the canvas-wrapped limb on the deck.

'We'll put it over the side,' said Cotterell. '*Sans ceremonie.*'

10

Hours had passed while Cotterell had been below in the cockpit. On deck again with the canvas parcel he was surprised to see the summer's dawn breaking. The sky was still swaddled in cloud all the way from horizon to horizon. The weather didn't look likely to change, though. The air felt fair and dry. The watch had changed, so Cotterell was surrounded again by his own watch or quart. Dead Mathelier was laid out on the gun-deck, like an extra ramrod, parallel to a cannon. His body was wrapped in a large white ensign with one of the new, three-coloured republican ensigns stitched in the corner. The French Navy was conservative, even in its chaos, and the revolutionary republican flag had been appended to, rather than replacing, the French marine service's traditional white ensign. Cotterell and Tom passed dead Mathelier, climbed onto the *galliard avant* and went to the head as the most discreet way of putting the canvas parcel over the side, though every member of the crew that saw them knew what it was tucked under Tom's arm. When they returned again to the gun-deck Second Auchard was standing at the quarter-deck rail. The two British sailors tried to duck swiftly under the ship's boats but Auchard had been waiting. The Captain was far away, by the helmsman's side, like a shadow. Auchard crooked his finger at Cotterell and Tom mouthing, *'Venez.'* Tom whispered, 'Here we go.' They mounted the steps to the quarter-deck like condemned men going to the gallows. As they climbed Cotterell looked up at the sails, a captain's habit. Above them the spread canvas drew steadily.

'Cotterell, where is my wife?' asked Auchard, glaring at him through his one good eye.

'She made some bandages out of spare clothing for Citizen Lefèvre, Citizen.' 'That is not the answer to the question I asked.'

Which was true. Cotterell didn't want to answer.

'Where is she?' Auchard repeated, glaring at them with his one eye. Cotterell was silent. Tom looked like he might pass out from indecision. The Captain was behind Auchard now, full of morning cheerfulness.

'Meester Cotterell. A very good morning to you, sir.' Dubarre spoke in English. Auchard was forced to stand in silence while his Captain addressed the two men. The air was cool, despite it being a summer's morning, and in consequence Dubarre was well wrapped in a huge sea cape, officer's hat and woollen scarf, though his feet were bare. A cutlass grip protruded from the sea cape – the traditional long officer's sword was not for Dubarre. The ensemble was very piratical, especially as Dubarre was next to one-eyed Auchard.

'How is Meester Lefèvre?'

'He seems well, Captain, all things considered.'

'What have you done with him?'

'We removed the limb for fear of Lefèvre's life.'

'Was that the right thing to do?'

'It was thought, sir.'

'But what do *you* think?'

'With your leave, sir, I just wouldn't know what to do. Mr Charles acted for the best.'

'Alone? This is some skilful negro we have found ourselves, Auchard.'

Auchard gave a little bow to agree. Dubarre turned to Cotterell again.

'The negro acted alone?'

'Not entirely sir.'

'You helped?'

'A little.'

Dubarre screwed up his brow and pushed his face close to Auchard's one eye. 'Is that part of a clerk's skill, Auchard?'

'Non, mon Capitaine.'

'No. I'm sure my clerk couldn't do it. I mean, Cordell, he could sharpen a pen. I should think he could make a stylus out of a bone. But take a man's leg off without killing him? That would be beyond Cordell. That would be the work of a very extraordinary clerk. Wouldn't it Auchard?'

'It would,' replied Auchard.

'Unless you had help. Someone who was used to handling a knife. Flesh. Bone.'

'The ship's cook . . .' Cotterell began.

Dubarre feigned surprise and slapped Cotterell, though like Auchard he must have known who was on the orlop.

'Ah, the cook. The cook you say? Is this true?' He asked Tom. 'The *cook?*'

'Yes, mon Commandant.' Tom replied.

'What a frightening thought! Does he have the required skill?'

'I believe so.'

'Only believe?'

'He made a good job of it.'

'Cutting up limbs is a cook's skill, Auchard, eh?'

Auchard didn't answer. Dubarre appeared to reflect before going on. 'Well, I suppose it must be. After all, who knows what goes in the stock-pot?'

'We put the limb discreetly over the side, mon Commandant,' said Tom.

Dubarre feigned shock. 'That's exactly what cook does with the salt beef! He tows it from the stern in a . . . what do you call it?'

'Un *cliavé?*' suggested Cotterell, who knew French ships treated their beef in this manner. As soon as the word left his mouth he wished he hadn't uttered it. *Cliavé* wasn't a French word.

'A what?' asked Dubarre, his eyes narrowing.

'A cage, sir?' Cotterell translated 'lobster pot' into the loosest

English he could. Ships often towed their salt beef for a few hours in a cage resembling a large lobster pot, to wash some of the salt off before it was steeped in the cook's freshwater tub.

'That's it. A cage.' Dubarre affected not to have noticed the Jerrais word for lobster pot, *cliavé*, but Cotterell knew he had. Dubarre went on, 'A cage is the best place for salt beef and Englishmen, eh English Tom?'

'Sir?'

'Don't look like that, Mr Tom, Mr Cotterell. It was a joke.' He laughed at Cotterell and slapped Auchard, so that they both forced a smile. 'Is everyone from Kent so serious?'

'I beg your pardon sir. I am unused to the ways of seamen.'

'Anyway it wasn't done so discreetly,' said Auchard. 'Everyone saw. Everyone knew it wasn't a turd you were taking to the place of ease in a canvas wrapper.'

'It wasn't a turd!' Dubarre repeated, laughing as he quoted Auchard with relish. 'Good, eh?'

Cotterell didn't reply. Dubarre seemed not to notice.

'What brilliance,' he went on in French. He liked to show off by speaking English to them, but always retreated into French for more difficult ideas. 'Lefèvre has kept his life and I have kept my station in Admiral Vanstabel's great convoy to save France. I have my heart's desire and Citoyenne Lefèvre has hers, all because of the presence on board of Charles the negro, you two Englishmen and the ship's cook. Lefèvre is favoured by fortune. How very brave,' said the Captain, rubbing his brow. He appeared lost in thought for a moment and repeated, 'How very, very brave.'

It was all fake, Cotterell knew. This monster Dubarre wouldn't be satisfied till he had broken the nerve of every man on the ship.

'Citoyenne Lefèvre can be proud of her husband,' said Cotterell, wanting the conversation to end.

'I meant how very brave you were. What if you had killed Lefèvre? I might have been forced to execute you.'

'We don't know for certain that they haven't killed him, Capitaine,' said gloomy Auchard, looking at Cotterell with his one unblinking eye as he spoke. He was eager for the conversation to take a turn for the worse and he was eager for the Captain to leave so he could press Cotterell and Tom further about his wife. The four stood in silence for a moment, then Dubarre looked up.

'I do believe the wind has veered half a point,' he said in French.

The Second looked up too, followed by Tom and Cotterell. The wind was steady from the south west, as it had been for days, certainly ever since Cotterell had come on deck today. The sails pulled well, as they had done for days. Nothing had changed.

'Second Auchard!' commanded Dubarre.

'Mon Capitaine,' responded Auchard.

'It has veered. Definitely veered,' said Dubarre. 'Brace up, Auchard. Brace up. We mustn't lose our station.'

Auchard leaned over the rail and called, 'Bosco!'

'Oui Citoyen!' replied the boatswain.

'Brassez!' ordered Auchard. He spat the word with real venom.

'Oui Citoyen!'

And the boatswain motioned to his mate, LeBlanc, who took out his whistle and began to call on it.

'To your stations, gentlemen. Come, come.' Dubarre spoke in English to Cotterell and Tom again. His voice was solicitous, as if he were asking them to go for a walk. Tom tugged his forelock and the two Englishmen ran down the companionway to the gun deck of the little frigate. But as he left the quarter-deck Cotterell looked back. Out of the corner of his eye he saw Dubarre smile at the Second. Did he tip his hat slightly? Cotterell didn't quite catch it. Auchard put his hands on the rail and stood overlooking the decks. By the time Cotterell was down the companionway and on the gun-deck he could see, even from there, that the Second's fingers were white from his efforts to control himself.

Cotterell began to make his way towards the *gaillard avant*, but the pockmarked Eustache stopped him.

'Bosco says you are to fetch wood for the stove,' he said, referring to another of Cotterell's regular tasks. 'It is well past dawn and the men have had no breakfast.'

On warships, French or English, dawn was met with some circumspection. Who knew what danger might have approached the ship in the darkness? A reef, a squall or an enemy might be revealed as the dawn displaced the night. Darkness hid danger. First light might reveal ships, friend or foe, just a mile away. For this reason, in time of war, stoves on the warships of all nations were dowsed overnight and only lit again in daylight. Providing fuel for the stove fire was now Cotterell's task, a job so simple and mundane it could be entrusted to an English *terrien*. In the hold Cotterell split some kindling for the range with an axe kept there for the purpose. He was standing on a pile of logs with a further pile banked up before him. The hold stank of dead men buried in the ballast. No doubt Mathelier would end up in the gravel here below his feet, once they found time for the ceremony. So many things were uniquely French on *Hortense*. The English preferred coal for their ranges. And they buried their dead promptly at sea. Interment in the ballast was a hangover from the old Catholic tradition, he knew. He wondered what qualified crew for burial there. They certainly couldn't have put half the crew in the ballast hold, those who had died suffering from the flux. Apart from the obvious danger from miasma, there would be a simple problem of space.

Cotterell had a glass lamp, without which he couldn't see in the hold. He held it down to the wood to check what was there. He knew from earlier visits there was a lot of chestnut, which wouldn't do. They had been duped by an American firewood dealer, or perhaps the ship's clerk Cordell had duped his Captain and crew. Chestnut was cheaper to buy (or supply) but more dangerous and unsuitable on a ship's galley stove because it spits.

Cotterell began to sort the pile for pine. The foremast passed through the hold close to where he sorted, a large hollow column of wood reflecting and reverberating each sound from the deck above. Cotterell could hear the creaks of the spars transmitted down it as he worked. If he leaned against the mast he could feel the noises too. He smiled to himself at the vision of Dubarre forcing Auchard to adjust the sails. If you rested your head against the mast you could hear the sounds transmitted from above. You could even hear men's voices, muffled and strange. He leaned against the enormous wooden column so that his ear rested against it.

'You're in no rush,' said a woman's voice behind him. Cotterell turned and saw Liberté.

'It's no good.' He indicated the wood. 'I was sorting. It spits. I don't know who took it aboard.'

She said. 'We'd better say someone dead, for fear of causing trouble.'

'That concerns you?'

'We need to keep our morale high,' she replied. 'Mathelier was brave. We'll blame him. A simple oversight. No one will speak badly of Mathelier.' She met Cotterell's eye. 'Don't look surprised. We're Republicans, not monsters, you know.'

'The Republic is a hard master. I have heard men are executed under it for very little offence.'

'We French have lived with fear and starvation for years. The Republic has to reflect that.' She sat suddenly on the stack of wood nearest. 'Oh, I haven't come down here for a Section meeting.'

'Which is?'

'Politics. It's how we are organised.'

'What have you come for?'

She smiled. 'Unfinished business.'

'What?'

'To help you fetch wood.'

'Does Eustache know you're down here?'

'What business is it of his?'

'He threatened me. When you boasted you'd made love to me.'

'Love had nothing to do with it! I stood your cock up. I brought you back to life! You should be grateful.'

'Should I be grateful if I wake with his knife sticking out of my ribs?'

'So it's true what they say . . .'

'What?'

'Englishmen are cowards.'

'Says who?'

'Eustache.'

'Your lover. '

'He may wish. He is nothing of the sort.'

'I think he'd like to fight me for you.'

'That would be fun.'

'It would presume I want you.'

She laughed. 'Well argued! You are a clever Englishman.'

'And you are a fickle Frenchwoman.'

Liberté stood again, whatever depression she had felt now lightened. 'If we talk all morning we'll never get this moved and the quart will never get their breakfast. If they get no breakfast they may as well serve as slaves, like the English.'

'The red cap you wear means you were slaves.'

'You are well informed. It is the badge of galley slaves, and we wear it to show we are free. I'll sort, you split.'

She went on her haunches beside him and began to toss the pieces of chestnut to one side, handing Cotterell pieces of pine to split as she found them. He trimmed the split pieces on an upturned log, larger than the others, then tossed the split wood into a large canvas-and-rope basket. He was aware of her all the time in the near darkness. Sometimes her body moved in front of the light and he had to move her slightly to prevent her shadow falling where the axe was aimed. Once he left his hand on her shoulder to hold her there. She did not resist. When they had split enough pine to start the stoves he began trimming pieces into kindling. She watched.

'Why did you come down here?' he asked after a while.

'I said. To fetch wood with you.'

'I don't believe you.'

'Citoyenne Lefèvre asked me to thank you and the others for saving her husband.'

'Can't she speak?'

'She is in her cabin and is distressed.'

'I accept your thanks.'

'But?' she looked at his features closely in the dim light, moving her face close to his to do it.

'We don't know that we have saved him,' said Cotterell.

'Not that ... something else concerns you?'

'What do you care, if I am a loyal Englishman? I thought the subjects of King George were your enemies.'

She was laughing at him. 'Would you throw yourself at his feet? Would you kiss the hem of his cloak?'

He bent and kissed her. She took the axe from his hand.

'Eustache sent me here. Did you arrange it?'

'No,' she said. But it sounded like a lie. 'Do you plan for him to kill me?' Cotterell asked.

'No,' she breathed.

'Death to the English?'

'When they are true enemies and a threat to the Nation, yes.'

She dropped the axe on the wood and pulled his empty hands inside her tunic. They kissed again. Cotterell could barely see Liberté in the near dark of the hold, which was lit only by the little hand oil-lamp he'd brought, now placed on a pile of wood, but he could feel her warmth, and the smooth suppleness of her body led his hands around her. They kissed again and she slipped her hands inside his fruques.

'Am I in danger?' he asked.

'I've handled this before and you have come to no harm, John Cotterell.' She clasped his penis in both her hands, thumbs uppermost, fingers touching around it like a penitent at prayer. 'Or don't you remember?'

'I do. I also remember you taking a bow and laughing about me with the entire quart when I took my place on the lower deck.'

She kissed him again. 'That won't happen this time.' She slipped out of her tunic entirely, then stepped out of her loose trousers. In the half light her body shone. He kissed her shoulder.

'You taste of olives.'

'I wash with oil on a rag-cloth. There is nothing else here on board ship.'

He tasted her again. She untied his belt.

'Come here and I'll kill you!' A voice roared from the deck above. Two men's feet ran across the deck, right above Cotterell's head. The feet were in shoes, which meant they belonged to officers or civilians.

The voice roared again. 'Ahaagh!'

And there was the humming, singing clash of metal with another piece of metal. It sounded like tempered steel, which has a distinctive 'ring' as it hits another steel or iron object. Cotterell immediately thought someone was swinging an axe or a cutlass. The maddened voice came again, 'Ahaagh!' then another clash and ring.

Liberté pulled on her tunic and rushed up the hold ladder. Cotterell extinguished the light and followed, with the hot lamp in the basket which he had slung on his back with a piece of twine. As he emerged onto the lower deck Charles and Second Auchard rushed past him. Auchard was roaring incomprehensibly and striking at Charles with a cutlass, Charles dodging behind the cast-iron deck support pillars to avoid the blows. It was contact with these pillars which gave the distinctive ringing sound to the cutlass blows which were missing Charles. Auchard's slashes were in deadly earnest. He meant to kill Charles, and swung at him with venom each time there was an opportunity to do so.

The two men rushed in this way as far as the after-companionway, where Charles stood and sheltered on one side of the stair outside the clerk's cabin while Auchard slashed at him around it, roaring all the while. The rising rail and steps of the wooden companionway took the force of the blows, which was as well, since any one of them would easily have removed Charles' arm. Charles had no weapon with which to defend himself. Eventually, frustrated by his inability to reach Charles with the cutlass, Auchard pulled back and lunged at him through the open rising of the steps. The cutlass, a weapon more suited for slashing in the open air than stabbing between decks, missed Charles and jammed in the wood of the clerk's cabin door. Charles was quick. He grabbed Auchard's arm through the open companionway and pulled. Now Auchard was trapped against the companionway by his sword arm, held fast by Charles.

'Stop!' Charles cried. Their faces were close.

'I'll kill you,' shouted Auchard.

'No you won't. Leave off, man!'

Auchard roared again as an answer. Charles punched him.

'Bravo!' cried the watch on the lower deck, which had turned out to view the fun. '*Bravo le negre! A bas les aristos!*' Auchard was far from popular.

Tom was by Cotterell's side. Cotterell went to step forward to stop the contest before Charles was killed. Tom took Cotterell's arm to prevent him.

'No,' said Tom. 'He will simply kill you both. And if he doesn't, they will.' He meant the sailors. At the back of the throng the fiddler scratched a few chords of '*Ça ira*'. Charles continued to punch Auchard through the companionway steps until Auchard loosened his grip on the cutlass and slipped to his knees. Charles rounded to the front of the companionway, pushed Auchard aside and began to climb. Auchard recovered himself, roared again and scrabbled on the deck for his cutlass, then followed the fleeing feet of Charles up the companionway steps. Cotterell, Liberté, Tom and most of the off-watch or quart followed, fifty persons at least, plus a fiddler.

On deck Charles had found a paying iron, a long steel rod with a ball moulded into the end, normally heated in a brazier and used for repairing tarred deck seams.

'Come here!' cried Auchard, as he emerged from the companionway, cutlass hanging loosely at his side. Charles turned and held out the iron like a quarter stave. 'Come here and I'll pay you, you dirty bastard!' Cotterell, among the first to follow Auchard from the companionway onto the deck, saw Charles lift the iron effortlessly. The ball end must have weighed six pounds, and the shaft a further six or eight, but Charles handled it as if it were a light piece of ash.

'I told you!' shouted Auchard and slashed at Charles, who parried the blow with the paying iron above his head. Auchard was no expert swordsman, but he was no fool either and he rained cutlass blows at Charles' head and shoulders, each parried by Charles with the paying iron. Auchard began to alternate the slashes with stabs, which Charles could counter with the iron or simply avoid with body movements. It was like a dance, with Auchard leading, but Charles in control. The fiddler started up again, 'ça ira, ça ira, ça ira' came the beat. The watch clapped their hands and stamped their bare feet. Dubarre was watching from the quarter-deck rail, grinning. The members of the duty quart were in the rigging or on the foredeck, also watching. Ship's work was suspended for the moment.

'I have seen an officer strike a sailor before,' whispered Tom into Cotterell's ear, 'and I have seen an officer strike another. I have even seen a sailor strike another, though that seems difficult to believe. But I have never seen an officer and a passenger come to blows. Which law will apply?'

He was right. A fight between the first officer – the British equivalent to Auchard – and a non-military passenger was unthinkable on a British ship, where in any case the squabbles would be short, brutal and ugly. The people of the *Hortense* seemed to

revel in the dispute between Auchard and Charles. No one
attempted to intervene. Captain Dubarre was at the quarter-deck
rail looking like a man attending a cockfight. He only lacked a
bookmaker to take his wager. Derray the boatswain didn't even
bother to tell the crew to get back to work.

'It is chaos, this ship.' Tom whispered. 'Absolute chaos. The
world turned upside down.' Tom loved saying it. Charles, meanwhile, had retreated below and between the ship's boats, which
had the advantage of sheltering his head from the slashing blows
directed from above, while the paying iron defended his legs.
Auchard was constrained to simple vertical slashes or stabs at
Charles' body.

'Calm yourself, sir. Calm yourself,' said Charles.

'I know what you did!' cried Auchard.

'Then you know nothing. I did nothing.'

'Dirty bastard!' Auchard flung himself bodily at Charles,
who responded with blows both from his fist and knee. Auchard
dropped his blade and punched back, then Charles grabbed
Auchard's head and pulled him onto the open space of the
deck, beneath the quarter-deck rail, holding him in a chancery
and serving him out with blows 'all around the physog but
especially to the lanterns', as Tom put it later, 'Or rather,
lantern,' he said, referring to the fact that Auchard only had
one good eye. Pugilism was the favourite sport between Jack
Tars on British ships and Tom's pugilistic vocabulary was vast,
barely challenged by the brief fight between Charles and
Auchard. A couple of English seamen would have fought all
morning. This was a shorter affair, where Charles beat, or
served out Auchard, till he dropped, dancing round the deck
to do it. The watching crowd or 'Fancy', as Tom described
the crew, grew quieter with each blow. Charles was immensely
powerful and each blow shook Auchard. Eventually the foot
stamping and clapping died away. The music stopped. Auchard's
face was a mass of cuts, contusions and bruising. The flesh
around his eyes had swollen so much that his good eye could

barely see any more. It was, Tom confessed, not exactly a right good turn up. He would have been happier if both men had their faces beaten to a pulp, noses broken and eyes swollen, then one had proved the conqueror by a narrow margin and both were carried away shoulder high by their supporters while sporting wagers were paid out between high and low alike. Charles merely damaged his knuckles on Auchard's face, watched by a now silent crowd. Eventually, believing the danger over, Charles allowed Auchard to drop. He gave Auchard's prostrate body a little bow, then turned and approached Cotterell.

'Would you be so kind as to fetch me a bucket of water,' he asked. Cotterell pulled a bucket of water from the sea and Charles washed in it, surrounded by the off-quart. The crew kept a respectful distance from Charles, who had displayed qualities they hadn't perceived in him before the fight. Merlet had boatswain's mate LeBlanc pull a second bucket of sea water to revive Auchard. LeBlanc was wary. He feared Auchard's temper when he recovered. When the water was tossed Auchard shook himself like a dog emerging on the shore.

'Now that was something,' said Dubarre to no one and everyone. At this sign of approval Charles was closely surrounded by the excited quart. He was cut on both his hands and arms, with a big wound on his upper arm. Cotterell helped him pull off his shirt. Blood flowed freely into the sea water which ran from the bucket to the deck about his feet as he washed. He tried to staunch it. Citoyenne Lefèvre appeared from the crowd, gave him a cloth to dry upon and thanked him profusely for the night's efforts with her husband.

'Lefèvre lives!' she said, sounding to Cotterell's ears for all the world like a short, fat, bourgeoise and Breton Mary Magdalene. 'Lefèvre lives, and we have you to thank for it.' Then she looked up and screamed as Auchard tried to push through the throng again. His face was distorted with rage and his features distended from the beating, cutlass held once more high over his head.

Charles turned and caught the blow on the bucket. Auchard slashed again and the crowded crew scattered to relative safety. Charles caught that blow on the under-part of the wooden bucket too.

'Stop!' cried Dubarre from the quarter-deck. They stopped. Every face turned to him. Dubarre grinned.

'That's not just,' he said. 'A bucket against a cutlass. And if he goes back below my ship's boats again you are going to damage them.' He signalled to a sailor, who drew a cutlass from the artimon mast-foot and handed it to Dubarre. Dubarre threw it to Charles. The steel flashed, reflecting light as it spun through the air. A seaman on the gun-deck caught it cleanly by the handle, then handed the weapon to Charles. The crew drew back further, forming a circle.

Auchard drew himself up and puffed out his chest. Like every officer of the old French Royal navy, Auchard had been schooled in sword fighting. He was angry and confident. '*En garde*,' said Auchard through broken, bloodied lips. 'I will finish you here today.'

Charles examined the blade of Dubarre's cutlass, then stepped back, looking thoughtful. He held the blade up in a guard position, like a short sabre. Auchard advanced, raining blows, intending to injure Charles's head or shoulders. Now, with the sword in his hand, Charles was calm and expert, much more expert than Auchard. He parried each of Auchard's blows with his blade. He was much the better swordsman, and seemed able to predict where the blows might land long before Auchard's arm descended. Charles parried, parried again, blocked, parried, then, at one of Auchard's slashes, Charles knocked the descending blade to one side as it fell and punched Auchard with the finger-guard of his own cutlass,.

'Enough?' asked Charles. He had hold of Auchard's left sleeve in his free hand and was keeping the Frenchman close, the two blades crossed before their faces.

Auchard merely roared for a reply and stepped back, twisting his arm free. The watching crew were silent now. Auchard slashed again, Charles parried again. Auchard delivered several further blows like this in quick succession, each parried by Charles, retreating steadily as he did so until he dodged the final blow, stepping aside and allowing it to land on the ship's rail. Auchard's enormous blow gouged a long mark in the wood. Charles clamped his free hand over Auchard's sword arm.

'Enough?' Charles asked again, standing side by side with Auchard, holding his wrist and facing out to the empty ocean. Auchard twisted, drew his blade off the rail and stepped back. Charles turned to face him. Auchard attempted to attack again. This time Charles fought back, both men slashing and defending furiously, each in turn, moving around the deck as they did so. There was an inevitability about it now, and Tom whispered to Cotterell, 'He didn't learn *that* working for a lawyer in Jamaic-ee, I know.' It was true. In the matter of pugilism, Auchard had been defeated. As a military man he had presumed he would better Charles with a sword. In fact Auchard had bitten off a great deal more than he could chew.

'The Second's best course now would be to stick his quid in his hat and quit to the better man,' advised Tom.

Cotterell scanned the thronging sailors. Tom had been right. They were more like a crowd at a fight than any military group of people. Cotterell saw Emily at the back of the crowd, watching, but impassive. She was making no effort to advance. Her husband made a desperate lunge and his cutlass went into Charles' thigh. He drew blood. It seemed to make something come alive in Charles. The black man knew now he would have to end it. As he straightened, Charles aimed one slashing sideways blow at the right side of Auchard's torso, which Auchard defended with the finger-guard, then a second blow reversed at the left or open side of Auchard's body, which Auchard parried with the back of his cutlass blade. Quick as a flash, as soon as he felt the pres-sure of effort in Auchard's blade and knew Auchard was committed to the parry, Charles bounced his blade off the steel and into Auchard's face. The tip entered Auchard's eye. Auchard staggered back a pace or two. Charles held his pose for a moment, frozen in action.

Auchard cried, 'I am blinded!'

The only other sound was the rush of the sea and the creak of the rigging. Bare feet shuffled uncomfortably on deck as understanding of what had happened dawned on the crew.

Auchard dropped his sword and fell to the deck. No one else moved. Charles took the rag Citoyenne Lefèvre had given him, wiped the blade and climbed quickly up to the quarter-deck, where he presented the cutlass to Dubarre with a very slight bow.

'Blinded!' cried Auchard from the deck below Charles and Dubarre. 'I can't see.'

Cotterell looked at Emily again. She was still at the back of the group, unmoving, and apparently unmoved.

'*Voile! Voile!*' came young Erique's voice from the main-top. 'Sail to the north east!'

'Where?' shouted Auchard and stood quickly, stumbling against a sailor, who held him.

'Take me to the quarter-deck, man,' said Auchard.

'Take him below,' said the Captain, and handed the cutlass to a sailor. Dubarre ordered the drummer to beat to stations, grabbed his telescope from its resting place beside the binnacle and began to climb the rigging.

'Where?' shouted Auchard again as the sailor led him to the steps of the companionway. 'Where?'

Erique, who had only had a perpendicular view of events far below on deck, and in any case had been loyally attending to his duty as look-out, had no idea the Second couldn't see. He leaned down from his vantage point on the platform and threw his arm out in the direction of the two British warships he could see.

'There, sir! Right there to the north east. As plain as I can see.'

After a few seconds Dubarre was with him. The Captain squeezed the boy's arm to encourage him.

'This will be interesting, Erique,' he said, and raised the telescope to his eye.

11

There were two sails, not one, and sails from that quarter could only belong to British ships. There were no friends of the French towards Iceland, the seas around which were ruled by the British. *Hortense* made no signal. In any case Admiral Vanstabel's precious fleet of warships and corn-carrying merchantmen was out of sight, over the southern horizon. Dubarre knew his duty; he was to engage and delay any British frigates he saw to the north, to lead them away from the grain fleet and to postpone or prevent any contact with the grain fleet. To that end he meant first to lead them a merry dance across the North Atlantic. Dubarre knew that in the end, if he could not escape, he would have to sacrifice himself, his crew and his ship in defence of the Revolution. Most of Dubarre's crew had divined that was their purpose too, as soon as they had stationed themselves so far to the north of the convoy proper. Less analytical souls or less experienced seamen, those who had been slow to either comprehend or believe their purpose were finally persuaded when the *Hortense* failed to change course at the sight of British frigates. Instead she ploughed her course, heading just north of east towards an inevitable confrontation with the British ships in some hours time. One sick frigate, lightly and inexpertly crewed, cannot fight two prime British men o'war. Even the most inexperienced of the revolutionary sailors knew that. And the old salts trembled. When the battle came they would be fighting with one arm tied behind their collective back.

The gun-deck was cleared for action. The main cabin, the

Second's cabin, Captain's sleeping cabin and other knock-down partitions on the frigate's gun-deck had their partition walls swung up on hinges and fastened to the deckhead. The spaces revealed were cleared of their furnishings, which were struck down in the hold in a few minutes by gangs of men. The possessions within the furnishings of the Captain's sleeping cabin were distinctly un-maritime in nature. They belonged to Emily Auchard, its temporary occupant. Like the lady herself, they were taken below for safe-keeping. The furnishings were stowed in the hold, the lady moved to a dark cuddy – hardly a cabin, though it was called such – above the hold, which had once been the sailing master's quarters. Blind, immobile and maddened Auchard had been put in the next cuddy, this time the quarters of the ship's clerk, who was himself on deck at the Captain's side and would have no need for sleeping quarters for some time to come. Lefèvre was brought up from the orlop too and installed in a cuddy. He wasn't dead and the little space on the orlop was the nearest thing the frigate had to a sick bay. It would be needed for other men if there were to be any action. Action, and the subsequent injuries to men, seemed likely.

The crews prepared the guns. Those on the quarter-deck were carronades, cast in a Yorkshire foundry and plundered from a British ship earlier in the *Hortense*'s career. They were heavy, short-barrelled, meant for close quarters and inaccurate at any distance. They were useless for the coming action. If *Hortense* found herself fighting two British frigates at close quarters she would be finished. Directed by Dubarre, who was everywhere, but especially at the shoulder of his gunner, giant black-haired Hanoverian Lang, the crew ignored the eighteen-pounder carronades for now. Instead they readied the light eight-pound cannons below on the gun-deck, which were manned fully without the ports yet opening. Braziers were lit. Liberté was like a species of *sous-cannonier*, rushing around the teams of gunners and preparing them for action. Liberté was an expert. She had seen plenty of action on both land and sea. The galley stove had not been lit, of course, so the crew were served cans of water and dry biscuit with a promise they would eat 'like aristos' after the inevitable action. It seemed unlikely, but none complained. They knew the die was cast. The action would come and there would be a victor and a vanquished, come what may.

That which remained of Mathelier went over the side without much more ceremony than Lefèvre's leg. At least the corpse was saved the ignominy of being poked through the heads as the leg had been. Number five gun crew disposed of it, under the boatswain's mate's instructions, with a quick salute and a heave onto a tipping plank. Dubarre and Merlet were too busy to spare time for readings and whatever atheistic prayers the revolution-aries had been able to cook up. Cotterell and Tom watched. As a gunner folded the ensign which had covered Mathelier, Tom suggested quietly to Cotterell that they would need dozens to cover the bodies which would be served up by action against the two British warships.

'This vessel has half the men, half the guns and what cannons exist are lightweight and lack exercise. It will be like firing ladies' face-powder pompoms against those British frigates.' He opined.

'There will only be action if we are caught,' answered Cotterell. He pointed to the quarter-deck, where Dubarre now had teams of men arranging tackles to heave the carronades over the side. Dubarre meant to run as far and as fast as he could, dragging the British frigates with him. Their courses were closing, but Dubarre was holding his. For a man standing on deck the British frigates were now easily visible on the northern horizon. Pierre Jan Vanstabel's fleet was over the southern horizon, out of sight now even of a mast-head look-out on *Hortense*. The fleet would be invisible to the British frigates. Dubarre intended to keep it that way. There were at least thirty miles between the British and the grain convoy. Dubarre told his boatswain to crowd all sail, then looked around the quarter-deck for Merlet, the new officer he had gained when *Hortense* had first met Vanstabel's fleet in mid-Atlantic. Merlet was *Hortense*'s last remaining navigating officer, apart from her captain.

'How far to Brest?' Dubarre asked. Though Merlet had been at sea since he was a boy or '*mousse*' (in the naval argot), he had been qualified as an officer for less than a year. Merlet had spent all his active life as a sailor on great ships where there had been an expert for each task. Usually the expert had a deputy who was just as skilled. Merlet had specialised in signals and yet had not risen above the status of second deputy to the officer of the signals on Vanstabel's seventy-four, *Rhone*. Of course Merlet had passed his sea officer's examinations. He was able to navigate as well as the next inexpert man. But abrupt commands and demands from his new Captain flustered him.

'Well?' asked Dubarre.

'About four hundred miles, mon Commandant.' The young officer answered.

'*About?*' Dubarre was incredulous.

'I didn't do the last sight, Citizen. The Second did it some days ago. He has estimated us . . .'

'Estimated?'

'There has been no chance to verify it, mon Commandant. There has been heavy cloud.'

'Don't talk to me about the weather.'

'Auchard has estimated us at 47°24' of latitude and 17°28' of longitude today. By his workings it's just over four hundred miles to Brest.'

'How many aboard?'

'Many?'

'People.'

'A hundred and thirty-eight, if we discount Citizen Mathelier, Capitaine.'

'Yes let's do that, Merlet. Since he's dead, and just gone over the side, I think we can presume he won't be joining us for meals or issues of drinking water. Say five day's sailing?'

'If all goes well, sir, and we make a direct course.'

'Which is unlikely. Say a week, and a week beyond that for a margin. We need a hundred and thirty-eight times twelve times . . . oh for God's sake, what do we ration water as?'

'I'm not sure.'

'Not sure? How long have you been on the vessel?'

'There's plenty, mon Commandant. We don't ration at the moment.'

'Well we are going to, Citizen Merlet. Do the sum, three pints a day, check it twice, then start the remaining fresh water casks and put men on the pumps to get the water over the side.'

'Sir?'

'Do it now man, or will I have to go down there with an axe and start them myself?'

'No, mon Commandant. At your service. Immediately.'

Merlet ran down the companionway. Dubarre leaned over the rail.

'Bosco!'

'Yes, mon Commandant.'

'You're my lieutenant now. What's your mate called?'

'LeBlanc.'

'He's boatswain.'

'Oui, mon Commandant!'

'Boatswain!'

'Yes, Commandant?' replied Derray.

'Not you, him,' said Dubarre.

'Mon Commandant,' replied LeBlanc.

'Run along with Citizen Merlet. Take an axe. He'll explain. Derray, you'd better get up here, man. Reassure me I haven't chosen another cretin.'

Derray issued his last orders as boatswain, mounted the steps and looked about himself. He looked as if he had just puffed his chest out a little. His stride had a strut in it. Me, a temporary Lieutenant? His expression seemed to say.

'Wipe the smile off your face. We're all about to die.'

'Capitaine?'

'I want to outrun those Englishmen, as if you didn't know. And if I don't out-sail them they'll make steak haché of the lot of us,' said Dubarre. 'What would you do?'

'On this point of sail, hose the sails, ease the masts to give them a bit more rake. Ease the braces. Throw everyone and everything we don't need overboard. I see we have made a start with the eighteen-pounders, Capitaine. Will we have to fight after we have run?'

Derray was a blond Parisian from the slums of the Marais, approaching thirty, with mousey hair and blue eyes. He was average height, about five foot four with a powerfully-built upper body, which reflected almost twenty years of running up and down the rigging, hauling ropes and developing expertise. There was no ship's task he asked of the men that he couldn't complete himself. The crew all knew it.

'If we have to fight it won't last long, Derray. I agree with your advice. Do it all. Start the hose, rake the masts, have men go through the holds looking for whatever can be jettisoned. But leave the supernumeraries where they are for now. I don't want to leave a trail of Englishmen and women in the sea behind us.' He grinned at Derray, leaned over the rail and bellowed, 'You two!'

He meant Cotterell and Tom, who were beneath the boats.

'What are you doing?'

'Begging leave, sir,' said Derray. 'That's their station. They are to man the foc when necessary and carry the wounded below in case of need in action.'

'Move them out of view. Two Englishmen on my deck while we are being chased by their frigates is an offence to the eye.'

Since there was no boatswain on deck to order, Derray's first task as a temporary Lieutenant was to go and tell them himself, then set about gathering men to set the sails to the Capitaine's order. He couldn't help revealing his new rank to Cotterell and Tom.

'Watch your step there. You are now receiving orders from an officer of the marine service of the French Republic.'

'He must be the only one there ever was who couldn't write his own name,' commented Tom to Cotterell, as they went below.

'I know at least one other,' Cotterell responded.

'Who?'

'Dubarre.'

'*No*?'

'I think so.'

'How do you know?'

'Have you ever seen him take a sight?'

'No. So?'

'So? Isn't it the commander's task to see the navigation is right?'

'There's seeing navigation is right and there's doing it yourself. For all that he expects to know where his is I don't suppose the gracious Lord Howe takes sights on the quarter-deck.' Tom was pleased with his own logic.

'Nor does King George light his own pantry fire in the morning. It's not the same thing, Tom. This is a sea captain.'

'I don't believe our Captain Nugent on the *Veteran* did it.'

'Light fires? Shoot sights?'

'You know what I mean. Some things just ain't done. No man keeps a dog and barks himself. That's why ships' commanders have sailing masters or commissioned officers, lieutenants and midshipmen.'

'But even a great man like Captain Nugent checked the workings of his navigator, I'd imagine.'

That stumped Tom. 'He did,' Tom replied. 'As does every captain.'

'Have you ever seen Dubarre do it?'

Tom thought. 'I don't follow his every movement.'

'This man never reads anything,' said Cotterell.

'I don't see how he could become a captain. It's impossible.'

'What about if your navy is a shambles, with the crews dancing Barnaby and their 'aristo' captains running away out of the country?'

'He still needs to know how to con the ship, Cotterell. To be a captain you must have served as an apprentice somewhere. And that means navigate it and know where he is and where he must be. How does Dubarre get round that?'

'Auchard. Or someone like him.'

'No. I don't believe it. Dubarre needs a warrant. There's exams, and boards and . . . there's *things*.'

'He has a warrant – *as a privateer*. Whoever asked a privateer for his qualifications, when he was surrounded by men holding pistols and boarding pikes, when he was staring down the muzzle of a twelve-pounder?'

Tom put his hand on Cotterell's chest and his finger to his lips.

'Be quiet when you speak like that. There are plenty of men speak sufficient English on this ship to hear you and know what you mean.'

They were on the lower deck, above the powder room and orlop. The open part of the deck was deserted, save for two men on the pump, two standing by for their turn, and two more men at the far end, part of the crew sent to rummage for items that could be jettisoned. These last two were arranging a tackle to lift their discoveries out of the forward part of the hold, ready to be pitched over the side. The rest of the crew were on deck or aloft, preparing guns, setting fly yet more sails, rushing around to follow the Captain's orders, following his officers', boatswain's and gunner's orders. The ship was alive. It was nervous with tension, like an eager horse. The thrumming of canvas and creaking of halliards, shrouds and stays reverberated down onto the lower deck. The masts, with their chocks loosened and their rake tuned, moaned to confirm the pressure of the wind on the sails. Cotterell and Tom could hear the sea water rushing by just outside the wooden walls of the hull. Cotterell felt, as so many times before, as if the ship breathed, as if she inhaled wind and exhaled speed. There was another sound; the pumps creaked and rattled as they lifted the spilt fresh water from the hold.

Near to Cotterell and Tom stood the companionway with the marks slashed by Auchard's cutlass as he attacked Charles. Beyond the companionway were the officers' and masters' cabins. Blind Auchard was in one. Lefèvre and his wife in another. Tom and Cotterell fell to whispers.

'A privateer needs no more ticket than a highwayman, save for the letter marque or warrant,' murmured Cotterell. 'Consider their position. If the so-called 'aristo' officers have all jumped ship, the Frenchies are short of experienced men. There would be no question of looking for men with warrants. There was already talk in St John about the French drafting merchant captains. What navy short of competent proven captains would turn down a privateer who had been chasing the English all around the Atlantic for twenty years? You wouldn't choose instead the master of some tubby little barkey to run your warship?'

'Tubby little barkey?' repeated Tom. 'That's salty talk for a store clerk.'

'I have been listening to you.'

'And St John, you say? St John? I thought you was from Halifax?'

Cotterell thought for a moment. Perhaps they were all about to die. Eventually you have to trust someone. 'When you were on the *Veteran*, did you ever keep company with the *Asia*?'

'The old *Asia*? Once or twice . . .' He looked at Cotterell for a long moment. 'You served on the *Asia*?'

'For several years.'

'When?'

'During the American war.'

'You were a boy.'

'I was the captain's servant.'

'Well I never. Put it there, matey.' He held out his hand. Cotterell shook it. 'How did you end up in the briney?'

'I told the truth. I was on a boat which sank.'

'Boat? Not ship?' Tom was sharp.

'Fishing boat.'

'You a fisherman? And you had me showing you knots?'

'I didn't want them to know.'

Tom was outraged. 'A fellow tar?'

'I didn't know who I could trust.'

'How did she sink?'

'In a storm.'

'How many men?'

'I don't want to talk about it. Think about Auchard. Follow my logic. Put yourself in his shoes. You are a qualified captain. You have stayed at your post when every other marine officer has fled to Jersey or over the Rhine. As a reward your government places Dubarre over your head; an uneducated, unlettered sea-robber. No wonder Auchard lost his taste for the sea, serving under Dubarre. No wonder he was angry. Why bear it any longer?'

'What will I do, as Auchard?'

'You determine this is your last trip. You will leave the sea. You buy a beautiful wife in Georgetown, Carolina to keep you company.'

'Company!' exclaimed Tom. 'Will she warm me on winter nights?'

'Undoubtedly.'

'Now that's something I could do with. I can feel myself retiring from this bastard seafaring life even as we speak, Cotterell. No more rotting salt beef. No more hard-baked biscuit. I will eat white bread, drink only the finest wines and spend my life exercising my beard splitter on my wife.'

'Exactly. You are going home to France to enjoy your wife and your estate.'

'Only the trouble is, it's not Auchard's cock in his wife or his nose out of joint he has to worry about *now*, is it?' Tom indicated the cabin door behind which lay Auchard in permanent darkness. 'He is blinded. Now he has all his life to regret his hastiness.'

There was a silence, then Cotterell let his voice drop so low it could barely be heard.

'You are exactly right, and you have arrived at the point of all this. I will tell you what Auchard's blindness and the Captain's lack of letters means to us, Tom. The Captain can't read. I believe it has left young Mister Merlet as the last navigator on this ship. There may be plenty of men who can sail on the *Hortense*. There may be plenty of men who can read that book of tables the Second uses,' he corrected himself, 'used. But I believe there is now only one man on this vessel who can handle that sextant, reduce the sight and find out where we are. Lieutenant Merlet.'

Tom was thinking. His face was screwed up like a bishop's chitterlings. 'You have soft hands,' he said, 'not fisherman's hands. That means it was your boat.'

'It was.'

'You were the captain.'

'Without its navigator *Hortense* will be lost. Just as lost as if there never was a chart aboard. Just as lost as if there was no sextant or regulated clock. Just as lost as if a dozen British frigates had pounded *Hortense* and served us out with their best. Dubarre will lose the ship. He won't know whether he is wrecking her on the Scillies or the Casquets light. But without a navigator at his side, wreck her he will.'

Tom thought again.

'Will you navigate her?'

'I am a loyal servant of King George. I will stand by and watch Dubarre wreck her.'

'Spoken like a true Englishman.'

'I never said I was an Englishman, except to this lot.' He indicated the ship. 'I am Jersey, me. Jersey born, Jersey bred.'

'And you won't navigate her?'

'No.'

Tom pulled his knife from his belt. 'Then my duty's clear. I must kill this navigator, Merlet.'

'Kill him?' It wasn't what Cotterell had meant at all.

'To disable the ship.'

'Hold hard, Tom.' Cotterell closed his hand over Tom's knife-holding fist. 'Let's not be hasty.'

'These beggars have chained me for weeks, spat in my face, made me dance their fucking fandango, insulted my Navy, my ship, my shipmates, my parents and my Sovereign. Now I find them in my hands. I can twist their ballocks if I want and I am going to. I will show them what Jack Tar is made of. I can wreck the lot of them, just as if I was the one on the gun-deck of the good old *Veteran* who loaded the hot shot, fired the flintlock and hit their hanging magazine. Bullseye. You have shown me how to hurt them, and by God I'm going to do it. We're at war.'

Cotterell pushed the knife hand down. 'That's not the English way, a stab in the back.'

Tom raised it again. 'Then I'll cut his throat.'

'From behind?'

'Face to face if it serves your conscience.'

'I wish I'd never told you.'

'It's my National Duty.'

'Now you are beginning to sound like a Frenchman.'

'Do not make sport with me about that, Cotterell. Save your humour for when you are standing on dry land, preferably somewhere in England.'

The crew at the forward part of the deck had a hatch out now and were moving heavy boxes with their tackle, calling commands to each other back and forth to the hold.

'Tom . . . Tom. Easy now. Where's your God-given conscience? Merlet's just a midshipman.'

'So was Mr Wills in Guadaloupe, but what mercy did they show him, with their pikes and their sabres and their *'a bas les Anglais'*? All is fair in love and war, they say and my King is at war with France. Which means I am at war. They say death to the English. I say death to the French.'

Now Cotterell had to hiss for quiet. 'Whisper, for God's sake.'

'You've changed.'

Tom turned to leave for the deck. Cotterell held him.

'Must I stab you too?' Tom said.

'There are British frigates hard on this ship's wake. Give them a chance to sink it at least.'

A door opened nearby. Emily Auchard emerged. She looked at the knife in Tom's hand, the two men caught in an embrace.

'What are you doing?'

'Going below to help Mr Charles, Madam,' answered Cotterell. He loosened his grip. Tom tucked the knife back into his belt.

'He's in here.' She pointed to the little room she had just left. 'I have bound his wounds.'

'And your husband? How is he?'

'He is in the furthest cabin.'

'He's in pain?'

'The wound is superficial, I believe.'

'But it's to his eye.'

'It is painful, and he can't see. But he will live, Cook assures me. Perhaps he will even recover his sight.'

'Emily!' cried Auchard's voice. 'Is that you?'

She turned away and began to climb the companionway.

'They won't allow you up on deck, Ma'am,' said Tom. But she ignored him.

'Emily!' cried the voice behind the door.

'They'll send you down,' said Tom. But she was gone.

'They won't send her down,' said Cotterell. 'Nothing would suit Dubarre better than to show off in front of that lady.'

'Emily!' called Auchard behind his cabin door. 'Emily!'

12

There were two British frigates. The pursuit lasted well into the afternoon. After the first hour the wind began to rise. Still Dubarre piled on every sail. The masts creaked and moaned their complaints. Gusts blew the *Hortense* onto her side and they lost a man overboard from the shrouds. He was a Swede. They all heard him cry out, they all saw him fall into the sea. He surfaced, arms held aloft. His mouth moved but no one on the *Hortense* heard what he said. He was too far behind. Then the Swede was lost in the waves and his only hope was the British, which was no hope at all. The *Hortense* ploughed on, leaning, bouncing over waves, men and objects shaken loose within her hull. The British pursued, steadfast, implacable. The Swede drowned.

Now there was sunlight shining on them for the first time in days and a cleared sky above them, but there was no place for Merlet to take the sight required to deduce their position. The *Hortense* sailed on her ear, every scrap of sail flying. The two British frigates strained every rope and fibre chasing her. In her turn *Hortense* strained more. Dubarre stood by the helmsman with a permanent rictus of exhilaration on his face. He climbed the windward artimon shroud and hung there like a monkey, watching his pursuers' every move and calling instructions to the helm and to the boatswain. But the British frigates were sailing just a fraction faster than the French vessel. Dubarre had his crew jettison as much baggage, water and cannon as he could over the side, he threw all caution to the wind, but still the

British frigates gained. Just before two in the afternoon the first, faster vessel furled its foresails and staysails. It could only mean a stay had parted. The certain cause was invisible at this distance. Dubarre, watched by Emily, Merlet and Derray, danced a little jig on the quarter-deck. He was happy as a sandboy in the city. Dubarre had thrown off his cape in the sunlight, wore two pistols in his belt and a cutlass in a leather sheath strapped over his shoulder. Dubarre's crew affected not to notice his jigging. He seemed to have lost his mind to some degree and no one wanted to provoke him. Dubarre held his glass to his eye a great deal. Once he gave it to Emily to view the British ships and slipped his arm about her waist to steady her as he showed her. She didn't resist.

'They are frigates.' Dubarre said.

'How can you tell?'

'They have just a single row of guns.'

'Is that all? Are there no other ships with a single row of guns.'

'Lots. But they are not frigates.'

'So what makes a frigate?'

'The shape over all. The seaworthiness. The rig. The size. The intention. They are sea terriers.' He sounded as if he approved of them.

'Will they catch us?'

'Perhaps. Perhaps not. They will lose time while they change the broken stay. And the other one is not so fast.'

'How can you tell?' she asked.

'I can judge,' answered Dubarre. 'It's experience, my dear. I don't need a workbook to tell me who is how far off, to whom I must pay attention and who may be ignored.' He sniggered quietly.

She took this comment to be a slight on Auchard's arithmetical bent, and was right to do so. Dubarre smiled and patted her arm before putting the telescope glass to his eye again.

'Look. Still not changed that sail. They'll never catch us like that. What are they doing, eh?'

But eventually the British sailors on the single-decker did change the sail. And meanwhile the other frigate gained on him remorselessly. It wasn't slower than *Hortense*, whatever Dubarre claimed.

Below, on the cleared gun-deck Cotterell looked out through an unmanned port.

'He is catching.' Cotterell said quietly to Tom. 'Like a man pulling in a long line of cod. We are on the hook.'

Cotterell and Tom spent an hour below decks. There Lefèvre slept, attended by his wife and a brandy bottle, to which she helped herself freely. Charles, in another cabin, sat sullen, unable to speak for anger. After one attempt at conversation and commiseration Cotterell and Tom left him. Auchard writhed nearby, his still-booted feet slamming on the foot of his little swinging cot. Eventually Tom and Cotterell were sought out by former boatswain Derray. They were sent up on deck again to lend a hand hauling where needed. Derray was careful to place them as far forward on the gun-deck as possible and tell them not to emerge on the forecastle unless called. *Hortense* did not carry so many men aboard she could dispose of their services at this rate, he said, but they were 'to keep out of the old man's way.' And Derray stressed again that Dubarre was not to see them.

From the gun-deck they could see the towering, full sails of the pursuing British vessels crowding down upon the *Hortense*. 'I'd give it another hour,' said Cotterell, 'before the first one fires.'

As if in answer there was a puff of smoke from the bow of the British ship and Tom laughed and cried out, 'He must have heard you.' But they knew it was serious, and that a reckoning was coming.

The gun crews heard the bang too. Several looked out and could see the puff of smoke. They cheered and danced and sang the *Marseillaise* because the British had missed.

'Where did the ball land?' asked Cotterell.

'I couldn't see,' said Tom.

'A long way short of us, then.'

'Was gunnery the subject for the Captain's boy on the *Asia*?'

'Never mention it again,' said Cotterell. There was a chill in his voice.

'I give it an hour before the first one hits us,' said Tom.

It took half an hour before the first blow fell. Between, *Hortense* had burst a foresail. The accident slowed her, much to Dubarre's agitation. The foc's'l men had to hand the other foresails while the thrashing cloth was brought back under control. The misaine, the foremost mast on a French ship, was almost bare of canvas stretching fore and aft. Tom and Cotterell, hauling with other beefy foc's'l men on deck, helped replace it. If Dubarre saw them he gave no indication. The *Hortense* ploughed on, unstable, while they fought the canvas. The ship was under main and artimon alone now. The vessel was unbalanced and two helmsmen fought the wheel, sometimes aided by Dubarre himself or by Merlet, the new officer. *Hortense* griped, but Dubarre could not, and would not, reduce sail further. He didn't dare. The lead British ship grew ever closer. It was less than half a mile behind them now. Emily could make out the white faces of the men on the ship. She could even see an officer supervising some men above the bow. He wore the characteristic uniform coat of a British naval officer and, more importantly, took no part in the work himself, merely directing. She realised the men were a gun crew and they were laying a light bronze gun there. Its polish glittered in the sunlight. Then the men stood back and the officer peered over the shining small gun. He stood back in his turn, there was a flash and they all disappeared in a small cloud of powder.

'They're firing at us.' Emily said to Merlet, the French words like stones in her mouth.

'They've been doing it for some time, Madame Citoyenne.' Replied Merlet, who hadn't a clue what to call the American wife of a French ship's officer, so covered all possibilities. Emily turned and looked again. The men on the British ship were reloading their bronze chaser.

Forward, the foc'sl men, including Tom and Cotterell, set about the backbreaking, sinew-pulling, muscle-drawing task of setting fly the sails on the misaine again without heading the wind. They fought and hauled the replacement sail, lashed onto the original halyard. It was bound up with small stuff but the rolled sail had enough surface to make it impossible to haul. Derray lost his temporary officer's '*sang froid*' while he screamed at them to get on with it, pushed the lead seaman aside and tied the bends himself. All the time the *Hortense* was making the best way she could under sails set on the mainmast and the artimon. The helmsmen struggled. Below deck Dubarre had arranged men and tackle on the tiller to aid the wheel. Dubarre stood at the head of the quarter-deck companionway, bellowing instructions to the men on the tackle below. Emily stood at the helmsman's shoulder, looking back towards the British ships. Her cheeks glowed with excitement. She wore her cream dress. She looked like she might be going on to a ball. She shook her hair loose and allowed it to fall over her shoulders. Little Merlet stood next to Emily and glanced at her from time to time. He could only admire her, Madame Citoyenne.

'Would you not be more comfortable below, Madame Citoyenne?' he asked. She didn't even answer. Spray flew along the rails and side-decks. It reached the quarter-deck like thick salty rain. Emily could taste it on her lips and feel it on her face. She loved the sensation. She'd have given anything to be a proper part of the crew, with knowledge and skill and a rope to pull or a gun to fire.

'It's done!' cried Derray as he stepped back on deck below his beloved filling foresails. As the power came from them the wheel eased fractionally. Now it needed only the helmsman and one other.

Bang! The crack of the chaser gun on the British frigate sounded quite clear now. The tell-tale plume of powder smoke rose above the British ship's bow. This time Emily saw the shot hit the sea behind the *Hortense*. She wanted to show Merlet, but he stood facing forwards, checking the helmsman's course. He wanted to look like a good officer when his new Captain re-emerged from the companionway.

'It's so fast,' she said. 'I never expected it to be so fast.'

'They reload very quickly, Madame Citoyenne,' Merlet replied. 'The British are known for it. They practise their guns a great deal.'

'Don't we?'

'We don't have sufficient powder. The French Republic has to guard its resources carefully.'

By now the foc'sl men had their sails set and trimmed. *Hortense* pulled forward. But it was too late. The first British frigate was upon them. Emily turned to look again at the frigate. It was close enough now to allow her to pick out individual men's faces, both on deck and aloft, managing the sky scrapers which would soon need to be furled. The officer at the bow chaser was so young, she thought, and his gunner wore a beard, so that they looked like father and son. She heard a 'swoosh' followed by the kind of cracking sound a broken squash makes underfoot. Something splashed her body and from the corner of her eye she was aware of Merlet dropping. Emily saw the small plume of smoke rise again from the bow of the British ship. The bang of the gun came across the water again, slow, relaxed and discon-nected with the plume of smoke and the violence. Then Emily was aware all at once that her cream dress was splashed with blood, and a small cannon ball was rolling harmlessly along the deck. It steamed. Merlet was at her feet. His head, crushed and severed from his body, had bounced along the quarter-deck towards Dubarre as he emerged from the companionway. Dubarre stepped aside and let it pass, falling to the gun-deck like a coconut and landing close to where Cotterell and Tom had taken their stations as surgeon's assistants again. Whatever was in that shattered severed head, hopes, ambitions, dreams of promotion, lists of codes and orders of signals, grasp of literature and geometry, was now lost forever. A seaman on the gun-deck called for the surgeon, which meant Cotterell and Tom. They were at his elbow. Tom approached and stood irresolute over the severed but calm features, not knowing for a moment what to do for the best. Only the back of Merlet was destroyed and that, like the ball which had hit it, steamed lightly. Then black-haired Gunner Lang picked the head up by what remained of the hair and pitched it through an open port.

'Its presence will make men lose their bottom.' He said, in English. He was a former Hanoverian soldier and like many of his kind spoke English.

'Frenchmen have no bottom to lose,' answered Tom. 'They might have fury, but only Englishmen have bottom.' By which he meant the stolid, hearts of oak determination with which his fellow countrymen fought. Lang grinned and turned away.

'Does it matter?' asked Cotterell.

'You're the one dressed like a Frenchie,' Tom reminded Cotterell. 'It may matter when Jack Tar comes over the side bearing pikes and pistols and takes you for a furious Revolutionary Timonyjit.'

'Timonyjit?'

'Regiwhatsit. King killer.'

'Jack Tar has saved you a decision, anyway,' said Cotterell.

'Being?'

'You can keep that steel on your belt sheathed. You won't be obliged by your National Duty to kill Merlet now.'

On the quarter-deck Dubarre touched Emily and said, 'You'd better go below, Madame,' almost as an aside, before yelling for his gunner to send a crew to lay the brass lightweight stern rail guns at the frigate, and counter the bow chaser, which was still firing.

'Merlet asked me already. I'd rather stay here.' She said.

'Your husband needs you.'

'I can't help him.'

'You could comfort him.'

'I don't believe so,' she said, with an air of finality.

'You saw what became of Monsieur Merlet.' Dubarre said,

but he did not insist on her leaving. Liberté came at the Gunner's order and instructed the gun crew, who were unfamiliar with the flintlock stern gun. Its usual crew and gun captain had died among those with the flux. The two women looked each other up and down as Liberté passed, one in a blood-spattered cream silk dress, the other in her short blue tunic and trousers, the red galley-slave cap of the sans culottes on her head. 'This thing,' Liberté whispered to the gun crew, 'will never reach that ship. But we must do as we are asked.'

Before Liberté and her assistant crew could lay the stern gun, the first British frigate wore and prepared to heave-to, a certain sign it was about to deliver a broadside. Liberté dashed below to her proper and useful place on the gun-deck.

'Wear ship!' came the call from the quarter-deck. The ship-handling quart ran to their duties and the ship turned as the wheel spun.

Rasselas Charles climbed the companionway to the gun-deck and tumbled as the ship turned. Cotterell picked him up. 'Are you well, sir?'

'I was until then,' answered Charles.

Tom explained, 'We have to take a broadside on the beam now. Running away won't help. We would just be battered from the stern and wrecked. One ball passing longwise down the deck of the *Hortense* would kill half the ship's crew, a second the other half and a bit of chain and bar will bring down the rig. A fight between two ships is a form of turn up, like two pugilists on the deck. Our only chance is to stand and fight and take our beating in the belly, not on the nose.'

Of course the chance Tom talked about was no chance at all. They were caught by the British frigates and they all knew it.

'Listen,' said Cotterell. They could hear a band on the closer British frigate playing *Hearts of Oak*. Cotterell looked at Tom, who struggled not to tap his fingers and nod his head to the music, which he had heard a thousand times before. Cotterell found the presence of the orderly British vessel somehow comforting, even if the result would be death and destruction on the deck where he stood. He looked across to the British ship. The calm red-coated marines, the neat and nice ship handling, the full, lusty crew manning the guns and in the rigging, the music, the sharp-shooting of the bow chaser; it all combined to give the impression *Hortense* would soon be fighting two British frigates in their prime and pomp. Unbelievably, since he stood on the British ship's target, Cotterell also found *Hearts of Oak* stirring, as if he might be walking with his mother or grandfather on St Aubin's strand in Jersey and heard the strains float on the evening air from a ship in the roads. Beyond the music, Cotterell fancied he could hear the slop of the sea against *Hortense*'s hull as she slowed and completed her manoeuvre.

'Come on,' cried Lang to the gun-crews. 'Let's hear it.' The fiddler on the gun-deck began to play *Ça Ira*, their favourite revolutionary song. The gun-aimers crouched over their weapons to see through the gun ports. Their assistants made a show of helping. At this range, though, there was no real aiming to do. They could see the ochre and black stripes of the British ship. They could see the faces of their counterparts too, peering through the opposing ports. Eye to eye, the two groups of sailors glared. Still there was no command to fire. The British ship's rigging was full of armed men, with nets set above and across the decks to save their comrades below from falling spars or sailors. *Hortense* lacked sufficient crew to do all this, or even to set out nets. Those who fell would have to take the consequences, as would those they fell upon. Falling spars and rigging would just have to be dodged as best *Hortense*'s crew could. The French gun-aimers could see the British officers on the quarterdeck, swords drawn, shouting orders. The gun-aimers could see the soldier marines there on the British frigate too, with their short naval muskets aimed at *Hortense*. *Hortense* had carried no marine soldiers since giving hers up to the garrison at Guadeloupe. Cotterell leaned to look over a gun captain's shoulder. He fancied he could see the heat rising from the frigate's braziers. They would be heating cannon balls to make sure they caused the greatest damage. The shouting of familiar English words of command carried across the water. They had a strange, eerie sound to Cotterell. Behind their opponent he could see the second frigate, some distance behind, flying signal bunting to pass some message to the first.

On *Hortense*, the crew prepared to meet the blow. Behind Tom the powder monkeys, boys and spare members of gun-crew – including la belle Hélène – were jigging about the gun-deck to the fiddler's single-handed rendition of *Ça Ira*. The crewmen sang their infernal fast-repeated revolutionary song, whipping themselves like dervishes with the words. The men – and Hélène – holding smouldering long matches jigged too, so that the whole looked like a war-dance such as Cotterell imagined Red Indians might make.

'*Ah! Ça ira, ça ira, ça ira!*

Ah! ça ira

Les aristocrates à la lanterne

Ah! Ça ira, ça ira, ça ira!

Les aristocrates on les pendra'

'They are frightened,' said Tom.

'Aren't you?' asked Cotterell.

'Why? We will soon be free, one way or another.'

'More, more!' cried the gunner in his thick German accent, waving at his crews. 'Encore!'

The fiddler began to play a different tune. The crew began to sing the *Marseillaise* with power and enthusiasm.

'*Allons enfants de la Patrie,*

Le jour de gloire est arrivé!'

The wind seemed to drop. The ships seemed to settle, though it could only have been an impression. 'Duck your head,' said Cotterell, glancing at the frigate through the gun port and making a judgement.

'It would be cowardly,' said Tom. 'What will the Frenchies think of us?'

'Just do it. We are not fighting and you are no use to anyone dead.' Cotterell felt a duty towards his companion and reached out his hand towards Tom's head to push it down. Charles didn't need to be told to duck. The crew were still singing.

Contre nous de la tyrannie,

L'étendard sanglant est levé,

At '*levé*' those wooden ship's walls of the *Hortense* which faced the British frigate exploded. The air on the gun-deck of the *Hortense* filled with shards of steel and splinters of painted oak, whooping and flying through the air like newly-released devils, cutting down gunner and non-gunner alike. A twelve-pound ball passed between Cotterell and Tom, a shadow or presence really, rather than a real, experienced danger. A long thin splinter of oak flew through Tom's outstretched hand, penetrating the palm between the first and second fingers. It stopped just short of Cotterell's face. Tom's gesture to take cover had saved Cotterell, though neither had actually taken cover. Cotterell was amazed to discover he was unharmed. He looked about himself. The walls of the ship were penetrated in half a dozen places by great ragged holes. There was nothing neat about the damage, which was mostly caused by tearing of the ship's oak by the iron balls. The oak inside the holes was fractured, torn and splintered. This had been the source of the flying fragments and splinters. Alarmingly, there were two holes torn on the far side of the hull, where balls had passed right through both walls of the ship. All the holes smouldered. The marks where some balls had pitched on deck were scorched. The deck ran with blood. Near Cotterell one man's arm was a mangled mess, another lay on the deck with his bowels in his hands. Belle Hélène had been peppered by thousands of small splinters, so that she was covered in blood and looked like a form of hedgehog, but she was still moving freely enough. Lang strode up and down the deck, checking on his crews. Dubarre appeared at the head of the companionway and shouted, heedless of the godless revolution he represented, 'Fire! For the love of the tabernacle and sacraments, fire!'

Lang repeated the order. 'Fire!'

The guns of *Hortense* flashed and roared fire and power, then were rolled back on their tackles ready to clean, swab to cool, load and fire again. The air on the gun-deck was full of smoke, dust and the smell of burnt powder.

The gunfire appeared to have stilled the wind entirely, so that the powder smoke was an age drifting away. As it cleared on deck and he could see again, Cotterell was aware that Dubarre was still looking down the quarter-deck companionway at him. Dubarre even had time and self-possession enough to grin at him. He looked euphoric, as if he had been born for this moment. Dubarre's mouth moved. Cotterell had been almost completely deafened, though temporarily, by the boom of *Hortense*'s firing guns and couldn't understand the Captain. He thought Dubarre may have shouted '*A bas les Anglais! Quel éclat!*' which seemed unbelievable.

The gun crews around Cotterell worked like devils to reload, harried by Lang and Liberté. Tom pulled the splinter from his hand. The flesh pumped blood. He clapped his free left hand over the wound to stop the coursing but this rendered him useless as a crew member, even as a mate to a man who was not a surgeon. Cotterell tried to speak to him but the words were muffled by their temporary deafness. The two men bent over with their heads together, bellowing at each other and misunderstanding. Then the second British broadside hit. Again the air was filled with hot steel and flying splinters. Men were cut down where they stood, spinning, bloodied, away from their posts or falling, limbs flailing out of their control. One man was beheaded. Another was cut in half by a piece of flying steel, another lived but was crushed below the waist. He would die soon, Cotterell knew. Cotterell bent to give a man water and was amazed again to realise that he himself was not hurt too. Two broadsides and not even a scratch. Cotterell was even more amazed by the speed with which the British vessel had re-armed and fired. Some of the *Hortense*'s guns were hardly past the

swabbing stage. Others simply lacked crews and were surrounded
by piles of dead and dying Frenchmen. One gun was dismounted
from its carriage. It must have been hit, for they hadn't fired
enough to stall and jump from heat, as Cotterell had seen a gun
do himself as a boy. The disarray about him was unbelievable.
Men skidded around the guns in rivers of blood. A sailor threw
a bucket of sawdust on the deck. Boys stumbled with their loads
of flannel cartridge or balls, sometimes dropping their loads or
falling. The surviving gun captains screamed encouragement or
oaths, according to their nature. Gunner Lang and his deputy
Liberté strode through it all unharmed, helping and encouraging
the crews, lending a hand where they could, making order of
the chaos. They seemed unassailable.

'Surgeon!' screamed Derray from the quarter-deck above.
'Surgeon. Get up here!'

No surgeon was available. Probably the nearest was on the
British ship. Charles was dealing with a man with a smashed
arm. Tom aided him. Cotterell climbed the companionway. The
chaos of the quarter-deck was even worse than Cotterell had
imagined. It looked like a mad butcher's shop. The British frigate
was almost invisible from the quarter-deck of the *Hortense*, hidden
by the smoke from her guns. But the damage wreaked by those
guns was clear. Liberté's stern gun crew, formed and ordered
there during the pursuit, had managed to fire little. They hadn't
discouraged the British at all. When the first broadside had
finally come from the British ship, the starboard stern gun crew
had stood by their useless lightweight bronze weapons and been
cut down by canister-shot aimed at the quarter-deck. Their parts
had been scattered around the deck, along with what seemed
like thousands of spent British grape shot and musket balls.
There was nothing to be done for the gun crew. Dubarre had
also received some of the canister material in his back. Blood
streamed down his legs, causing him to leave bloody footprints
wherever he moved, mingling with the blood of his crewmen.
Dubarre could not walk easily and dragged himself around the

deck on the arm of a sailor or by pulling himself along the rail,
but he did not allow the injury to impair either his leadership
or his lungs. He leaned against a rail shouting instructions to
those members of his crew who hadn't been torn to pieces by
canister, ball or splinter. The helmsman appeared conscious, but
was slumped over the wheel and was being assisted to keep in
his place by Emily, who was now covered in other people's blood
but seemed unhurt. She was blackened by powder, dishevelled
by the action but steady on her feet. She seemed cool and aware
of all that was going on around her. The decapitated Merlet still
lay at her feet. Before them was the wreck of the binnacle,
smashed where a ball had passed through it. At each volley,
concentrated and powerful, crashing from the British ship, ragged
and disjointed from the French, a great deal of gunpowder
smoke drifted over the deck of the *Hortense* or over the water
between the two ships. At times the attacking frigate disappeared
from view only to reappear a few seconds later. At times even
the sea around them was invisible. The *Hortense* might as well
have been in a Channel summer fog for all they knew of their
surroundings. Then the smoke parted for a moment, leaving
Hortense sitting alone in crisp clear air. Another zephyr blew for
a second and the powder smoke surrounding the British ship
blew away too. Another volley followed and again the British
vessel was wrapped in gun smoke. The attacking ship was dark,
dangerous and filled to the tops, it seemed, with men whose
only desire in life was to kill those on the *Hortense.*

Immediately they had a view of the *Hortense* the British frigate's
marines began to fire. It was uneven fire, made at will instead
of in volleys. The ships were close enough for Cotterell to pick
out the marines' individual features, their eyes squinting down
the barrel, their red coat-sleeves leaned against the British ship's
rail to control the fire better. Near to the marines was the boarding
party, an officer and forty or fifty men crammed against the rail,
pikes, cutlasses, pistols and boarding axes to hand, the sailors'
heads covered in their traditional black boarding scarves. They

looked ready, and more than willing, for the fight to come. Cotterell knew such a force would sweep aside the crew of the *Hortense* and was surprised, momentarily, to feel a pang of regret about this. Cotterell could see other men with pistols and short muskets in the British frigate's rigging. He knew there should be marines on their own quarter-deck firing back and ready to repulse them. There should be men with muskets above him in *Hortense*'s rigging, blasting away at the British deck. But there were no marines aboard *Hortense* and no sailors to spare for either task. This meant the deck of the *Hortense* was a much more dangerous place than the deck of the British ship. Musket balls flew past Cotterell like bees or small birds. Others bounced up from the wooden deck like hail. Time passed slowly. Cotterell's movements were deliberate. Each step took an age. He couldn't believe he was still uninjured. On the way to the rail he saw a red-coated British marine in the press by the quarter-deck rail reload. The man on the British ship was cool, unhurried, biting the cartridge and pouring, then pushing in the ball and wad, using the thin ramrod as if he were on the training ground or a field day. The smoke cleared further for just a second and Cotterell could see the second British frigate half a mile behind the first, signal flags flying, sails backed. How odd, Cotterell thought ... sails backed and keeping station behind the first British frigate. Didn't they want to fight? It wouldn't be fear, so what was it? Honour? A pre-arranged division of prize money? Would the other frigate come in to attack them second? It was a puzzle.

Derray pointed at a bundle under the quarter-deck rail. Erique was there, motionless.

'Help him!' shouted Derray.

The marine on the British ship fired. Cotterell saw the flash in his musket's muzzle. Derray spun, hit in the arm. It looked like the marine had shot him, though Cotterell knew he couldn't connect the events in that way. A musket at that distance, a couple of ships' lengths away, was hopelessly inaccurate. Cotterell bent to see if Erique was alive. Then another tremendous crash came from the British frigate, like a thousand hammers landing at once. This time it was chain and bar, aimed at the masts and rigging. A piece of bar bounced off the artimon mast and fell at Cotterell's feet. The mainmast and its rigging seemed to take the worst of it. Now it creaked, leaning over like a drunken sailor. Its spars slipped and its cords were for the most part cut. Cotterell knelt by Erique. He was at a loss what to do for the best. He couldn't fight against his countrymen. He had no surgical skill and couldn't save the men and women around him. Behind him, Dubarre leaned against a rail, seeming almost delirious with a kind of battle joy. Derray moved about the quarter-deck, running the ship. Cotterell felt for Erique's pulse, but there was none. It was gone, the lifeblood drained away by a wound in his chest, no doubt caused by a musket ball from one of the British marines, from the look of the wound. If Cotterell looked up to the maintop of the frigate he could see the 'lobsters' still firing. Erique felt fragile in death to Cotterell, like a bird brought down by a hunter's gun.

A man in officer's uniform and hat appeared at the rail of the British frigate. He held a speaking horn to his mouth. Some of the words were whipped away, but his intention was clear.

'You there, you must strike. *Vous devez . . .*' and it was lost. 'You must surrender, sir.'

Dubarre leaned over his ship's rail too, as far as he could from the quarter-deck, as if he was trying to reach the British frigate and strike at the British officer with the mouth horn. He had a cutlass in one hand and a pistol in the other and he waved the cutlass above his head for emphasis as he screamed in English, 'Never! Never! Never!'

There was a moment when the guns were silent, and neither Dubarre nor the English officer was shouting. In it Cotterell could hear the ship around him. The *Hortense* was full of screams and cries and pain. Cotterell wondered if the British had finished firing. He didn't believe so. They seemed as if they would fire their guns into *Hortense* until every man was dead aboard her. Cotterell felt suddenly intensely furious with the battle-maddened Dubarre, as if they were all here because of some form of wilfulness on the Captain's part. This was quite separate from the need for revenge over his father and the first *l'Imprevu*. This was red-hot anger, immediate and almost unbearable, appealing direct to his soul without pausing in his rational mind. Cotterell wanted to take the cutlass from the Captain's hand and beat him with it, even though he knew that was pointless, would be fruitless and was anyway something he probably couldn't achieve. Cotterell eyed a cutlass in the rack at the foot of the artimon. If he could just reach it and swing at Dubarre, the battle might be over. Cotterell knew he would probably die if he did it. These thoughts rushed through his mind all at once, like a crowd fleeing a runaway bullock and, as if in sympathy, the ship seemed to shudder. Then the mainmast groaned, moved, paused and fell, broken despite its enormous size about twelve feet above deck. Part of the mast fell into the sea, most was fastened to the ship by the rigging. Below him, on the gun-deck, Cotterell heard the French ships' guns fire again, ragged and few, hardly a volley. The powder smoke swirled once more about them. Cotterell felt sure they must be boarded now. Dubarre was still bellowing orders, but they were ignored by those of his deafened and shattered crew still standing. Instead men did what they could or what seemed right. They hacked at the cords retaining the broken mast while others grabbed pikes, guns, cutlasses, even oars and boat poles to resist the expected assault. Guns fell silent again. The cries of the wounded, the creak of rigging, the chopping of axes as men tried to cut away the fallen mast were the only sounds. Then Cotterell could hear Liberté yelling at a gun crew below his feet. Her high-pitched voice cut through the fog of the action.

'Don't leave it there. Move it. Move it.'

Move what? He wondered. The chopping of cords on the mainmast continued. The mast fell away with a splash. One of

its spars fell on the quarter-deck with a crash, narrowly missing
Cotterell, but crushing the hen coop. Hens flew. Some were
crushed. More blood ran onto the deck. The British vessel fired
again. The crew of the *Hortense* waited and waited, but no invasion came from the British ship, which was now lost again in
a cloud of its own powder smoke. Emily stood by her helmsman,
supporting him. Dubarre fell from the rail that propped him,
still bellowing orders few could hear and fewer understand.
Derray the former boatswain took his place. As he did so the
powder smoke cleared again, as if some great invisible hand
had pulled a curtain aside. The parting smoke revealed an extraordinary sight. The British ships were sailing away. Cotterell could
just make out the name of the frigate which had attacked them,
Circe, carved in the stern works and picked out in gold leaf.
Once clear of the powder smoke the ship's name-board glittered in sunlight. The vessel bearing the name looked neat and
proud, ready to take on and wreck a navy, let alone a mere
convoy escort. The band on *Circe* was playing music again; 'God
Save the King' this time. He could hear her crew cheering, even
from this distance. But there was no more gun-fire. Before, and
to the west of *Circe*, now perhaps a mile away from *Hortense*,
the companion stand-off frigate was still signalling. Cotterell
could see *Circe*'s midshipman running the flags up the signal
halyard to answer the signal. No sense could be made of the
flags without the code book, but Cotterell guessed *Circe* had
been ordered off by her companion. One captain always outranks
another. The captain and crew of the frigate would be furious.
Hortense represented prize money for the crew of *Circe*, and she
could only be ordered off in extraordinary circumstances. They
were here to find a convoy, not chase down single and individual French warships without bringing a general action. No
doubt they would be back soon to finish their victory. Wrecking
Hortense was triumph enough for now and the business they
were about was sufficiently urgent to allow no time for prizes.
Vanstabel's giant corn convoy would be prize enough. Cotterell

looked around himself at the ruined and smashed upper works of the *Hortense*.

'Derray.' Dubarre called, and waved at his second in command, his voice hoarse and his face grimacing with pain. Derray bent over his prone commander with difficulty. His arm bled. His blood trickled onto Dubarre, who was clearly in great pain.

'Keep them here, Derray. Keep them here. Fire the guns. Go below and fire them.'

But below there was no one able to fire the guns. And soon, in the sea around them, there was no one to aim them at. The British sea terriers left their wrecked and ruined victim *Hortense* and sailed as close to south as they could lay a course.

Derray approached Cotterell. Erique was his favourite too. Cotterell shook his head.

'Dead.'

'They have finished with us.'

'No,' said Cotterell. 'They have got us where they want us. They think we will sink, and they don't have time to save us.'

'I won't let us sink.'

'Then they will be back to pick over the wreckage. Either way, they have won.'

13

The smashed French frigate *Hortense* wallowed for fully twelve hours. Derray, the former boatswain, in sole command for the time being, was at first unable to raise a sufficient number of fit men to handle the ship's rig, though it had been reduced to two masts, artimon at the stern and misaine in the forward part. The British frigate's fire had damaged rigging, running cordage and the hull. With his hand forced, Derray had whatever sails he could carry reduced until the ship just kept steerageway.

The *Hortense* was lucky. The Atlantic weather was kind. The dominant south-west wind stayed light for now, though the sky had become blue and had taken on a kind of crisp clarity which Cotterell's fisherman instinct found threatening. He told no one about it. The date was some time at the very end of May, 28th or 29th as Cotterell and Tom had reckoned the English calendar against the Republican version used on the ship. So, though the vessel was a ruin, there was still plenty of light left in the day to begin to put her right. The sea air was balmy and the water calm. No other vessel approached during the twelve hours of wallowing, though if the crew had listened carefully, and had not been already deafened by their own gunfire, they might have heard distant cannon fire. Cotterell thought he heard guns. It was hard to be sure. No one else reacted, probably due to their post-battle muffling deafness. But Cotterell heard something from the south. The British frigates had sailed south, as near as damn it. Cotterell knew *Hortense* was west and north of Brest – he'd

overheard Dubarre and Merlet. Vanstabel's convoy, which was
to their south, had been heading for the French port, while
Dubarre had taken a more northerly station to draw off British
ships falling upon them from Iceland, Ireland or St George's
Channel.

Cotterell knew that if *Hortense* continued on an easterly course
from this point they would pass into the English Channel. Or
perhaps founder at Scilly. As soon as they had way, they needed
to head south and east. He imagined that the moment at which
to make the change of course would represent a problem for
Derray and Dubarre. They would be forced to head south at
some point – *Hortense* was not stationed in Torbay – but Dubarre
would have had strict orders from Vanstabel, Cotterell knew,
that his position should be well to the north of the convoy,
heading east. Those orders would have held good until they'd
been attacked. But now? It was difficult to imagine how *Hortense*
would represent any significant delay to any British warship she
met. The French frigate was in no position to defend herself
from Tom's apocryphal 'bum-boat full of Lascars with blunt
pikes,' and on her present course she would certainly meet more
British ships; frigates, double and triple-deckers from the Channel
fleet, armed East Indiamen convoying home. Some tough little
armed Cornish lugger could take her, without doubt. The south-
west coast of England teemed with British naval ships. He imagined the very least the crew of the *Hortense* would want to do
was stay alive long enough to cheat the crew of *Circe*, their
tormentors, of the prize money.

Cotterell supposed there would be a fleet out looking for the
French. And if the rumbling he thought he had heard indicated
contact had been made, how much longer should Dubarre allow
the *Hortense* to remain the sacrificial pawn of Vanstabel? The
rumbling meant marauding British warships had found something, even if it wasn't Vanstabel's convoy. Perhaps there were
other so far unrevealed ships in a French defensive screen flung
out from Brest. If they were desperate enough to import corn

to feed their Revolution, they were desperate enough to risk all in this way. But it would be a big risk. It meant the British could defeat them in a day. And if the *Hortense* and her performance in battle was any indicator of the more general French fleet, the British *would* defeat them. Cotterell thought about the crowd of men with pikes, pistols and swords on the *Circe*, dressed to board, right down to the famous black scarves. He shuddered.

None of these distant, soft-booming gun sounds was easily audible over the sea to those on the deck of the *Hortense*. None gained a physical presence in the form of a sail on the horizon. The French ship sailed slowly, crippled but undisturbed, across a seemingly empty ocean, her crew oblivious to the action around them but aware of the danger in which they stood.

After their beating by the *Circe* the crew of the *Hortense* had turned in on their ship, like a family filled with grief, concerning themselves with saving those of their fellows they could and repairing their vessel to meet the inevitable change in the weather. Derray assigned some crewmen to the task of burying those they couldn't help. The dead men were given a swift muttering about the Nation, the debt the Maritime Service owed its 'children' and those children going into the arms of the 'great mother the sea.' Then they were slipped over the side. It would have been impossible to put them all in the ballast as French tradition expected. It was even impossible to sew them up in canvas and drop them over the side with a shot at their feet as ballast. There were just too many dead.

Other more-or-less fit sailors pumped the bilge, cleaned the decks, stowed the fighting equipment and returned the ship to the best order they could. The Portuguese carpenter attacked the worst damage around the waterline himself, aided by a mate and followed by a small crew with caulking materials. The carpenter also gave instruction to other men to make what repairs they could higher up the wooden wall of the hull. The whole crew did their best to put the ship back in order. They knew that soon their lives might depend on it.

Derray was a practical sailor, a man after his Capitaine's own heart. He ordered the stove lit and the assistant cook was put to work on it, since his boss Pascal was already occupied deep on the orlop, demonstrating his new skills as a temporary surgeon. When he'd finished those who had been carried down to his little surgery there were plenty more customers on the gun-deck. Meanwhile the crew needed to eat. As a temporary solution they were issued with cold pressed salt beef, biscuit and water where they stood. Many, exhausted, sat down at their work to eat it. Derray didn't argue or chivvy them. He knew nothing could be achieved if the crew were fainting from hunger. Among the Captain's possessions a small boxed compass was found, which would serve in place of the wrecked ship's compass. It was placed on deck on the centre line of *Hortense*, wedged there for Derray to observe where his new command was headed. He organised a system of steering, for the helm itself had been smashed, along with the helmsman. Emily had, in fact, been propping up a dead helmsman, and he had toppled as soon as she had stopped helping him. Tackles were arranged on the lower deck tiller – it was too heavy to work without tackles, and in any case was above head height for most of the crew. Two men were set to work the tackles, with a third sitting at the top of the companionway steps calling or repeating orders from the quarter-deck. Not that they were going anywhere yet.

The broken deck equipment, dismounted cannons and wrecked boats and binnacle were put over the side, along with everything else deemed beyond repair. The hen coop had been completely smashed. The dead birds were taken down to the assistant cook to be plucked and gutted and turned into broths and soup for injured men. The living hens had been chased down and returned to the remains of their coop. A tarpaulin was stretched over the structure to save them, as best they could, from heatstroke, high wind or a simple repeat escape. The crew – especially those injured – would have need of all the fresh sustenance they could get over the next week or two.

A shot had passed through the manger, the lye tub and two cows. The cows' guts and their bloodied contents, along with some gallons of lye and blood, had run back down the gun-deck during the action, leaving much of the forward surface coated as if with slow-drying pitch. To avoid waste the animals were roughly butchered where they had been cut down. The butcher Gaston and cook Pascal, the only men with real skill in this business, had long been on the orlop with Charles and Tom, doing their best for their shipmates in their unskilful and unlearned surgical way. Rurally-bred seamen simply did the butchering of the freshly dead and mangled cows with as much skill as they could muster. It wasn't much. They used seaman's knives. They didn't even have hot water yet.

Teams of more-or-less fit men splashed sea water and scrubbed the deck, so that all this blood, guts and lye was washed away, along with the blood of the men who had died on the gun-deck. The exposed foredeck, quarter-deck and gun-deck were all scrubbed too, scrubbed clean of blood, body parts and black powder. Once the frigate's gun-deck was clean the swing-up and knock-down partitions were let back into place, so that the Captain's cabin, sleeping quarters and his Second's quarters were re-established. The partitions were barely damaged, even to the extent of their lime white paint, so that when they were replaced, and the doors fitted, the after-part of the deck seemed extraordinarily normal. Furnishings which had not been jettisoned during the chase re-emerged from the hold, blankets and paliasses were found and a cot arranged in the Captain's sleeping quarters, the whole made as comfortable as it could be. Then, by the quarter-deck rail, Dubarre – who wasn't easily able to move unaided – was laid on a sheet of sail canvas and carefully taken down the companionway by a group of sailors. His face was twisted with pain, even though the sailors' movements were as smooth and gentle as they could be.

Emily took charge of making Dubarre comfortable once he had been carried below. The piece of British canister shot had entered his upper back, then travelled to his lower back where it had exited. The shot had clearly damaged his spine en route. Dubarre claimed the spine-bones grated when he was moved. He said he felt as if there was something broken inside him, though unless he moved or was moved he wasn't in a great deal of pain. Dubarre had lost all feeling in his legs, which was why he couldn't stand.

Charles and Tom came up from the orlop to lay out injured men on deck and to see to Dubarre. They were both covered from head to foot in other men's blood. Charles, with his dark features and white surgeon's apron soaked red, both with his own blood and that of the *Hortense*'s crew, was an extraordinary sight. When Cotterell had first seen him he'd been a crisp, almost dandyish man in a wig who acted as if his mode of dress was a necessary extension to his natural good manners. Cotterell had been naked from the sea. Now Charles was dressed like a battle surgeon, while Cotterell wore the bloodstained fruques of a French matelot. Cotterell was holding a tourniquet on a dying man's leg, keeping him on earth for a few minutes longer. He didn't know why. The damage to the man's leg was beyond repair, and far too high on the thigh for their crude attempts at surgery to be effective, so the man had gone to the end of the queue for treatment and was now dying. When Charles emerged he had immediately gone to Dubarre. Tom stayed to help Cotterell. Tom said the butcher Gaston and the cook Pascal had quickly become expert surgeons below, and had abandoned the books they couldn't read once they'd got the hang of leaving a flap of flesh to be sewn over the amputated stump, usually by Charles or himself.

Despite the evidence to the contrary Tom said in baby French that the man with the tourniquet on his leg had little to fear, he would soon be as right as rain and dancing, confessing to Cotterell, 'though obviously a bit hoppity. We have got the hang of it now. Probably he will live with a simple wound like that, though he will not dance their blessed *Carmagnole*, stamping just the one foot.'

'You are a real Joab's comforter, Tom.'

Tom whispered to Cotterell, grinning all the while, 'I do my best. Keep a smile on your face for these poor bastards, matey. I have seen things down there you would not wish on an enemy. I have never after any action seen so many grievous wounded men spilling their guts on the deck. I have never seen so many with smashed legs and arms. It's what happens when you can't defend yourself proper. I can't tell you how many have perished. We lost count, and Charles only allows us to work on someone if there's a good chance he may be saved.'

'This fellow?' Cotterell gave no sign he was talking in English about the man below his hand.

'I don't believe so,' answered Tom, keeping up the same pretence. It didn't matter. The man was barely conscious from loss of blood. 'We are lucky, you and me.' Tom said. He pointed at his wounded hand. 'Me with my hole in my hand to remind me of my mortality, like the Blessed Saviour himself before he rose, and you with your open head have got away light, I can tell you. I reckon those Jack Tars weren't even trying to kill we two.'

Cotterell felt the crown of his head, where Tom had indicated. His hand came away wet with his own blood. He'd had no idea he'd been injured. He had felt nothing, and presumed the blood on his clothes came from other men.

'Did you see who she was that fired upon us?'

'*Circe*,' answered Cotterell. 'I don't know about the other.'

'*Circe*, eh? I have seen her hanging off the hook in the Downs, but never with her guns run out like that, and I have never spoken to one of her company, well, never knowingly.'

'I don't suppose anyone was settling personal scores, Tom.'

'But they fired smartly, eh?'

'They did.'

'And this rabble was no match for them?'

'That's right.'

'Didn't I say the first British ship that found us would serve us out in fine style, Mr Cotterell?'

'Yes.'

'I wonder they didn't make us prisoner.'

'They want to find and wreck the grain fleet Dubarre showed us, not some mean little French frigate.'

'Of course. But there's prize money.'

'They will be back for us, I expect.'

'How many guns, did you see?'

'Twenty-eight.'

'Twenty-eight?' said Tom, who had of course seen her too, 'Just twenty-eight? She's a flighty little thing, *Circe*. But she fights, eh? You'd have thought she was a seventy-four firing one deck after another, with the speed those guns were loaded and fired. Are you sure the other fellow wasn't firing too?'

'Other fellow?'

'The other frigate.'

'He stood off the whole time.'

'Is that a no?'

'He would have had to have fired *through Circe*.'

'*Circe*, eh? *Circe*. Good old fellows. *Circe*. Nearly as good as those on Captain Nugent's *Veteran*. Here's to them. King George should create every man-jack of them Knights of the Realm. If these mean French bastards carried any grog I'd drink their health in it.'

Failing an issue of grog magically appearing beside himself Tom raised his hand in salute to the south, the direction in which the frigates had sailed. Tom was very proud of the British frigate which had attacked them, though it had killed half the complement of the *Hortense* and would have sailed away ignorant, with her crew-members' consciences clear, if her ball and case and bar and chain had torn Tom and Cotterell apart too, just as they had done to so many others. Few seemed without injury aboard *Hortense*.

'You are falling down on your stitching duties, Tom. Here, let me.' Charles was with them again, and wiped his hands on his bloody apron for cleanliness before accepting a needle and catgut from Tom and stitching Cotterell's head. It took only a few seconds but the needle stung badly and Cotterell was ashamed to be hurt like that when surrounded by men with broken and smashed bodies.

'If we had vinegar and brown paper we'd have made a perfect job of that wound, Cotterell,' said Tom. 'But this vessel is woefully short of medical supplies. And Mr Charles has to do the best he can.'

He turned to Charles. 'Can't you give him some of your Red Indian dirt, as a poultice?'

'It is finished,' said Charles. 'And, frankly, so am I.' It was true, he looked ready to drop from exhaustion. No hour or watch had rung on board since the bell had been shot away, but Cotterell guessed that about four hours had passed since the battle.

The action was ended and there were so many injured men on the gun-deck it was neither helpful nor necessary to carry each of the injured down to the orlop. Instead that had been reserved for amputations, splinting, digging out of splinters and pieces of shell, the binding-up of wounds and the dispensation of brandy and sympathy, the main medicine available to Charles and his fellow amateur surgeons. Charles would have dispensed other strong medicine if he could, but most had disappeared before he had joined the ship.

Derray appeared to be a capable commander, given his and the ship's limitations. He could handle the ship under sail and had done so for over a year. Dubarre and Auchard had restricted themselves to simple orders, leaving interpretation and execution to boatswain Derray and his mate LeBlanc. This meant both men were used to commanding the crew on a day-to-day level. It was just as well, for with Merlet and Mathelier dead, Auchard blinded and Dubarre incapacitated, promoted boatswain Derray was effectively in command of the vessel. There were no other officers, no sailing master. The ship would have to be run by Derray, his deputy LeBlanc, Gunner Lang and the cook, Pascal. There simply was no one else.

'It is a committee, like their bloody Republic,' said Tom, watching as the four men and Liberté met on the quarter-deck. 'Any minute now they will set up a machine and start cutting men's heads off. Starting with their Captain. A committee will finish off the work our frigates started.'

'They won't get the chance. The sea will do for us,' replied Cotterell.

14

Dubarre was in his sleeping quarters, resting in almost complete darkness. Next door, in the Captain's cabin, Emily and Charles pored over books, tables and charts. She had changed and now wore a black frock and white shawl. Charles had removed his bloody apron. In the sleeping quarters Dubarre twisted and turned uncomfortably. He was only able to move his upper body and he felt deathly cold. He was still in the clothes he'd worn during the battle. The dried blood stuck to him. He was wrapped in his cloak and had a blanket on top, but he just couldn't get warm.

'Well?' Dubarre called. 'Well?' No reply came.

'Madame Auchard,' Dubarre called. 'Madame Auchard.' Emily put down her book in the cabin and entered the sleeping quarters.

'Come here.' He said in English. Emily and Dubarre looked at each other in the darkness for a moment. She approached him and knelt by the cot.

'Is there another blanket?' He asked in English.

'I will find one directly.' She answered. 'This will help for now.' She took off the shawl and laid it on him, then took his hand.

'You are freezing.' Emily said.

'I am.'

She made to stand, but he spoke again. 'Don't go yet. I am dying.'

'No,' she said. 'Never.'

'It's true. I am wounded and am cold to my core. I know what it means.'

'I will fetch Charles and the Englishman.'

'For what? They're no surgeons.'

'There are books. Lefèvre is doing well under them.'

'Good for him. But I am not Lefèvre and a knee is not a spine. Listen. There is important work to be done. Your husband and I are the last officers on the ship. I cannot get up and if he goes on deck he has to play the colin-malin.'

'The *what*?'

'He cannot see. Blind man's buff. He is blind, and so are we. But somehow the ship must be navigated until it's in sight of land. We must not reach the land in the dark. We must not sail onto shoals. Your black would be better turning his precious reading brain to that than to digging lead out of me.'

'He can't command a ship from a book.'

'He won't. Once we are within sight of land Derray can get *Hortense* into port. He has done it many times with only a word from me or your husband. Can you read a chart, my dear?'

'I can read what is written there.'

'Then you could establish our position.'

'It seems unlikely.'

'You just need to read the book.' Dubarre was becoming exasperated.

'There are several manuals aboard, sir,' said Charles from the doorway. 'Any one of which would provide the information we require. However, each represents several years' work to master.'

'Not for a man like you, Monsieur Charles. You will be master of one before noon, I am sure.'

'I could read them all. I could read the navigation book. I could read the tables. I could read a clock. I am probably capable of the mathematical workings. But Captain, really, I am no navigator.'

'Auchard will help.'

'Help *me*? The man who blinded him?'

'He knows his duty. Auchard will help his ship.'

Charles thought about it for a moment, then said, 'There must be sailors aboard who can read.'

'There are. But none has learned the art of navigation.'

'Nor have I.'

'But you are an educated gentleman.' Dubarre was a man who was never ashamed to flatter, if it got what he wanted. 'You have languages and sciences. You said yourself, you are in correspondence with members of the Convention and others. Can one of my little matelots compare with that?'

Charles didn't answer.

'You do it,' said Dubarre. 'When you are on the quarter-deck open the sextant box. Derray will show you where it is. There are notes in the box for the use of the navigator. You have used one before?'

'Captain, if I held the sextant in my hand and was advised by this highly literate and intelligent lady I could no doubt point it at the noon sun. Even I can find the noon sun. I could consult these books we have laid out in the cabin, it's true. Properly checked and aided I could do some navigator's sums. I might even be able to make a mark on the chart. But whether I could actually use the device to establish a position for the ship is another matter.'

'You are a man of learning.'

'But I have never learned *that*.'

'You have seen one used dozens of times on this ship.'

'We all have. But I have never been *taught*,' said Charles. 'And I never took notes. I never imagined I'd have to do it myself. By the time I have done the various reckonings we could be a day later or a hundred miles out.'

'Then we will all drown on some rocky shore, most likely,' said Dubarre. They were silent. 'In that drawer.' Dubarre pointed into the gloom. 'Is the regulated clock. Take it.'

Emily took the clock. It was in a wooden box.

'There are two keys to the clock box.' Dubarre said. 'Here is mine. Give it to Derray when you are done.'

'Where is the other?' asked Charles.

'Auchard has it.'

That night, in the darkness of his little cabin, Auchard had decided to take command of the *Hortense*. The night had been awful, full of men moaning, crying out and dying. Even the smallest sound carried to Auchard and tortured him further with the frustration of his blindness. Light and dark meant nothing to him, but sounds loomed out of the darkness like lighted beacons warning of rocks or shoals. He was drawn to them and could not shake off a vision of his body smashed against the shore, more vivid than if he had seen it with his own eyes.

Auchard knew the young officer was dead, Eustache had told him, and that meant there was no navigator. Eventually he decided he must act or go mad. He raised himself from the cot and bellowed, 'Eustache!'

Since his injury Auchard had been attended by, and led everywhere, by Eustache, the pock-marked sailor who'd held a knife to Cotterell's throat.

'Eustache!'

The Second blundered about the little cabin, waiting for his attendant.

'Eustache!'

Cotterell could hear the shouting but did nothing. He wanted nothing to do with either Auchard or Eustache. Cotterell had also spent the night listening to men die. He'd watched them, helped them, held their hands, promised to inform sweethearts or mothers, then assisted in throwing their bodies over the side. There was little choice in the matter of disposal, or in its manner, though it seemed enormously significant to the remaining members of the crew. Burial at sea was hated by French sailors, however rabidly republican.

Derray, acting as Second and now in command, had the ship set up as skilfully and tidily as he could. Cotterell, one of the few fit men, had taken his part in that too. Fewer than seventy fit men remained on *Hortense* and no one who could stand was excluded from the physical duties of the matelot. An hour before dawn one last night task remained for Cotterell – wood for the ship's stove again. As he was on his way down to the wood-hold with Tom he passed Auchard and Eustache, who had found each other. The pock-marked sailor held a flickering candle. Eustache had lost his red headscarf somewhere and gained a wound on his right arm, which was in a sling. He had a hangdog look. He had gone from rabid, jealous revolutionary to a limping blind man's helper in just an afternoon, with the visit of the British frigate. Auchard had his hand on the sailor's left arm. The blinding wound on Auchard's one good eye had been band-aged with a strip of blue cloth. Arm in arm they looked to Cotterell like a strange form of wedding party. The battle with the English frigate had not made pock-marked Eustache any better disposed towards the English, and he scowled at Tom and Cotterell as they passed.

'He can pull all the faces he wants,' said Tom, when Auchard, who understood English, was out of earshot, 'he is no threat to King George now and neither is his ship. He is reduced to playing blind-man's buff with that other silly beggar.'

'Like us,' said Cotterell.

'Us?' said Tom.

'This ship.'

'I remember when you called me a signed-up Frenchie seaman for saying *us*.' Tom was unhappy. 'And now you are making sport of me.'

Cotterell smiled. 'Better I do than 'nasty face', eh?' Cotterell clearly meant Eustache.

'He has had to change his ways and adapt, like others on the *Hortense*. He can't hold a knife strong enough to cut the stuff they serve as meat on here. Mind you,' he smiled, 'who can? I believe the carpenter has a saw which may serve.'

Auchard seemed intent on a one-man mutiny. Eustache and Auchard played their form of blind man's buff all over the ship; on the quarter-deck, where Auchard was politely refused command by Derray and escorted off by sailors who a day before would tremble before him; on the foredeck, where the surviving foc's'l men were on watch and refused his invitation to rebel; eventually to the lower deck which echoed like an empty chamber when in his blindness and ignorance he called the names of men who were already dead, while those who heard him rocked in their sleeping hammocks in dumb silence. Eventually, commanded there by the Second, Eustache led Auchard by the arm to the gun-deck and the reconstructed Captain's sleeping quarters. They climbed past Cotterell and Tom on the companionway.

Cotterell stood and said quietly to Tom, 'I want to see this.'

They followed Auchard and Eustache through the wreckage of the ship into the Captain's cabin, where Charles and Emily were reading charts spread over the great table there, as ordered by Dubarre. Auchard of course saw none of this, nor did he see Cotterell feigning a lack of interest in the charts. Cotterell could see from a glance that the chart workings were out of date.

Eustache sneered at the black man and the American wife, 'We have come to see the Captain.'

Dubarre's bunk was in a cuddy adjacent to the cabin. There he moaned and tossed but couldn't rise from the cot unaided.

'What do you want, Auchard?' he asked when he saw the Second enter the cuddy.

'You are indisposed, Citizen,' said Auchard.

'And?'

'I believe you should cede command of the ship to me.'

'Do you?'

'Yes, Citizen. It is in the code.'

'Do you think I'm mad? Give my ship to a blind man? I am not *that* indisposed.'

'Capitaine Dubarre, I must insist . . .'

'Go to your berth, Auchard. I command the ship. Derray acts for me.'

'How?'

'What do you mean – how?'

'How can a Bosco command for the Captain?'

'Have you taken leave of your senses, man?' Dubarre asked politely and softly. He was always at his most dangerous when he was calm. 'Do you think you can question me, because I am injured?'

'If you recover I would hand back command, of course ...'

'If I recover ... so you have it planned.'

'Of course, Citizen Dubarre.'

'Derray commands because I say he does.'

'But I'm your Second. It's my role.'

'Get out, you cretin!' bawled Dubarre in a sudden and complete burst of fury. The wooden chamber reverberated as if someone had fired a gun. 'Get out.'

Auchard didn't move. 'They say you are shot in the back.' His voice was cold and harsh. Dubarre's reply was expressed gently again. But it didn't lack menace.

'They say ... but you wouldn't know, would you, Auchard?'

'How long will you last, Capitaine. Just how long? They will have to come to me soon.' Auchard leaned over Dubarre, wagging his finger for emphasis. It looked like he might attack Dubarre and this was too much even for revolutionary Eustache, who barred the Second with his free hand.

'Citizen,' Eustache hissed. 'Take care.'

'If the Captain is indisposed the Second commands,' insisted Auchard. 'It's the law.'

In the great cabin beyond Dubarre's cuddy Emily and Charles stood up. Their chairs scraped as they rose.

'Get out of here,' said Dubarre. 'Get out or I'll have you tied to the rigging for a week, blind man or not. Get out!'

'I know what is going on.' Auchard began to fumble around the little room. 'It's that whore, isn't it? She's here somewhere, poisoning your mind.'

'Out!'

'I know she's here. I can smell her,' said Auchard. 'Who else wears scent on this ship?'

Cotterell stood in the cuddy doorway watching. LeBlanc pushed past him with two fit sailors.

'Come on sir. Rest in your cabin.' LeBlanc said to Auchard.

'Who's that?' asked Auchard. 'Who's that? LeBlanc?'

A sailor took him from Eustache.

'Don't you touch me, LeBlanc. Let go of me.' Said Auchard. LeBlanc indicated that the sailor should lead the blind man to the companionway.

'Put him in a cabin on the lower deck and look after him there,' he said. They all filed out.

As Eustache left he caught Cotterell's eye.

'It's your fault,' he said quietly. 'All your fault. If most of the crew had their way . . .'

'Who is that?' asked Dubarre, who'd overheard from his cuddy.

'Just a seaman, mon Commandant.' LeBlanc replied.

'Which?'

'Me,' said Eustache. 'Eustache Verney. I accompanied the Second.'

'So you did. 'Me' did you say?'

'For brevity, Citizen.'

'How long have you been under my command, Eustache Verney?' came the voice from the cot in the darkened sleeping quarters.

'Months, Citizen.'

'Long enough to know how to address me?'

'I use the revolutionary forms, Citizen Commander. I intend no discourtesy.'

Outside in the great cabin, observed by Cotterell, Charles and Emily, Auchard tried to move, stumbled, then called, 'Where's my man? I can't see a damn thing here. Eustache? Eustache?'

'I must go, Capitaine,' said Eustache. Now he was desperate for the conversation to end. He knew where Dubarre was leading him.

'Have I dismissed you?'

'No Citizen.'

'Where is he?' called Auchard from the great cabin. 'Eustache? Eustache?'

Eustache was eye-to-eye with the Captain. 'If you don't mind, I was just telling the truth.'

'Am I weakened because I'm wounded and in this cot?'

'Citizen?'

'It's a simple enough question,' said Dubarre. 'Am I no longer your Captain because I'm wounded and on my back in this cot?' It was almost a whisper in the darkness. Eustache couldn't see Dubarre's face, but he was no fool. He knew his Captain was a dangerous man.

'But I don't know what you mean, Citizen Commandant.'

Dubarre was in pain. He could feel cold sweat running down his face. But he would not lose control of his ship.

'I have killed dozens of my crew today, Eustache Verney, by fighting the British. Most were better men than you. Do you understand?'

There was silence.

'Do you understand?' Dubarre repeated.

'Yes, Citizen.'

'Do not allow yourself to believe, even for a moment, that I would hesitate to spill your blood too.'

'The Convention orders, Citizen . . .'

'Bosco! Hold him!' shouted Dubarre.

LeBlanc grabbed Eustache.

'Damn the Convention, Monsieur,' spat Dubarre, 'and damn you. I command on this ship. I command. One more word of insubordination and I will have you hanged from the rigging right now, right at this moment, without regret or a second thought.'

They stood in silence for a moment, not knowing whether they could move. The seriousness of Dubarre's threat had frozen them. They were under no illusion, he meant it. Outside Charles looked at Emily. Auchard left, making his way alone along the deck, barking his shins and cursing, pushing sailors out of his way.

'Begging your pardon, mon Commandant,' said Eustache in a belated show of humility. 'Begging your pardon . . .'

In the cot Dubarre waved weakly at Eustache. 'Shut up.' Then to the boatswain, 'Bosco. Tie him to the rigging. Windward, mind you, not leeward.'

'Mon Commandant. For how long, mon Commandant?'

'Until I say.' Said the ice-cold voice in the dark.

In the great cabin Cotterell found himself alone with Charles. They were both exhausted but Cotterell wanted to see the chart.

'Mr Cotterell,' said Charles, 'we are lost.'

'Lost sir?'

'We have Mr Auchard's calculation of our position for some days ago, fixed while the sun shone. No one can calculate where we are now.'

A long silence followed, which Charles broke by saying, 'Will you?'

'Me?'

'Calculate.'

'I am a poor English clerk.'

'They all know what you are. They can see it. It was obvious from the first moment you set foot on this ship. You are an English sailor and your smooth hands say 'officer'. You owe them your life. They saved you. Now save them. For pity's sake.'

The sea slopped against the hull, unbroken and calm. Cotterell had heard French sailors say the cannon-fire calms it. He went to the stern gallery. Dawn was breaking. To the west a mackerel sky reflected back orange bars from the rising sun. Even in the early light the sky looked more crisp than usual. Cotterell knew what the mackerel sky and crisp-looking air meant. He remembered the loss of *l'Imprevu* and a shiver ran down his spine. She was much bettered prepared than the *Hortense*.

'Won't you?' asked Charles.

Still Cotterell didn't answer. If he saved the ship it meant saving Dubarre too.

'We'll all die, man,' said Charles. 'Innocent and guilty together. Is that right?'

At last Cotterell spoke. 'You are mistaken, sir. I can't help you. I'm not the man you think I am.'

'No, you are not,' said Charles. He pushed back his chair, stood and left the cabin. Cotterell was alone. There was a sound. Emily emerged from the Captain's sleeping quarters.

'You were lucky, being found by this ship,' she said.

'I have lived several weeks longer than expected. But you may have noticed what kind of creature a man is. As soon as we find we are not dead yet, we want to live for ever. Well, it can't be done. There is an end to everything.'

'Look about you, sir. The ship is a wreck. The Captain is almost dead. Half the crew is gone. You have won.'

'Me?'

'You English. King George doesn't need everyone to die, surely.'

Cotterell looked at her in the half light. He thought about his father. He thought about Dubarre. The ship still smelled of gore. She went to speak again, but he held up his hand and said, 'These ports will need to be shuttered. There's a storm coming.'

15

Before the storm came, they reached soundings. They had swung a lead since dawn. The sailor who was responsible felt the tremble of the line as it touched bottom. Richter, the sailor, was a small dark-haired man from Dunkirk who had served a lifetime on merchant ships before being pressed by the Navy, and wanted to be sure before he called it. He pulled the lead up a few fathoms and then let it fall again. The same sudden lessening of weight came into his skilful and sensitive hands. It had touched, and the sensation carried quite distinctly up the seventy or so fathoms of line in the sea. The shiver of the line's movement through the resisting water was quite different from the drag of the lead weight on the ocean floor. Richter checked the length of cord they had out with his lead-swinging mate, then turned, filled his lungs and called, so that everyone on the *Hortense* could hear, '*Fond! Fond! Soixante-huit brasses! Mouiller de soixante-huit brasses d'eau!*'

Sixty-eight fathoms of water lay between the keel of the *Hortense* and the continental shelf. But where on that shelf were they? Somewhere to the east or possibly north-east of them was England. Somewhere to the south and east was France. The distances were indeterminate, but Cotterell wasn't unduly concerned. Though the possible size of inaccuracy in their reckoned position grew by the minute, they had travelled only a couple of days since Auchard had fixed their location from the sun and the clock. And there was plenty of sea room from the first soundings to the first land, whether that land was Cornwall or Ireland. Their main task now was to save *Hortense* from being overwhelmed by weather, and to keep her from finding the land in darkness. If they blundered into a position where the ship was on a lee shore she would be in no condition to claw off.

In the Captain's day cabin, Cotterell and Derray consulted a chart together. Cotterell had a great cloth around his head covered by a scarf so he looked like a white sepoy. Derray's arm was massively bound against bleeding. They seemed almost comical, though their situation was very serious. The chart was spread on the great table in the centre of the cabin and the Captain's dining chairs, such as had survived the sea-chase and battle, were pushed to one side. Holding down one side of the chart was a box of navigation instruments, bound with brass bands. Holding down the other was the leather and buckram-bound ship's log. Cotterell took a protractor, a wooden rule and a stick of graphite from the instrument box.

'We are somewhere along here.' Cotterell drew a line with his finger along the western approaches. 'This is where the lead line finds the bottom.'

'We can't be more precise?' asked Derray, meaning 'you can't?'

'No.'

'Our lives will depend on it.' Derray said.

Cotterell looked at Derray but didn't answer. Every navigator knows that at some point his life will depend on it. Cotterell had been well taught as his father's apprentice. Derray didn't trust Cotterell. He had no choice but to do so, and that made him feel very vulnerable. He felt it was sure to go wrong and, having gone wrong, would rebound on him. He hadn't spent all these years getting to this point, plucked from the ranks to be a temporary officer on a ship of the French Navy, just to have the cup dashed from his lips. But Derray had little choice. He couldn't navigate. Derray could sign his name and read script, but he wasn't fluent. His poor reading certainly would not allow him to interpret a chart. Derray was a serious-looking young man and furrowed his brow as he focussed on the chart, which may as well have been covered with carpenter's or mason's hiero-glyphs as far as he was concerned. He had never even seen such a document close to before. He glared at the paper, willing the hieroglyphs into his mind. Cotterell pointed to one end of the imaginary line he had drawn with his finger.

'Four days ago Citizen Auchard took a sight and fixed this place on the chart. He had no further opportunities for fixes because of cloud covering the sky.'

'Can *you* work the device to measure the sun's angle, Cotterell?'

'Yes.'

'We could do it now.'

'It has to be at the apparent solar noon.'

'Has to be?'

'For simplicity the tables are set for noon, when I can shoot the sight and find the position in one simple calculation. There are other methods to get the fix . . .'

'How?'

'We don't have time for them now.'

'But still, how?'

'I can measure the angle from stars, or even the moon, and calculate a running fix, but I need several hours to do that and some more time to calculate. And there is no moon and stars out there.' Cotterell pointed through the window to the sky outside. It was late afternoon. The high clouds still spread evenly across the blue in waves, underlit with a golden, threatening light by the sun. 'From the look of the heavens the ship is unlikely to provide a steady platform for me to do that tonight. And we need to make a plan now. So we use the information we have. Look,' he pointed again, 'twenty-four hours before we fought the English frigate *Circe*, Auchard estimated our position here, 47°24' of latitude and 17°28' of longitude. It's in the navigation log. If he was accurate . . .'

'Do you doubt it?'

'Not at all. But we can all make mistakes in this matter. It doesn't take much. That's why a good captain checks his navigator's sums.' They both knew there was no chance Dubarre had done this.

Cotterell went on, 'By extension from Auchard's workings, which I presume for now are accurate, when we fought we were approximately two hundred miles west and north from Brest. There is no reason to doubt Auchard's ability with a divider, but remember it is only an estimation. We could have been here, here or here.' He pointed around Auchard's mark on the chart. 'And the form of his mark indicates this. Since then we have been sailing north and east, to escape the British. How many miles do we sail in a day?'

'I don't know,' said Derray. He'd never considered the matter. It simply wasn't his task on ship.

'How fast does *Hortense* travel through the water?'

'We were sailing at five knots to keep our station with the convoy. The Captain was very particular.' That *was* Derray's job so he knew about it.

'Does one hundred or one hundred and twenty miles a day sound right?'

'Yes. It must.'

'But which?' asked Cotterell. 'One hundred, or one hundred and twenty?'

'I don't know,' said Derray.

Cotterell pointed to the open page of the ship's log. 'But I saw men running the log off the quarter-deck.'

'I ordered it.' Derray said proudly.

'Who wrote down the result?'

'The clerk or the officer.'

'Auchard or Cordell?'

'Usually.'

'It's not noted in the ship's log. Is this Auchard's hand?'

'I don't know. I can't read handwriting very easily, as you well know. But I know who kept the ship's records. Cordell, the Captain's clerk wrote that book up every day from rough notes he kept.'

'Where is Cordell?'

'Dead. Killed by the British frigates.'

'Where are the rough notes?'

'No one knows. Gone.'

Cotterell shook his head. He sat by the table on a dining chair, sighed and ran his hand across the chart, as if the deeps and lands could be felt. Cordell was beyond questions and Auchard seemed deranged. Dubarre was dying. Questions seemed superfluous.

'You see where the vagueness comes in.' Cotterell said to the former boatswain. Derray didn't see, no matter how able he was at handling ship, sails and crew. Cotterell went on, 'Twenty miles more or less a day is sixty miles in three days, which is a second of arc out.' He pointed again at the chart. 'One hundred miles north east from Auchard's mark, which may or may not be correct, is approximately here. Give or take sixty miles.' He made a mark on the chart with the graphite stick. 'Considering how much store the Captain sets by sailing an accurate course, and discounting any current, we should consider this area very likely as our position before we fought the frigate. Agreed?'

Derray nodded thoughtfully. He agreed. He had no choice. Cotterell drew a circle around the place he'd been indicating.

'Before the pursuit we were somewhere in that circle. When we ran before the British ...'

'... we continued north east. The Captain commanded it.'

'Eight knots?'

'Yes.'

'Six hours?'

'Seven.'

Cotterell marched dividers across the chart. 'So we fought about here?' He pointed to the chart again and drew a bigger circle.

'Yes,' said Derray. 'The circle is bigger.'

'It is an estimate, based on an estimate. It needs to be treated with a great deal of caution. I have not included an allowance for currents or for leeway.'

'So what's this?' asked Derray, pointing to the outline of Cornwall on the chart. He'd never looked closely at a chart before.

'Britain,' said Cotterell, 'and this is Ireland. And this is Brittany and there, Brest. And we are here between them and to the west. But none of it is certain.'

'What do you suggest?' asked Derray.

Cotterell pointed to the chart. 'Brest is somewhere to the south. But it is too dangerous to head that way. We need to approach it from the west. We don't want to find either the islands or the coast in the dark, and we are so uncertain of our position that we may do that. We don't want to find ourselves too far east at dawn and have to come back down the coast.'

'I know that coast.'

'Then you know it's dangerous. I don't want to beat west at all if I can avoid it, and I don't want to find ourselves having to creep around the coast and navigate the *Chenal du Four* in a broken-down ship.'

'You know the coast well.'

'Do you want my advice or not?'

Derray did. 'So what to do?'

'Ideally? We take *Hortense* to a point due west of Finisterre. We first raise the land in the morning, at a point where we're about fifteen miles out.'

'We would reach that point tonight?' asked Derray.

'No. It's too far. Tonight we could safely make all sail, if it were not for the weather. If we must go to Brest I suggest we make our best course south east tonight and tomorrow. Then tomorrow during darkness heave to, if we have not already seen the land. Then we should continue in this way until we find Finisterre. *If* it is in your orders that we *must* find Brest.'

'They are the Captain's orders.'

'But you are bound to them, aren't you?' asked Cotterell. He wanted Derray to say 'no'. Derray certainly didn't look as if he felt bound to Dubarre's orders.

'It's dangerous,' he said.

'Well, Captain Derray, it's all dangerous. But I think if we try to work this ship into Brest the odds are much better that we will fail than that we will succeed.'

'Are there alternatives?' Derray asked.

'To continue on our present course may take us into the bay of Mont St Michel.'

'*May*, you say?'

'You only know more or less where you are, sir. Given our condition I would not recommend entering the bay. We are not able to claw off and find sea room again if we become embayed with contrary weather.'

Derray nodded sagely. 'The bay is a ships' graveyard.'

'Then we must head a little to the north of our present course, which direction may take us to Cherbourg or Le Havre du Grace. Another day's sail would reach Cherbourg, two Le Havre.'

'You sound as if you prefer that.'

'I do.'

'What would be the advantage of that course?'

'Two good ports open to the west we can enter, no matter what the condition of either the ship or the sea. Plenty of opportunity along the way to find ourselves. Cherbourg is attractive. Deep water off, no reefs once we have avoided the Casquets, which are lit with a brazier, complete shelter once we reach the harbour, a great deal of room to manoeuvre.'

'You know it well.'

Cotterell did not reply.

'For Cherbourg wouldn't we have to pass before the British Channel fleet?' asked Derray.

'They are not off Cherbourg or Le Havre. They are in the Atlantic, hammering Vanstabel's convoy, just as they hammered us.'

Derray thought about it, rubbing his chin. 'What do you recommend now, right now, as a course?' he asked.

'Head east. There will be more sea room. We will have a better chance to see the coast and establish our exact position. We will allow an opportunity for the sun to emerge and give us an indication of where we are.'

'You are certain we won't meet the English coast.'

'I am not. I think we *should* not. But nothing is sure in navigation until you are tied up in harbour. Discuss it with the Captain and give me your instructions.' Cotterell indicated the door to the Captain's sleeping cabin behind them.

'He is indisposed. I must decide,' said Derray.

'Is the problem the ship's orders?'

'I haven't seen them, and daren't ask the Captain for fear of being lashed to the rigging, like Eustache.'

'Whatever the orders are,' said Cotterell, 'you will serve no one if you don't save the ship.'

Derray leaned on the chart and considered again, fists on the chart supporting his weight as he did so. Above them Cotterell could hear shouts, thumps and the sounds of men heaving masts and rigging. Derray had ordered the top parts of the two remaining standing masts struck. A gale was clearly coming, though the sea outside the windows was quite calm for now. Cotterell would have merely reefed. The boatswain was a very careful sailor, but he was in command of a near-wreck and the responsibility weighed heavily upon him.

'I will make it east.' Derray said. 'It is more important to save the ship than make our intended port. We're not carrying corn. Just men.'

He stood. Cotterell rolled the chart. Derray watched him. He couldn't resist saying. 'The Captain had you down for a ship's officer since you first spoke.'

'Did he?'

If the French Captain had had any idea how far he stood into danger he'd have tossed Cotterell back into the sea straight away, or left him chained in the nask until they reached France. As if responding to Cotterell's mind, Dubarre moaned behind the lime-painted door.

'Will he live?' asked Cotterell.

Derray shook his head. He touched Cotterell's back. 'He was hit by canister balls. One entered here and travelled down and out. You can see the path. The other went in here.' He touched the small of Cotterell's back now. 'But has not emerged. I've never seen anyone survive such injuries.'

Cotterell was disappointed. He needed Dubarre to survive. There could be no revenge on a dead man. Derray mistook the look for sadness.

'It comes to everyone in his turn, my English friend. Will you help me?' asked Derray.

'I'll help you save lives. That's all.'

'You are a ship's captain or navigator, Cotterell. Where did you get that skill?' Derray asked.

Cotterell looked at the lime-painted door again. Dubarre was beyond his reach now, he decided.

'On a fishing boat,' said Cotterell.

Derray smiled. 'I knew it. Seconde Auchard said you were Royal Navy but the Captain said you were a Jersey fisherman. They wagered.'

'How much?'

'Thirty ecus.'

'Not revolutionary money?'

'No. The Captain is very traditional when it comes to money. He prefers gold or silver.'

Cotterell laughed.

'Did no one think I was a clerk?'

'No one.'

He turned away. Cotterell opened a drawer in the cabin's sideboard and stowed the chart, the log and the box of instruments. When he turned again Derray had gone. Cotterell heard his voice calling orders on deck. It was unnecessary. LeBlanc was perfectly competent.

Cotterell was left alone in the Captain's great cabin. He sat in the armchair and stared at the door into the sleeping cabin. Not a sound came from beyond the door now. Cotterell thought about Dubarre, about his father and the dead Goffs floating in the Newfoundland surf. He considered for a moment going into the Captain's sleeping cabin. He needed a reckoning with the man. Something held him back for now. He didn't know what. Perhaps for the first time since *l'Imprevu* went down, his own life meant something. He had survived the sea, and then survived a battle with a warship, both against the odds. Cotterell wondered if he was fated. He certainly knew he needed to see the story of the *Hortense* played right out. He needed to be part of it. Cotterell had found her, or she him, two specks attracted in an ocean. God, or whatever more logical being with which the French had replaced him, had brought man and ship together especially for the purpose. And Tom was right, *Hortense* was the world turned upside down, like France. She had no Captain, more than three-quarters of her crew were dead, and Derray could hardly raise forty uninjured men out of those left alive. *Hortense* couldn't fight again. The half-wrecked warship depended on Cotterell, if those aboard her were ever to safely gain the shore. She had saved him, and apparently now he must save her. Instead of owing God a life he now owed it to a ship. Cotterell had resisted the idea until this moment, though it had always been there. Even now his mind was partly revolted at the thought of delivering Auchard, Dubarre, Lefèvre and Charles to safety. His dealings with the traitorous negro, as Charles must surely be seen in England, disturbed Cotterell most. The two men had formed a respectful, confessional relationship of a sort Cotterell couldn't define. If Charles hated the English enough to go to war with them, and God knew he had good reason, why was he so sympathetic and easy to Cotterell? The Jerseyman found the African an enigma, but a strangely familiar one.

Before the battle Cotterell had wanted them all to go to the bottom of the ocean, and so defeat both his own and the King's enemies in one stroke. But what were the crew of the *Hortense*, but men and women? They had rescued him, fed him and shared their experiences for better or worse. They had given him the clothes on his back. Cotterell knew that the longer he spent aboard the ship the more these French terrorist sailors became people, humans with faces. They all had fates he could influence. He could save them. He remembered the faces looking up towards him from the deck, before Lefèvre had fallen. Their upturned faces had looked like children's, had seemed so far from the madness of France, or the ferocity of their songs and their guillotines. What reason was there to let every man jack aboard drown, including himself? None. The ship was flotsam tossed across the ocean. The men and women aboard her had fought and struggled against their fate, repaired her, cherished her and clung to her boards, just as a man clings to his nation, whether he lives in his country or elsewhere. Though he was the complete antigallican, and would fight the French to the last drop of his blood, Cotterell knew he was bonded to the men and women of the *Hortense* and their fate. In the matter of nations, Cotterell thought, we sink or swim together. In the matter of ships, the same rule applies. *Hortense* was a nation and he was part of her.

16

Cotterell stood again in Dubarre's cuddy. A trickle of blood had run from Dubarre's body and dried on the side of the cot. It looked like a dribble of misplaced paint staining the lime-white woodwork. The Captain was asleep in his cot, but the Jerseyman spoke anyway.

'I am Jean Cotterell,' he said.

Dubarre opened his eyes and smiled. 'The Chouan[1]? Don't look surprised. We get the papers here in Charleston, sir, even if they are delayed.'

'We're not in Charleston.'

'You are not the Chouan?'

'No. Who is he?'

'An anti-revolutionary. They're looking for him everywhere. All ports are closed to him. He has been condemned to death in his absence.'

'Has he?'

'The paper we had in Charleston said.'

'I thought you couldn't read.'

'Who told you that?' asked Dubarre, fiercely.

'It's a view commonly held by the crew.'

'What do they know?'

Cotterell said nothing.

---

[1] Jean Cottereau (also known as Jean Chouan) was an anti-revolutionary resistance leader in the area of Fougéres and Laval. He was active until the summer of 1794.

'Anyway,' Dubarre went on, 'I used to have a Charleston whore read to me. Hélène. So whether I read or not isn't the issue. Wait till Lefèvre hears we have been sheltering a counter-revolutionary.'

'Listen to me, Capitaine. I'm Jean Cotterell from Jersey.'

Dubarre looked disappointed. 'You've never been to the Couesnon?'

'No.'

Dubarre closed his eyes for a moment and smiled to himself. When he opened them again Cotterell was leaning over him. 'Ah the Couesnon,' he said. 'Many is the happy hour I spent fishing on its banks as a child. It's my home. All gone now. All gone. I won't see it again. Have you been there?'

'No.'

'But am I mistaken? You are from there?'

Which didn't quite make sense to Cotterell. It wasn't a mistake so much as an entire illogical departure from the Captain. He leaned forward and touched Dubarre's brow. The movement was like bursting through a membrane. Like gutting a fish. Dubarre's brow was cold and beaded with sweat. The Frenchman's eyes closed briefly as Cotterell touched. Then he looked directly into Cotterell's eyes.

'Well?'

'No.' Said Cotterell.

'But you are Jean Chouan.'

'No.'

'Ah, you lie,' said Dubarre in a matter-of-fact way. 'They are known to be big liars, the Chouans. It's a characteristic of anti-revolutionaries. That, and a lack of 'civism'.'

His watery grey eyes focussed on Cotterell's for a time, as if Cotterell was the one speaking nonsense and Dubarre the one seeking signs of normality in him. Neither man moved.

'Civism?' asked Cotterell.

'Commitment to France. To the Revolution.'

'Then civism has nothing to do with it. I am from Jersey,'

answered Cotterell, and I am utterly antigallican, leave alone anti-revolutionary.'

'But we have met before?' asked the Captain. And he sniggered softly at some joke inside himself. Cotterell could see no reason for laughter. Dubarre went on, 'What makes an anti-revolutionary Chouan, eh? What have you got against us?'

'Us?'

'The Revolution.'

'There is no 'us', Captain. 'Us' is a delusion.'

'We are the Revolution.'

'Are you?' asked Cotterell.

'Ask any of my crew.'

'The Revolution is nothing but a collection of thieves and blackguards allowed license to rob, ruin and execute good men and women.'

'Oh-ho. Daring words, Jean. Now we see your true face.'

'You were a privateer. What else is this Revolution but a whole country gone privateering with neither moral force nor conscience?'

'Ungrateful cunt. I saved you from the sea. I hove my ship to and plucked you out when you were dead. You shut your mouth or ... or ... or I will have you lashed to the rigging.'

'No you won't. I will cut your throat first.'

Cotterell took out his knife. He meant it.

'Stop that Jean Chouan,' said Dubarre. '*Arrete ta Chouannerie*, Jean.' He laughed a hollow laugh again while Cotterell looked on in silence. 'Thank you. And now a little drop of Calva, I think,' said Dubarre. There was no Calvados and no glass in the cabin, which was bare, apart from the cot and a chair. Cotterell continued to look down on the Captain, knife in his hand.

'Just imagine, eh?' said Dubarre. 'The world is all within our reach, neither of us knowing what would happen after.'

'After?'

'You don't listen,' spat Dubarre, with venom.

He didn't make any sense to Cotterell. There was a silence

between them for a while, then the Jerseyman said, 'It's not by the Couesnon you will have heard my name, but on a beach in Newfoundland.'

Another silence. Cotterell looked at the knife in his hand. He should use it. Then the world, somehow, would be in balance again. Dubarre looked at the knife too.

'Have you ever cut a man's throat?' asked Dubarre. Cotterell didn't answer. 'I thought not,' continued Dubarre. 'It feels like cutting silk. Quite unique. Once you've felt it and heard the sound it never leaves you.'

Dubarre seemed completely lucid again, though ordinary conversation with the Captain always took its own tortuous and highly particular course.

'You killed my father in Hope Bay.'

'Where is Hope Bay?'

'Newfoundland. I should kill you.'

'One of your countrymen has already laid claim to that honour, my young friend. I am killed. Instead, you will have the duty of transporting my body to France, should you wish it.' Dubarre winced in pain and closed his eyes again. 'I don't think a burial by the Couesnon will work, do you? Perhaps they'll find me a corner among the monks in the Mont St Michel. Have you been there?'

'No.'

'Nor I, since I was a small boy. Though we could see it rise above the marshes from the fields where I was raised. I went to Granville to go to sea and find my fortune and I never went back. I suppose Coutances would be too much to hope for.' His voice trailed off, as if he was musing where he might build a cathedral. In his mind Dubarre had a rather grand tomb waiting for him. But where?

'I have money, you know.'

'I expect you have.'

'Ask Derray.'

'I won't help you.'

Dubarre ignored him. 'Or there's a little corner in a little church outside Pontorson. That would be nice. Do you know Pontorson?'

'No.'

'I'd be among friends there. Welsh archers and English adventurers. The scum of the earth.'

'I was on *l'Imprevu*,' said Cotterell.

Dubarre spoke with his eyes still closed. 'What is *l'Imprevu*?'

'That which is unforeseen.' Cotterell said in English. 'A St Helier Terre-Neuvian. A small cod fishing boat. She belonged to my father.'

'And she's called 'the unforeseen,' eh? He's a wag.'

'He's dead.'

'Cotterell, eh? First name?'

'Jean-Jacques.'

'I'll pass on your regards when I see him.'

'He had a crew of four, plus me as the boy. You killed them in Hope Bay.'

'When?'

'Seventy-six.'

'No.'

'You must remember.'

'I do not.'

'A black hull. She was called *l'Imprevu* and you burned her down to the ribs.'

'I don't remember.'

'You were on the *Galipétan*. You killed my father, two Cornish sailors from *l'Imprevu* and pressed two others. Dumaresq and Gallichan.'

'Dumaresq?'

'Yes. Do you remember him?'

But now Dubarre seemed to sleep again. The wind whistled outside. The seas built. Cotterell had to grab a beam to stop himself tumbling as the ship lurched for the first time. He dropped his knife. It slid across the deck. This was it. The storm was coming in. Dubarre stayed reclined and apparently comfortable, with his eyes closed and the very beginnings of a smile on his lips. Was he dead? Cotterell wondered. He could be. He was ghastly pale. There was a little chair near the cot with Dubarre's coat on it. Cotterell took up the coat and sat. He felt hot bitter tears in his eyes and on his cheeks. He missed his father and even saying the words, that Jean-Jacques had been murdered by this wretch, hurt more than he could have imagined before he spoke. He had never said them aloud before. He dropped the coat to his lap and rubbed his face with his hands. Outside he could hear the wind howling in the rigging. Inside the ship the pumps creaked over and over, almost without pause. Creak creak, creak creak, creak, creak. It sounded like a giant in new boots was marching between decks.

Cotterell clasped the coat in his lap. There was blood on it, and a ragged hole where the shot had entered the Captain's body. The coat was sticky with blood. He felt for his knife again. It was now or never.

'You killed my father.'

Dubarre didn't respond. Cotterell shook him. Dubarre didn't wake. Cotterell punched Dubarre in the chest, once, twice. Still no response. Cotterell lifted the Captain from his cot and shook him.

'Wake up. Wake up, you bastard.' But the Captain was dead. A large sticky pool of his blood was congealing on the cotton ticking of the little mattress below him. His life had bled out while they spoke. Cotterell had hold of the Captain by his shirt front. The man's head lolled backwards and his mouth was open, revealing rotten teeth. He was unshaven and stank, even now, of strong drink. His plaited hair hung over his shoulder. Cotterell was seized by a desire to wake Dubarre to kill him again.

'What are you doing?' asked Liberté behind him. She held two crocks, one of soup and one of water, both gripped through the handles in her right hand while she supported herself with her left against the doorframe. She wore no bonnet rouge now and she stood with one hip cocked as she braced herself against the ship's movement and waited for Cotterell's reply, though she knew what it would be.

'He is dead,' replied Cotterell. He let Dubarre go. The body fell back. The head cracked like a wooden bowl on the edge of the cot. 'So that is that.'

Cotterell bent and picked up his knife and Dubarre's coat. He tucked the knife in his belt, then folded the coat carefully and placed it on the chair. The garment seemed smaller in his hands now its owner was dead. Liberté hadn't moved. Cotterell looked into the crocks, took the soup from her, drank a few mouthfuls, then handed it back.

'Are the topmasts down?'

'Yes.'

'All secure?'

'As much as LeBlanc and Derray can make it.'

'The pumps keeping up?'

'Yes.'

'Sick and injured secured?'

'Secured? How should they be secured?'

'Tied up in a bundle if you have to. Lashed into their hammocks. If they won't have that put them in irons.'

'The *sick*?'

'We don't want to fight a storm in a crippled ship with amputees and dead men rolling about the place.'

'I'll get it done.'

He kissed her. She responded. He thought, for some reason, of toothless Hélène, peppered with splinters like an American porcupine.

'Who brought your lover aboard?'

'*Who*?'

'La belle Hélène.'

'She's not my lover.'

'The entire lower deck believe she is.'

'I expect they do, Cotterell. They'll believe anything. Not long ago they believed other men should rule and tax them. Men are like children.'

'And women?'

She shook her head. 'I don't know why I'm talking to you.'

'They are frightened of you, the sailors,' he said, 'when the two of you go into the byre.'

'Frightened? Why?'

'When Liberté delved and Hélène span, who was then the gentleman.' He spoke in English.

'What? Translate it.'

'I can't. They think when you two are alone you are delving into each other. You are dealing in dark secrets.'

'We talk.'

'You talk?'

'We sit in the byre with the animals and talk. And Capitaine Dubarre brought her aboard, is the answer to your question.'

'Why?'

'She was trapped in America with no money, and no way of getting to France. He felt sorry for her, I believe.'

'Can she read?'

'Read? Of course. She loves to read, and write too. We are not all ignorant fools, no matter what your government tells you.'

'Almost none of you are ignorant fools, I find. That is the trouble.' Cotterell went past her, walking away through the great cabin and onto the deck. Underfoot the deck heaved as he walked He could hear the tiller men struggling below his feet. He had to hold the rail as he climbed to the quarter-deck. He didn't look back once. On deck Derray stood with a 'helmsman', the two looking down at the boxed compass lashed to the deck and then looking in turns at the horizon. The sky was dark and brooding now. The sea was grey and filled with white capped waves. Spray was beginning to fly off the wave-tops. Cotterell stood next to Derray and pointed to the deck below his feet, meaning the cabin below that.

'The Captain is dead,' he said simply. Derray walked away, to the windward side of the quarter-deck, and leaned against the rail there looking out over the waves. After a few moments Cotterell followed. Eustache, lashed to the rigging, watched them both.

'You have to be the Captain now.'

'I know,' answered Derray, then he could contain himself no longer. 'I sailed with him since I was a boy.' He wept for a moment, then recovered himself.

'I'd imagined you were regular navy,' said Cotterell in surprise.

'No. Just Dubarre's boatswain.' Derray bowed his head against the rail, like an old-fashioned penitent in church. Cotterell looked at the former boatswain, bent in a moment of grief and appre-hension. He saw the boy at sea, as he himself had once been. He couldn't resist a question.

'So, if you were with him when you were a boy, you were on the *Galipétan*?' asked Cotterell.

'You've heard of her?'

'Yes.'

'As a youngster. I was. Dubarre took me in. I don't have any parents and had made my way from Paris to Dunkirk, hoping to get a place on a ship.'

'Do you remember cruising Newfoundland?'

'Yes. Many times.'

'You burned a fishing boat. *L'Imprevu*.'

'When?'

'Seventy-six.'

'I was on board then. Just. Was it British?'

'Yes.'

'We burned many British fishing boats.'

'Two men were pressed from her. Gallichan . . .'

'Dumaresq came from a fishing boat,' Derray interrupted, '. . . with Gallichan. He died. He fell from the rigging in a storm.'

'Dumaresq?'

'Gallichan. He died at my feet. Dumaresq is the captain of an American privateer now. I saw him only last winter in Charleston. Do you know him?'

'This Dumaresq is from Jersey. He speaks French perfectly. He has an accent which sounds like Dubarre's. He speaks English too.'

'The same man. He was a particular favourite of Capitaine Dubarre. I never knew he went to Halifax. Did you know him?'

'I knew his grandson.' He thought of little Thibault. Cotterell turned and found himself eye-to-eye with Eustache.

'Is he fit?' he asked Derray over his shoulder, meaning Eustache.

'He has an injury to his arm.'

'We need every fit man, Captain Derray,' Cotterell said. He knew he had been the first to use the form of address. He turned and looked at Derray, who nodded. Cotterell took out his knife and crossed to Eustache. The Frenchman was soaked in spray.

'You held a knife at my throat once,' Cotterell said. He held the blade before Eustache's eye with one hand and gripped the rigging with the other. The pockmarked skin of the Frenchman's face blanched.

'Did I?' asked Eustache. His voice sounded like he had a brick in his throat.

The ship bowed to the sea. The spray flew even over the quarter-deck. Eustache kept his eye on the knife. The tip wobbled as Cotterell struggled to hold his position against the movement of the ship.

'If you threaten me again I won't hesitate to kill you.' Cotterell said.

'Perhaps you should do it now, while I'm trussed.'

Eustache knew he wasn't taking a risk.

'Not I,' said Cotterell, 'I'm British. But just because I release you now, don't think you're safe. I will kill you if I have to.'

Cotterell reached up above their heads and held the knife against the cord binding Eustache's hands. He sawed. Their faces were close, their bodies pressed together. Eustache's dislike of Cotterell poured out through his eyes. His skin seemed to reek of distain. Now his hands were free and he dropped them to his side. Both he and Cotterell were soaked in spray. Eustache made no attempt to move away.

'To your duties,' ordered Derray. Then he leaned over the rail and called, 'Bosco! All hands on deck. Every fit man on the gun-deck now!'

Eustache had left. Derray and the helmsman were alone with Cotterell. Derray explained, 'Someone has to tell them.'

17

The wind had moved to the south west. It blew a full gale. The sea heaped up, smashing and crashing against itself in the darkness outside of *Hortense*. Derray gave the news of the Captain's death, then ordered everyone not engaged in a task off the exposed decks and below. They should get in their hammocks if there was nowhere else to go. The crew cowered between decks. It wasn't an attempt to care for their comfort, or keep them dry. Derray simply did not want the risk of needlessly losing one of their few fit men. In any case there was little shelter, even below decks. The seas penetrated everywhere, streaming across the decks, foaming about the legs of the Captain and helmless helmsman and falling on those below deck. The crew were soaked wherever they stood or lay, and the misery of being soaked over and over with no hope of drying off was only relieved by the misery of turns on the pumps and the fear of being overwhelmed by the water rising steadily in the hold.

In the night the gale turned into a storm, and the storm swept the little ship over and over with sea water, punishing those aboard, pushing them to the edge of destruction. She rolled violently from side to side and seemed ever slower to recover. Men clutched at any handhold and, having found one, stayed there. Some lay on the deck for want of anywhere better to rest and be still. The rolling, yawing ship ran east. When there was any south in the wind she ran north east. They were moving further and further from France.

The spars were bare but presented a surface to the storm. The wind drove the ship at nine, ten, even eleven knots. Derray, screaming above the roar of sea and wind, wished out loud to Cotterell and LeBlanc that he had taken the spars down as well as the topmasts while they could. The sea was slowly wresting control of the ship from the men. They couldn't move freely about her, leave alone accomplish tasks. The cook doused the fires. The men on the tiller below the quarter-deck hung on for dear life and had little idea what instructions were passed down to them. Derray put away the box compass for fear of losing or smashing it. They couldn't set a course anyway. All they could do. was run with the wind and the seas, go where they were taken. There was no hope of making Brest or St Malo or any direction with south in it now, even if they'd wanted. Derray and Cotterell had taken the right decision to let the ship have her head. But where would it end?

Derray had the gun ports opened, so that the sea water might pass through and out of the opposing port rather than be trapped in her and swamp her. The vision of rising bilge water occupied them all. The ship was beginning to wallow, at least that's what the sailors convinced themselves. The change in motion is insidious. Both men and women pumped, continuing each spell on the pump handles as long and hard as they could manage. It wasn't long for any of them. There wasn't much space to organise a pump gang and those who crowded about the machines were exhausted before they took the handles. Their rest periods didn't allow enough time to recover, nor enough comfort in which to recover. They pumped until they were exhausted, and then the boatswain's mate would call down a new gang from their hammocks. The people of the *Hortense* pumped and pumped and pumped, but still the water rose, slowly, steadily. They strained at the handles until they fell down and rested on the deck beneath the pumps. When recovered enough to stand again they dragged themselves up and pumped with the strength of fear. There was a great deal of fear on the *Hortense*.

The misaine main sail, lashed to its spar, broke in the night and immediately tore, cracking like a wooden block splitting, sounding like a gun firing in the gloom above them, then letting forth a fusillade of smaller shot sounds as the canvas flapped and ripped. LeBlanc didn't hesitate, but immediately led a team of the fittest and most experienced seamen up into the darkness to cut it away. None refused. They knew it had to be done. The ship's rolling was now at its most violent. She felt as if at any moment she would refuse to recover. Derray clutched the quarter-deck rail. It was useless to give orders. The crew on deck watched LeBlanc and the others climb from the foredeck. Derray's crew were unable to hold a course, unable to meet a wave. The broach seemed imminent. The ship simply ran at more than ten knots with the Atlantic wind and waves around and above it. Each time *Hortense* rose from a wave she seemed to shake like a dog leaving the water. LeBlanc's climbing men rose from the dim light of the deck and disappeared into the night above. Tom was among them. Mixed rain and spray flew across the ship and rigging in sheets as they moved from the loom of the deck light into the gloom above. The only sound of their work was the ceasing of the gun-fire-like sounds from above, then one single awkward flap of the sail as it was swept away into the night. They went up empty-handed and came down the same way, gingerly and silently, like cats leaving a roof. They eased themselves back onto the deck as the ship's bow plunged again and the rigging trembled uncontrollably, trying to shake them off. They held on, then the sea greeted them with a renewed soaking.

'Well?' Cotterell asked Tom when he returned. He had to cup his hand to the matelot's ear to make him hear.

'It could be worse,' said Tom.

'How?'

Tom held onto the rail and thought about it while sea water swept about their knees, then left them as suddenly as it came. Eventually he nodded and yelled back. 'I'm considering.'

Cotterell went below.

'What happens if this continues?' Charles asked when Cotterell checked on the sick and wounded. Charles had abandoned the cockpit when the bilge water was swilling about his feet, carrying what medicines and possessions he could up to the lower deck. His 'patients' were already there, firmly tied into hammocks.

'It won't,' responded Cotterell. 'These things blow themselves out.'

'We found *you* in the sea.' Charles reminded him. 'Your ship turned over.'

'Do any of these speak English?' asked Cotterell, pointedly.

'I expect so.' said Charles.

'I'd rather not make it worse, if you follow my drift.' Cotterell indicated the bundled-up men in their hammocks. There was no way to know if they were asleep.

'So what has improved?' asked Charles.

'We are not being fired upon,' replied Cotterell. 'We are not being pursued by anyone. And we are not dead yet.'

Their situation could barely be worse, except if the crew panicked. Even the pounding from the British frigate had only been dangerous to *some* of the ship's people. This storm, if it continued, would kill them all.

At dawn, Cotterell was in the great cabin with the chart pinned down again. Tom fetched him coffee in a can with a lid on it, bracing himself and moving across the cabin like a drunk to deliver it. Cotterell was sitting before the table. Both his chair and the table shook and shuddered each time the ship descended and smashed into the face of another wave.

'This is the old man's special stuff, this. And it's made with the last of Pascal's hot water. So enjoy it,' he said as he passed Cotterell the can.

'Give it to one of the wounded.'

'They would rather you had it. They live in hopes you will save them.'

Cotterell sipped the lukewarm coffee, which had been

sweetened. 'Live in hopes, die of despair.' He smiled as he repeated the old saw, one of his grandfather's gloomy favourites.

'Is it so bad?'

'We can't steer the ship for fear of breaking her up. She is sinking no matter how much we pump. The crew are dead and dying and I am drinking the last of the dead Captain's coffee.'

'Is there no good news?'

'If we stay on this course I believe we will drown not far off the Isle of Wight.'

They both smiled.

'Does this dead captain fellow have any rum?' asked Tom.

'Brandy. In there.' Cotterell pointed to a cupboard. Tom opened it, took out a flask and poured himself a large cupful. He tasted.

'Good stuff, this is. Captain's brandy, no surgeon's muck.'

'Good stuff, Tom.' Cotterell repeated, mocking him gently. 'I seem to remember you thought the surgeon's stuff was above average. This ship is a regular floating vintners.'

'People think Jack Tar is the scum of the earth, but he can be as refined as the best of gentlemen. It is the opportunity to show off the good manners he is lacking.'

Tom took one more polite taste, then drank the cup of brandy down. He smacked his lips, dispensed with the cup and drank from the bottle. He stopped when he saw Cotterell looking at him. Tom looked as if he thought he'd been caught in something.

'Want some?'

'I have my coffee.'

'Is this all right?'

'If Derray doesn't catch you.'

'Will you tell him?'

'What do you think, Tom?'

'Nah.'

Tom took another swig, then put the flask away, closed the cupboard door, then changed his mind, took the flask out and drank again.

'I'm a *real* cap-a-barre,' he said, wiping his mouth with his hand. 'I'm a thieving matelot.'

'He won't miss it.' Cotterell indicated the sleeping cabin, where the dead Captain rested.

'I don't care. If we keep on taking water like this we can't last another twelve hours. So,' Tom continued, 'this is it. The end. I sit here drinking until their bloody old barky founders on the Owers.'

'Not if Derray or LeBlanc catches you.'

'I can only die once. Anyway,' Tom peered into the flask, 'it's nearly gone.'

He staggered to the cupboard as the ship lurched and put the flask away, then turned.

'How is the ship?' Cotterell asked.

'Awash in the hold. The ballast has shifted, which is why we are sailing a bit down on one ear. LeBlanc has men down there shifting it back with shovels. But it's ugly work. They are up to their chests in water. Some of the Frenchmen they buried in the ballast early in the cruise have shaken loose and are bobbing about in it, which makes it stink worse than you could imagine. The food is all gone foul and LeBlanc has had water butts hoisted up out of the hold, so that we may have something to drink at least. The fires are out in the stoves and will stay out for want of something to cook.'

'Any good news?'

'Oh it's not all despair. It's not far to go now, so we might be a bit hungry when we drown but we won't be starving. The fiddler broke his elbow falling down the stair so we won't have to listen to their wretched revolutionary songs any more. Instead Lefèvre sings your praises, as if you were his beloved Jeanbon whatever.'

'St André.' Cotterell offered.

'Himself. The revolutionaries are convinced you will save them. You are the new Robespierre that they love so much.'

'Is Lefèvre fit?' asked Cotterell.

'He's not mad, if that's what you ask. I think he'll live. He don't bleed and Mr Charles says the wound is clean. They have decided also to idolise the black because of his work with the wounded. He can do no wrong too.'

'Can he walk on water?'

'You can. In Mrs Lefèvre's mind you are as good as a Frenchie, which is saying something. Give her another day and she will convince herself you *are* a Frenchman.'

'Well I don't want to be. If anything I am anti-gallican.'

'Which is?' asked Tom, his vocabulary exceeded.

'Anti-*French*,' explained Cotterell.

'It'll be our secret. Derray and LeBlanc put their trust in you.'

'Then they are fools.'

'No. You know where we are.'

'I'm just not as thoroughly lost as they. How is Auchard?'

'Locked in his cabin.'

'With the American lady?'

'He never was, why start now? She has borrowed some pantaloons and works with the crew at the pumps. Half a day more and she will join the bonnet rouges. I think she is clearing her conscience so she meets her maker with a stainless soul. But her position has come from so many dead niggers and so much misery. I don't believe she can ever achieve it.'

The ship shuddered. A dribble of water ran through the deckhead where the tarred paying had parted.

'None of us chooses our parents. Neither you nor Madame Auchard.'

'You wouldn't want my father,' said Tom.

'He lives?'

'I believe so.'

'Then be grateful. Your parents are a long time gone.' Cotterell stood. 'I should take a turn on the pumps.'

'You should not. LeBlanc expressly says to leave you be. You are a precious commodity on this here ship. If they could wrap you in lint cloth and only fetch you out to work the navigation instruments I believe they would do so.'

A voice called indistinctly from the deck above.

'Did he say 'ship'?' asked Tom. Cotterell was already rolling the chart ready to leave.

18

The little British ship stayed with them until the wind dropped in the afternoon. She was about a mile off their starboard beam on a parallel heading. She had her topmasts rigged and the sails still bent on the spars, though furled. She looked smart and spanking-new compared to the floating wreck Cotterell stood upon. Though she was shaken and tossed by the sea her movements had a tightness and regularity which *Hortense* lacked. Cotterell presumed her bilge was dry.

Though the wind dropped, the seas did not. The little British ship bobbed along in the giant swell, raising sail as the wind decreased and eventually making a signal. Perhaps she thought *Hortense* was in distress. Perhaps she thought she had found a friend. Derray didn't want her to approach too close, for fear, as he put it, of being made prize and prisoner by a six-gun merchantman. They raised a new ensign on the stern of the *Hortense* and laughed when the merchant ship took fright and changed course, speeding away while *Hortense* wallowed in the heavy seas and her pumps creaked. Cotterell never saw the little British ship's name.

'That's another chance gone,' said Tom gloomily. Proximity at least to an English ship, if not England, had turned Tom's thoughts homewards.

'You'd rather be on her?' asked Cotterell.

'I'd rather be on an ice-bound whaler with a hole in the side. I'd rather be hanging on to a bit of seaweed off Beachy Head.'

'You may get your wish.' Cotterell couldn't help but be amused. Tom's emotions were so heartfelt.

'What's funny about it?'

LeBlanc paused beside them. 'On the quarter-deck, Cotterell.'

'See?' said Tom, when LeBlanc moved on straight away. 'Now he knows you are officer material and he knows we are relying on your skills, but does he bother with a little extra politeness?'

On deck Derray consulted with Cotterell. 'We will pump her out before we change course. What is our position?'

'Somewhere in the Channel, Captain. Shall we go aloft?'

'I'll send someone. You stay on deck.'

'Will they recognise the English coast? We can deduce our position from the coast.'

'You think it is near?'

'That little merchantman wasn't going to Cherbourg, was she?'

Derray thought for a moment, then picked up the telescope and pointed at the artimon ratlines.

'Come on.'

They climbed.

The two men sat in the rigging, arms wrapped around the shrouds, while the ship, lacking its mainmast and hove to under staysails alone, with no way, rocked madly from side to side in the rough seas. From the swaying top the southern coast of England, invisible from the deck of *Hortense*, could be clearly seen as a thin dark line on the north-eastern horizon. On the easternmost point of the horizon the line seemed to be composed of white cliffs. Or were they? Derray and Cotterell took turns staring at what might be white cliffs with a telescope.

'Well?' asked Derray, while Cotterell stared through the device.

'The slim white line . . . see? I think it breaks there which, if it does, means the Solent and the Needles. The Isle of Wight. You see the way the dark horizon line dips before it? That's Poole, I think.'

'Are you sure?'

'No. I'm not sure.'

'I have heard English sailors talk of Hamoaze. It's not Hamoaze?'

'No. Plymouth is to the north west of here.'

'You are sure of that?'

'Yes.'

'I can't see any warships.'

'Do you want to? We could sail into Portsmouth and surrender?'

'Never!'

'Hm. I thought that would be the case. So, what to do?'

'Is that your affair?'

'No, Captain Derray.' Cotterell admitted. 'It is not.'

There was a silence, then Derray said, 'It is a good thing that you help us and it is a good thing that you show proper respect for me. I will treat you the same way. But if you mention surrender again I will have you tied to the rigging, no matter what your skills as a navigator. We will make a course as we discussed before. For Cherbourg.'

'It's to the south,' said Cotterell.

'Good. We can't stay here. The merchantman will report us as soon as he finds his convoy, or a warship,' said Derray. They could see the little ship crashing through the waves some three or so miles off. 'We will stay no longer than it takes to pump ship.'

'We will never make a course to Cherbourg. It's almost due south and into the wind. And if we delay, this tide will take us up the coast towards the Isle of Wight. We will be intercepted by the British.'

'Then what would you do?'

'If it's not impertinent . . . as soon as she is pumped enough to make way, I should make sail and leave this coast with the best course we can make.'

'That means Le Havre.'

'Possibly. More likely Calais.'

Derray bowed his head against the rigging. 'There's no room to work down to Le Havre?'

'Look at the horizon. Has this storm finished with us?' It had not. 'So you know the answer, Captain. The bay outside Le

Havre calls for a ship to be under control or she'll land on the sands. Even if we avoid that we could easily find ourselves embayed and unable to make Le Havre. Then what, sir?'

'What do you suggest?'

'The tide is carrying us up. Our own windage is speeding us on that tide. By the time we have pumped again we will be ten miles, or even twenty, further on. Too far to lay a course with the wind that much in the south. To begin with we will have to beat and tack even to Le Havre. Then, if the storm begins again, the wind will veer round to the west or south west. We would have to take it on the beam for fifty or sixty miles. Not in this ship, Captain. She will fall apart.'

'Then?

'We stay at sea. Make for the middle of the Channel. When the storm wind veers, we run. We let the storm blow itself out, even if it takes us to Calais or Dunkirk.'

'Calais it shall be.' Derray said.

'And God preserve us. You are sure you don't want to go to Portsmouth? I could fetch us in there easily.'

'Just one more word,' threatened Derray, but when he turned away he smiled.

They clambered down the heaving, tossing shroud. The movements were violent and sudden, lacking rhythm. Cotterell was amused to see Derray get on the ratlines first, as if to better protect his precious navigator from falling. Cotterell had the telescope stuffed in his shirt. He paused as he descended and took one last look at the horizon. He was too low now to see the thin blue-grey line which meant England. He wiped the lens and tried again. Nothing from this height except the little merchant ship – probably a Channel Islander like me, thought Cotterell – running for its life against a grey sea and a white, washed-out sky over England. But he knew the further horizon was there and he knew it meant England. He tucked the telescope away again, and looked towards the French horizon. There was nothing to see. Not a mast, not a coast. The Channel was too wide at this point. A seemingly endless grey expanse of sea tossed white 'moutons' into the air. Above them towering darker grey clouds indicated the storm had not yet finished with the *Hortense*. Cotterell began to descend.

The wind blew on Jersey too. Angharad Le Bignan stood on the hill above her granite cottage and worked her hoe, weeding around rows of leek seedlings. She leaned into the unseasonably strong wind as she worked. She wasn't going to allow a bit of weather to slow her down. Angharad was a small, intense-looking woman with grey-brown eyes, and a sharp, enquiring mind behind them. She had grey hair cut short and tucked into a bonnet, which was tied below her chin. She was careful and methodical. She continued to work the hoe, leaving no scrap of weed above ground level. Angharad had an old willow basket on the ground by her feet, and every few minutes she would pause, crouch down on her haunches, pick up the pieces of cut weed and put them in the basket. Angharad Le Bignan moved forward a couple of feet, still crouching. She remained lithe, though she was one month and three days short of her fiftieth birthday, a widow, and the mother of two living grown children. Two others had died as babies. For most of her adult life Angharad had lived on Jersey, and for most of that time she had abandoned Breton dress and worn the plain cotton frock, bonnet and pinafore of a Jersey countrywoman. But for the past two years she had worn dark clothes, usually a brown woollen knitted shawl over her shoulders and a black frock under the pinafore. She felt these clothes were appropriate for her widowhood. She sometimes longed to wear Breton clothes, a black frock and a starched coiffe, as she had when she was a young woman. But she didn't do it. Such an act on Jersey would be ridiculous, Angharad thought. She had a strong sense of the ridiculous. But still she pined for the old clothes and the old religion, which she kept in her heart. There had been few other Catholics on Jersey before the Revolution in France.

Angharad lived with her father-in-law, Jean Cotterell. He was in his eighties and therefore usually called Old Jean. They had a stone-built cottage in St Ouen which had been in old Jean's family for generations. Old Jean called Angharad 'Ann,' as had his dead son, her husband. Breton names didn't come easily to the lips of Jerseymen, who spoke what was, to Angharad's ears, a form of Gallo-French. The widow and the old man lived together in harmony. They kept the cottage pin neat, with the fire cleaned out every morning, the pot scrubbed with sand every night and fresh straw daily on the *terre battu* floor. In a pen outside the back yard they had a couple of pigs, and in another enclosure some hens. They had a cow, crops growing on the fields, and two Breton clerical lodgers, expenses paid by the recusant Bishop of Dol. Though Ann and old Jean were not rich, their lives were comfortable. They owned a French bible and a seaman's almanac and read both.

Angharad rested on her haunches on the little plot of land overlooking the cottage. The wind plucked at her face. She knew the priests were somewhere in the lane, returning from their daily constitutional. She rocked slightly on her heels, her hand grasping the shaft of the hoe for balance. She could see Old Jean now, sitting in the sunlight by the back door of the cottage. He was smoking his pipe. An occasional whisp of blue smoke slipped away from him. She could see them in a shaft of sunlight. Old Jean could sit for hours, neither speaking, nor showing any need for company. He was typical of the Grand Banks fishermen produced by Jersey. Calm, Protestant and implacably anti-French, he appeared entirely self-contained. He never conversed with the Breton priests who lived in his cottage, though they and Angharad all spoke French in the house out of respect for him. Jean was stubborn. He didn't like priests living with him and he didn't trust them, despite the payments from the Catholic Bishop. In Old Jean's eyes all Catholic priests were a form of Frenchman, which was untrustworthiness incarnate.

Old Jean looked up towards the hillside. Angharad caught his

eye. He raised a hand in greeting. If the wind got no worse she
would take Old Jean down to the shore with the cart when the
tide fell. They would check their beach lines for sea bass or eels,
whatever God had seen fit to provide. She would collect a cartful
of kelp to dry. But that would be later. It was the month of
May and there was plenty of light after dinner.

Beyond Jean, and beyond the granite cottage, Angharad could
see the sea. It was studded with white caps, while the waves
themselves flashed like jewels. Despite the wind, despite the
clouds in the western sky it was a dazzlingly clear day. The clouds
stood out, looking as if they had been sculpted and placed in
this crisp blue sky by some brilliant artist. In the far distance,
twelve miles or so out towards the horizon, lay Sark, Herm and
Guernsey. God had allowed Angharad good enough sight to see
them clearly. Two ships sailed slowly past Sark and Herm, emerging
from the Grand Rousseau. They were well reefed and were
moving slowly. Angharad thought they were no doubt guard
ships from the British fleet. The French would never allow themselves to be caught between the islands like that. There were
strong British naval forces both in Havelet Bay in Guernsey and
St Aubins in Jersey.

The sun spread a serene yellow glow over sea and ships alike.
Light flooded onto the upper slopes of Sark, to the north west.
Beyond Sark lay Guernsey. Angharad thought of her son the
fisherman, out on the Grand Banks. 'Saint Anne intercede on
his behalf', she whispered, then said the Hail Mary five times.
Ave Maria, gratia plena, Dominus tecum. As she finished praying
she raised her eyes again. She could see the priests in the lane
now, holding on to their broad hats. They bobbed above the
hedge, half a mile away and below her. Angharad stood. She
would have to go down and prepare their dinner. The breeze
from the sea seemed to strengthen as she descended the beaten
earth steps. The clouds beyond Guernsey and to the west had
darkened. She suspected the weather would get worse. The
invisible men on the British guard ships south of Sark agreed

with her. Angharad could see the ships turning back into the Russell.

'That's more wind coming, on top of this.' Angharad said to her father-in-law when she reached the cottage.

'That's right. That's a storm. And those French crows will need to get a move on, or they will wet their cassocks good and proper.'

'French crows' meant the Breton priests. Angharad didn't answer, but looked nervously at the sky. Old Jean knew she was thinking about her son.

'He is thousands of miles away, Ann. A storm here isn't a storm there. We don't even know what the weather is like in England, leave alone the Grand Banks.'

She began to weep, despite herself. She had woken in the early hours that day with a cold dread in her heart that her son was drowning. She hadn't wanted him to go to sea again at all, and God was punishing her weakness by allowing her son to drown. Old Jean had no way of countering her logic. And he knew, anyway, that Ann's feelings on this subject were not a something she could discuss in a rational manner. She was a fisherman's mother and a fisherman's widow. He went into the house, knowing she would not want to embarrass herself by allowing him to watch her weeping.

Later Angharad went to the animal shelter outside the house with the priests to pray. She did this in secret, though Old Jean knew what they were doing. He pretended ignorance. The wind blew and the rain fell into the thatch roofing of the little shelter. Angharad and the priests, one old, one young, stood among swaying strings of drying garlic and early onions and prayed. A pregnant goat watched them suspiciously. Non-juring priests were only tolerated in Jersey on condition they didn't practise their faith openly, neither preaching nor proselytizing. So the prayer had to be secret. The wind blew, the rain fell and Angharad prayed with the priests by the light of a single candle behind a glass. A little statuette of St Anne, the Breton patron of fish-

ermen, stood on a plank, ready to receive their prayers and intercede on their behalf, via her daughter, the Virgin.

Later, when the priests had gone to bed, Old Jean went out
to fetch his daughter-in-law. She was kneeling in the dirt by the
little statue, weeping and praying both. The candle had gone out
but the moon lit her. Old Jean put his arm about Angharad and
picked her up.

'There, there, mother. I'm sure he's safe.' He said. 'Your boy
is a lucky boy, and a good sailor too. He will come home to
you.'

He led her into the house, arm about her shoulders. He told
her she had no way of knowing her son was in any danger, that
she was unreasonable and irrational to believe he was. But
Angharad was inconsolable.

19

When *Hortense* struck the sand the blow was violent. They knew they would likely be stranded but still, when the ship hit the sand shoal, the force was a surprise. It felt as if the sea was angry with the men and women aboard her. Some fate was certainly dealing them false. How long could one ship continue to have no luck at all?

The blow came and those sailors standing were thrown across the deck. Those sitting were thrown on the floor. The wounded rolled in their hammocks. The timbers of *Hortense*'s lower part gave way immediately on contact with the packed sand of the 'ridens'. There was a loud splintering sound from deep within *Hortense*'s hold. It felt as if her very backbone had broken on the first contact. Everyone heard. Everyone aboard, landsmen and sailors, men and women, those who were sick and those hale and hearty, knew they were finished. *Hortense* would not come off the shoal whole.

When they had parted company with the British merchant vessel *Hortense* had set sails, though Derray did not raise the mast-tops nor rig the lower yards. The weather was still too rough to rig a jury main. Derray, like Cotterell and every knowing sailor aboard, was afraid *Hortense* would fall apart as soon as she was strained. Two deep-reefed sails, one on the artimon, one on the misaine, drove the ship and gave her steerage way. *Hortense* slipped further away from the invisible English coast as dusk came. Cotterell marked a position he estimated on the chart, some twenty miles south and west of the Needles. Then he walked around the ship to see that everyone and everything which could be secured was secured. It wasn't Cotterell's role but he couldn't resist doing it. They would be punished by heavy weather again soon and they should be prepared.

The second part of the gale came in darkness. The ship bowed her head before the weather. Their only choice was to run, as Cotterell had argued to Derray, turning the vessel due east towards the Straits of Dover. If they tried to work against the wind at all *Hortense*'s timbers eased and water came in. So run east they did, and the water came in anyway. *Hortense* wallowed, swaying and yawing out of time with the seas and the wind. She failed to respond to tiller or sails, as she had in the approaches. But here in the chops of the English Channel there was less margin for error. Shoals awaited their mistakes, and beyond them rocky shores.

The crew of the *Hortense* pumped as best they could, but they were exhausted. And though they pumped, the water still rose in her hold. They pumped until they fell. But this time they did not defeat the rising water. They had pumped more-or-less full-time since the hours after the battle with *Circe*. The only food they had consumed was whatever happened to be in the cook's store, above the level of the flood water. Biscuit, a couple of hams paid for and stored there by officers, some onions and spices were all he could supply. Derray ordered that the food be rationed fairly to the whole surviving crew. It wasn't much of a meal, spread so thin, and was served cold. Their fresh water supply, taken from casks which had been under the rising bilge water, had become tainted and was undrinkable, but they had raised a cask from the hold, under Dubarre's orders, before they fought *Circe*, and Derray rationed this. They wouldn't survive long without food or, more importantly, water. It hardly mattered. *Hortense* was approaching her crisis. During the next few hours either the storm would abate, or they would find a port, or they would sink.

As exhaustion came on, the crew pumped slower and slower, and to less effect. Soon after midnight the tribord pump broke down, halving even this effectiveness. The breakdown was inevitable; indeed it was a miracle the pumps had lasted so long. But one pump alone couldn't cope. The bilge water, which they had once driven right down to the ballast, was now four feet deep in the hold, and rising, if slowly. It was with the greatest relief that the people of the *Hortense* saw the Calais light about an hour before dawn. The sea was still rough, but the wind had eased a little; a very little. Derray decided to anchor and wait for the dawn. There was no hope of taking *Hortense* into Calais in darkness and the sea outside the port is littered with sandy shoals.

'We are drifting.' Derray told Cotterell after half an hour. It was true. The ship now lay head to the wind with the sails furled. When they first anchored Cotterell could line up an artimon shroud with the Calais light from the quarter-deck. Now the light was off the beam and remorselessly moving forwards as *Hortense* slid with the wind and falling tide. Behind Cotterell he could hear the leadsman calling the depths.

'Six brasses. Five. Six brasses. Seven.'

Cotterell lined up the compass with the Calais light. He had the chart on deck and plotted on the chart. Derray leaned over his shoulder. The seamen standing around him watched carefully as the two men studied the chart.

'There is the light.' Cotterell told Derray, pointing to the chart in the light of a little lamp. 'And there we are.'

'You are sure?'

'Yes,' answered Cotterell. 'I am sure. We can see Dover too. Over there.'

'So this,' Derray pointed to a pecked line on the chart, 'is a shoal?'

'Yes.'

'How close are we?'

'A couple of cables, if the chart is accurate.'

'French charts are accurate,' protested Derray.

'But the shoals move,' said Cotterell, quietly. 'It could be a mile away, it could be a hundred feet behind us.'

'Richter!' called Derray. The leadsman answered, 'Citizen?'

'Is there a shoal there?'

'Somewhere, Citizen.'

'You can't see it?'

'Not for certain until there is daylight.'

Derray immediately turned and spoke quietly to LeBlanc. 'Put out the second anchor.'

LeBlanc went forward to give the order, a series of whistles and calls. Someone cut the cord securing the anchor. It splashed in the darkness. Cotterell could feel the capstan turning and the sound of feet as the sailors controlled the cables and attempted to distribute the load. But they all knew it wouldn't save the ship without a huge stroke of luck. The ship slipped back a little further, then trembled to the cables.

'The wind is easing.' Derray told Cotterell. It was. But not fast enough.

'Four! Quatre brasses!' cried the leadsman.

'Two under the keel.' Derray said to no one.

'She's holding.' Cotterell had one eye closed and was looking at the Calais light again. It was a couple of miles off and to their south-south-west now. But it was steady.

'Four!' came the call from the leadsman.

Dawn came. They could see the shoal close behind them, broken water on its surface. To landward they could see the tops of the banks, then smoother water, then a wide, shallow beach. The dryness and flatness and solidity of the beach looked very welcoming, but it might as well have been a hundred miles away. Beyond the beach Calais was a line of buildings with a tower for the light, which still glowed, but now it seemed yellow. A fort guarded the harbour entrance. On the long beach it looked as if the whole town had turned out to watch the fate of the stricken ship. A line of men and women waited, watching, almost motionless. The women wore aprons. Cotterell could see them clearly. The wind was dead in the west and plucked at their bonnets and apron strings. *Hortense* hung on her two anchors, straining, not swinging at all. Waves crashed across the ship's bow. Charles climbed the companionway. The ship bucked to the anchor, pitching him onto the quarter-deck.

'Where is that?' he asked when he recovered.

'Calais.' Cotterell replied.

'Well done, sir.' Charles said, in English. The meaning was clear to Derray. Charles pumped Cotterell's hand. 'Congratulations.'

He repeated the performance with Derray, but in French. Both Cotterell and Derray were impassive. Their lack of emotion was not lost on Charles.

'It is well done. Isn't it?' He asked.

'We're not there yet,' said Derray.

'But we'll get there?' asked Charles. He knew the answer now. Derray met Cotterell's eye but said nothing.

'Do you know Calais?' Cotterell asked the temporary captain.

'Richter does. He's from Dunkirk.'

Cotterell turned to the leadsman.

'What will happen?'

Richter lay his lead on the deck. He looked at the shore and the banks before answering. 'We will be here for some hours until the tide is at the bottom. Then, when it's making, if the wind has dropped, we have a chance to make the port.'

'Will it drop?' asked Charles. No one replied. None of the sailors on the quarter-deck thought it would any time soon.

'We can't reach Dunkirk?' Cotterell asked Richter.

'No.'

'There's a channel on the chart,' said Cotterell. He unfurled and held up the chart for Richter to see. The wind whipped at it. Rain spotted it. Richter turned his back and heaved the line again.

'I don't believe he thinks much of your question,' said Charles.

Derray walked away too, to lean anxiously at the rail over the gun-deck. His first command looked like it would be lost. He was distraught, Cotterell knew. He'd had the same feeling, a hole in the bottom of his stomach, a sense of disbelief, when *l'Imprevu* was lost. He'd seen it in his father when they'd caught sight of the charred remains of the first *l'Imprevu*. Now Cotterell and Charles were alone on the quarter-deck, where the smashed wheel and binnacle should be.

'How is Lefèvre?' Cotterell asked, struggling for some ground they could share.

'He'll live.'

'Auchard?'

'How would I know?'

'Does Madame Auchard say anything?'

'She is anxious. We all are,' said Charles.

'And she has her grief for her husband's blindness to contend with.'

'Something like that,' answered Charles.

'I hope she has a bag packed,' Cotterell continued.

'Why?'

Then the anchor cable parted and they knew 'why.'

'Best bower's gone,' called LeBlanc from the gun-deck. The ship veered and rolled about the single remaining anchor for a moment. The anchor cable slackened, took up the tension, slackened again, then juddered as the waves bounced the ship about as if she were a toy boat or a simple piece of flotsam.

'Is there another anchor?' asked Charles.

'In the hold, I expect. But there's no time,' said Cotterell. He walked to the shroud and looked over the side, gripping the pin-rail. He felt drawn to see the shoals. Emily came on deck.

'What's wrong?' she asked.

The single anchor dragged as if to demonstrate what was wrong. *Hortense* slipped like a skater fallen on ice. She glided backwards, away from Calais and towards the North Sea. If there were no shoals she might have glided all the way to Holland thus. Those on deck steadied themselves for a moment. They braced, knowing what would inevitably happen. She struck the shoal, and the blow was powerful. The ship had landed on hard-packed sand. It might as well have been a sheet of granite. When it came, Charles and Richter were thrown across the deck. Cotterell held the shroud and grabbed Emily, drawing her to himself. Derray held on to the rail but stumbled. That blow had made men sick to their stomachs. All the sailors knew instantly there would be no recovery from such a violent grounding. Another big wave crashed into them. The ship groaned and turned, pivoting half-afloat, half-grounded on the bank. The timbers of *Hortense*'s lower part gave way immediately. There was a loud splintering sound from deep within her hold as she broke. Sailors immediately appeared on deck from every stair or aperture, half climbing against the angle the vessel had taken up. They all looked up to the quarter-deck. Cotterell could feel Emily's breath. The two looked into each other's eyes.

'Thank you,' she said. Cotterell could feel her heart thumping. He released her.

Derray's reaction to the stranding was immediate.

'Get the boat out.'

Some of the ship's boats had been smashed into firewood by the action with the *Circe* and subsequently jettisoned, but two whalers remained on deck. *Hortense* was at an angle on the shoal, perhaps thirty degrees. She bounced in the sea a few times more, then steadied. She lay with her back broken at that angle. Derray led the crew in launching a whaler. It was chaotic. Crewmen fought to get aboard. LeBlanc and Derray fought the sailors back, beating them with flat cutlass blades or with the pommel of their cutlass handles. Tom helped, swiping at men with a bronze belay pin. Citoyenne Lefèvre appeared in the crowd supporting her husband. Cotterell pushed him into the un-launched whaler, the one-legged revolutionary's only chance. They manoeuvred the boat to the rail with little Lefèvre inside. His wife cried and prayed aloud. Cotterell promised to send her down once it was launched. Fear gripped the crew. They grasped at the whaler's gunwhale and were in danger of tipping the contents, Lefèvre and the oars, onto the deck before the boat was launched. The people of the *Hortense* pressed to climb aboard the whaler, which would have made the launch impossible, and only subsided temporarily when Pascal, emerging from the lower deck, leading Auchard and another man blinded in the battle with the British, plunged his knife into a man's chest. The man staggered back, looking surprised at the flow of blood onto his shirt, then collapsed.

'Make way!' cried Pascal. 'Make way!'

'No!' responded the small crowd of sailors. Cotterell, Tom, LeBlanc and Derray had the boat over the side now and on its way down to the sea. The crew stood around and upon the ship's rail. They were above the boat, which was now dangling half in and half out of the sea. The sailors ignored it and began to fight among themselves for precedence.

'Make way!' cried Pascal again.

'Make way for me!' shouted blind Auchard. His wife stood near to him in the chaotic crowd. She was impassive, but he did not, of course, notice. She made no move towards him.

'Lower!' cried Derray.

Now the whaler was in the sea, sheltered by the bulk of the stranded *Hortense*'s hull. Men scrambled over the tilted ship's rail and slipped the few feet into the whaler, or the sea next to it. Helene and Liberté were by the rail. Derray beat some of the men back, then grabbed Hélène roughly.

'You get in. The two of you.'

Hélène needed no second asking. Liberté backed away. Derray held Hélène's hand as she climbed the rail. The men in the whaler pulled a couple of their fellows from the sea, left a couple more to drown, arranged themselves around the prone Lefèvre, then were ready to pull. One sailor stood prepared to cut the cord from the ship, though the whaler was at best half-loaded.

'Not yet!' called Derray. Hélène was dangling a few feet down the rope. But the cut was made below her feet. The men in the whaler pulled at the oars. Now there was nothing but sea beneath Hélène. She realised her predicament – that she was descending to the bitter end of a cut rope. She screamed, slipped further, then grabbed the rope again and stopped sliding. Her fingers grew white on the rope. Behind her the six men in the whaler pulled as hard as they could for the shore. The wind shrieked in the rigging. As soon as they left the shelter of *Hortense* the sea tossed the whaler, once, twice. It turned, first onto one side then the other, tipping out sailors and shedding oars as it went. Then there was only one man left in the whaler, holding an oar, half standing. Cotterell recognised Eustache.

'Help me!' cried Hélène. Strong men's hands reached out to her as she swung against the hull, but she was out of their grasp.

'Hold on!' Derray cried to Hélène, but it was too late. Her grip loosened and she fell and was swept away. He felt, rather than saw, Liberté at his side. She called, 'Hélène!' But she'd gone.

Cotterell looked at the whaler again, bobbing about in the enormous waves, sometimes visible, sometimes hidden by spume. Eustache balanced with the aid of the oar. He was alone, a dark figure in a dark boat outlined against the grey tossing sea. The other men were nowhere to be seen. A wave broke over the whaler, knocking Eustache momentarily to his knees. Another wave followed. The boat turned over and stayed inverted. Cotterell recognised the bearded face and dumpy figure of Lefèvre in the sea next to the inverted boat. He waved once, then was no more. It was like a dream.

Cotterell turned. LeBlanc raised and fired a pistol near Cotterell's head. The report deafened him. The crowd of sailors staggered back, though it was unclear whether that was from the shock of the gun being fired or from watching the others drown. Derray aimed a pair of pistols into the melée.

'Fall back!' shouted LeBlanc. They parted and reeled away from Derray and LeBlanc, courage gone, nerve broken for now in the face of the more imminent death.

'I want you to take Monsieur Charles ashore.' Derray said to Cotterell. 'Take the Second and his wife too. And Richter to guide you. Get them there safely and see if you can't come back to us. Bring help, for God's sake.'

Protected by Derray and LeBlanc, Richter and Tom let out the second boat. Charles let blind Auchard, then the sobbing Citoyenne Lefèvre down into it. The others followed; Emily, Liberté, Richter, Charles himself holding a packet wrapped in oiled paper, Tom, cursing his wounded hand, then two of the fittest of *Hortense*'s sailors, then Cotterell. Cotterell crouched in the stern of the whaler, holding the tiller, timing the waves, judging them. Liberté and Richter took the oars just before him. Charles and Tom cut the cords holding the bucking, bobbing boat to the ship. They rocked for a second in the lee of the ship, then Cotterell picked the back of the biggest wave, which he knew was followed by the weakest and yelled: 'Pull, pull!'

The men and women pulled at the oars. Cotterell grinned at Liberté, who had lost her red cap. His grin had fear, hope, exhilaration and fellowship in it. He realised he felt extraordinarily happy. Why? He pushed the thought out of his mind.

'Pull!' he yelled. 'Pull, for your lives depend on it.'

Now they were out of the relative shelter offered by the hull of the tilted, grounded ship and heading for the shore. The sea between *Hortense* and the beach was like the surface of a boiling cauldron.

'Pull! Pull!'

The sea tossed them this way and that, from side to side; the whaler yawed, plunged and rose. Cotterell had seen an angry young horse behave like that, but never a boat. He didn't believe for an instant they could survive it. The whaler see-sawed. At one moment the rowers seemed below Cotterell's feet and he looked out at the flying spray ahead. The next moment Citoyenne Lefèvre, crouched sobbing in the bow, was above his head. Cotterell clutched the tiller but had very little control of the boat.

'Pull! Pull!' He cried. 'Pull!' Only speed would save them. He noticed Auchard, sitting side-by-side with Emily, both pulling like demons. In front of them were two sailors Cotterell didn't know, but they were strong men. Tom and Charles were in front of the two strong young sailors, also side-by-side, teeth bared, hands clenched around their oars. Closest were Liberté and Richter. Beyond the rowers Cotterell could see what he knew was the sandbank. The seas broke, boiled and bubbled across its expanse. The whaler was heading directly for it. Cotterell couldn't steer. He knew that to turn was to broach. The rowers had to pull with all their strength just to keep the whaler from being overturned. The sandbank rushed towards them as if it had a life of its own. Beyond it, Cotterell could see smoother, though still dangerous water, beyond that another sandbank, then even smoother water, then the beach, perhaps half a mile away. He didn't believe they had the smallest chance of reaching the beach, but they had to try. One wave broke over them, half-filling the whaler, but they couldn't stop. The hard-packed sand of the bank awaited them but still they couldn't stop. On and on they rowed, waves crashing and breaking around them, spray flying over them. Then the sea lifted the boat as if it were weightless. Fate held them in its palm. To Cotterell it seemed for a moment as if all the oars pulled against the air. Liberté lost her oar. Fate lost patience. The sea threw the small boat forwards. The packed sand rose to meet it.

These events passed very slowly before Cotterell, so that he felt he had plenty of time to prepare himself for the impact to come. He didn't. They collided with the sandbank with a bone-jarring crash. Cotterell felt the boat flex and weaken and was convinced, for a second, it was over right at that moment. His knees banged heavily and painfully against the gunwhale. Then another wave smashed into his shoulders. The little boat drove forward into the boiling white water on the bank. He was aware of the rowers' faces looking up at him, horrified. Cotterell knew they could see the seas behind him. That's what horrified them, he realised in an instant. He half turned, in time to see another giant wave breaking over them. Cotterell held on to the tiller for dear life. The wave seemed to break on his shoulders, then smash the rowers flat on their thwart-seats. It felt to Cotterell as if it would suck the people out of the whaler. Then the huge wave was gone and Cotterell rose, surprised to find himself still alive, surprised to see they were halfway across the bank and in the middle of the white water.

'Pull!' he cried. 'Pull!' He had no idea whether they could hear him. The rowers were recovering of their own accord. Another big wave came and pushed them forward again, this time another thirty or forty yards.

'Pull!' cried Cotterell. They pulled. It was another fifty yards to the end of the first sandbank and the beginning of the smoother water. Another wave hit them, then another. They rowed for their lives. Cotterell could see a figure floating in the smoother water. Lefèvre.

Now they were free of the bank and into quieter water. Cotterell could steer, though the seas were still wild. He guided the boat through the heaving waves until it was by Lefèvre's floating body, then called, 'Stop rowing!'

'What is it?' shouted blind Auchard.

'Lefèvre in the sea,' replied Tom. Citoyenne Lefèvre immediately sat up and began to wail, 'Hirnan, oh my Hirnan.' Her Hirnan was face down in the surf.

'Is he alive?' asked Auchard.

'Unlikely,' one of the sailors answered.

'Leave him,' said Auchard.

'Get him in,' ordered Cotterell. Emily fixed Cotterell with a stare, judging him, Cotterell felt. All the time the boat was crashing up and down in the seas. The unconscious Lefèvre might be crushed at any moment. A wave broke over the whaler, reminding them of the danger they were in, if they needed reminding. Charles, Liberté and the others tried to bail the boat with their bare hands.

'Are you mad?' Auchard called. 'Row. Row!'

No one rowed.

'Row, for the pity of the tabernacle row!'

But they ignored him, waiting on Cotterell's command. Tom and one of the French sailors dragged Lefèvre onto the boat's gunwhale. He fell across their knees. His wound bled, suggesting, if nothing else did, that he was alive. Now Cotterell cried again, 'Pull!' They shoved at Lefèvre's unconscious body until he fell beneath their feet. The rowers pulled again, now with Hirnan Lefèvre between and under them. No one made any attempt to revive him, not even Citoyenne Lefèvre, who couldn't reach. Another wave broke over them, pinning the rowers to their seats. Some tried to bail again.

'Leave it!' called Cotterell. 'Row.'

'Row, row!' echoed Auchard, and dug in his oar. They pulled, somehow finding a rhythm, and somehow staying afloat in the half-flooded boat. Cotterell crouched to see over the rowers. Before him was a second sandbank, covered with whipping, whirling, white water. Richter met Cotterell's eye. He twisted in his seat to see, then called. 'We can't get across this. You have to row towards the fort and then turn.'

They did it. Rowing into the heavy seas was more secure than being chased by them, though the effort they expended in rowing was quickly bringing the men and women on the whaler to the brink of exhaustion. At last they reached the point where they must turn, a few hundred yards from the beach. Half a mile in front of them was the fort, and behind it the lighthouse. To Cotterell's starboard lay the heavy seas and the broken ship, to his larboard the citizens of Calais lined the beach, ready to rescue them. Sandbanks separated them from both, seeming almost to funnel the storm upon the whaler. Before them was the foment, the breaking storm seas outside Calais. One more throw of the dice would see them safe. Richter was watching the coast and the surface of the sea carefully, looking for the end of the larboard sandbank. He saw what he wanted.

'Now!' called Richter.

Cotterell timed his turn so it would fall between two waves. As he put the tiller over, blind Auchard, taken unawares, lost his time just for a beat. His oar clashed with that of the sailor before him. They missed a stroke. The boat stalled, just for a second, just at the worst possible moment. A big wave, carrying the full force of the storm, rose and spat at them. The whaler began to broach. It turned about its axis and kept turning. They lost their oars and tumbled. Cotterell was pitched headlong into the sea. Now it was really every man for himself, '*sauve qui peut*'. The water was freezing. It knocked Cotterell's breath out of him. He struck out for the surface, broke through, breathed in a lot of flying spray, was tumbled once, twice, three times by waves, felt the touch of another crew member's body brush past him in the sea, then felt the brutal impact as the sandbank hit him every bit as hard as *Hortense* had been hit. He wondered, idly, slowly, if he would be punished and break up too, then he was slammed one last time onto the sandbank. The blow, which he took on his head and shoulders, jarred his teeth and spine. He'd bitten his tongue, he knew. Did it matter? Cotterell thought. Perhaps I have no further use for it. He could taste his own warm salty blood. The sea lifted him one more time. Then darkness came.

Cotterell came to on a beach. He had sand in his mouth and eyes. He'd lost his shirt. His head hurt. The storm still roared overhead. An old woman was kneeling by his side. She had beautiful blue eyes. She wore a purple skirt with a white blouse and had grey hair tucked into a black-painted straw bonnet. The bonnet was secured by a ribbon. Her clothes were plucked by gusts of wind. She wore a blue-grey apron and, unbelievably, had a little teapot in the apron, cupped in her hands. She put the pot on the flat sandy beach by Cotterell's side and lifted Cotterell's head with her hand, gently brushing the sand away.

He turned his eyes towards the sea. The waves still rolled and roared up the beach, bursting on the sands. Beyond the foam he could see the *Hortense*, listing over a long way now. Even from this distance he could see the seas were breaking over her. One furled sail had torn loose from its reevings and trailed in shreds from its spar on the misaine. He could see no movement on board her. Cotterell closed his eyes briefly. How long had it taken him to come ashore? He should go back and help, but his limbs were weighed down, almost immovable.

'Would you like some tea?' asked the woman with his head cradled in her lap.

Cotterell would have laughed had he not been so exhausted. He coughed sea water.

'Yes. Thank you mother,' he whispered. He tried to sit but couldn't. A shadow fell over Cotterell's eyes. A uniformed man with a musket stood over him. The man was middle aged. He wore a blue uniform and bicorn hat, marking him out as a coastguard, in all probability. The musket had its bayonet fixed and was pointed at Cotterell's throat. He held the bayonet at Cotterell's throat for an age. The woman watched dispassionately, holding up her little pot of tea in one hand and Cotterell's head in the other.

The man who held the gun finally spoke. His voice trembled. 'That man says you are English. Is that so?'

Cotterell turned and focussed on the man indicated. Behind the coastguard stood Eustache.

'Make one false move and I'll shoot.' The coastguard said.

Now Cotterell did laugh, despite his headache, the sand in his eyes and his painful tongue.

20

Jean Cotterell stood on the foredeck of the Channel Islands packet, *Robert Wace*. His tousled light brown and blond hair had been cut within a week and combed just that morning. The bone comb was in his pocket, resting against some silver pieces, paid over by an agent in Dover when he first arrived in England. Cotterell was clean shaven. He wore new clothes; grey cotton trousers, a blue serge jacket, cotton shirt with silk kerchief, knitted jersey wool socks and new leather shoes. The socks reminded him of Thibault. The shoes were uncomfortable and creaked whenever he moved. But they shone and they had silver buckles. They marked him out for a passenger, not a sailor.

Cotterell imagined the *Robert Wace* might well be the same little British ship he had seen from the deck of the *Hortense* two weeks before, when she was on her way towards the shallows of the English coast and a form of safety. She was smartly kept and smartly sailed by her crew of expert Jersey sailors. *Robert Wace* was painted, polished, holystoned and sailed more like a Royal Navy ship than some sloppy merchantman. That made her crew a prime target for Royal Navy captains, short of experienced seamen. *Robert Wace*'s Captain, Chandler, was a wise old sea dog who'd served twenty years on coasters before going into business on his own account with a group of St Helier investors. Chandler kept to hand in his cabin a copy of a 'letter of protection' written by the secretary to the Admiral of the Channel Fleet and signed by the great Lord Howe himself, just in case they encountered a British warship on the press. The crew, at least, should have nothing to fear. Cotterell would have to hide behind his silver buckles and gentleman's clothes, if a press gang boarded. It might serve.

No protection was available to ship or sailors from marauding French vessels, of course, and being pressed would be the least of their problems if taken by one. The jeopardy then would have been reversed, since Cotterell had in his bag a 'laissez passer' from the port Captain of Calais which described in glowing terms John Cotterell's attempts to save the crew of the *Hortense*.

Failing a warship to convoy him to Jersey, Captain Chandler, the packet's master, followed a cautious course. He spent two days making westwards from Portsmouth into light, flukey, usually contrary winds, creeping the ship along the English coast with the tide, anchoring when it was contrary and eventually reaching Lime Bay. They headed south when the slant to the wind was open, passing at night west of the three steady glowing beams of the Caskets light. That had been the point they would go by closest to the French coast, save for their arrival in Jersey itself, which would be under the guns of the militia and regiments stationed there. The safest places in the Channel Islands were the closest to France.

Dawn found the little ship sucked southwards on the swells of an oily-looking black sea. She was among the Channel Islands at last. Harbour porpoises visited and played around her bow wave. They were a common sight in the bay. Alderney and Cap de la Houge were far away to larboard. Guernsey beckoned. Once the sun had burned off the early morning mist Jersey became a thick smudge on the south-eastern horizon. Captain Chandler had left a small promenading space open to passengers on the foredeck, when it was not required for the foc'sl men's work. Cotterell paced there full of anxiety, accompanied by a French exile returning from England. The man, who was thin, dark haired and in his late twenties, refused to give his name, asking instead to be called Pommelier, because he was an apple dealer. He gave Cotterell no indication why a French apple dealer would undertake the hazardous journey either from Portsmouth to St Helier or vice versa. There was no market in apples between the two. Cotterell barely heard the man's unceasing, nervous chatter. All of his energy was instead channelled into watching the smudge on the horizon grow more distinct. Each pool and eddy they passed seemed to greet him like an old friend. He had fished most of them with his grandfather and sister. Two patrolling British frigates anchored, waiting for them at the head of the Russell. The *Robert Wace* couldn't avoid passing under their guns if she'd wanted. The tide would take her there. At a couple of miles' distance, Chandler responded to the frigates' private signal. The frigates stayed at their anchors. A slight change of course fetched the head of the *Robert Wace* round so she headed past Sark for Jersey. Landfall would be Groz Nez point, which Cotterell could make out an hour later. Soon the towers of the island's churches began to appear behind Groz Nez and Cotterell could pick out St Ouen's. He couldn't help but feel that old, homecoming anxiety in the pit of his stomach. As the island grew and filled the horizon he found himself scanning the fields, hoping to catch sight of his mother or his grandfather. It was a ridiculous hope, but one he couldn't resist.

'Do you know what is the difference between the English and the French?' asked the apple dealer, speaking in English. Cotterell didn't answer. Unimpeded by this lack of a willing audience 'Pommelier' went on, 'The French are chaotic. Everyone knows that. Every Frenchman pushes for himself. Everyone in France grasps, grasps, grasps. Imagine, if you can, a nation like that, with everyone just getting what he can from everything. There had to be an end to it somewhere. And do you know where that end is?'

Cotterell didn't.

'The end is the Revolution. Endless revolution. The result of revolution is the scaffold. The result of endless revolution is innocent men, women and even children on the guillotine,' said the apple dealer. 'Look at me. I freely admit to you, I am a

Royalist. Why else would a simple man like me have quit France
and come to Britain? But I tell you, my friend. We loyalist, Royalist
Frenchmen have brought it upon ourselves, this endless revolutionary war. How's that, you ask? If the French were only a bit
more orderly, if they'd been a bit less greedy, if the King had
been a little bit stronger . . . not much, just a bit . . .' He threw
up his hands. Cotterell noticed they were dirty, like the apple
dealer's clothes. He wore a white shirt with a frilled front, a black
scarf about his neck. He hadn't shaved in days and probably
hadn't washed, for he had such a pungent mix of sweat and
perfume about him that Cotterell was constantly trying to
manoeuvre upwind of him. Not that there was much wind. The
Frenchman smiled. 'You know the story. What's your name again?'

'Jean,' said Cotterell.

'It's a sad tale, Jean. My country is in chaos. The poor man
lost his head for want of a bit of discipline among my countrymen, his subjects. His Queen, too. And thousands of my
countrymen have made the same unhappy climb up the scaffold. Do you see?'

'No,' answered Cotterell flatly, 'I do not.'

'It's our own fault. We have been invaded from within. Imagine
how that makes me feel.'

Cotterell did not imagine. He did not answer.

'What a disaster. We are . . . what do you say? Devil take the
hindmost. Imagine a country as a dining table. France is everyone
head-first into the pot. The English, on the other hand, are
systematic. The meal is served out in an orderly fashion. King
George and the English Milords make sure the pot is divided
fairly, having served themselves first, of course. Very little is
served to the other diners, but it is done equitably. *That* is the
difference between the two countries.'

'You sound as if you don't like either England or France,'
suggested Cotterell.

'On the contrary,' replied the apple dealer. 'I said I am a Royalist.
I am jealous that you English have kept your royal family, that

you have a great king on his proper throne. God is in his place, parliament and the laws are in their place. Would that it were so in France. I admire England and I love France.'

He watched Cotterell for a moment. The tall Jerseyman stood in silence, watching the approaching island.

'And you?' asked the Frenchman.

'I am a Jerseyman, not an Englishman sir.'

'You are indifferent?'

'Not at all.'

'You are a loyal subject of King George?'

'Indeed.'

'You are a lucky man. And the English? You are loyal to them too?'

'I share my King with the English,' said Cotterell, and turned away. He didn't like the prying Frenchman at all.

The *Robert Wace* swung to her anchor without a flutter of the sails, and was at rest. They were in St Aubin's Bay, anchored in the deeper water just east of the Vier Fort, surrounded by fishermen and their boats. The only other ship of any size was a gun boat, *Lion*. By her position Cotterell presumed she was a shallow draft, and by the level of activity on deck she seemed unoccupied, save a watchman. *Lion* hung on a buoyed mooring, tied to a floating cask. The familiar drying harbour and little town of St Aubin was to their west, St Helier was to their east. On the eastern side of the bay, showing above Elizabeth Castle, Cotterell could see the masts of ships in the St Helier small road. The strand between the two, St Helier and St Aubin, which also served as Jersey's main highway, was busy. The sun was well in the west. There was no wind. Lacking wind, the *Robert Wace*'s crew had towed her with boats from the Corbiere headland while the flood was making . They couldn't tow against the Jersey ebb, so the only thing for it was to come to off at St Aubin and wait for the turn of the tide.

The Captain came forward to satisfy himself the anchor had

a good hold. The apple dealer cast his eye over the ship's disposition and said to Cotterell with the air of an expert, 'We will
have to wait for the tide now.'

Cotterell leaned over the side and called in Jerrais to a passing
fisherman, 'Hey, Pierre! Will you take me ashore?'

The man looked up, recognized Cotterell, and ten minutes
later he was walking up the sandy beach towards the shore. The
water was warm. His shoes and Jersey hose were in a ditty bag
over his shoulder. The sand squeezed between his toes. Cotterell
didn't pause when he reached the shore but continued up the
Mont de la Rocque, the road which climbed out of St Aubin.
He climbed fast, and his footsteps were as light as a child's. His
feelings on approaching Jersey had been mixed. He had lost his
family's main asset, *l'Imprevu*, and dreaded passing the news of
ruin to his mother and grandfather. He had lost Thibault
Dumaresq but had news of the boy's father. He could barely
imagine the conversation he must have with Widow Dumaresq.
But as his feet trod the road up the Mont his step became lighter
with every passing yard, and his heart was lifted by the thought
of seeing his grandfather, mother and sister again. When the
road became rough he stopped and slipped on the fancy leather
shoes, keeping the buckles in his pocket for fear of losing them.
Cotterell reached his grandfather's house an hour and a half
later. Angharad, his mother, was in the yard. She stood perfectly
still when she saw him coming down the hill. She couldn't move.
She felt as if she was seeing a ghost.

'Now don't cry,' he said, but it was no good. He wrapped his
arms about her and they both cried.

'I've lost everything, mother. I've lost the boat. I lost the crew
too.'

She pressed her finger to his lips.

'You're here. You're alive.'

They went and sat on the hill, overlooking the cottage and
the sea.

'Where is Grandfather?'

'He has gone to visit Marie.' Cotterell's sister had married a farmer called Falla in le Coin Hatain and the old man was in the habit of visiting her for a couple of days a month, rather than allow her to become bored to death by Falla, whose chief entertainment, according to Old Jean, was 'counting his money'.

Angharad and Jean, mother and son, sat on the hill and watched the sea together. They were happy just to be in each other's company. Below, the Breton priests went hungry for once, or found something cold to eat. Angharad didn't allow herself to think about them. She sat with her arms about her son as if he were her little boy again. They talked about what had passed. He told her how he had been sure he had drowned on that day in May, what it was like to be attacked by a British frigate, how the *Hortense* had sunk before Calais. She was amazed to hear it all, but most amazed to have news that Dumaresq still lived. If he did, why did he not write to his wife and children? Cotterell couldn't answer. He'd heard news of Dumaresq, not seen him. And even if he had seen Dumaresq, would there have been an answer?

The sun sank low and changed to a dull red. Its rays shone a heatless red line from the west towards them.

'I knew you were in danger,' said Angharad. They could see the lane. A group of men were walking down it. The men were about a quarter of a mile away, above the shore where the Catholic priests liked to promenade. Angharad could see two of the men were carrying muskets. Red evening light reflected from their barrels, which were high above the hedge. She wondered if someone suspected her priests. Angharad knew the priests were beyond reproach and would not misuse the trust the Jersey people had put in them. But plenty of Jerseymen suspected there were revolutionary agents among the refugees, and what better disguise than a cassock? She squeezed her son's hand. 'But I prayed. And the next day I knew you were safe.'

'I wish I had known I would be safe,' said Cotterell and smiled.

'It's the power of prayer,' Angharad said. 'I expect you kept your prayers up.'

'It would have been difficult, in a revolutionary warship,' he replied.

'God knows what is there, in your head and in your heart. That's what matters.'

She kissed him.

'Make me a promise.'

'What?'

'That you won't go to sea again.'

'I have to work, mother.'

'We can find work for you.'

'As?'

'Marie . . .'

'I'm not working for my sister,' he responded sharply, 'or her husband. Anyway, I'm no farmer.'

'Promise me you won't go to sea again.'

He was silent.

'Please.'

'Ask me tomorrow, mother.'

'Thank you. You must be hungry,' she said. 'I expect the priests wonder where I am.'

They climbed down the beaten earth steps in the hillside. Watching his mother, holding her hand as they went down, Cotterell was aware the steps had been cut and beaten by the feet of his ancestors, the cottage built and the roof laid by the hands of his ancestors. He felt as if the Jersey earth would suck him in and make him one with itself. He feared it as landsmen feared the sea. Each time he came home he felt like that. Each time he felt as if he never would leave again. But he always did.

The last red rays were on the cottage as they reached it. Inside was dark. Cotterell saw one of the priests light a lamp. They could hear the soldiers in the lane. Then they emerged, led by a very young naval officer. The soldiers' uniforms, unclear in the gloom, looked like they belonged to the Jersey Militia, not Englishmen sent over to guard the island. Two carried muskets, the third was a Sergeant with a sword.

'I am looking for Jean Cotterell,' said the naval officer. He was English.

'And you are?'

'A representative of His Majesty. Are you Cotterell?'

'Yes.'

'You are to come with me,' said the youthful sailor.

'Why would I do that?' asked Cotterell.

The young man gave a small movement of his hand. The Sergeant drew his sword and the militiamen levelled their muskets at Cotterell.

'Because I say so and I carry the King's warrant. Come with me,' commanded the naval officer in his half-throttled, youthful English voice. He sounded determined. It was hard to make out his features in the gloom. Cotterell kissed his mother, slipping her his money and his silver buckles, then turned again, picked up his ditty bag and said to the officer.

'Let us go.'

21

They took Cotterell to Mont Orgeuil castle, which was about as far from his mother's cottage as Jersey's geography permitted. The five men arrived in the small hours. They had made the journey in something like silence, following the young officer. He didn't speak either French or Jerrais and the Sergeant had to translate the slightest order, since the soldiers had little English. They stopped twice for militiamen guarding crossroads. The password was '*crapaud*', which caused amusement each time the non-French-speaking naval officer gave it. When he asked the Sergeant what it meant he replied 'Guernseyman,' causing more suppressed mirth in the darkness. Once at the castle Cotterell passed through several more guarded doors, then into a court-yard, then into a form of keep. Eventually he was led upstairs in the keep and left alone in a room. It had very small windows, hardly better than slits, and was bare save for a long fruitwood table and four rush chairs. There was one candle. The soldier who fetched him there said nothing, offered no clue, no food or drink, merely left and turned the key in the lock. Cotterell's feet were sore from walking the seven or eight miles in his new shoes. He waited for half an hour. When it seemed quite clear he was to remain alone and would receive no dinner, he put out the candle and slept on the table, wrapped in his serge jacket and with his shoes inside his ditty for a pillow.

He was woken by the dawn light coming through the east-facing windows. He lay for some time like a dead king, arms folded across his chest and eyes closed against the light. Then he got up, aching. One little window allowed a glimpse over the town of Gorey below the castle. Small boats lay on a drying beach to the south beyond the town. Another small window in the stone castle wall, the one admitting the most sunlight, looked east, over the roadstead. Cotterell knew the waters around Gorey well, but had never seen them so crowded. Close to the castle, on the inner road, was a series of armed luggers, armed fishing boats and the like. They were well kept and neat, which meant they carried Royal Navy crew as well as fishermen. Fishermen do not carry neatness beyond utility. Beyond the luggers a miscellany of warships was afloat on the outer road. They ranged from gunboats and brigs to an ancient frigate. The larger ships, though armed, did not look prepared for sea, which surprised Cotterell. They wouldn't be much use for the defence of Jersey, if that was their purpose. One had no sails on her spars, another had her topmasts struck. Like the vessel moored off St Aubin, they did not appear well manned. Two warships clearly had no crew at all.

The door to Cotterell's room clicked open. The young naval officer was there. He carried writing materials: a sheaf of papers, a stylus, a bottle of ink. He put these on the table. He was followed by the militia Sergeant, who carried a tray with a cloth over it and looked the most unlikely butler imaginable. This man also put his tray on the table.

'There is some food,' said the young officer. He waved for the Sergeant to leave, then sat and watched Cotterell eat. There were apples, a piece of cheese, a piece of bread and some small beer. Cotterell was ravenous.

'You were on a French warship,' said the young officer eventually.

'I was.'

'The *Hortense*. She was shipwrecked.'

'How do you know?'

'We have our sources.'

'We?'

The youth smiled but said no more. This intrigued Cotterell. This flaxen-haired boy, with blue eyes and no beard, was amused by him. Cotterell asked, 'I have the honour of addressing . . .?'

'The Earl Leigh.'

Leigh stood and bowed slightly. Cotterell put down his apple and followed suit, saying, 'My Lord.'

'Can you write, Cotterell?' asked Leigh.

'Yes, My Lord.'

'Write down what happened.'

'All of it?'

'All of it. From when and how you first boarded the *Hortense*. There's plenty of paper and plenty of time, sir.'

Cotterell considered for a moment.

'Am I to do so under duress?'

'We are at war. All visitors are to report to the proper authority. You didn't report on arrival. So we will hold you here until that matter is cleared up. That could take some time.'

Cotterell picked up the stylus and reached for the sheaf of paper. He dipped the stylus and began to write. Leigh sat opposite, sanding and reading each page as Cotterell finished it. After five pages he stood and left, carrying the pages. Cotterell paused for a moment, then continued.

After another hour the Sergeant appeared and picked up the papers Cotterell had written subsequently. He had completed the last page with: 'These were the events on the French ship *Hortense* of Floréal and Prairial, an II of the Republican calendar or, as we know it, May and June of the Year of our Lord 1794.' Cotterell had signed each page 'Jean Cotterell.' The Sergeant made no attempt to read any of the pages. He looked at Cotterell, then at the next blank page which lay under Cotterell's hand. He looked at the ink and at the stylus on the table, but still said nothing. The Sergeant was clearly a very careful man. He left.

Cotterell stood and went to the small window overlooking Gorey. He saw, far below him, a man ambling about the road. The man looked as if he was cooling his heels, waiting for something. It was unquestionably the apple dealer, even seen from this superior and unfamiliar angle. The Frenchman was holding a fore and aft hat with a white cockade in it, the badge of office for counter-revolutionaries in Jersey. So much for dealing apples, thought Cotterell. He sat again at the table and rested his head on his hands. He ached from sleeping on the table. He closed his eyes.

What seemed like ten minutes later a man in his fifties burst in. He was Phillipe d'Auvergne; small, intense, florid with sharp blue eyes and white hair. He was dressed in a brown coat under which he wore a white shirt and naval officer's trousers. He shook Cotterell's hand. 'Jean . . . how are you?'

'A little tired.'

'I'm sorry. I was away, in Guernsey, otherwise I'd have met you myself.'

'Captain d'Auvergne, I am very pleased to see you, sir.'

'How's your mother?'

'I lost our boat.'

'I read your report. You're a lucky young man. The others were all lost?'

'As far as I know, sir.'

'And then you conned a French ship. Well, there's an experience. But your statement doesn't say, how did you get out of Calais?'

'I was brought home by an English man of affairs who was a regular visitor there.'

'Smuggler?'

'I couldn't say . . .'

'Hodges? Tall chap with a big round black hat. Sort of gruff. Wears a thick blue seaman's mantle in all weathers.'

D'Auvergne had described the seaman who had brought Cotterell back to England to perfection.

'Hodges is one of a type. We have several on that coast. We use him, and the French use him to get people out whose presence would otherwise be embarrassing.'

'And here?'

'Here it's different. There is a war between the Bretons and the French. There are no truces.' He considered. 'Hodges usually needs paying.'

'An American lady paid, sir.'

D'Auvergne smiled.

'A good friend, was she?'

'Apparently. She is married to the Seconde of the *Hortense*. I am told she was grateful I got her party ashore.'

'You were told?'

'I never saw her sir. I was kept in a guardroom in the lighthouse of Calais for a couple of days, visited by various sea officers and soldiers, each requiring my story to be told, then just once at night by the gentleman you describe. The smuggler. He told me the French didn't know what to do with me. So it had been arranged that the guardroom doors would be left unlocked and unattended for a few minutes after midnight. I was to leave and walk as fast as I could to the beach, where I would see a light. I followed his instructions. The streets were empty. Eventually I reached the shore and followed a light across the beach to a small boat. Once aboard, this smuggler gentleman you call Hodges, gave me a 'laissez-passer' issued by the port Captain of Calais and a letter to an English banker in Dover. It was the English banker who told me my expenses had been paid by the American lady.'

'Her name?'

'Madame Auchard.'

'Where will we find this paragon?'

'I really don't know, sir.'

'No address?'

'The last time I saw her she was swept from the *Hortense*'s whaler and appeared to be drowning.'

D'Auvergne thought, burying his head in his hands theatrically as he did so. Eventually he reached a decision. 'Follow me.'

Cotterell did as he was asked and followed D'Auvergne downstairs to the yard. They passed a sentry, who saluted.

'Don't salute, you fool,' said D'Auvergne to the sentry. 'How many times?'

The man looked confused. D'Auvergne marched on. Cotterell followed.

'Tricky situation with the Mont,' confided D'Auvergne. 'Do you know my cousin, Fall?'

'No sir.'

'He's the Lieutenant Governor. He controls the castle. He's a bad hat.'

'Yes sir.' Cotterell had no idea how Fall was a bad hat, and was disinclined to ask. The Lieutenant Governor's disposition was not a subject which much exercised the minds of fishing boat captains.

'I command here, but he has to sign all the vouchers. And he controls the castle. It's not good enough.' D'Auvergne and Cotterell had now passed outside the main gate of the castle. They descended a granite cobbled path and were soon on the street below the castle. The apple dealer had disappeared, cockade hat and all. Instead a pair of priests stood waiting for D'Auvergne. They were elderly and wore white ribbons in their lapels. They wanted to speak, but D'Auvergne held up his hand.

'Not now, gentlemen. Not now.'

Then he whispered to Cotterell, 'They want transport from me. I can't help. My task here is a 'closely guarded secret'. Could you imagine such a concept in Jersey? We have more than our share of island gossips.'

He guided Cotterell a few yards further down the road. He pointed to a small gunboat, perhaps a little over forty feet in length, in the inner road. 'That is *La Niege*. She was commissioned in Nantes to prey on our inshore traffic in this bay. She's a miniature privateer, not even six months old. We captured her in April, high and dry on les Ecrous. I think it must have been her captain's first time in the bay. The speed with which the tide ebbed surprised him.'

The idea of a French seaman's embarrassment really amused

D'Auvergne. *La Niege* was smart and shipshape. She was brigantine-rigged in the French style. She had not been allowed to
deteriorate once in Jersey hands. The spars shone with newly-
applied oil, new tanned sails were already bent on and ready to
go. The hull was painted black with a thick red ochre band round
her waist, as if she was a miniature three decker. Two cannon
muzzles showed through gun-ports in the red ochre band and
would doubtless be matched by two more in the seaward side
of the hull. Men moved about her, busying themselves. Two
sailors hung over her sides on rope and plank seats, painting out
the red ochre band with black paint.

'The red is showy,' explained D'Auvergne, 'and unsuited to
our task, which requires discretion. It is important that anyone
who sees our ships thinks they are fishermen. We don't want
people alerted to our real task.'

D'Auvergne looked towards the two priests, who were loitering
by the strand, waiting for a signal from him that they might
approach. He turned back to Cotterell. They were outside a
cottage facing the sea.

'What do you think? We are fishers of men, Jean Cotterell.
We move men and material to France on behalf of King George.'

D'Auvergne opened the door to the cottage.

'Now – luncheon.'

Cotterell went in. He noticed two tough-looking saiors strolling
towards the cottage as he did so. D'Auvergne made brief eye
contact with the sailors, then followed Cotterell into the house.

22

Cotterell was surprised. The outside of the cottage appeared simple, but D'Auvergne had the inside set up in some style, with fine plasterwork over the stone walls painted in pink distemper. There were thick curtains, lamps and easy chairs in the drawing room. The dining room was arsenic green, with engraved pictures of naval and military actions in frames around the walls. The dining table was plain, with four chairs set about it. Leigh was already there, waiting for them. Lunch was served by the cook herself, a diminutive black-haired woman who glared at Cotterell as if his presence was a personal affront.

'Ignore her,' said D'Auvergne. 'She serves out every one the same way. She feels put upon to wait at table.'

'You have no maid?' asked Cotterell.

'I am of the opinion the fewer people visit here, the better,' replied D'Auvergne.

'You are honoured, sir,' said Leigh to Cotterell.

The pages of Cotterell's account were spread on the table, along with tureens of lamb chops, bacon and vegetables. There were sauce boats, home-made hot rolls and three bottles of Burgundy wine.

To one side of the table a picture had been taken down and placed to face the wall. There appeared to be no reason for it, and Cotterell was puzzled.

'I can promise much for this wine,' D'Auvergne said. 'We took it off a French merchantman outside St Malo.'

D'Auvergne poured 'dear Leigh' – as D'Auvergne referred to

him – a very large glass of wine. He poured one for Cotterell too. But Cotterell noticed D'Auvergne drank little. The chops grew cold and the sauce grew a skin as the two Royal Navy officers questioned Cotterell closely about every detail of life on a French revolutionary vessel. His experience was rare, and they wanted to draw every piece of information they could. D'Auvergne was friendly and open. These men lived inside artifices. When the meal and the interrogation was ended D'Auvergne asked Leigh, 'Well?'

'I believe he will serve, Captain.'

'So do I, Leigh. Will you fetch our parcel?'

'It is lodged in the castle. I will send a soldier.'

'No. You go, My Lord.'

It was formed as a friendly suggestion, but all three men knew D'Auvergne was commanding. Leigh pulled a face, but said no more and left. D'Auvergne was not only his commanding officer but was old enough to be Cotterell's father, let alone the youth's.

He said, 'I expect you can guess the project.'

'Not at all,' replied Cotterell.

D'Auvergne stood and draped his coat carefully over the painting. 'I have a certain amount of authority here, invested in me by their Lordships at the Admiralty. I am the commodore of the fleet protecting our islands now.'

Cotterell stood and raised his glass. 'My very best congratulations to you, sir.'

D'Auvergne clinked his glass with Cotterell's. 'I can appoint and promote men, subject to their Lordships' later approval. It is my intention to make Leigh Lieutenant, pending that approval, and place him in command of the vessel we saw, *La Niege*. He will need a sailing master, of course. I propose to rate you master's mate, if you will go to sea with him. I can't just take you off a fishing boat and put you in command, but that's as near as dammit.'

'I am honoured to be considered.'

'That sounds like the prelude to a refusal. Your work for us in Newfoundland was extremely useful.'

'You are too kind, sir. I kept my eyes and ears open, as asked, but ultimately I was a failure.'

'Nonsense, Jean. You were a signal success. I trust you, I admire your seamanship and now I want you to carry out a most secret and important mission for me. Do it and you stand to gain his Majesty's warrant. Become a gentleman. You will win prize money, Jean. There are a lot of small vessels in the bay of Mont St Michel. One adventure, one stray French merchantman,' he tapped a wine bottle to remind Cotterell of its source, 'and you could make your fortune.'

There was a silence. 'Well?' asked D'Auvergne.

'You have no sailors. It's clear from the manning on your ships, which are mostly, by the way, broken down.'

D'Auvergne waved away Cotterell's objection. 'Their Lordships are aware of the situation with the fleet. I have replacements en route from Cowes as we speak.'

'Will you be allowed to keep their crews?'

D'Auvergne was silent. He would not, they both knew. After a moment he said, 'After a period with Lord Leigh, you will pass for a commissioned officer yourself.'

'Or a nursemaid, sir. One or the other.'

'Don't be such a hard arse, Jean. We are at war with France, and His Majesty's Navy has need of men who know the waters around here well. Reflect on your duty to your country.'

'I have. I cannot go to sea for you.'

'Why not?'

'It's impossible.'

'You lost your vessel,' said D'Auvergne. 'You cannot go to sea at all, unless someone employs you. Why not let that person be the King?'

Cotterell didn't answer. D'Auvergne poured him a glass of wine and once more tapped the bottle against the glass, to remind him again of its source. Eventually Cotterell said, 'I promised my mother, is the reason. She depends on me.'

'Depends?'

'Sir?'

'How will you provide for this dependency?'

'This is a miracle which is yet to be revealed. But she has my promise.' Cotterell stood. 'Are we finished?'

'No, we are not.'

'I may not leave?'

'I don't like to do this. But I will. In your statement you say you navigated a French warship to port.'

'She sank.'

'That may be your defence. And it may or may not succeed.'

'My defence? Against what?'

'Sit down, Cotterell. Even my stupid cousin Fall would accept that a subject of King George who acts to save a French ship when we are at war has a charge to answer. If you walk out of that door the sailors outside will arrest you and the Lieutenant Governor will incarcerate you in his beloved castle.' He paused for effect. 'Don't be alarmed. No one will be allowed to execute you forthwith. There will be a trial. You will spend a good deal of time in prison while someone, presumably in England, decides whether that trial should be in Jersey or England. Or you could be Lord Leigh's sailing master.'

'Wet-nurse.'

'Perhaps. You don't have much of a hand to play. Now which is it to be, sir?'

Cotterell sat. D'Auvergne held out his hand. 'Well chosen sir. Well chosen.'

Leigh returned half an hour later with his parcel – the apple dealer.

'This is Monsieur Prigent.'

Prigent bowed deeply and swung his hat to the ground as he did so. He stank of brandy.

'This gentleman is Mr Cotterell, Prigent. He is an expert pilot in these waters. He will take you to your rendezvous. Can you read a chart?'

'Of course,' said Prigent.

'Show Mr Cotterell.' D'Auvergne rolled out a chart of the bay. Prigent pointed at St Brieuc.

'Do you know this part of the bay?'

'Yes,' said Cotterell.

'The grève de Rosaires?'

'I know it.'

'We have to arrive at night. Two night's time. There will be a light. It will only show for ten minutes. If we don't answer, they will leave.'

'And if we miss it?'

'We mustn't.'

'What do you say?' asked Leigh.

'We can get there.'

After they had gone, and D'Auvergne was alone again with Cotterell, he said, 'Don't trust that fellow.'

'No sir. I won't,' Cotterell answered.

D'Auvergne took his coat off the framed picture.

'Help me put this up again.'

It was an etching. 'After Copley' was written on the bottom. It showed an idealised view of St Helier Market Square with red-coated militiamen and French soldiers firing at each other across the square.

'I paid for the copy to be made myself,' D'Auvergne told him. 'Do you remember the event?'

'No sir. I was fishing on the Banks. We stayed over that winter in St John.'

The event depicted in the etching was famous, an invasion of Jersey by French forces under the Baron de Rullecourt on January 6th 1781. The French were repulsed. The Jerseymen won, but in doing so their commander, brave Major Pierson, was shot in the breast. Rullecourt was killed too, as well as some dozens of his soldiers. The picture depicted Jersey soldiers collected around the fallen body of Pierson. A woman and child ran away from the battle. In the middle of the crowd of soldiers, who themselves stood at the centre of the picture, was the tall figure of a soldier with African features. He was firing into the French.

'So you've never seen the painting?'

'No.'

'But you've seen the African?'

'Yes, sir. I've seen him.'

'He's so vain,' said D'Auvergne, referring to the African. 'He was staying with a friend in London and heard about the painting. They were going to use some warehouse porter to stand in for him, but he had to sit himself. I told him not to.'

'Where is the original painting?'

'At the Academy in Piccadilly. Now every French agent who sets eyes on that painting will have seen him in a British uniform. And I can't guarantee that every French agent is scrupulous. In fact, I can guarantee that some are not.'

'Prigent?' asked Cotterell. 'Is that why you hid it?'

'I am not sure about Prigent. And I don't expect their paths will cross. But you never know. How many blacks have you met in France?'

'Not many,' considered Cotterell. 'One of the Calais officers. And there were a few on the *Hortense*.'

'Very few then,' said D'Auvergne.

The picture was secure on the wall now. D'Auvergne let the hook take the weight. It was big, the size of a full sheet of art printer's paper and was in a heavy frame of gilded wood. The two men stood back, looking at the etching on the dining room wall. Though ten years younger, the dashing African soldier standing over Major Pierson's body, defending St Helier from Rullecourt's invading French soldiers, was undoubtedly, unmistakeably, Rasselas Charles.

The end

Historical Note

1794, l'an II in the Republican Calendar, is the year of the Terror, which is considered to have begun in the summer of 1793 and ended with the coup of 9 Thermidor and the fall of Robespierre. Though the great naval events during that period, Toulon and the Glorious 1st of June, are well known, the French perspective is less well represented in print than the British. The French naval point of view is hardly represented at all in fiction. The reason is simple. Writers and readers of fiction set on British ships during the French Revolutionary and Napoleonic wars are spoiled for choice with historical sources. The Herculean work done by modern British naval historians allows access to knowledge about the sailors' conditions and the organisation of King George's Navy. His sailors' thoughts, feelings and recollections are widely available in book form. But there are fewer clues on the French side. There is no French publishing equivalent of the Naval History Society. Notes and autobiographies of French sailors exist, and some are in print, but it is a much shallower pool. Perhaps for this reason the interior life of French vessels is rarely depicted in sea novels. In any case the history is little enough known outside the world of the professional historian that I may allow myself a few words of explanation of the world in which my novel is set.

In 1793 and 1794 the French Navy was chaotic, and often in a state of near or actual mutiny. In 1793 there had been a full-blown mutiny among the sailors on ships 'guarding' Quiberon. Their task – to patrol the seas between Belle Isle and the Quiberon peninsula – was pointless, and strategically useless. Their conditions were awful. Their admiral complained they suffered from *fievre putride* (typhoid fever). Their food was foul and of poor quality. There were shortages of fresh water on the ships, and even shortages of the equipment to replenish them. The experience of revolution had predisposed French seamen to express grievance; they were the sans culottes of the sea. They mutinied. The response of the authorities in Paris was to send *Conventionnel* and former merchant seaman JeanBon St André as an emissary charged with reorganising the Navy in the west of France. He did this through a mixture of force and argument. A guillotine was set up on the strand in Brest. The Republic wasn't slow to execute those who challenged its authority in 1793/94 and St André was no more patient with opposition than the next revolutionary. But he was measured in his actions. St André was careful not to destroy that which he'd come to save. He certainly did nothing to dampen sans-culotte revolutionary ardour, wanting instead to marry it to naval discipline and produce a *'furia Francese'* of the sea.

In April 1794 a grain convoy of over a hundred ships sailed from Chesapeake in America to Brest in France. It was escorted by a small force of French warships commanded by Admiral Pierre Jan Vanstabel. The grain was intended to feed revolutionary France.

France was changing in 1794. There was a power struggle expressed through summary and irrational executions – 'The Terror.' The struggle was resolved in the coup, and subsequent execution of Robespierre and St Just on 9 Thermidor (July 27th). After 9 Thermidor sans-culottism of the type displayed by Liberté and the Lefèvres in the novel disappeared in an 'anti-Terrorist' backlash. But neither the crews of French ships, nor the British ones who fought them in the early summer of 1794, knew that the power of revolutionary zealots would end any time soon. Therefore in the novel they act as if it wouldn't.

Admiral Lord Howe's Channel Fleet attempted to block

Vanstabel's convoy, of which the British had intelligence. Howe didn't find Vanstabel, but instead met and attacked the fleet of Admiral Villaret-Joyeuse, who had emerged from Brest accompanied by Jeanbon St André. Villaret-Joyeuse risked his ships in the Atlantic in an attempt to conduct Vanstabel's convoy to safety. It is fair to say Jeanbon St André went along to make sure the naval elite followed orders. Howe's and Villaret-Joyeuse's fleets were more or less matched at arms. The battle between them was a set-piece sea fight, probably the greatest of the revolutionary wars – the Nile and Trafalgar belong to the period of Napoleon. We might see the actions on the *Hortense* as peripheral to the greater battles on 1st June 1794.

The actions which the British know as the 'Glorious First of June' and the French as 'Les Batailles de Prairial' were a Phyrric victory for the French. Villaret-Joyeuse's fleet was smashed, though not beyond repair. According to *l'Histoire Ignoree de la Marine Francaise* (Etienne Taillemite, editions Perrin), 3,300 Frenchmen died or were wounded in the fighting, with another 4,000 taken prisoner. This is set against 1,000 killed and wounded in Howe's fleet. The British won the battle but the French received their grain.

The layout of the frigate *Hortense* in the novel is based for the most part on the *Flore*, sometimes called *l'Americaine*, a French frigate built in the American style twenty years before. The vessel is not to be confused with *l'Amerique*, a ship of the line seventy-four which took part in the Quiberon mutiny of '93. A model of *Flore/l'Americaine* is in the Musée de la Marine in Paris. On the subject of ships and confusion, *misaine*, the foremost French mast and *mizzen*, the rearmost on an English ship are *faux amis*, described by Jean Merrien (Dictionnaire de la Mer, Editions Omnibus 2001) as '*source d'innombrables erreurs de traduction*.' It certainly is. The foremost mast on a French three-master of that period is the *misaine*, the second the *grand-mât* and the rearmost the *artimon*.

French naval crews had become chaotic and almost ungovern-

able during the period leading up to 1794. The French marine
service had been, to a great extent, stripped of its competent
officers by the Revolution. French merchant captains were taken
into the French Navy in 1793 in an attempt to replace the losses,
where they were unsurprisingly discovered to be lacking in the
skill necessary to handle a warship, which must be both manoeuvred and fought at the same time. A former Charleston French
privateer captain like Dubarre, willing to serve the revolutionary
authorities, would have been a find beyond value for the French
Navy in 1793 or 1794.

The form of address 'mon Commandant' was used in the
French Navy up until Trafalgar (1805) but not after by order of
the Emperor himself (again according to Taillemite).

Jersey and Guernsey fishermen visited the Grand Banks for
more than 400 years, fishing cod on both hand and long lines.
Traditionally they dried and salted their catch in bays on the
Newfoundland and Nova Scotia coast, then imported the fish
to Europe. It was usually sold in Catholic countries, where days
of abstinence from meat were still common at the end of the
18th century. There was also trade in salt cod as a cheap source
of protein for African slaves in the West Indies. To this day salt
cod is a favourite dish in the Caribbean, as it is in southern
France and Portugal. The Grand Banks fishermen were preyed
upon by French privateers, but they also supplied crews for their
own fearsome Channel Island privateers.

There was no Jersey packet in 1794.

If there was a Grand Banks fisherman like *l'Imprevu* I hope
it was more seaworthy than the tubby old barge of that name
I spent a winter moored next to in Redon harbour. *Galipétan* –
Dubarre's privateer – is the name of the French forerunner to
the *Flying Dutchman*. Bretons called the same legendary vessel
Meou-Meou.

Though the euphemistically named 'sailors' wives' were gener-
ally confined to port visits, there were some women at sea in
the British Navy of the period. There is no reason to presume

there were none in the French, indeed a naked French woman was rescued from the sea during the battle of Trafalgar (*Sailors and their women*, David Cordingly). She was not an exhibitionist, but had taken her clothes off because she had been scalded with hot lead.

Resistance to the Revolution was always strongest in the west of France. The most important revolts before 1795 were those formally organised by Royalist forces of the Vendée and informally 'organised' by irregular Chouans of the forests between le Mont St Michel and Laval. Later the word Chouan would come to mean any Royalist, Catholic and anti-revolutionary force in the West. Phillipe d'Auvergne, otherwise known as the Prince de Bouillon, organiser of the Channel Islands Correspondence is a well known figure in Jersey and in naval history.

Cotterell, Tom, Emily, Liberté and Charles will be back to continue their adventure in France, Ireland and the Channel Islands.

Thanks to Carlo Gébler, Michael Harris, Bernard Hetherington and Sarah Milne for reading all or part of the manuscript. All standing gybes, Irish pennants and fouled lines are my own.

PIRATES & PRIVATEERS

Tom Bowling

From Robert Louis Stevenson's *Treasure Island* to Errol Flynn in *Captain Blood* on to today's *Pirates of the Caribbean*, the romantic image of pirates in modern Western popular culture has long been with us. But of course pirates come in many guises and not all of them as charming as Johnny Depp.

Pirates are outlaws who move quickly, a form of lawlessness based on the application of immense short term power by mobile forces which fade away, similar to guerrilla warfare.

In *Pirates and Privateers* Tom Bowling offers a lively history of piracy, from ancient times through the 'privateers' such as Morgan, with their Letters of Marque (an early example of State-sponsored terrorism), to the still real and flourishing threat of contemporary pirates that patrol the less well-regulated shipping lanes of the world today.

To order your copy

£9.99 including free postage and packing
(UK and Republic of Ireland only)
£10.99 for overseas orders

For credit card orders phone 0207 430 1021 (ref A)

For orders by post – cheques payable to Oldcastle Books,
21 Great Ormond Street, London, WC1N 3JB

WW1 AT SEA

Victoria Carolan

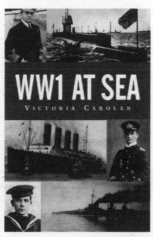

Images of WWI in the popular consciousness normally involve the bloody attrition of trench warfare, the miles of mud, the shattered earth, the tangled miles of barbed wire. However there was another significant arena of war - the battle for control of the sea.

In 1914 at the beginning of the war, Britain's maritime supremacy had remained unchallenged for around a hundred years. Many expected another Battle of Trafalgar but advances in technology saw a very different kind of warfare with the widespread use of mines, submarines and torpedoes.

This book examines the events that led to war and the naval arms race between Britain and Germany. It traces the events of the war at sea looking at the major battles as well as the effects of unrestricted submarine warfare and the sinking of the Lusitania. It also profiles key figures such as Fisher, Beatty, Tirpitz and Graf von Spee.

To order your copy

£9.99 including free postage and packing
(UK and Republic of Ireland only)
£10.99 for overseas orders

For credit card orders phone 0207 430 1021 (ref A)

For orders by post – cheques payable to Oldcastle Books,
21 Great Ormond Street, London, WC1N 3JB

LUCA ANTARA

Martin Edmond

'Luca Antara is a book-lover's book, a graceful and mesmerizing blend of history, autobiography, travel and romance.' – *JM Coetzee*

Part memoir, travelogue, history and part detective story, *Luca Antara* is a rich tapestry of history and the present. It parallels the life of the author, an émigré to Sydney, and the life of an historical figure, António da Nova, the servant of a Portuguese explorer who in the 1600s sends him to find out more about Luca Antara (now Australia).

New to Sydney, Martin Edmond finds himself impoverished and displaced. He earns money as a taxi driver but spends his spare time frequenting second hand bookshops trying to learn more about the history of Australia and the wider region. The people Edmond encounters in his taxi and in his search for rare books are varied and strange, offering the reader a voyeuristic glimpse into Sydney's sub-culture.

Sent to discover more about Luca Antara, António da Nova's crew mutiny and dump him on the West Australian coast. He is found by Aborigines, who take him on an epic walk across northern Australia. Eventually he manages to return to his master in Portugal who awaits news of his explorations.

Edmond's reading centres upon da Nova, but each book he reads leads to another and the subject becomes broader and increasingly fascinating. The lives of the two men and the strange customs and unique social mores of each man's culture and time intertwine throughout the book, ending with Edmond literally walking in the footsteps of da Nova across northern Australia.

To order your copy

£9.99 including free postage and packing
(UK and Republic of Ireland only)
£10.99 for overseas orders

For credit card orders phone 0207 430 1021 (ref A)

For orders by post – cheques payable to Oldcastle Books,
21 Great Ormond Street, London, WC1N 3JB
www.noexit.co.uk